Dear Reader,

This month we're delighted to welcome best selling author Patricia Wilson to the ***Scarlet*** list. With over 40 romance novels to her credit, we are sure that Patricia's new book will delight her existing fans and win her many new readers. You can also read *Resolutions*, the conclusion of Maxine Barry's enthralling 'All His Prey' duet. And we are proud to bring you books by two talented new authors: Judy Jackson who hails from Canada and Tiffany Bond who is based in England.

You will possibly have noticed that some of the ***Scarlet*** novels we publish are quite sexy, while others are warmer and more family oriented. Do you like this mix of styles and the different levels of sensuality? And how about locations: is it important to you *where* an author sets her ***Scarlet*** book?

If you have written to me about ***Scarlet***, please accept my thanks. I read each and every one of your letters and I certainly refer to your comments and suggestions when I am thinking about our schedules.

Till next month,

Sally Cooper

SALLY COOPER,
Editor-in-Chief – ***Scarlet***

About the author

Judy Jackson spent her childhood in Alberta before her family moved to the coast of British Columbia. She married her highschool sweetheart and they live with their two terrific sons in the Vancouver area.

All through school, Judy could never decide on her future. Since then she's worked at so many jobs she can't remember them all, though most have involved bookkeeping. At age thirty she threw a 'what do you want to be when you grow up costume party.' Judy, of course, couldn't make up *her* mind, so printed 50 different jobs on slips of paper and pinned them to her maternity smock! Now she lives vicariously through her characters' professions.

With hindsight, Judy knows her career began as a child, entertaining her friends with imaginative stories. Telling 'stories' was so much fun, Judy never stopped. Thanks to ***Scarlet***, she can continue to entertain people with her stories and get paid for it!

Other ***Scarlet*** titles available this month:
AN IMPROPER PROPOSAL – Tiffany Bond
RESOLUTIONS – Maxine Barry
A DARK AND DANGEROUS MAN – Patricia Wilson

JUDY JACKSON

THE MARRIAGE PLAN

Enquiries to:
Robinson Publishing Ltd
7 Kensington Church Court
London W8 4SP

First published in the UK by Scarlet, 1997

A copy of the British Library Cataloguing in Publication data is available from the British Library

ISBN 1-85487-907-3

Printed and bound in the EC

10 9 8 7 6 5 4 3 2 1

To Bert, David and Mark for their love and support. To my parents, Don and Donna Jackson, who believed and gave me that first typewriter. And to Kay Gregory, friend and mentor beyond compare.

CHAPTER 1

'You can't take my home!'

Becky Hansen detested the shrill disbelief and panic in her voice. She sucked in a deep breath to compose herself, then tried not to gag on the mingled odors of musty paper and sweet cologne that always thickened the air in the bank manager's office.

'I am sorry, Rebecca. Bank policy requires you to make all mortgage payments or we will be forced to foreclose. However, if you sell it yourself, Lilac House will probably realize a considerable amount beyond the mortgage value.' Tom Ellford leaned back and squeezed his thumbs into vest pockets stretched across his paunch.

'I don't want to sell it.'

'You might not have any choice and I'm sure you would rather collect the profit yourself, if there is any. At the moment residential properties are selling better in Richmond than in most Vancouver suburbs. Indeed, real estate prices are higher here than anywhere else in Canada.'

His smile raised goosebumps on her skin and Becky shuddered. Why did her future lie in fingers as mottled and pink as raw sausages?

His black eyes gleamed and his red lips glistened wetly in his pudgy little face as his gaze drifted down her legs and fastened on her ankles. Feeling as if something clammy had crawled across her skin, she tucked her legs back under the chair out of sight. She didn't think she'd be able to keep her mouth shut if he hinted even one more time how he could be 'persuaded' to help with her money problems.

Like he did the time she needed a loan because the roof leaked and the roofing company told her that even with another patch job it wouldn't keep out morning dew. Like he did the day she had to buy the used station wagon because the mechanic swore only voodoo would get her old van running again.

She wondered how many other people left this office positive that 'loan' qualified for a high place on the list of four-letter obscene words.

He coughed and pinched his lips together, forcing lax muscles into the proper and carefully sympathetic half-smile he habitually wore. 'We regret there is no alternative. No matter how I feel personally about your problems, my hands are tied.'

'But Eric, my ex-husband, is responsible for the mortgage payments.' She fought to keep her voice even and reasonable.

'The result is the same. If he doesn't make the payments you will have to leave. When it became obvious he would not remit the proper amount, we contacted you. You allowed two weeks to pass before informing us you were unable to locate him.'

How shockingly easy it was to hate another human being, she marveled bitterly. First Eric had taught her a lesson she would never forget; now this man clearly enjoyed his position of power. To keep Lilac House she'd force herself to be polite, but it left a bad taste in her mouth.

As both a young child and a young woman Becky had often accompanied her grandmother to afternoon tea at the old house. She'd sat in awed silence, absorbing the atmosphere of whimsical Victoriana while the elderly ladies gossiped about dead or absent cronies. As a teenager she'd often walked blocks out of her way to visit the house, falling more in love with it every year.

Stuart Smythe built Lilac House in 1913 as a monument to his wealth and importance, even though both had existed mostly in his own mind. After his death the family money evaporated slowly but inexorably. Stuart's only surviving child, Emily, lived elegantly, if slightly out of touch with reality. The house aged gracefully, suffering benign neglect through the last twenty years of the owner's life.

Eric had reluctantly agreed to buy the house when Emily's distant cousins sold it after her death. He'd complained constantly that the house's upkeep was too expensive and too much work. But Becky believed the house returned her love, sheltering and comforting her through the painful years of marriage. Now it belonged to her alone and she'd go to almost any lengths to keep it.

'Please give me some time, Tom. I'm sure I can work out a way to make the payments.'

He shuffled the computer printouts, cleared his throat, and ran one finger down a column of figures. 'You have three children.'

'Yes.' As his fingers drummed an uneven beat on the desk top, she wondered if his grimace of distaste conveyed his opinion of children in general or her lack of restraint in particular.

'Do you have any source of income other than the trust fund?'

'I create and sell crossword puzzles.'

He raised a derisive eyebrow.

'I make pretty good money,' she replied defensively, naming a figure that lifted both of his eyebrows.

'Very well. You have two weeks. If you can provide us with a financial plan including the income from the past year and your projected income.'

She released the breath she had been holding. 'Thanks.'

'But you must allow me to advise you, Rebecca.' The squat man centered the papers on his desk and squared the corners with finicky nudges. 'I feel your best option – '

Becky felt that if she stayed in that room one more minute she would suffocate. She swung the long strap of her bag over one shoulder and jumped to her feet, leaving Ellford with his mouth hanging open, in mid-speech.

'I'll be back in two weeks.' With the money, she added silently. No matter what she had to do, no one would force her and the kids out of their home. 'Thanks for your time.'

His jaw snapped shut and he glared.

She ignored his indignant requests for her to return to the office and strode quickly through the bank. Spine stiff and head erect, she tried not to see the sympathetic glances from those she knew on his staff. That's the trouble with small towns, she thought.

Everywhere she went . . . bank, lawyer, doctor's office, or her children's school . . . she couldn't do personal business or deal with family problems without running into someone who knew her personally. Meeting them in another setting and looking them in the eyes when you knew they knew your most private problems, seemed to double the situation's level of embarrassment.

Once through the glass doors, fat drops of rain hit her face. She hurried to the shoe store beside the bank and sheltered under its striped awning, searching the depths of her oversize bag for the collapsible umbrella.

When she opened it one of the spokes snapped, tearing through the fabric and ripping a gaping hole across its top. Grumbling under her breath, she tossed the ruined umbrella into the trash can on the corner as she sprinted to her car.

In the parking lot across the street she bent to put the key in the lock, becoming soaked while she jiggled the key with practiced ease. As the door opened, a battered pick-up full of teenagers zoomed by. Their truck hit a pothole, splashing a wave of muddy water all over her and the inside of her old 'woody' station wagon, Matilda.

She ruefully inspected her mud-coated body. Vanity had persuaded her to leave her only coat, an old slicker, in the closet at home and now greasy, muddy water soaked her to the skin.

So much for vanity.

Behind the wheel of the car, with the door firmly shut, she peered in the rear-view mirror. Rain was streaming off her hair, streaking her mascara and flattening her curls. Her hand trembled as she used a handful of tissues to make a few ineffectual swipes at her cheeks and chin.

The urge to laugh at her appearance evaporated and a sob shook her frame before she sucked in a huge breath and pulled herself upright.

She had to get home.

Briskly she blew her nose and stuffed the tissues into the plastic garbage bag hanging from the tuning knob of the broken radio. This was simply a little setback and a little mud. Nothing she couldn't handle. Nothing she couldn't fix.

The old wagon rattled and vibrated as she turned the key in the ignition. Becky threw a grateful prayer heavenward when the engine finally caught.

Stalls, backfires, and other assorted mechanical foibles enlivened the drive home. Eventually the car hiccuped and died in the driveway before she could turn it off. A practiced hip check slammed the door shut.

She booted the front tire on her way past but immediately felt guilty when the car coughed and wheezed. For the five hundred she'd paid for her, Matilda had given good service. The old girl deserved better than a kick in the retread.

She opened her front door and went inside. A small backward smack with her heel shut the door behind her. She leaned her shoulders back against the wood as the warmth and welcome of Lilac House surrounded her. Safe home at last.

'I'm what?' Ryan's tone rose and the man opposite winced at the volume of sound.

Eighteen years in Canada had not entirely erased from Ryan's voice evidence that he had spent the first half of his life growing up in Texas. The lingering drawl was always stronger when he was upset. Right now he was very upset. 'Y'all must be insane.'

'Please, Mr McLeod. There is no need for you to become overwrought.'

Ryan gaped incredulously at the skeletal man with the dry-as-ashes voice, then scanned the engraved and embossed business card that lay on his desk. Mr Agnew Withers-Bright, of Rutherford, Smithers and Withers, Attorneys-at-Law, practicing in Boston, Massachusetts.

About Ryan's age of thirty-six, Mr Withers-Bright obviously lived and breathed all the whereases and whyfores of a lawyer more than twice that age. He even smelled dusty. The man had been sitting in that same chair, precisely centered and knees pressed together, talking about Ryan's cousin for the last forty minutes.

Mildly fond of Ron and his wife, Marcia, Ryan regretted their deaths. Their will, their money, and their progeny didn't interest him. Deciding that enough was enough, he had been about to terminate Mr Withers-Bright's interview when the man dropped the bombshell.

'Overwrought? I've been appointed the guardian of a child, without my consent, and you tell me not to get overwrought?' Ryan leaned forward across his paper-strewn desk, impatiently swept his hair out of his eyes, and glared directly into the bulging eyes of Agnew Withers-Bright.

He watched the lawyer pull the might of the legal world around his shoulders and clasp his shaking fingers together. Obviously supported by moral rather than physical courage, the thin man recoiled slightly at the anger emanating from Ryan but refused to retreat from his position.

'Yes, Mr McLeod. Mr Ronald McLeod specifically named you as the child's guardian.'

'But why, dammit?'

'At the time they drew up the will, I asked that same question. Do you recall some years ago when you responded to Mr and Mrs McLeod's request for funds with a large donation? For their research into a now defunct society in Africa?'

'Vaguely.'

'Your liberal contribution to their research safari evidently convinced them of your generous nature. They felt you would be the most suitable person to take care of their child in the event of their deaths.'

Ryan fell back in his chair. 'This can't be legal! I wasn't asked . . .'

'It wasn't necessary,' the lawyer interrupted. 'They worded it more as a bequest than a request. Not strictly correct, I know. Of course you are not legally obliged to accept guardianship.'

'Do you expect me to take this seriously? I can't believe they would make so important a decision about their daughter's future based on something so ridiculous. I gave them that money because my accountant advised me I needed a tax deduction and their research qualified, for Chrissake.'

'Your intent doesn't invalidate their response.'

'I'm a bachelor, almost forty years old, and a very busy man. It's absurd to expect me to take care of a seven-year-old girl! Texas and Louisiana are littered with their relatives. There has to be someone more suitable than myself.'

'I'm sorry. On the McLeod side, there is only yourself and your parents. They have retired to Florida and don't wish to, ah, be saddled with your responsibilities.'

'That sounds like a direct quote.'

A faint smile crimped his visitor's lips.

'Yes, it is, unfortunately. They were slightly indignant when we approached them. Mrs

McLeod's family, two of whom have alternated in providing a home for the child since her birth, believe they have done enough and have refused to continue.' He hesitated. 'I believe it wasn't a happy situation for the child.

'They made it clear, however, that if you made funds available for the little girl's care, education, and any other expenses, one of them would agree to be responsible for her upbringing. Of course they expect some recompense for their effort.'

'You mean none of them want the kid because there will be no money left after the estate is settled?'

'That's correct.'

'But if I supplied sufficient cash one of Marcia's relatives would then be willing, if not pleased, to continue giving the kid a home?'

'That is, ahem, precisely the case.'

Dragging his gaze away from Withers-Bright's face, Ryan stared at his graffiti-decorated blotter, then swung around to face the corner window. On the twenty-second floor in the middle of the high-rent district of Vancouver, his office provided an expensive view of Stanley Park and North Vancouver's waterfront.

But rather than the scenic panorama he saw his mother's gaunt, cold face.

'I don't want to go. They're mean.' Five-year-old Ryan knuckled the tears from his eyes.

'You are invited to the Rowland boy's birthday party.' His mother loomed over him, holding his one good suit. 'You will stop snivelling, put this on, and go to little Harry's party. While you are at their home you will be a credit to me. If we make a good impression Mrs Rowland will invite me to help organize the church fair. Only the best people in town are associated with the fair.'

Tears trickled down his face.

'Come on, Ryan, do this for Mommy,' she wheedled. 'It will make me so happy and I'll love you to bits.'

The tears came harder but he shook his head, slowly backing away. His mother slapped him hard, on the arm where it wouldn't show, handed him the suit, and pointed sternly to his bedroom door.

That memory faded and he was eight, an unwilling witness to yet another battle in his parents' ongoing war.

'You demand a raise or else!' His mother waved her dinner knife in the air, her voice precisely enunciating every syllable.

Ryan winced as the sound sliced through his skin like a scalpel.

'I told you. The company is letting workers go. No one will receive a raise this year.' The angry pleading in his father's voice made Ryan's stomach twist. 'There's nothing I can . . .'

'Either you earn more money, or I'll leave you. I will not stay with a man who will not support me in proper style.'

'Bloody hell, woman . . .'

'Reginald! There will be no more discussion.'

The meal continued in a dark silence that invaded Ryan's soul. Three weeks later his mother's voice was sugar sweet when his father arrived home with two paychecks from working two jobs.

Then Ryan was eleven.

'Ryan? Ryan!' The shriek of his mother's voice rose over the heavy beat of rock and roll blaring from his record player. The door crashed open.

'Why didn't you answer me?' his mother asked. 'Never mind, it doesn't matter. Your father and I are leaving now.'

'But, Mom, I haven't had any dinner.'

'Oh.' She tapped her foot, visibly annoyed at this reminder of his needs. 'There's some leftover fish in the fridge, eat that.'

'I don't like fish.'

'Is this your gratitude?' Defensive anger put a red patch high on each cheek, making the rouge she'd brushed there look garish. 'Thousands of children starving in the world and you complain about the good food your father buys for you?'

She twitched the skinny fox stole higher around her shoulders and he avoided looking at its glassy eyeballs. 'If you don't want fish, then stay hungry. I'm leaving.'

'Where are you going?' he asked. He refused to shed the tears building up behind his averted eyes.

'Mrs Rowland has invited us for coffee,' his mother preened. 'At last your father and I are moving into society, where we belong.'

He thought about his old granddad who ran the small market at the other end of town and his uncle, who spent most of his life drunk or fighting or both. Ryan laughed, the sound strangely adult and scornful, even in his own ears.

'That's enough, Ryan . . .'

His mother's voice, coldly enumerating his faults, faded into another memory.

'Ryan McLeod?'

Heart thumping in his chest, hating the hope that refused to die, fourteen-year-old Ryan looked through the bars at the uniformed officer. Arrested as an accessory, as lookout for older kids who robbed jewelery stores, he was the only one who'd ended up in jail when the others fled, leaving him behind. He'd told the cops his parents were attending a party at the Rowland ranch. Maybe this time . . .

'Your parents will be here tomorrow.'

'Mommy's boy gotta sleep on a hard bed, eh?' The jeers and laughter of the two big, dirty men who shared his cell rang in his ears. 'Leave him to us, cop. We'll make him comfortable, won't we, bro?'

'We're full up, you'll have to stay in that cell. One of the guards will check on you as often as possible. I'm sorry.'

The sympathy and regret he saw in the officer's eyes terrified Ryan.

During that harrowing night in jail, Ryan finally lost all faith in the myth of unconditional love. It was also the last time he'd wept. The legacy of that night was the lingering memory of terror and anguish that, over twenty years later, still occasionally woke him from a sound sleep.

His father bailed him out at four the next afternoon. Ryan ran away the next morning and for three years wandered the Southern states, hitchhiking from Houston to Miami. He lived on the streets in every city he passed through, finding a group of kids like himself to hang out with. This usually lasted until the group's nominal boss felt threatened by Ryan's natural ability and instinct for leadership and he was forced to move on.

In Miami he got lucky when he tried to extort protection money from a wealthy and well-connected businesswoman. She admired his pretty face and body as much as she respected the way he controlled the pack of street toughs he'd banded together. After they'd known each other one day she made him an offer he was too hungry to refuse.

For the next few years she clothed him, educated him, and used him. As her confidential errand boy he learned everything there was to know about the dark underbelly of high finance. He slipped into places he wasn't supposed to be, saw and heard things the participants wanted concealed. His youth, looks, angelic manner, and charm usually brought him off safe with the information she needed.

He didn't give a damn if her orders fudged or even broke laws. He only cared that survival no longer depended on his ability to be better with his fists or a knife than the guy who wanted his coat or food or body. Success and survival now depended on a whole new set of skills. Skills he'd acquired while working for her.

When he was eighteen she'd discovered him using these same skills to increase his influence in her organization and threw him out. He went peaceably enough. He'd already used up eight of his nine lives and was beginning to fear his luck was about to run out. He went as far away as her cash would take him, ending up in Vancouver six months later. Only an inner sense of his own worth and an out-size measure of determination had brought him to where he was now.

From petty crime to successful businessman.

Could he live with himself if he didn't try to give this kid a happier start than he'd had? Although he knew nothing about taking care of a kid, he was willing to try.

'I'll do it.' He spun around to face the lawyer again.

'Sorry?'

'I will assume guardianship of Ron's daughter. What did you say her name was?'

'Danielle.'

'Danielle,' Ryan repeated. He sat silently for a moment longer, then shoved himself away from his desk and stood. 'Make arrangements for me to pick her up in three weeks. In the meantime I'll have my secretary start making preparations for . . .'

'I'm sorry, Mr McLeod. That will not be possible.'

'What do you mean, not possible? It has to be. I need some time to rearrange my life. You tell my secretary where Danielle is living and Hallie will take care of everything.'

'She's outside. In your reception area.'

'Of course she is. That's where her desk is. Now, if you don't mind, I'm very busy.'

'I'm sorry. I have not made myself clear. *Danielle* is in reception.'

'Outside? Right now?' Ryan plopped down in his chair and covered his eyes with one hand. 'What in hell am I going to do?'

For a few minutes, Becky let herself enjoy the calm of Lilac House, then peeled herself away from the wooden door and skirted the graceful, curving staircase on her way to the play room archway.

'Oh, Mrs Hansen! What happened to you?'

'Pretty bad, huh?' She smiled at Ann, the young student who baby-sat her children. 'A truck splashed me as I was getting into my car.'

The kids were concentrating on a board game, sprawled in the center of the old carpet. Faded and worn, the Persian rug was still the most comfortable spot on the hardwood floor. Five-year-old Nicky waved to his mother from his perch on Ann's lap. Sarah, her eight-year-old daughter, muttered hello but didn't look up.

'I hope it was after your appointment at the bank, Mom. You look awful.' Mike, already trying to be the man of the family at twelve, had risen to his knees and anxiously awaited her answer.

'Yes, it was after my meeting.'

Nicky started to bounce up and down in Ann's arms. 'Ann'n' me are partners and we're winning, Mommy.'

'Very nice. Here's your money, Ann.' Becky put it down on the table.

'Thanks, Mrs Hansen. I'll stay until the game is over, okay?'

She glanced out the window at Ann's house across the street. 'Will your mother mind?'

'No problem. I'll call her.'

'I'm going to take a shower. Mike, would you please get some old towels out of the garage and try to wipe the worst of the mud out of the car?'

'All right, but only because I was losing anyway.' He jumped to his feet and raced out of the room at the same time as his mother left.

As soon as she was around the corner and out of her children's sight, her shoulders sagged and she rubbed the back of her neck with one hand while she dragged herself upstairs. She pushed open the doors to her bedroom suite, the sanctuary she'd created for herself on the second floor of the tower after Eric had left for good.

In her own room Becky had allowed her love affair with Lilac House full rein. Wallpaper lilacs in full bloom climbed a painted trellis. Lamps with fabric shades and silken fringe cast a pinkish glow. Portraits of her family in antique frames clustered with fragile glass perfume bottles on almost every flat surface. Ivory crocheted lace trimmed the pillows, quilts, and linens on the high bed.

The fireplace in the corner was unusable so she'd heaped dried flowers inside its cavernous firebox, occasionally refreshing their delicate scent with potpourri oils. A faded photograph taken of her grandmother and Emily on the day of their debutante ball took pride of place on the mantel. The two laughing girls stood arm in arm wearing long white dresses and lacy wide-brimmed hats with trailing veils. Lilac House in its prime formed their background.

Becky shut the doors, then stood beside the bed, waiting. Eventually she sighed deeply. The peace she needed, the peace she usually felt in this room, wasn't coming today.

In her bathroom she pulled off the clinging dress, dropped it into the laundry hamper, added her pantyhose and underwear, and closed the lid. While she waited for water to fill the claw-footed tub, Becky wrapped a towel around her body. She leaned back against the tiled wall and silently endured as tears began to run down her cheeks. Fear and despair fought in her stomach, threatening to consume her as she wept.

If she paid, no, when she paid the two outstanding mortgage payments she would have only eighty-six dollars and fifty-two cents to her name. That money had to last until the end of the month when the check from the newspaper arrived. How could she feed her family? Where would they live if the bank took the house?

'Damn you, Eric!'

The three words echoed back at her. Cursing her ex-husband felt so good she repeated it. Twice. Why had he disappeared? Where was he? Was he ever going to make another mortgage payment or had those gone the way of the child support payments?

She felt a twinge of old pain at the thought of those support payments. She let her mind rest lightly on that memory, much as another person would probe gently with their tongue at a broken tooth, testing to see how much suffering would result if it was touched. Even after nearly six years her mind shied away.

Resting back against the cool tiles, she slid down to crouch on the floor as racking sobs tore through her body. The roar of the gushing water echoed the thudding of her heart and the throbbing pain in her head. She wrapped both arms around her stomach and tried to hold in the misery. She was so tired of being alone. Never having anyone to share midnight trips to the hospital or Christmas morning exhaustion. No one to comfort her or to care only for her.

Sometimes, not often but sometimes, she even got desperate enough to wish for a man in her life to hold her through the long hours of the night.

'Mom? Are you almost done? It's dinner time.'

Becky jerked upright and slammed her head into the wall behind her. Rubbing her scalp, she slid back up until she was standing and could reach over to turn off the water. She dropped the towel and stepped into the tub.

'I'll only be ten minutes, Sarah.'

'Okay.'

After Becky was dry she used a towel to wipe the steam from the long mirror on the back of the door and examined her image. Mid-brown hair, mid-brown eyes and a mid-sized body carrying ten extra pounds.

You are a sight, she scolded herself. Her curly hair was in wild disorder because of the brisk rub with the towel. The dark purple marks under her eyes would soon be so noticeable make-up would no longer be able to cover them up. Laughter had created the lines radiating from her eyes but worry and stress had carved the grooves between her eyebrows.

She turned sideways, pulled back her shoulders and sucked in her stomach, trying not to see the stretch marks. You have to lose weight, she admonished herself, then laughed without real mirth while she pulled on jeans and a sweatshirt and headed downstairs. If she didn't look so much like a tired old housewife Ellford might give her the money she needed but then he would never leave her alone.

'What's for dinner?' 'I'm starving.' 'Can we have fried chicken?' The minute she entered the room, the kids began clamoring for their favorite meal.

'I made stew for today. I'll heat it while you guys get cleaned up and set the table.' A chorus of groans arose.

'Gee, Mom, we had stew twice this week already. Why can't we have McDonalds' hamburgers tonight?' asked Mike.

'And fries.' Nicky jumped up and down. 'And milkshakes.'

'Sorry. Maybe we'll eat out tomorrow, *if* I get some co-operation tonight. I'm tired so I want you all to be good, then go to bed early.'

'Mom, how come we have to go to bed early when you're the one who's tired?'

She laughed. Sarah, as usual, had cut right to the heart of the issue.

Later Becky gently closed Mike's bedroom door, arching her spine while massaging her lower back. All asleep, finally. What a day! She straightened and started slowly down the stairs. First she needed some cocoa while she worked on the budget, then some sleep.

In the kitchen she stirred a big spoon in the pot of hot chocolate, idly scanning the headlines of the local paper and enjoying the calm and quiet. When steam rose from the pot she reached for a large mug and, after a moment of indecision, cut open a new bag of marshmallows.

Today was definitely a marshmallow day. She dropped in one and then defiantly added two more before she firmly twisted the bag closed and put it back on the top shelf. The diet could start tomorrow.

She burned her lip on the hot liquid when the doorbell rang. She put down the mug and ran for the front hall before the unexpected caller rang the bell again and woke the kids. Through the window beside the front door she saw the light from the old carriage lamp glinting on the fly-away coppery hair of her best friend. Becky swung the door wide and Jan immediately started chattering.

'Hi, I know it's late but I couldn't wait to tell you. You remember Ryan McLeod, the man my Aunt Hallie works for? He needs day-care for a little girl, his niece I think, and I told Hallie you'd be perfect. He's loaded and desperate so you can charge him the earth.'

'Come in, Jan.'

'I can't,' she answered, then turned, smiled, and waved at a shadowy figure in the passenger seat of her car. 'I've got a date.'

'What's this one's name?'

'Simon. And I'll have you know that this is our fourth date.'

'Four dates? He's going to beat the record.'

'Becky!' She put her hands on her hips and glared. 'I didn't drop by so you could nag me.'

'I worry about you.' She reached out to touch Jan's arm. 'Ralph's been dead six years. Isn't it time you accepted the fact that no matter how many different men you date, how many years you wait, none of them can *be* Ralph?'

'How many times do I have to tell you that you've got it all wrong?' Jan shook off Becky's touch. 'I don't want to talk about . . . about Ralph.'

'Jan . . .'

'Drop it, Becky.'

She saw the pain in Jan's eyes, the stiffness in her posture. 'Okay. For now. No promises about tomorrow, though.'

Jan's eyes closed. A moment later she sighed and when she looked at Becky again she smiled brilliantly.

'I wanted to let you know I'd solved all your problems. You love kids, you need money. The guy's rich and he needs you.'

The car horn blared and Jan glanced over her shoulder again. 'Look, I gotta go. My date's getting impatient.' She winked and laughed suggestively. 'For that matter, so am I.'

'But . . .'

'Listen, okay? Ryan's bringing the little girl here, Monday morning at ten, for an interview.' The horn blared again and Jan dashed down the front steps, calling good-bye over her shoulder. Becky waved, locked the door, and sipped her cocoa as she wandered toward the kitchen.

Work for Ryan McLeod? Surprising he'd want to even talk to her after the strip she'd torn off his ego two years ago.

Becky and Jan had just turned thirty and Hallie sixty, so Jan had hosted a combined birthday party. The friends of all three women crowded into Jan's condo. Becky wore pantyhose and a nice dress for the first time in almost four years.

As much as she loved her life, she was feeling positively drunk on freedom. She was enjoying intelligent conversation with other adults. No kids demanded her attention. The small glass of wine she'd allowed herself only added to her giddiness.

When the drop dead gorgeous man walked in near midnight she noticed him immediately and detested him instantly. The past qualified her as an expert on his type and she had no doubt he would be a selfish, cold-blooded jerk, just like Eric.

He hugged Hallie, shook hands with Jan, and smiled graciously when Hallie introduced him to Becky. Ten minutes of party conversation ensued, mostly consisting of light-hearted banter. She probably owed her own recklessness to the glass of wine, but she hadn't been able to resist joining in. The shock that tingled up her arm when he casually touched her elbow scared her to death and she froze instantly.

During that conversation and throughout the first part of the evening, he showed signs of wanting to know Becky better but she was resolutely unresponsive and eventually he mingled with the crowd. Throughout the evening she saw several different women clinging to his arm, hanging on his every word.

Shortly before midnight she decided to go home and phoned for a cab. Freedom was fine in small doses but her head was beginning to hurt. After telling Jan she would wait outside in the quiet, she put on her coat and left. She took two steps into the fresh air and reeled as if hit by a sledgehammer. She didn't know whether to be glad or sorry when Ryan's arm supported her tottering steps to a nearby garden retaining wall.

'Thank you.' She put one hand to her head.

'My pleasure, Ma'am.'

'I feel terrible.'

'You'll be better in a few minutes. It's the combination of a stuffy, over-crowded room and too much alcohol.'

'I'll have you know – ooohh.' She winced and pressed her fingers to her temples as her strident tone caused pain to ricochet through her brain. After a moment she finished quietly, 'I only had one drink.'

'Even one can have that effect if you're not used to it.'

She sat in silence until the ache in her head began to subside. Then she looked up at him suspiciously.

'How did you know I was out here?'

'I saw you leaving and told Jan I'd see you safely into the cab.'

'Why?' She didn't care that the question was bald to the point of rudeness, especially considering she'd needed his assistance.

'It seemed the gentlemanly thing to do.'

'It's unnecessary. You can go back to the party.'

He laughed. 'I like you, Rebecca Hansen, though I don't know why. How about dinner tomorrow night?' And then he smiled.

She felt the world reel sideways again. She gripped the rough stones with her fingers and gritted her teeth. This time she was grateful for the pain that bloomed in her head. It diluted the effects of a smile that was potent, brilliant, and entirely too sure of itself and its power over women.

In two succinct sentences she told him what he could do with his dinner invitation and his liking and his southern charm. The cab arrived; she left. She never saw him again.

Becky scowled. Apparently she was going to see him again on Monday. Determined to find some way to avoid the meeting and possible job, she sat down at the kitchen table in front of a pad of paper and Mike's calculator. With so few places to trim her family's expenses, she had to find another source of income.

An hour later she frowned at the note paper covered with scribbled numbers and the empty marshmallow bag crumpled on the kitchen table. All this time spent fiddling with the budget and not much to show for it. Except perhaps a few extra pounds when she got on the scale tomorrow morning.

The cork squeaked when she tacked the short list to the memo board. Then she carefully folded the empty marshmallow bag into a tiny square and shoved it deep inside the garbage can so the kids wouldn't see it. She was going to bed and when she got there she was going to sleep. The budget could wait until tomorrow.

Her hand swept down across the light switch and the kitchen went dark. On her way upstairs to bed, a thought meandered across her tired brain. If she agreed to take care of Ryan McLeod's niece, she'd be seeing him every day.

Was he still drop dead gorgeous?

CHAPTER 2

'Is she asleep?' Carol asked as she leaned forward to pick up her wine glass. She curled her legs beneath her and reclined into the sofa pillows. She smoothed the skirt of her suit down over her thighs.

'Yes. Finally.' Ryan stood just inside his living room and watched her with a detached, impersonal admiration. She was a very elegant woman.

He'd noticed that whenever anyone talked about Carol Hill, they mentioned her elegance and her intelligence. Her beauty. Her ruthlessness. Her drive. Strange how he was beginning to notice how every mention of her, good or bad, bespoke her distance from the world. Almost since the beginning he'd been aware of a lack of warmth in their relationship, even in bed. Passion, yes, but no heat. Which probably explained why he hadn't initiated sex in a long time.

She smiled and patted the cushion beside her.

He briefly considered accepting the blatant invitation in her eyes but couldn't find any enthusiasm or energy for intimacy. Besides, who knew if Dani would stay asleep for any length of time? He sank into the leather chair on the opposite side of the room and let his head drop back. 'This parenting stuff is difficult.'

'It's only your first night.'

'Don't remind me.' He rolled his head sideways and smiled at her. 'Sorry about our date tonight. You should have used the tickets anyway.'

'Alone? I don't think so. I'm sure Paul and his wife will enjoy the performance and the evening away from their children.' She ran her fingertip around the rim of the glass for a few minutes. 'Have you ever envied them? Marriage, the picket fence and a few children?'

'Paul and Sheila? No way. That life's not for me. I like our arrangement just fine.' A strange look crossed her face. 'Why? Do you envy them?'

She studied him over the rim of the wine glass. 'Have you considered that if we were married I could help with some of your problems?'

'No, I hadn't. I couldn't ask you to do that.'

He noticed an odd expression flash briefly in her eyes. Was she angry?

'Carol, if you've decided to cut me loose and look for a man who wants those things, I'll understand.' Odd. He found himself hoping she'd say yes.

'No. Our arrangement stands.' She tipped up the glass and drained its contents. Silently she held it out to him. He refilled the glass in the kitchen and when he came back she seemed her old self. She took it from him with a soft smile.

'What are you going to do about the child? Boarding school?'

'She's staying with me. Hallie's finding someone to take care of her during the day.'

'She's going to live with you?' Her eyebrows rose. 'That's going to be an interesting experience.' She sipped the drink. 'How was the rest of your day?'

'Bad. That bastard Pastin won the bid on the hospital's reorganization project. Hallie's sources told her that their bid was only five hundred dollars lower than ours. Plus Susan quit today. She was lured away by a friend of his.'

'Isn't that the sixth time you've lost a bid to Harold Pastin?'

'Yeah.' He rolled his head, trying to ease tense neck muscles. 'There's definitely a pattern. All six lost bids were undercut by less than a thousand dollars. She's the fourth key employee I've lost to Pastin or his friends. All four were in a vulnerable financial position and couldn't refuse the offer.'

'It sounds as if someone is giving Harold Pastin inside information.'

'Yeah. It does.'

'Hallie would have access to all the bid information. Her pseudo-maternal manner means she also knows your employees' personal problems.'

'It's not Hallie!' Ryan immediately regretted raising his voice when Carol looked surprised. 'She's as much a part of McLeod's as I am.'

'Okay, okay.' She held up her hands in surrender. 'I was only making a suggestion. You know her better than I do.'

'I know the tension is no excuse, but I am sorry.'

'Of course.' She set down her glass and picked up her purse. 'I'd better go home.'

'You don't have to go so early. We could watch one of those movies Hallie is always buying for me. She's still determined to educate me on what she calls the "real" world. Although I don't understand what Hollywood movies have to do with the real world.'

'No, thank you. I'd better be going. You're tired and I've got some more work to do before my trip tomorrow.'

'I can't leave Dani here alone to drive you home but I'll call for a cab.' He held her coat. When she'd slipped her arms into the sleeves and fastened the buttons, she went on tiptoe to kiss him good-bye.

'I'll call you when I get home from my trip. Good luck finding a baby-sitter.'

'Thanks. I'll probably need all the luck I can get.'

Females!

Ryan's frustration level rose another notch as he wove the silver Mercedes through Sunday morning traffic, the intermittent thwap of the wipers the only sound in the car.

Now, when he needed to concentrate all his resources on a plan for his company's survival, this happened. Now, when he needed to spend time at work he'd be distracted like the parents he knew. He scowled. Recitals. Meetings with teachers. Car pools.

He shifted to pass a bus, snagged his passenger's ruffled skirt on his fingers, and bit back a curse as he disentangled himself.

'Sorry.'

His apology netted only a nod as the atmosphere inside the car sank another chilly degree. Every man who thought he knew females should have to spend a few days living with one like this. For two days and two nights she'd barely said a word beyond yes or no.

Not for the first time he regretted Ron's and Marcia's deaths and questioned his cousin's wisdom in naming a bachelor as guardian of their daughter. He looked down at the child who sat so quietly beside him and made one more attempt at conversation.

'I think you'll like Mrs Hansen.'

'Yes,' Dani responded obediently.

Ankles crossed, fingers linked in her lap, long black hair held back tidily by a blue velvet ribbon, she sat perfectly still. Too still. She didn't fidget or talk endlessly the way he'd expected. The only comment she'd volunteered was that she preferred the shortened version of her name. He knew very little about children but this one didn't seem quite normal.

Giving up, he pulled a slip of paper from the pocket of his jacket and scanned first the address typed there, then the house numbers flashing by.

How could a seven-year-old who seemed so docile make life so difficult? After nearly two solid days' visiting possible baby-sitters, Dani had rejected every applicant for a sometimes absurd assortment of reasons. Rebecca Hansen was the last name on his secretary's list. He'd really hoped to hire one of the other women.

He was amazed Hallie had managed to convince her niece's friend to agree to an interview. Why Rebecca became so irate over a simple dinner invitation, he didn't know, but when he'd met her two years ago she hadn't minced words in her opinion of him. Too bad circumstances had placed him in the position of asking her a favor.

He shrugged. He'd have to charm Becky into acceptance.

Of course all the charm in the world was useless if she or the other children failed to meet Dani's requirements. If Rebecca went the way of the other applicants, he was in big trouble. Capital B, capital T.

He checked the address one more time then slowed down in front of a huge white house on the corner. Its three levels stood out in a neighborhood where every other house was one or two floors. The house bulged out on one corner in a round tower that culminated in a pointed cupola. An ironwork rooster crowed silently and endlessly on its peak. An ornately carved wooden sign that read 'Lilac House' hung from the veranda roof.

Must have been a nice house once, he thought as he rolled to a stop in a driveway lined by straggly bushes. A shame it had been allowed to get so run down. The only exterior paints not faded or peeling were the rich purples, blues and greens on the sign.

In addition to multicolored paint on the walls there was a rusty old station wagon in the cracked driveway and a jungle in the side yard. Not an attractive picture.

As the low rumble of the engine died away the house's disrepair made him doubt the wisdom of leaving Dani here. A moot point because she probably wouldn't stay. She'd already rejected two possibilities because she didn't approve of their homes.

A head popped up from behind the vine-covered rail of the veranda encircling the house. Big brown eyes monitored their approach and Ryan squeezed Dani's fingers when she slipped her cold hand into his. As they climbed the stairs a small boy with unruly brown curls stepped out in front of them. A streak of chocolate adorned his chin and grass stains discolored the bare knees poking out of his torn jeans.

'Hi. What's your names? Why did'ya come here? Can I sit in your car?'

'Nicky! Be polite.' An older girl with smooth brown ringlets that reached the waist of her frilly dress opened the weather-faded screen door. 'May I help you?'

'My name is Ryan McLeod and this,' he tugged lightly at Dani's hand until she was standing in front of him, 'is Dani. I had an appointment to talk to Rebecca Hansen about day-care.'

The girl looked Ryan over with a hint of disapproval in her gaze. 'Mommy told us you were coming tomorrow.'

'I'm afraid I will be unavailable tomorrow. I tried to call but your line has been busy since eight this morning.'

'I guess it's all right for you to come inside. May Dani come upstairs? Nicky can show you where Mommy is.'

He saw the corners of Dani's mouth tip up into a smile, the first since he'd met her, and allowed himself to feel relief. Perhaps, finally, here was a family and house she would deign to spend time with. 'If you're sure your mother won't object.'

'She won't. Come on, Dani.'

He followed the children inside. Breathing deeply of the apple and cinnamon scents wafting through the house, he paused to admire the stairs' wide parallel railings while Sarah led Dani sedately upstairs. On either side of the spacious entry way were matching double French doors with glass panels.

A narrow table against one wall held an assortment of gloves and hats while the ugliest urn he'd ever seen did duty as an umbrella stand. The gilt mirror over the table reflected the magnificent chandelier that hung from the high ceiling.

To his left he saw what he guessed had once been a formal dining room. Currently the upholstered chairs and an ironing board were pushed against the far wall. A sewing machine sat at one end of the wide table's mahogany surface, surrounded by drifts of fabric.

Beyond the doors on his right he could see the ground floor level of the tower. Though it had probably once been a formal parlor, its curved walls surrounded a living room comfortably furnished in a jumble of styles. A heavily carved mantel enclosed a small fireplace. Faded rose velvet drapes framed elegant windows that reached a ceiling ten feet high. His lips tightened as he noticed that both rooms, though clean, showed evidence of the same neglect as the outside of the house.

He felt a tug on his pant leg and looked down at Nicky.

'Mommy is in the play room fixing the fireplace. She can fix anything.' He paused and appeared to re-think what he'd said. 'Almost anything. She promised we could eat lunch in front of the fire 'cause it's so rainy out. Like a picnic.'

Nicky took Ryan's hand and urged him down the hall. At the archway with another set of double doors opening into a large room they stopped. 'Mommy?'

This must have been a magnificent library once, Ryan decided, as he studied the elaborate plaster ceiling, the multi-paned windows, and the heavy oak shelves stacked haphazardly with toys and games. A long, low bench under the window held a large aquarium that appeared to have been adapted for three turtles. Colorful throws concealed the well-cushioned furniture grouped around the television.

'Not now, Nicky. You march back out and play quietly or no picnic. I told you it would take a while.'

Ryan stepped around the corner, seeking the owner of the voice. At the opposite side of the room a second furniture grouping faced another fireplace, this one with a large cavity and plain mantelpiece. Her back was to him as, unaware of his presence, she removed fireplace tools from a cast iron stand.

His heart missed a beat and he felt an unusual constriction in his throat as he struggled with the unwelcome and unreasonable sucker punch of attraction.

Brown curls as unruly as her son's brushed the shoulders of her baggy white cotton T-shirt. Silky pink shorts clung to her hips and derriere, leaving bare the slender legs curving gracefully into small bare feet. He caught a glimpse of toenails painted a vibrant red. His fingertips tingled as he wondered if her flesh was as firm and satiny as it appeared.

'But, Mommy . . .'

'No, young man. I swear you've been in here ten times already to check on me. Not another word, or else.'

Nicky opened his mouth to protest, then evidently thought better of it and bolted as ordered.

Ryan's physical reaction to her presence overwhelmed his first attempt to speak, a mortifying development for a man of his age and experience. He cleared his throat and tried again. 'Rebecca?'

Loud banging drowned out his voice.

She was balanced precariously, with one knee on the raised black slate hearth and one hand on the bricks, with her other hand up inside the chimney. She prodded its depths with the poker in what appeared to be an attempt to force open the damper.

Whatever the reason, she couldn't hear him and his gut clenched as he tried not to stare at her bottom rocking back and forth with each thrust of her arm. The surge of desire he felt shocked him. Where was his mind, his control? He barely knew this woman!

His footsteps made no sound on the old carpet as he moved closer.

'Let me help you.' He reached for her hand on the bricks as he spoke.

Becky felt a large hand cover hers and heard a man's deep voice close to her ear. Shock and panic stifled the scream in her throat. Her knee slipped from its shaky perch as she snatched her hand away from his.

Alarmed she might be hurt against the rough bricks, he wrapped both arms around her middle and jerked her back against his body. Though he had moved fast he was unable to stop her momentum entirely. Her head and shoulders fell forward and the hand holding the poker jammed further up inside the chimney. A discordant clang assaulted his eardrums as the damper jarred open. A cloud of soot and ashes billowed into the room, enveloping them both.

Shock kept them still until he tightened his grip, hauling her upright against his body, her curls tickling his chin. Her weight shifted and they both gasped when the full weight of her breasts came to rest on his forearm and her bottom rubbed against his groin.

Becky's mind went blank and the poker she still held clattered to the floor. Under his hand her heart pounded, rough and fast, as she fought the waves of panic.

He turned her around, never loosening his hold. She gazed up into silvery blue eyes and her heart thudded in her chest as she told herself over and over that this stranger was not Eric. Eric was gone.

Slowly her fear turned to anger, anger that grew stronger as he began to laugh, revealing gleaming white teeth in his soot-coated face.

'Let me go!' Ignoring the fact that only his hold kept her from falling, she pushed against the rock-firm muscles of his chest and twisted in his arms, striving to put some space between their bodies. Her flailing foot knocked over the stand holding the rest of the fireplace tools. He staggered and abruptly stopped laughing as his hands tightened again.

'Be still or you'll get hurt.'

Ignoring the allure of the deep voice with the slight drawl, she glared up at him. 'Then let me go.'

'Yes, Ma'am.' He shifted his grip to her upper arms and slid her down his body, only releasing her when he was sure she was steady on her feet. He took two steps backward.

'Who are you and what are you doing in my house?' The poker scraped along the bricks as she snatched it to hold in front of herself protectively.

'Ryan McLeod. Sarah let us in.'

'Ryan? Oh.' She glanced behind him. 'Us?'

'Your daughter took my ward upstairs and Nicky brought me to meet you.'

'He should have told me you were here.'

'He tried.' His lips twitched, tilting upwards at one corner in what was almost a smile. 'But you told him if he said one more word he wouldn't get his fireside picnic.'

'Oh.' Becky could feel herself gawking at him but couldn't drag her gaze away. She wished she could see his face but it, his upper chest, and his arms were as filthy as she knew her own must be.

Long legs, narrow waist and hips, broad shoulders. Her brain catalogued what she could see. He wore old jeans faded at thigh and crotch, an Oxford cloth shirt that used to be white, and a grey tweed sports coat. These covered but didn't conceal a body guaranteed to make any feminine heart miss a beat or two, even one as guarded as hers.

Obviously not much had changed in two years.

'Why didn't you phone?' Her instincts ordered caution and she looked away.

'I tried. Your line was busy.' He strolled over to replace the phone receiver she hadn't noticed was knocked off its base by a pillow.

'Oh.' She realized she was still holding the poker and put it down. 'Sorry about this. You scared me.'

'No problem, Rebecca. I understand.'

'I prefer to be called Becky.' She picked up the rest of the fireplace tools and replaced them on the rack.

'Jan told me you needed day-care for a child. Why don't you stay for lunch and we'll talk afterward?'

'Thanks. That would be nice but what about . . .' He held his hands out from his body. 'I'm a little dirty to be sitting in your house.'

'Oh! I guess we should get cleaned up. If you follow the hall past the kitchen there's a shower you can use.'

'Sounds great.' He bowed slightly and waved his hand.

She had to stifle a nervous laugh when she realized the courtly gesture indicated he wanted her to precede him out of the room. Polite, but singularly ridiculous, looking the way they did. After a self-conscious tug at the hem of her shorts, she edged past him.

He followed her to the bottom of the stairs and she could feel him staring at her.

'You have to go the other way.' She paused with one foot on the bottom stair and pointed down the hall.

'Thanks.' His drawl was thicker than she remembered it and he lifted one hand to his forehead, as if to tip an invisible cowboy hat.

His eyes glinted as they traveled the length of her bare legs and she felt her cheeks heat beneath the soot. So ridiculous to feel under-dressed when she often wore similar shorts and a T-shirt to the mall.

'I'll be as quick as I can. You should find towels and everything else you might need under the sink.' She hesitated when he didn't leave. 'Do you want me to show you?'

'Thanks, but I'm sure I can find them.'

'Was there something else?' She didn't care that he might hear the annoyance in her sharp tone.

'No, Ma'am.' He grinned but obediently sauntered off down the hall toward the kitchen.

Becky dashed into her bathroom and stepped into the shower still wearing her clothes. The metal rings rang along the rod when she yanked shut the plastic shower curtain. Black water pooled around her feet before it swirled down the drain. After most of the soot had rinsed clear she tugged off her clothes and kicked them to the opposite end of the tub.

She filled her palm with shampoo and scrubbed it into her scalp. Who did he think he was? Marching into her home and scaring her out of her mind. Becky turned and tilted her head back so the spray could rinse out both shampoo and any lingering madness generated by the touch of his long fingers.

Even more difficult to understand . . . why hadn't she called Hallie to cancel this interview as soon as she knew Jan had set it up?

The water pressure dropped. Becky twisted the hot and cold knobs, evening out the temperature of her shower.

Darn this old, crummy plumbing anyway, she thought. She should have remembered that anytime someone turned on the taps in the shower downstairs, it cut off most of the water upstairs. Suddenly visions of Ryan, his body naked and wet in the other shower, filled her mind. Heat pooled deep in her belly.

Needs and sensations long forgotten, and not regretted, began to revive. Forcibly she reminded herself of Eric's beautiful face and black heart. She shivered uncontrollably.

No! She'd learned her lesson and, whatever her body and Jan argued otherwise, she didn't need a man. Becky grabbed the bar of soap and scrubbed vigorously at that same traitorous body. The sooner she got clean and dressed the sooner she could get Ryan out of her house.

She fought the unwelcome cravings back into the dark place she had hidden them. He would have to find someone else to take care of the little girl, Becky swore to herself. She hadn't wanted to date him two years ago and didn't want him around now. If it wasn't for her financial circumstances she wouldn't have even considered taking his baby-sitting job. She'd listen to him since he'd come all this way, but seeing him, being touched by him, strengthened her doubts.

She dried off quickly, then opened her closet to find her oldest jogging suit. Once a beautiful yellow gold, a laundry mishap had created something horribly misshapen and the color of mud. It would cover her totally. No way would she give Ryan McLeod even the remotest signal she was interested in him. She wilfully ignored the fact that, for the first time since Eric's actions had cauterized her needs and instincts, her body had responded to a man, any man.

On her way downstairs she stopped by Sarah's room to collect the girls for lunch, then hesitated with her hand on the knob.

'Why do you live with him?' Sarah's voice was matter-of-fact as always. She wanted to know so she asked, without thinking of what her questions could mean to other people.

'My parents are dead.' The quiet voice was equally blunt.

'When did they die?'

'Three weeks ago. Their plane crashed in Peru.'

'Why were they in Peru?'

'Mother and Father were scientists.'

Becky knocked on the door and went in before Sarah could ask any more questions that the other child probably found painful.

'Hi. My name's Rebecca Hansen but everyone calls me Becky. What's your name?' She smiled down at the pretty little girl who sat in the chair beside Sarah's bed.

'Danielle Anna Mary McLeod but I like to be called Dani.' She got to her feet and shyly held out her hand.

'Let's go downstairs,' Becky said, after solemnly shaking her hand. 'I've invited you and Ryan to stay for lunch. Would you like to eat with us?'

'Yes, please.'

'Well, let's get moving then.'

Becky herded the girls downstairs and sent Nicky to find his older brother. She was determined to make sure she was surrounded by kids for the rest of Ryan's visit.

As they passed the play room she paused. Someone had swept up the mess and now a fire burned merrily in the grate. She paused to marvel at the flames and clean room. She had been so sure she had him pegged correctly and yet Ryan must have done this. Eric would never have cleaned it up, even if asked.

In the kitchen Becky sat the girls at the big table and put ham, cheese, peanut butter, jelly, and bread in front of them, along with a selection of knives and plates.

'You guys make the sandwiches. I'll heat up the chowder.'

Before long the four kids were seated around the table preparing a portable feast of sandwiches, raw vegetables and potato chips. She stood at the stove, stirring a big pot of her own seafood chowder. It was her kids' favorite and Dani had said she liked chowder, but would the man in the shower enjoy a simple family meal?

Hah! Men like him ran screaming in the opposite direction when faced with a room full of children.

'Hey, mister. Do you like peanut butter and jam or ham and cheese in your sandwiches?' Nicky's voice piped shrilly.

'I like both. Anything I can do to help?'

She stiffened when she heard his deep voice answer her son. Becky had to pry her suddenly numb fingers loose from the ladle and place it on the counter top before turning to face him.

He was unbelievably beautiful. Golden hair fell in a careless wave across his wide forehead. The two years since she'd last seen him had etched a few lines around his eyes and beside his mouth but they added to, rather than detracted from, his looks.

He was barefoot and naked to the waist. Faint traces of soot were still visible on the jeans he wore low slung on lean hips, revealing the concave curve of his belly. His shoulders were lightly muscled and his broad chest furred with a golden pelt that narrowed until it disappeared behind the buttons fastening his jeans.

Becky gulped. The man made Michelangelo's David look like a homely wimp.

Ryan almost laughed aloud when he saw what his hostess wore. Old baggy sweat pants the color of mud were topped by a matching jacket, zipped tight to the neck. Her hair was scraped back in an effort to tame her curls.

So she thought she could hide her assets, did she? Thanks to their earlier encounter, he knew Rebecca Hansen was an attractive woman. Very attractive and still unattached, according to Hallie.

Forget it, he reminded himself. You're here to meet the baby-sitter, not the woman, no matter how delectable she might be. Then he saw how, despite the wariness in her eyes, her gaze flicked over his body, away, then back again. Perhaps the attraction was mutual.

He wiped any appreciation of her feminine attributes from his expression when he noticed the look of revulsion on the face of an older boy seated at the table.

'Ryan, you haven't met my son Mike. Mike, this is Mr McLeod.'

The boy nodded without losing any of the scowl. 'Where are your clothes?'

'We had some trouble with the fireplace. The process left me so covered in soot your mother allowed me to use the shower to clean up.'

'You kids better get those sandwiches finished if you want to eat.' Becky frowned at her son, shaking her head when he shrugged off her disapproval.

'I used the pail and rags from the porch to clean the soot off the floor,' Ryan said, 'then dumped the ashes and rags into the garbage can outside. The fire is burning fine now.' He walked toward her, seemingly oblivious to his state of undress. 'There's one problem.'

She glanced at the kids, hoping for some distraction in that direction but the children had obviously lost interest in the adults' conversation. Their attention was once again directed to the important task of preparing their food and arranging the sandwiches on two platters in the middle of the table.

'Whaa-at?' She backed away until her spine pressed against the counter.

'My clothes are filthy.'

He kept stepping closer and Becky kept sidling away until he had her backed into the corner between the stove and the door. He stopped only inches from her and leaned over the soup pot, giving it a stir and sniffing appreciatively. 'You made the chowder?'

She nodded.

'Good food and a beautiful woman,' he said, his voice low and husky. 'A perfect meal.'

She stared as he rubbed a careless hand across his chest and down his lean stomach. He hooked a thumb into the waistband of his jeans, drawing her helpless gaze to his waist and hips.

Ryan felt himself responding to her gaze. This would never do, especially in front of a room full of children. Back off, you fool, he warned himself.

'I can't eat lunch or drive home like this.' His voice was louder now, the hint of intimacy gone. 'I need a shirt to wear and a plastic bag to put my other clothes in. The soot is so fine it flies everywhere.'

When she didn't answer him, simply stared wordlessly, he chuckled again and touched the tip of her nose with his forefinger. 'Do you have another shirt like the one you were wearing earlier?'

'Sarah?' Her daughter's name came out on a croak. 'Would you please get one of my night – ' she stumbled over the word, blushed, then continued, 'shirts for Mr McLeod?'

'Sure.' Sarah jumped up and hustled out the door.

'The bags are in the cupboard under the sink,' Becky mumbled. 'In the box.'

'Thanks. I'll get it,' he said.

His teeth flashed white in a grin and he turned away to open the cupboard. Like a rabbit wary of the fox, Becky wasn't sure if she would be safer running or keeping still.

His shoulders were smooth and wide and lightly freckled; muscles rippled across his naked back as he stooped. The waistband of his jeans gaped and she caught a glimpse of a low tan line and white skin before he stood up.

'I'll go get my clothes and put the bag in the car.' He met Sarah on his way out of the room and she handed him a folded shirt. Judging by Becky's blush and verbal stumble, it was one she slept in.

'Here, Mr McLeod. It was the last one in your drawer, Mommy.'

Ryan tucked a corner of the plastic bag into his pocket and held the over-sized shirt in his hands, fingers rubbing gently against the fabric. This one was washed as thin as the one she had worn earlier.

'Maybe I shouldn't. I wouldn't want you to have to go without, especially on such a cool, rainy night.'

His grin glinted wickedly at Becky and she visualized something, or rather someone, entirely different keeping her warm that night. As she was sure he meant her to. For a moment or two she was fascinated by the way his hands caressed the shirt.

'No.' Her voice was scratchy so she cleared her throat. 'No, go ahead.'

He unfolded the shirt and held it up by the shoulders so he could read the words printed above a small yellow cartoon bird on the shirt's front.

'"Have you kissed your Tweetie today?"' Ryan read it aloud then lifted an eyebrow at her.

'It was a present from the kids,' she explained defensively.

She watched as Ryan pulled the shirt over his head. Over-long and baggy on her, it stretched taut across those shoulders. Poor Tweetie would never be the same. Staring at his tousled hair and sparkling grin made Becky afraid that neither would she.

CHAPTER 3

How could a woman sulk and still look adorable, Ryan wondered. After consuming more food than he'd thought possible, the kids were playing games in the other room. Becky washed dishes in the kitchen, trying and failing to hide how much his presence unsettled her.

He slouched in one of the mismatched kitchen chairs, his long legs stretched out in front of him and crossed at the ankle. Every time she crossed the room she had to step over his legs or walk gingerly around his bare feet.

Every time it happened she glared.

Every time she glared, Ryan grinned.

'A wonderful meal. I have never had such delicious apple pie. And the chowder was amazing. You're a great cook.'

'Would you please move your legs? I might trip.'

'I'd catch you.'

'Why don't you make yourself either scarce or useful?' She tossed a dish towel at him. 'Dry the dishes.'

He caught the towel in mid-air before it slapped him in the face and nodded in the direction of the olive green dishwasher built into the cupboards. 'Why don't you use that?'

'Because it's broken. Do you think I put my hands in this water because I want to? Washing dishes is tedious and if you're not going to help, you can go sit with the kids.'

He let his gaze wander from the curve of her hips, barely discernible under the bulky outfit, to her hair. As it dried the strands had pulled loose from the elastic and now curled around her face. His body stirred as he visualized her wearing only a man-sized shirt like the one he'd borrowed. Not one of her own.

His shirt. In his bed.

Casually he dropped the towel in his lap, hiding the more and more obvious evidence of his arousal. What was it about this woman that excited him so?

Never a man to fool himself, from the age of fourteen he'd known what attracted women. His face. His body. Success and money, once he'd acquired both. Women had seldom, if ever, cared about the man behind the facade.

Young and desperate, he'd done what was necessary to survive. As an adult the using had been mutual. Now a mild distaste for that lifestyle had become so strong he seldom responded to the most subtle approach. He'd preferred to maintain a mutually convenient association with a woman who was a busy executive with her own successful public relations firm.

He'd met Carol occasionally through mutual business clients. Then one night, at a large cocktail party hosted by the Chamber of Commerce, she'd approached him after observing him repulse Sally, the drunk wife of a colleague.

Carol had smiled and offered him one of the two champagne glasses she held. When he hesitated she assured him she was offering a drink and escape, nothing else. A quick peek over his shoulder confirmed Sally's relentless advance, her silly grin and wavering walk proving she was far beyond the point of discretion.

He took the offered glass along with Carol's hand, grateful for her intervention. With her arm hooked in his they circulated for an acceptable length of time, then left to go their separate ways.

The next morning he'd been surprised when Carol phoned to invite him to dinner. He'd warily but politely refused until she'd explained she had a proposal they might find mutually expedient, strictly business.

That night he'd been stunned when she suggested they allow their acquaintances to see them as a couple. She'd been fighting off unwanted advances for years and some clients' wives saw her as a threat. His presence at her side on public occasions would solve many problems for them both.

He'd eventually accepted her proposition. After several months the platonic relationship had evolved into something more physical. Their arrangement had not been exclusive, although lack of time and interest had rendered it so. Carol neither wanted nor needed more from him than a presentable escort and, occasionally, a safe sexual partner. And lately even that superficial connection had been withering through lack of attention from both sides as they concentrated on work.

If the subject of marriage came up, she'd seemed perfectly satisfied with the status quo, agreeing with him that an unfettered life was preferable to the hassles of mortgages and children.

Spending time in Becky's home made him wonder how either Carol or he could have been satisfied with so little in their personal lives. Abruptly Ryan shook his head in disbelief. Marriage and a family weren't part of his plan.

So why was he thinking differently now? What was it about Becky that brought on these crazy thoughts?

Lust, he answered himself. This thing between them was physical, plain and simple. Easily remedied, if she was interested, resulting in mutual pleasure. He'd make sure she enjoyed their time together while it lasted.

'What's it going to be? Leave or work?'

'I think I'd rather stay in here with you, even if it means work.'

'Get started.' Becky turned her back and plunged her hands in the soapy water. She heard his chair scrape back, the old floor creaked and he was standing beside her. His clean masculine scent tantalized her nostrils and his nearness made her skin tingle.

No! Becky shouted in her mind. She worked faster in an effort to shut down her body's awareness of him.

'You better slow down. You're going to break a dish and cut yourself.' He was so close his breath stirred her hair and she shivered.

She dropped the dish she was scrubbing back into the water and stepped away from him. 'Why are you doing this?'

'What?'

'Coming on to me. Almost everything you said during lunch was . . . was suggestive. And you kept smiling that . . . that smile.'

He leaned back against the counter and crossed his arms on his chest. 'I'm sorry if I made you uncomfortable.'

'Well, you did and you don't sound sorry at all.'

Intent on kissing the frown off those extremely tempting lips, Ryan pulled back. It appeared he was heading for a showdown of some kind. His instincts told him he needed to keep his wits sharp and off the appealing idea of kissing her, thoroughly, until she kissed him back. But it was going to be damned hard. How could someone like Rebecca Hansen rip right through his control so easily?

'You come into my house, scare me to death, and then bother me most of the afternoon.'

'That's fair,' he murmured. 'You bother me. A lot.'

'What did you say?'

'Nothing.' He noticed the way she paced back and forth across the long room, always careful to step wide around him. The fire had been hot while they ate lunch and she had lowered the zipper on her jacket a few modest inches, revealing her white throat and the beginning of the shadowed valley between her full breasts.

He deliberately brought out his most charming smile, the one that tipped up one corner of his mouth and crinkled the corners of his eyes. The smile, he'd been told many times, that no woman could resist.

The impact halted Becky in her tracks.

'How do I bother you?' His voice was heated and dark, conjuring up visions in Becky's head, visions she'd rather not have.

His hand stretched across the space between them and slid a caress down her arm. She felt the electricity snap and crackle inside her, threatening to thaw frozen emotions. Remembered pain helped dissipate his allure. She stiffened and pulled away.

'Can't take rejection, Mr McLeod?' She turned her back on him. 'Two years ago I wasn't interested. That hasn't changed.'

'Becky?' His voice curled around her senses like a warm tropical breeze.

'There.' She swung around to glare at him. 'That's what I mean. A simple phrase or even one word and you make it into . . . into . . . into something else. I think you had better leave and you can find someone else to take care of Dani. I'm sorry because she's nice and I like her. But I will not be sexually harassed in my own home.'

'Harassed?' Shock wiped the confident grin off his face. 'I thought you felt . . . I didn't mean . . .'

'I'm sure you didn't. Men like you never do. It's as natural as breathing to come on to a woman. Any woman. You can take your flashy goods and . . .'

'What did you say?'

'You can take your *flashy goods* and peddle them elsewhere. I was married to a handsome man and one is enough for me.' Becky's voice became cooler and more distant. 'I'm not interested.'

'Flashy goods?' Ryan felt the tide of dull red that swept up his neck and across his face as his mouth gaped open. He snapped it shut, tossed the dish towel onto the counter, and stepped away, curbing the urge to shout at her.

'If the shoe fits . . .' Becky plunged her hands back into the cooling water.

'I'm sorry you feel that way.' His chair's legs scraped on the worn linoleum when he shoved it back under the table. His heels thumped the floor as he moved across the room. 'Thanks for the meal. I'll have Hallie return your shirt.'

She acknowledged him with an abrupt nod but didn't look up. He spun on his heel and stalked down the hall to the play room where the children were sprawled around a board game.

'Dani, we're leaving now.'

'Yes, sir.' She immediately put down the dice and picked up her jacket. 'Thank you for teaching me to play Monopoly, Sarah.'

'After school tomorrow we'll play something else,' Sarah said.

'That won't be possible, I'm afraid. We have several more interviews scheduled for tomorrow.' Ryan forced himself to disregard the way Dani's shy smile faded into hurt. He also tried not to think about Hallie's list, the one with every potential baby-sitter's name crossed off. 'Good-bye.'

Smiling farewell in the general direction of the other children he followed Dani down the hall to the front door. He almost bumped into her when she stopped abruptly.

'Why do we have more interviews? I like Becky and Sarah.'

'Because . . . because . . .' Ryan rubbed the back of his neck. What could he tell her? He couldn't let Dani think Becky's stubbornness was her fault. 'You told me you wouldn't stay at the last lady's house because it was dirty. This house is messy, too. I want to make sure we make the best choice.'

'Becky is the best. She's perfect.' Her eyes filled with tears. 'I want to be with Sarah. Sarah said she would be my friend. Lilac House isn't messy, it's . . . where people *live*.'

She was right, Ryan thought as he glanced around. Children in this house wouldn't be screeched at every time they left something in the wrong place. Faced with Dani's misery, he was forced to examine his actions with painful honesty.

Rebecca Hansen was a single mother supporting three kids . . . a nice woman, nothing like Carol Hill or any of the other sharks who swam in the deep waters of his own world. He'd been acting like a presumptuous ass.

He took only seconds to evaluate what he had done and what it had cost this child.

'Look, you go back and play. I'll talk to Becky.'

'Can she take care of me?'

Ryan pulled a crumpled but clean tissue from his pocket and crouched down to wipe awkwardly at her eyes. 'I can't promise, but we'll see.'

While Dani settled back on the floor beside the others he stood outside the kitchen, watching Becky slam dishes onto the draining board beside the sink.

'This is not going according to plan,' he said under his breath. He sighed inaudibly as he walked over to pick up a wet bowl and the dish towel he had thrown down a few minutes earlier.

'I told you to leave.'

'Yes, you did.' He searched out and held her stormy gaze as he rubbed the towel over the bowl's surface.

What could he say to convince her? Dani wanted to stay and he needed to concentrate on work. Becky might be the only baby-sitter the kid ever approved of. If he tried renewing their search then he'd be back in the middle of Big Trouble. Capital B, capital T. 'My behavior was inappropriate.'

'Yes, it was.'

'Look, I don't know much about children but today I met three kids who love and respect their mother. It's clear you love them and do your best to make them happy. I believe you would do your best to extend that same affection to any child in your home and under your care.'

'Of course.'

'Please listen to me, Becky.' A rueful grin lifted one corner of his mouth. 'Dani needs someone like you. Give her, give me, a chance. I thought the attraction was mutual. I won't make that mistake again. I promise.'

He reached out to touch her shoulder but instead waved at the chair behind her. 'Please sit down so I can tell you about Dani's life.'

She huffed but allowed herself to be persuaded to sit.

He walked around to sit down on the opposite side of the big table, purposely putting several feet of sturdy wood between them. No sense sitting within reach of temptation when he needed to maintain a clear head. He rested his forearms on the scarred surface and clasped his hands together, his body tense.

They eyed each other in silence. Becky's body language told him she was doubtful but willing to listen. He glanced down at his hands then back up, his own eyes intent.

'My cousin and his wife were dedicated anthropologists who noticed little beyond their research. After Dani was born they dumped her on Marcia's relatives and disappeared back into the interior of South America. From what I have been told Dani saw them about twice a year when they came back to report their findings or to raise funds for more research. They died last month while on another expedition.'

'I heard her tell Sarah they'd died in Peru.'

'So we've been told. I hadn't seen Ron and Marcia since their wedding. Their lawyer said they named me as Dani's guardian because I once sent them a donation for some damned scientific safari. They thought I was generous.' He shoved his hand through his hair.

'And you disagree with their assessment?'

'Dammit, it was a tax deduction. I didn't even know they had a daughter. The first I knew about her was when the lawyer showed up in my office a few days ago, Dani in tow.'

'That's atrocious. How could any parents have been so careless with their child's welfare?'

'Exactly my reaction when the lawyer told me. Ron and Marcia died penniless and Marcia's relatives wouldn't keep Dani unless I paid them a very large sum of money. A sum so large it was clear they expected me to support their entire household. I would have done it, if she'd been happy.'

'Were they unkind?'

'She won't talk about her life with those people but the lawyer told me something of how she was treated. They barely tolerated her and didn't try to hide it from her.'

'That's terrible!'

'So there we were . . . a bachelor and a little girl.'

He stopped talking and searched her face for some clue that hearing Dani's story had altered her attitude. Would he be able to change her mind?

'Dani is a good child from what I have seen. Quiet and able to entertain herself. She won't be any trouble for you and I promise, neither will I.'

'It's ridiculous for you to drive her all the way out to Richmond, five days a week.'

'I'll work out something. Maybe I can hire a part-time chauffeur.'

'You could find another baby-sitter for Dani, one closer to your apartment.'

'She wants to be here.'

'You sound like you care what she wants.'

'I damned well do care. I know how abandoned she feels, none better.' For a moment bitter disgust almost overwhelmed him as he stared over her shoulder into his past.

'What – '

He shook his head and cut off her question about the meaning of his comment.

Becky didn't mind. She didn't really want that question answered because she might learn more about him. Knowledge meant intimacy and intimacy with a man like him frightened her.

'Dani wants to stay with you.'

She looked into his eyes, seeking a hint of deceit, a glimmer of the sexual intensity he'd surrounded her with since he had first touched her hand on the bricks. The money he would pay her was crucial to her future but she was afraid to believe him.

He felt her doubt and concern and groped for something he could say to convince her he meant what he said.

'I regret, deeply regret, if anything I have said or done kept you from accepting Dani into your home.'

'But – '

'I'll pay you well,' he said, and named a generous sum that made her head spin. With that much money she wouldn't have any trouble making the mortgage payments. Her children wouldn't lose their home. She hesitated, then nodded, positive the turmoil in her stomach was caused by relief now she knew he would leave her alone.

'Okay.' She extended her hand across the table. 'Dani can start here tomorrow.'

They shook hands, both hiding their reaction to the touch of the other.

'This is not the way I expected to make our arrangements,' she said. 'Maybe we should pretend this afternoon never happened and start over.' She pushed back a niggling doubt such a thing would be possible.

'Whatever you want.' He stood and walked around the table to halt at her side.

'Hello, Ma'am. I believe you were expecting me.'

Becky sharply repressed a twinge of regret as she gazed up into his smiling face. Heavens, he's gorgeous, she thought, before reminding herself he was Dani's guardian and nothing else. Her answering smile was bright and she chuckled.

The light, cheerful sound startled Ryan, making him painfully aware she hadn't laughed once that day and it was probably his fault.

'Hello, Ryan. Call me Becky. I have a few questions and I need some information about

Dani. Why don't you sit down and we can take care of it now?'

'Terrific idea.'

He looked down into the brown eyes so clear he felt he could sink into their depths. A strong sense of relief coursed through him. He felt like he had signed the biggest deal he would ever negotiate, in a long career filled with important and difficult deals. Only one thought kept intruding, worming itself into his mind.

Where did they go from here?

That night, her children finally in bed, Becky was relaxing in front of the fire with a mug of cocoa and a blood-curdling mystery when the doorbell rang.

When she opened the door Jan pushed past and marched straight into the living room where she plunked herself down on the couch.

'Well?' She looked at Becky who had followed her into the room. 'Tell me all the gory details.'

'What are you talking about?'

'Aunt Hallie called and said you agreed to take care of the kid.' Jan's manner showed she felt she was dealing with someone either half-asleep or slightly dim-witted. 'Am I good, or what?'

Becky perched on the other end of the couch. 'You're crazy, you know?'

'No way. I set it up and it came together.' Jan's shoulders lifted as she spread out her arms. 'As it always does.'

Becky shook her head and grinned. 'You'll never change, will you? How do you manage to fool your bosses that you can do that big fancy, corporate job?'

'I'm an idea woman with an assistant who's darn good at detail work,' Jan chuckled. 'Right now I'm waiting to hear what happened, so talk, woman. Did you throw that gorgeous man on the floor and have your wicked way with him?'

'Of course not.'

'You don't have to sound so shocked. I can't help hoping you'll take advantage of the job's potential fringe benefits. Either way, you'll get some extra cash plus one more little girl to mother without suffering labor pains. Hog heaven, for you.'

'I guess so.' Becky bent forward to pick up her mug, took a sip and grimaced at the cold liquid. She got to her feet. 'I'm going to reheat this chocolate. Want some?'

'You bet. Why do you think I show up here so often in the evening? I know you always make that delicious hot chocolate.' Jan trailed her into the kitchen and watched her pour milk and cocoa into the pot that still stood on the stove. 'He's drop dead handsome and single. Don't you regret freezing him out when I set you up two years ago?'

'Jan, stop. I don't want or need a man.'

'Yes, you do. There are some things a man is good for that allow no substitutes.' Jan started opening and shutting cupboard doors. 'Sex and dancing are only two of them. When was the last time you . . .'

'Jan!'

'. . . went dancing?' Jan finished smoothly with a grin.

'Sometimes you make me so mad! What are you rooting in my cupboards for?'

'The marshmallows. I know you've hidden them around here somewhere.'

'Behind the cream of celery soup.'

'Thanks. Hiding them from the kids, again, huh?' Jan ripped the bag open and dropped some in their mugs. 'Of course, we have to get rid of that other woman first.'

Becky choked on the mouthful she had just swallowed. 'He's involved?'

'With Carol Hill.' Jan poked at a marshmallow that had melted onto the edge of the mug. 'My aunt says she's an icy blonde barracuda who uses him something awful, poor man, and he can't see it.'

'Yeah, right. No one could use that man unless he wanted them to.'

'I only know what Hallie told me. Anyway, as far as I'm concerned, all relationships are based on either the convenience or the needs of one or both partners.'

'Thank heaven not everyone's as cynical as you.'

'Not cynical . . . practical and realistic. Even you have to admit a rich husband would solve all your problems. Especially since all you ever wanted to be was a mommy and a wife.'

'You don't have to sound so disgusted,' Becky laughed. 'I will say this one more time and then I don't want to hear any more about it.' She waved her mug in the air to emphasize her point. 'I don't need a man.'

'But . . .'

'No. The crossword puzzles bring in some money and the trust fund from my parents covers the rest. Although baby-sitting was a good idea.'

'Good? It's terrific.'

'You have no idea how terrific. Eric hasn't made the mortgage payments in two months and now he's disappeared.'

'Oh? What did Tom Ellford have to say? Nothing good I presume.' Jan followed Becky back to the living room.

'They're going to foreclose.'

'Nobody knows where Eric's gone?'

'No.' Becky sipped at her cocoa and stared at the blank wall between the front windows where her great-grandmother's upright baby grand piano used to stand . . . before she'd had to sell it. 'He quit his job at the hotel bar and he dumped the woman he'd been living with. I think she's finally given up on him.'

'I suppose Ellford came on to you again, the louse.'

Becky linked her fingers over an imaginary paunch, and looked down her nose at Jan, assuming a fatuous leer. 'Rebecca, you know I'm always willing to help *special friends*,' emphasized by a wink, 'with their financial difficulties.'

'You should report that man to his boss.'

'He's always vague enough. He could claim I'd misunderstood his natural professional concern.'

'I'd like to get my hands on Eric.' Jan's vehemence made Becky smile. 'Are you going to try to find him?'

'How?'

'A detective might . . .'

'Where on earth would I find the money to pay a detective?'

'I would – '

'Absolutely not.'

Both women fell silent and sipped their chocolate.

'Mom?'

They twisted to look where Mike hovered in the archway, bony wrists and ankles sticking out from faded pyjamas.

'Yes, honey?'

'Can I talk to you?'

'Have to run.' Jan leaped to her feet. 'Bye you guys.' She shadow boxed with Mike on her way past, drawing a small grin from him. The outside door banged shut behind her.

'What's the matter?' Becky looked at her son with concern. He was getting so tall and lately he positively enjoyed wrapping his arm around her shoulder and looking down at her. 'Trouble sleeping?'

'No. At least not really.' Mike sat down beside her on the sofa and drew his legs up so he could wrap his hands around his ankles. 'Last week I decided Dad should give us some money, because of the furnace repairs and all, so I tried to call him at Sally's place and at work.'

'And?' Becky asked, her stomach knotting.

'It was a waste of time.' Mike hunched his head down between his shoulders. 'She hasn't seen him. His boss said he quit months ago. Is he gone for good?'

She hesitated, unsure what her son needed to hear. She had learned a long time ago that shielding her children from Eric's actions usually caused more problems than it solved.

'I don't know.' At her blunt answer his lips trembled then firmed.

'I hope so. We don't need him anyway.' He jerked his shoulder away when she tried to hug him.

'You're right.' She rubbed his back. 'Besides, whatever goes wrong, you know I can fix it.'

'Oh, Mom, you always say that.' His grin was weak but she was glad to see it.

She pulled back in mock reproof. 'And I'm always right, aren't I?'

'Oh, yeah? What about Nicky's tricycle? When most people try to fix something, they don't end up with more parts than they started with.'

She chuckled, partly because of the remembered incident but mostly because the crisis seemed to have passed. 'He needed a two-wheeler anyway. The tricycle was too small.'

'You always say something like that when you've tried to fix things and it goes wrong.'

'Get to bed, buster.' She stood and tugged him up. 'We have lots to do tomorrow.'

'Mom?' He stood on one foot, the other balanced atop its mate to keep it off the cold hardwood floor.

'Yes?'

'Ryan McLeod isn't going to be around here much, is he?' Mike asked.

'No.' Becky thought about the icy blonde then reached over and snapped off the table light, plunging the room into darkness. 'No, he's not.'

CHAPTER 4

'Becky? Where are you?'

So much for her promise to Mike. Some days she wondered if Ryan created excuses to linger when he picked up Dani. She sat up and scrubbed her sleeve across her eyes, but it was too late. He'd seen her tears.

For two painfully long weeks she'd managed to be cool, impersonal and slightly disapproving whenever he was at the house and now all that effort was wasted. Maintaining the tone of disapproval had been difficult because she'd agonized over whether she should apologize to him for the harassment accusation. As soon as she'd cooled down she'd had to accept that she might have been sending mixed signals.

A man like him couldn't have missed the way she looked at him or the other little signs of attraction she hadn't had control over. On the other hand, no way could she afford to give him the slightest encouragement.

Becky grabbed a tissue and tried to scrub away any mascara streaks beneath her eyes.

'Are you crying?'

'No.' She stared straight ahead, focusing on the flickering television screen, trying to avert her head so he couldn't see her red nose and blotchy cheeks.

'What's wrong?' he asked as he perched on the arm of the sofa beside her.

'Nothing.'

'Are you sure?'

'Yes! What can I do for you?'

'Mike said you were in here. I wanted to thank you for keeping Dani while I took my client to dinner and I wanted to drop off the check for next month.'

'Dani is always welcome.' She knew he was staring at her, trying to read her expression in the half-light of dusk.

She flinched when he reached out and flicked on the imitation Tiffany lamp.

'You *were* crying.'

'So? It's no big deal.'

'Can I help?'

'Will you stop badgering me?' She glared at him for a minute before she turned away to stare at the television again. 'Haven't you ever seen anyone cry because of a show before?'

Ryan glanced at the screen where a woman was throwing dirty laundry at a man sprawled on a couch. 'That's a sad show?'

She grimaced at the note of doubt in his voice but didn't answer him.

'Be straight with me, Becky. Let me help.'

She jumped to her feet and punched the button that silenced the sitcom. 'Thanks for the check. I'll walk you out.'

'Not until you talk to me.' He leaned back and crossed his legs, obviously prepared to sit there until she told him the truth.

'You mean it don't you?' Becky crossed her arms over her stomach and tapped her foot.

'Yes, I do.'

'Why should you care?'

He looked startled for a moment, as if he didn't know why himself. 'Hallie told me she'd make me sorry if you were unhappy. You and I both know it's better not to get Hallie in a snit. So, if you have a problem, let me help.'

She glowered at him but he only smiled, impervious to her annoyance.

'There's no problem,' she mumbled. 'It was only the commercial.'

His eyebrows rose and she felt the blush start at her chest and rise slowly until she knew her face was fiery red right to her hair line.

'A commercial?' When he saw she was telling the truth he started to chuckle.

'Yes, damn you. This mother was all alone 'cause her kids had grown up and moved away. They set up a telephone conference call for her birthday. Sometimes these things strike a chord. I think about my own kids and . . .' She stumbled into silence as his chuckle became a full blown belly laugh.

Her eyes narrowed in a fierce scowl. 'I'll have you know that lots of people cry at commercials. Lots and lots and lots. Furthermore, the advertising agencies earn big money from their clients if they make it happen.'

'A commercial.' He was laughing so hard he could barely speak.

'You had better stop right now,' she warned.

He gasped and choked with the effort to hold it back but in less than a minute he was howling again.

She picked up the check. 'You can see yourself out when you're finished having your little joke. I have work to do.' He was still trying to control himself when she straightened her back and marched grandly to the door.

How dare he laugh at her like that, she asked herself as she stamped away. What colossal nerve.

'Wait!' Ryan vaulted over the back of the sofa and seized her arm. 'I'm sorry. I've stopped now.'

She looked him over. 'Are you sure?'

'Ye . . . yeah.' He gulped suspiciously mid-word but there was a new tenderness in his gaze when he looked at her.

'Good.'

'Don't be mad. It's rather sweet.'

'Sweet is worse than cute and I despise cute.' She was disgusted. 'I hate it when someone makes fun of me.'

'I wasn't laughing at you, truly. Or maybe a little but more at myself for worrying about you because of some advertising ploy.'

'Worrying about me?' She looked away, surprised at the rare feelings of security and comfort his explanation evoked. She carefully eliminated the foolish emotions. 'You needn't bother.'

'I can't help it.'

'You must,' she answered sharply. He was still holding her arm, but gently now, his thumb making small circles on the sensitive flesh. She realized she liked it. Too much.

'Let me go,' she demanded as she tried to jerk loose. 'I'll call Dani, she's upstairs.'

'I know. I needed to talk to you about a couple of things.' He released her and she backed away.

'What about?'

'Last night at dinner, Dani and I talked.'

'That's good.'

'It was rough. I couldn't get her to tell me what she wants to do.'

'Do?'

'Yeah, you know, all those activities that keep kids busy and their parents go crazy organizing? The people at work are always going on about this stuff so it must be important. I was wondering if you would talk to her?'

'Sure, but I wouldn't force her to enrol in anything right now. There've been a lot of changes in her life lately. Allow her time to recover. Someday she'll want to do those things.'

'She also asked me what she should call me.'

'Call you?'

'She announced it was difficult to always wait for me to look at her before she says anything, especially when I'm busy working.' He chuckled when Becky smiled. 'Yeah, I'd been wondering why she had so little to say.'

'How did you answer?'

'It's tough.' He hesitated. 'I don't know what to say to little girls. Heck, what do I know about kids?'

'What did you say?'

'I told her it didn't matter, the waiter brought the food, and she dropped the subject.'

'Ryan, you should have – '

'I know. I should have told her something, but her question threw me. I intend to talk to her tonight about it but I hoped you would tell me what to say to her.'

'What does she want to call you?'

'She thinks Uncle Ryan is out because I'm not a real uncle and "plain" Ryan is not respectful.' He avoided her gaze and picked up the miniature action figure lying almost under his shoe, concentrating on straightening its limbs.

'And . . .'

'She wondered if she should call me Dad.'

Becky noticed him wince as he said the last word. 'How do you feel about that?'

'I'm not her Dad.'

'Don't you think she knows that? Probably, from how you've described her parents, you are the closest she's ever come to that relationship.'

'I know but I can't be her Dad.' He put the toy down and shoved his hands in his pockets. 'I don't have what it takes.'

'What it takes is caring.'

'I care about her. I want her to be happy. I buy her everything she could possibly need.'

'And now she has more "things" than any little girl I know. Maybe you should stop buying and start giving.'

His questioning gaze and furrowed brow made his puzzlement clear. Obviously he was unable to see the difference. 'Never mind. Decide what you want her to call you and give her an answer. Tonight. Okay?'

'Fine. It won't be "Dad" but I'll try to make sure she knows I care about her. I'll have to convince her that she can use my name.'

'This will happen again, so be prepared. Many times as she grows up she's going to want to talk about something she finds deeply emotional.'

He blanched. 'Emotional?'

'You'll be scared about saying the right thing but don't worry, all parents are. All you have to do is be there for her. Encourage open communication and provide nurturing and support.'

'That's all?' he asked in a strained voice.

'What else did you want to talk to me about?'

'What? Oh . . . I have to go to Miami for six days, beginning tomorrow. Can Dani stay here? I'll pay you extra for the inconvenience, of course.'

'Six days?'

'Yes. Hallie can't stay with her overnight, Carol will be out of town, and my housekeeper won't. There really is no one else I can ask.'

'I don't know.' She refused to acknowledge the strange sense of loss she felt at the knowledge he'd be in another city, thousands of miles away, for almost a week. Not because she'd miss him, of course.

She wouldn't!

She caught herself wondering who he was going with and snapped that thread of thought off short.

'Please?' His eyes lit from within and his lips started to lift at the corners.

She jerked her gaze away. Oh, my Lord, he's going to smile. Be strong, Hansen, be strong. Do you really want to take care of four children for six nights and six days, regardless of how much you need the money?

She looked back. He was smiling.

When she shut the door behind him half an hour later he still had an amused tenderness in his gaze and she was committed to six days of twenty-four hour day-care. Becky couldn't help smiling a little bit herself. Oh, heavens, she was starting to like him.

Her grin disappeared. How could she have done this to herself? She had to find some way to kill the liking before it infected her life.

Ryan blinked burning, bloodshot eyes as he stood outside Lilac House. No one had answered the front door. He stepped back out into the rain and looked up at the windows. The mostly bare branches of the oak tree were no protection from the wet weather as he scanned the house and yard for occupants. Where was everybody?

He'd been surprised by how much he'd missed Dani. But accustomed as he'd become to living with the kid, he'd been shocked by how much time he'd spent on the trip thinking about Becky. Before, no woman had made such an impact in his life that he missed her when he, or she, was gone.

Through six frenzied days of meetings, lunches, and dinners she'd been on his mind. So much so that he'd come straight home from the airport when he should have gone to the office to put in another four or five hours.

Home. Reality check, McLeod, he reminded himself. Home is a luxurious apartment on the West side, not this run down, imitation Victorian. He headed around the side of the house and stopped outside the low gate into Becky's back yard.

A milling crowd of short people, all dressed in brightly colored raincoats, moved up and down the yard. Smiling faces and laughter proved they didn't care about the drizzle or grey skies.

Ryan pushed open the gate and walked closer, curious about the source of their merriment. One glimpse and he was laughing as heartily as the children, his exhaustion eased.

Becky was kneeling on the wet grass at one end of a miniature race course staked out with Popsicle sticks and purple yarn. Rain dripped off her eyelashes and she cheered lustily as Nicky's turtles, each with a different number taped to their shell, either crawled the course or imitated rocks.

Her head jerked up to meet his gaze when she heard his voice. His unexpected presence had obviously caught her by surprise and for a moment she shared with him the enjoyment and the exuberance she felt, forgetting to shut him out.

His grin faded. What was it about this woman?

The connection between blue eyes and brown broke when Dani slipped her hand in Ryan's. He bent his head to listen while the little girl chattered happily about the First Annual Rainy Day Turtle Race Becky had organized for the neighborhood children.

When he looked back again Becky still wore a smile but the happiness and the sharing were gone. The connection between man and woman had vanished.

It hurt that her smile wasn't for him, was never for him. Once again she was the brisk, efficient caregiver. Within seconds she was on her feet, collecting Dani's school books and suitcase, and ushering them out the gate. She returned to her back yard before he and Dani were in his car.

It hadn't been that long since they'd had the run-in with her fireplace and ended up covered in soot. How come it felt like forever?

He'd only seen her for a few minutes when either picking up or dropping off Dani, but the urge to touch Becky wasn't easing. This obsession was totally irrational and definitely not part of the plan. Maybe when Carol returned from her business trip he could get his social life back to normal.

Well, as normal as life could be now he had a little kid to take care of, he thought as he helped Dani put her belongings in the trunk.

Driving away, he looked back once at the big white house before forcing his eyes forward, concentrating on Dani's chatter to distract him from his thoughts. At least, thanks to Becky and her family, the kid's lengthy silences seemed to be over.

Dani talked about the other kids in her class all the way home in the car. In the parking lot she told him how Becky had enrolled her in Sarah's dance class, then listed the new clothing she needed. In the elevator she rhapsodized about her teachers and as they walked down the hall on their floor she regaled him with the latest antics of her class' pet hamster.

He felt pleased she was finally using his name, if only occasionally.

It wasn't until he had the keys in his hand that he noticed the damaged lock.

'Ryan? Aren't we going in?'

His hand dropped and he stared at the round hole where the key slot used to be.

'What's wrong?'

'Give me a minute, kiddo.' He stepped back, putting himself between Dani and the door. 'Let me think.'

'Ryan?'

The fear in her voice made him realize he had to do something. He couldn't follow his first impulse and enter the apartment to check for intruders. He had a seven-year-old child to protect.

'Shh, Dani.' He quietly placed their suitcases on the floor against the wall and wrapped an arm around her waist, hoisting her high against his chest as he retreated to the elevator. 'We have to call the police.'

'Are there robbers in our apartment?' She squeezed her arms around his neck.

'I don't know.' He took out his cellular phone with his free hand. 'But I think we'd better let the professionals find out.' He punched out the emergency number and they waited together for the police.

'I'm Constable Draper, Mr McLeod. Can you tell us what's missing?'

'My computer, an antique abacus, and a golden ceremonial mask are all I've noticed so far.'

He absently patted Dani's back as he studied the chaos in his living room. She still clung to his side even though the police search had confirmed that any intruders were long gone. At least she'd stopped crying. Nothing in his entire life had made him feel as helpless as her silent tears.

'A golden mask?'

'It hung there, over the fireplace.' He shook his head. 'I really liked that mask. It was unique. I kept the abacus sealed in the glass case.' They both looked at the oak framework which now held only gleaming shards of glass.

Draper, the older of the two uniformed officers, scribbled in his notebook. 'Anything else?'

'I've only had time for a quick look around the rest

of the apartment. With all the mess it's hard to tell. I'll have a more thorough look when things calm down.' He indicated Dani with his chin and the cop nodded sympathetically.

'I have two that age at home myself. At least they left her bedroom alone.'

Ryan glanced around the living room, grateful that Dani's room didn't look like the rest of his apartment. Once there'd been artwork hanging on the walls and most of the room's flat surfaces had held some kind of modernistic sculpture. Now two of the paintings dangled from broken frames and the rest were impaled on a figurine. Most of the sculptures were smashed or dented.

'You have several valuable articles here that were damaged rather than taken. Is there some significance to the mask and abacus?'

'Only to me. I acquired the abacus to celebrate my first multi-million dollar sale after I opened McLeod Systems. I bought the mask a few years ago. Something about it . . .' His voice trailed off as he remembered.

He'd seen it in a New Mexico art gallery and hadn't been able to forget the compelling juxtaposition of sheer female beauty and utter lack of humanity in the mask's features. A week after he came home, he flew back to buy it.

'So the other objects in the apartment didn't have the sentimental value of the missing items?'

'You could say that.' Ryan looked at the foul language the intruder had scribbled on the wall with

Dani's crayons. His toe nudged the stuffing that had been pulled out of the slashed sofa cushions. 'Is this kind of thing common?'

'No. Usually this kind of vandalism only occurs when the motive is vindictive or if the intruder is looking for something he knows is hidden.' He stopped writing and looked Ryan straight in the eyes. 'Do you have any enemies, Mr McLeod?'

He stared back for a moment, then crouched to Dani's level. 'Could you take the other nice police officer – ' He looked up at the younger cop. 'What's your first name?'

'Jimmy.'

'Could you take Jimmy to your room for a minute, sweetheart? He'll help you check that your dolls are okay.'

Her arms tightened on his leg but she smiled uncertainly at the police officer's bright grin and extended hand.

'Come on, tiger. We'd better make sure your dollies are behaving themselves.'

After a moment of hesitation she released Ryan and wrapped her hand around the young man's fingers. Draper and Ryan waited silently until they left the room.

'My company has been subjected to some . . . extraordinary problems lately. I believe they are part of an attempt to ruin McLeod Systems and myself. There have also been several offensive, anonymous messages on my e-mail.'

'Threats?'

'They could be interpreted that way.'

'Do you know who is behind these actions?'

'I believe so. Let me show you something.'

Ryan crouched in front of the elegant rosewood cabinet beside the couch. He lifted off the table lamp and telephone, laid them on the floor, then simultaneously pressed two of the many roses carved into the wood. A steel cylinder rose slowly and silently out of the cabinet's top.

His fingers danced across the digital control pad inset on one side of the otherwise perfectly smooth metal surface and a previously invisible door swung open.

The officer's mouth fell open.

'My safe,' Ryan explained. 'Once I began to see a pattern in the events of the last eight months, I kept copies of everything pertinent.' He shifted through several envelopes and folders, placing them on the floor beside the table.

'Damn!' He leaped to his feet and stood staring at the safe's empty interior.

'Is something wrong?'

'The file's not here.'

'Could you have left it somewhere else?'

'No. I know it was here because I worked at home the night before I left on my business trip and I haven't been in the apartment 'til this evening.' He shoved his hands through his hair as he studied the mess he'd made but the motion was arrested.

He dropped to his knees and rummaged frantically through the disks on the floor. 'Dammit to hell!'

'Is something else missing?'

'Only my whole future.' He sat back on his heels and closed his eyes. 'Computer disks. New programs I'd written with business applications which were to be marketed by my company. Top secret.'

'How many people know the combination of that safe, Mr McLeod?'

'Only myself. Or so I thought.'

'Are there any signs of tampering on the safe's exterior?'

Ryan slid his hand over the smooth steel, then examined the delicate wood carving. 'No.'

'How many people knew of the safe's existence?'

'Its existence? A handful. Its hiding place? None . . . I thought.'

'Then I'd say we're dealing with a deliberate act by someone familiar with your home. The missing computer could be related to the theft of the file and disks. The mask and abacus were both valuable and important to you personally which might explain why they were taken. Judging by the damage done to your apartment I'd say you were the victim of a highly vindictive personality.'

'What happens now?'

'I'll call in. The lieutenant will assign a detective to your case. They may want to go over the apartment again to see if the perp left some clue as to his identity. You'll have to give us the name of your suspect plus as much of the missing information as you can remember.'

'And then I'd better call my housekeeper and tell her she'll need some help with this mess in the morning.' Ryan sat down to wait as the cop used the phone to call his superior officer. It was going to be another long night.

One night almost a week later Ryan lay in bed, staring at the ceiling. Midnight. Dani had been asleep for hours, thank heavens. At least she was finally able to sleep alone in her room, though she still used the night light and left her door ajar. It had taken four uneventful nights to ease her fears after the robbery.

He, however, had tossed restlessly tonight until the once crisp sheets were tangled. Wondering when or if he'd hear something from the police. Worried about Dani. Concerned about business. Obsessing over Becky.

Trying to sleep was getting tougher every night.

The silence was heavy, broken only by the ticking of the grandfather clock in the hall and the faint sound of traffic from the streets far below. He needed sleep and he desperately needed release from the tension that gripped him. Too bad the only release he craved was impossibly out of reach.

Finally he cursed, climbed out of bed, and pulled on an old pair of jeans to cover his nakedness, one of many concessions to having a little girl living in his apartment. Since he was awake, he might as well work. In the darkened living room of the penthouse Ryan jerked open the balcony door to get some fresh air.

He drew in long, slow breaths of the salt-flavored air, exhaling slowly, trying to empty his mind of thought and relax his muscles. A light wind began to swirl around the apartment tower, tantalizing him with its elusive touch. As light as a woman's touch. As he imagined Becky's touch.

Tension flooded his body again as cold droplets of rain water splattered across his bare chest. He went inside and slammed shut the sliding glass door.

Why couldn't he get her out of his mind?

What's so damned irresistible about Becky?

He slumped into the solid comfort of his leather easy chair and stretched out his legs until his ankles dangled off the other side of the matching ottoman. He watched as water drops hit the window and raced down the glass, blurring the lights outside. More rain. It had rained non-stop for weeks now. Ever since the day he'd met her.

He felt like he had his own personal ghost. But ghosts never crouched in tall wet grass to organize a turtle race for twenty children or cried at the sentimental vignette in a commercial. Ghosts never got filthy racing children down a muddy hill, sledding on wet grass with plastic garbage bags. Angrily he tried to shove the memories away. The attempt proved futile so he gave in and allowed her image to form on the inside of his closed eyelids.

A froth of rich chocolate curls, eyes that one minute snapped and sparkled and the next melted with inner warmth. Not too tall, not too short, her body lines composed of lush curves as dangerous and thrilling as any switchback mountainside road.

A pert nose and a generous mouth with full luscious lips he craved, that he prayed would someday join his in a senses-drugging kiss. Haunted by visions of pink silk under white cotton, he groaned aloud as his body hardened against his zipper . . . again. Even weeks later he was still so obsessed by the phantom memory of what she'd worn that day that he hadn't, couldn't, call Carol for a date.

He wanted only Becky, needed only Becky.

He propelled himself out of his chair and slammed open the balcony door. As he stepped outside into what had become a driving downpour, nature's freezing version of a cold shower, he hoped it would cool the hot longing aroused by images of Becky.

She's driving you mad but, damn it man, he berated himself, you promised her you'd leave her alone. Heedless of the rain that drenched his skin and made the faded jeans cling to his legs, he stared out across the black waters of English Bay at the distant lights that ringed the harbor. His fingers curled into fists where they rested heavily on the waist-high railing.

Since that first disastrous Sunday, except for one too brief interval during the turtle race, Becky had treated him as a mere acquaintance. He'd rarely approached her when he picked up Dani, afraid he might say or do something to offend her, wanting to bask in her presence and hear her voice.

Knowing any move he made to bring her closer might drive her away. Wanting to touch her, to kiss her, to make love with her.

On the outside peering in. These feelings were too much like those he had suffered through as a child and a teenager. He hated it. Oh, how he hated it.

He tossed back his head and let the rain drum on his face as he laughed grimly. He had regressed to the level of a young boy afraid to do more than worship his own particular goddess from afar.

Why now?

He'd never even thought of having a family. Now, when the business that had been his whole existence needed his undivided attention, he inherited a child to care for and met the woman he had thought didn't exist. Why now?

More to the point, why was he standing here torturing himself when he could be using this time more productively?

With a relief he refused to analyze, he focused on the string of betrayals he'd suffered at McLeod Systems. Over the past year more than half of his deals had gone suspiciously awry and PasComm, his most bloodthirsty competitor, had seduced away a few of his biggest clients. Key employees had received outrageous employment offers he couldn't meet and most of them had ended up working for PasComm or one of Pastin's affiliates.

When he'd pointed out the trend to Hallie and told her about the robbery she'd been shocked. Since then she'd watched everyone like a hawk, trying in her own motherly way to track down their traitor.

With the crisis coming at a time when he was already stretched thin because of recent expansion, his financial backers were becoming understandably nervous. Harold Pastin, owner of PasComm, was out to get him and the break-in made it obvious he had the help of someone Ryan trusted.

But who?

Carol was definitely wrong to blame his secretary. No way was it Hallie. Sixteen years ago when he started McLeod Systems, she was newly widowed and forty-six years old. Excited about her first job, she had been absurdly grateful to him for hiring her. Tired of being told she was not suitable everywhere she applied, she knew that her out-of-date skills and her age were the reasons many, if not all, the employers refused to hire her.

As his secretary she had worked the same long hours as Ryan, helping him when he was struggling to establish himself. If she wanted to sabotage him she'd had innumerable opportunities over the years. Even now he relied on her like no one else in his life. She knew he valued her. Hell, he paid her as much as other companies paid a top executive. Her advice had always been sound. Perhaps she could help him discover who was out to destroy him.

Deliberately he raised both fists shoulder high and slammed them down hard on the filigree iron railing. Pain streaked through his hands and up his arms but he barely noticed it.

Damn them. Damn them to hell!

Ryan left the balcony, changed out of his wet jeans, and switched on the light over his desk. He couldn't, he wouldn't, let his company fail. His breath rasped his throat as he swore to uncover the person who had sold him out.

All he needed was a plan.

CHAPTER 5

Dawn was glimmering behind thinning clouds when he was once again stretched out naked in his bed, woozy from lack of sleep and back sore from too many hours spent at his desk. He knuckled his eyes, yawned until his jaw cracked, and moved around until he found a place where the rumpled sheets were relatively smooth.

He couldn't wait on the police to identify the intruder and implicate Pastin. He had to move now on his fight with PasComm. With the work he'd done tonight McLeod's had a viable business plan ready to go.

He'd roughed out a new program that looked good, damn good. He hadn't worked his way to the top of this business without more than a few original ideas. He believed it would be enough. It had to be.

Tense and exhausted, his mind touched on Becky, glanced off and slowly returned. Tentatively, then with more strength of purpose, he concentrated on her. Her face, her body, her heart all called to him.

Rebecca Hansen was a woman made for passion. Once she decided to make love, he thought she would probably be like a child given free rein with buckets of paint. The result would be a delirious kaleidoscope of emotion and sensation. If only he hadn't made that damn promise. Ryan stretched out, enjoying the slide of smooth cotton against his naked skin. If only . . .

He snapped upright in bed. She thought he was a jerk. Of course she didn't want anything to do with him. But what if he showed her he was one of the good guys?

He lay down again, smiling to himself. When she got to know him, she would want him as much as he wanted her. He would convince her. He flopped over onto his stomach, punched the pillow into shape and buried his face. A minute later he flipped onto his back again.

Emotions, bah! Emotions sure made life uncomfortable. How was a man supposed to understand his own feelings, much less a woman's?

He'd had absolutely no experience with the emotion currently turning his world upside down. He supposed what he felt must be . . . Could this be love? Or merely a very meaningful lust? He snorted. Ha! Since when was lust meaningful? Never, that's when. If it wasn't lust that left only love.

Love? The word, the emotion, was a shock. He hadn't thought of going so far, so fast. Attraction, of course. Caring, yes. Affection, certainly. Passion, without doubt.

He lay there in the bed and thought back over the past few weeks and accepted the truth. Second by second, day by day, somehow his feelings for Becky had grown. Maybe, someday, if things worked out, they could get married . . .

He jerked upright in bed again. Married? Where was this woman leading him? Married, for Chris-sake? She had three kids! And then he thought of how jealousy struck every time he saw the warmth and acceptance she radiated . . . toward other people.

But married?

Did he want her enough to marry her? Yes, damn it, he did. He wanted her with him, day and night. The only way to achieve that with a woman like Becky was marriage. The first step was to convince her she liked him. Then he had to convince her that she wanted to marry him. What he needed was a plan, a *marriage* plan.

Of course he'd have to deal with being responsible for four children. He lay down on his side, propped his head on his bent arm. Sarah and Nicky were good kids. Mike could be brought around if Ryan tried hard enough. He had one of his own now anyway, he thought as his eyes drifted closed. Taking care of Dani was proving to be a training ground complete with mines, but he was coping.

Married with four kids. Who would believe it? Certainly not Carol.

His eyes blinked open. Carol. He'd have to break things off with her immediately. Plus he'd promised to be her escort to several functions in the next few weeks.

He shrugged. Carol was a good friend. She'd understand, as he would have if she had been the one to meet someone special. As soon as she returned from her London trip he would finalize what was left of that relationship. In the meantime there were plenty of sufficiently innocent events where he could be with Becky. He'd make his first move at the girls' ballet recital tomorrow night.

Soon enough he'd have his life in order. Then he would teach Becky to trust him. And then he'd marry her.

Rring. Rring. The warble of a cellular phone cut through the thumping drums, scraping violins, and dancers' stamping feet. Ryan scrambled for his jacket pocket.

'Shh.' 'Sshh!' came at him from all sides. It rang once more before he managed to silence it.

Hallie leaned close and whispered in his ear. 'That was classy.'

He glanced around at the fond parents and grandparents seated in the auditorium, several of whom were still staring at him disdainfully. 'I forgot to turn it off,' he whispered back.

His voice was drowned out by thunderous applause as the orchestra, ages ranging from eight through fifteen, abandoned their instruments and climbed onto the stage to form a ragged line. They all clasped hands and began bowing, the dipping heads moving down the ranks like a wave.

'Dani and Sarah looked cute as could be, didn't you think so?'

'They were part of the group of birds who buzzed around the tall girl and boy, right?' He straightened in his seat as the orchestra scrambled back down to the floor and the dancers took their place under the lights.

'Swans, Ryan. They were swans.'

'Swans. Right. Too bad Becky had to go to Mike's soccer game. She missed a great show.'

'And so you offered to escort both girls to the recital. Did I thank you for telling her I would be happy to help tonight?'

He grinned at the wry tone in her voice. 'You're glad you came.'

'Just don't start thinking I'm going to be able to step in like this all the time.'

The swan pack stepped forward and curtseyed to thunderous applause. Ryan realized he was grinning as he watched Dani perform hers without a wobble. She'd practised that particular move over and over this last week and he'd assured her that she'd get it perfect when it counted. Seems he'd been right.

Hallie and Ryan joined in the applause as the dancers filed off-stage. He turned in his chair to face her as the lights came up.

'You look terrible,' she said. 'Did you stay up all night working?'

'And all day. But it was worth it. First thing Monday morning I'm going to get Paul and Jamie in on this. Pastin won't know what hit him.'

'Paul is the best and he's been there almost from the beginning but are you sure about Jamie? He's only been working for us for eight months and we still don't know who is passing the information to PasComm. Or who robbed your apartment.'

'No. I'm not sure about anyone. I'll be observant and ensure security is tight.'

Hallie glanced at her wristwatch. 'Time to go help the girls change.'

'I'll wait here.'

Ryan settled back in his seat in the almost empty auditorium, opened his briefcase, and reactivated his cellular phone. He'd just disconnected from a call when someone spoke.

'Ryan?'

He looked up. 'Paul! I was just mentioning your name to Hallie. Don't tell me you're also related to one of those very talented performers?'

'My daughter played the cymbals. Sheila was helping behind the scenes.'

'Hallie just went to help Dani and Sarah change.'

'I saw her leave.' The slight man fidgeted with the program. 'Look, Ryan, can I talk to you? I was going to call you tomorrow but when I saw you here I thought I'd just do it now.'

'Yeah, sure.' Ryan noted the sweat beading his senior programmer's forehead and the way he was rolling and unrolling the program. 'Sit down.'

Paul pushed down the seat next to Ryan's and sat on its edge, staring down at the program he held between his hands. 'I don't know quite how to say this.' He turned his head to look at Ryan. 'I am fully aware of what I owe you. You took a chance on a kid who'd struggled just to graduate high school. You've paid me well to do work I love.'

'And . . .?'

'PasComm has offered me a job at almost twice my salary plus six weeks holiday and a company car. Every other time I've told them what they could do with their offer but Sheila and I need the money. We found out last week that her father . . .'

Ryan felt the ice invading his guts as he listened to the man stammer out his reasons for considering Pastin's offer. He listened silently, as if from a great distance, as Paul talked himself to silence.

'I'm really sorry to hear this. You've been an important part of the team.' His lips moved stiffly in a face that felt frozen. Did this mean that Paul was the traitor?

'I hate doing this, especially since Dick and Susan have also left McLeod's. It's just . . . We really need the money, Ryan.'

'I can't match that offer, Paul.' He lifted his hand from where it had been gripping the armrest and slowly began to flex his fingers, trying to work out the numbness.

'I didn't think so.' He looked absolutely miserable. 'I thought maybe . . . Never mind.' He stood up. 'They said, if I want it, the offer has to be taken immediately but I could tell them I had to work out my notice if . . . if you want me to.'

'No!' Ryan moderated his tone before he continued. 'That won't be necessary. Come into the office

Monday and show Jamie what you've been working on. Hallie will have the paperwork ready by noon.'

'Okay.'

They both stood up and when Paul extended his hand Ryan looked at it for a few long seconds before he gripped it briefly.

Paul took a few steps away before he spoke again. 'I feel really bad about this.'

'So do I. Good luck.'

Ryan was still standing when he heard Hallie approaching from behind him.

'The girls are saying good-bye to their friends. They'll be right out. Was that Paul?'

'Yes.' Ryan scooped his phone and a few loose papers back into his briefcase, then snapped it closed. 'His daughter was part of the orchestra. The cymbals.'

'I guess she was responsible for that lovely clang and clatter when the evil magician was defeated. On Monday I'll have to tease him a little.'

'On Monday you'll have to prepare his separation certificate and final check.'

'What?'

'He just quit McLeod's. PasComm made him an offer he couldn't refuse and I couldn't match.'

'Oh, my, oh, my, oh, my.' She pressed her handbag to her chest. 'Do you think he's the one who's been betraying us?'

'I don't know. I hope not. Either way, he's gone now.' Ryan forced his lips into a smile when he saw Dani and Sarah racing up the aisle toward him. 'I don't want to talk about it now. Tonight's for the girls and here they come. Put on your happy face. We'll deal with this Monday.'

'We're home, Mom.' Mike's voice rang out over her head, startling Becky so much she almost fell off the couch.

She clutched the paperback to her chest and closed her eyes, counting and sucking in deep breaths until the adrenaline surge died away. This was Monday afternoon in her own home, not midnight on a Scottish moor, she reminded herself.

She'd been so deep in the novel she hadn't noticed the passage of time. Of course she wouldn't have been so startled if the bad guy hadn't been sneaking up to kill the wimpy heroine.

'Mom? Where are you?'

'In here, Mike.' She pushed aside the laundry basket she been using as a footstool and stood up. She closed the book to look at the blood-stained knife on the austere white cover. Enough of that, she thought. No more thrillers like this one if the mere arrival of her children home from school was enough to scare the air from her lungs.

Two pairs of large teenage feet thumped down the hall to the living room. The welcoming smile slipped from her face when she saw the white curly hair of the young man with her son. She hadn't met him before today but Mike's enthusiastic descriptions left no doubt as to his identity.

'Mom? This is Joe Brasky.'

She nodded. 'Where're Nicky and the girls?'

'In the back yard with some of their friends, playing in the fort. Mom, can I go with Joe and some of the guys to the video arcade in the mall?'

Her son's smug grin told her all she needed to know. He was flattered and excited to be invited into the coolest group at school. If she refused permission he was going to be embarrassed and furious.

'Nice to meet ya, Mrs H.'

Standing slightly behind her son, Brasky looked her up and down in such a way she felt as if he'd mentally ripped off her clothes and intended to make use of what he saw. Her skin crawled and she shifted uncomfortably, clutching the book against her chest. He smirked, as if enjoying her unease.

'Nice house.' He sauntered over to look inside the curio cabinet against the wall. He spent several moments examining the glass perfume bottles she kept downstairs in the living room, a small part of the collection started by her mother. Thank heavens she kept the semi-valuable ones upstairs in her room where the kids wouldn't accidentally break them.

'You got some nice stuff.'

'Thanks but it's not worth much. I usually pick most of them up at thrift shops or garage sales.'

She felt the urge to sigh in relief as he shrugged and moved away. She'd been folding the laundry before she'd allowed herself time to read. Now she cringed when Brasky touched the panties and bras piled beside her T-shirts and sweatshirts.

'I'm sorry, Mike.' She dropped the book and swept the clothes off the couch into the hamper. These would go back into the wash the minute she got this person out of her house. 'You can't go out today. You have chores.'

'But, Mom . . .' Mike's voice trailed off into a whine.

'We need this boy, Mrs H. Mike's got the best hands in town,' her son blushed, 'and we've got a bet going with some other guys we're meeting later at the arcade. We need him on the team.'

Brasky stooped to fiddle with the stereo and television knobs. Thank heavens one fell off in his hand. His behavior was more like someone casing the joint than a visiting frie⌐d.

'No.' Becky spoke firmly. 'Now, I'm sorry but you'll have to leave.'

She stepped toward the front door and paused. His eyes met hers and he grinned, telling her he knew and relished just how nervous his presence made her. Her breath caught in her throat until he finally moved out of the room.

Mike sulked silently while she escorted Brasky down the hall and out of Lilac House. Her son burst into noisy protests the minute the door closed but she held up her hand and waited for him to stop.

'No. This isn't open to discussion. You know I don't approve of that person. You also know you're not allowed to hang around at the mall. And you'd promised to finish all your chores right after school today. The very same chores you've been putting off for the last week.'

'I'll do them later.'

'I'm really tired of hearing "later" every time you want to avoid your responsibilities. "Later" just isn't going to cut it any longer.'

Becky hid her relief when Mike capitulated. He stomped into the hallway, opened the cupboard, and dragged out the broom. He grumbled, but he did it. At least for now he was still willing to listen to her and follow direct orders. What would happen when he out-weighed her and towered over her, she had no idea. Hopefully by then he would be old enough not to be taken in by people like Joe Brasky.

Oh, well . . . One of her mother's favorite sayings seemed appropriate for today, though she couldn't quite remember the right words. Something about there's sufficient evil every day so don't worry about tomorrow's? Or, sufficient unto the day the evil there of? She wasn't sure. Either way, an excellent sentiment.

She left Mike to it and went to find Nicky and the girls. She'd suggest they come in for a snack as soon as they got tired of playing in the rain. Maybe by that time Mike would have stopped brooding and be willing to invite some of his more acceptable, and younger, friends over to play.

'Hello.'

The deep voice cut through the usual noise and confusion to be found in her home every day between school and dinner. Mike had called two friends, Dani and Sarah had invited one and Nicky had three.

Typical for most weekdays at Lilac House. Becky was crouched on the floor, helping Nicky's best friend, Timmy, take off his boots and wet coat while the older kids put away their own.

Ryan. Here. She stiffened and her hands stilled on the tangled strings she held while she listened to the heavy thudding of her heart. Was she ever going to be able to stay calm when he showed up unexpectedly?

'Please hurry, Mrs Hansen. They're going to start without me.'

She started as Timmy's voice jarred her back to awareness of what she was supposed to be doing. Keeping her back firmly to Ryan, she patted the little boy's shoulder.

'Sorry, Timmy. There you go. Make sure to hang your coat on a separate hook this time.'

'Yes, Mrs Hansen.'

She stood, wishing she could follow Timmy as he ran to join the others in the play room.

'Hi.' Ryan's voice sounded closer. She drew in a deep breath before she stuck on an impersonal smile, determined to hide how glad she was to see him, to bring her reaction under control before she turned to face him.

'Hello, Ryan. Dani isn't ready to go yet.'

'Neither am I.'

'You're early.' Becky pinned her gaze to a point on the wall behind his right shoulder, willing her eyes to look everywhere, anywhere but at him. One glimpse was enough.

In jeans he had been appealing but, damn him, if she looked at him again she was afraid her eyes might pop right out of her head.

Today his charcoal grey suit had a narrow red pinstripe and his shirt was muted silver. His tie and the scrap of cloth that peeked out of the breast pocket of his jacket were scarlet silk. The typical business executive's power suit but with a hint of the inner man's flamboyance.

Not that this executive needed to add anything to the presence he exuded from every pore. His face and body, wrapped up with all that charm, were striking enough with no enhancement.

'I'll send her out.' Doing her best to ignore Ryan, she tidied the rest of the children's boots and coats and headed into the play room. She half-hoped he would take the hint and take a hike.

But when she had them all settled he was still waiting for her in the kitchen, leaning against the wall, arms crossed on his chest and an expectant grin on his lips.

Ryan found it amusing to watch her pretend he wasn't in the room. Her hair was as unruly as ever. Her cotton pants and blouse were a pale peach hue. Bare toes painted with peach polish poked out of fuzzy white slippers. As she moved around the room, first bending then crouching, her clothes moved around her body, pulling tight across her thighs, outlining the curve of her bottom or emphasizing the shape of her breasts.

His breath shortened and his heartbeat sped up. He reminded himself to approach her carefully with none of the sexual intensity that had made her so defensive. If she was cautious because of a bad marriage he would have to move carefully. Let her get to know him and like him before they went any further.

He reined in his rampaging libido, reminding himself that her cheeks had flushed then paled when she heard his voice. At least she wasn't indifferent to him.

'Yesterday I forgot to thank you for taking such good care of Dani. She's enjoying herself here.'

Becky opened a cupboard and started putting dishes away.

'She's no trouble at all.'

'Would you have dinner with me tonight? I'd like to thank you properly.'

He sensed she was about to reject his offer so he jumped in before she could speak. 'With the children of course. For all you've done.'

'No, it's not necessary. You pay me very well.'

He stepped closer to where she stood.

Becky swallowed a sigh of reluctant admiration when he undid the buttons of his suit jacket and thrust both hands deep into the pockets of his trousers. His action revealed scarlet suspenders and pulled the trouser fabric taut across his thighs. The stack of dishes in her hands rattled slightly so she moved slower, forcing her muscles to behave.

'No, not necessary but I thought it might give you pleasure.'

'Sorry, I'm busy tonight.' She edged past him sideways, careful not to let her body touch his.

'Tomorrow night?' He angled his arm, blocking her movement.

'No. Thanks.' He kept coming closer and she could smell the tangy fragrance of his cologne.

'Next week?'

Becky spun around and marched over to the back door. She twisted the knob and jerked it open. 'Please wait in your car. I'll send Dani out to you.'

He buttoned his jacket. On his way past he paused, toe-to-toe with her. Her fragrance, light but compelling, and her lips so near were heady stuff. He had intended only to say a friendly good-bye. Coming that close was a mistake.

He forgot the plan and lost control.

'You know why I asked you to dinner. I'm not alone here, I know you feel this connection too.' His hand lifted, curved, and hovered in the air beside her cheek.

The electric surge between their bodies made the fine down on Becky's face stand on end. Would he kiss her? A potent mixture of anticipation and fear tingled down her spine.

'See you. Soon.' The word was a promise, his voice low as his breath touched her lips.

Then he was gone. The damp air wafted through the open door and she shivered. But she couldn't be sure if she shivered because of the chill in the air or if she felt chilled because he hadn't touched her.

Children spilled into the room. Becky had always thrived on the pint-sized turmoil around her and right now she was grateful for the herd of children who all wanted something different. The noise and confusion allowed her to concentrate on what was really important. Her children.

'Dani, Ryan's outside waiting for you. Get your stuff together. Everyone else go down the hall to the play room. Only half-an-hour until most of you have to leave.'

Ten minutes later she shut the heavy door behind Dani and slouched weakly against the wooden panels until she heard Ryan's car pull away.

How on earth was she going to get through this every day? She shook her head and rolled her shoulders before she stepped away from solid support. Her knees quivered. She drew in a deep breath, imagining his scent still hung in the air.

Remember Eric, she told herself. Then you will be immune.

As the car pulled away from the house Ryan shifted gear recklessly, wincing at the harsh grating noise.

Way to go, idiot. Make this great plan, he berated himself, and then let an excellent strategy fly out the window as soon as you're in the same room with her.

Keep it subtle, McLeod. Make her trust you.

Yeah, right. It had been a good plan right up until he was within arm's reach of her.

He glared out the windshield at a car whose driver dared to dispute the right of way.

Stupid, stupid, stupid, he raged silently. More than a little pushy telling her you knew the attraction was mutual. What to do now? He wasn't ready to give up. He had to show her he honestly cared about her.

An old Barbra Striesand, Neil Diamond duet came over the radio and as he listened he began to smile. He'd finalize things with Carol tomorrow, then court Becky the old fashioned way. Send her flowers, buy her presents.

He would woo her!

Ryan studied the cold, still face of the elegant blonde sitting beside him on his office sofa. Had he made a mistake? Had this relationship meant more to Carol than he'd realized?

'I'm sorry. I never meant to hurt you.'

'You didn't. We both know it was I who persuaded you into what was, at the time, a sensible arrangement. I knew one of us would end it some day. Although my ego wishes I had been the one to do it.' She lit a cigarette and waved the smoke away from her face. 'I can't imagine you married. With children. Who is she? Anyone I know?'

He noticed how her smile didn't reach her eyes but that didn't worry him. He had never known any woman whose smile did. Until Becky.

'No.' He swallowed a sigh of relief and relaxed. 'I met Becky a few weeks ago. She's Dani's baby-sitter and a friend of Hallie's niece.'

'Becky?' She stubbed out her cigarette. 'Her name is Becky? How . . . cute.'

'Yes, or rather Rebecca, but everyone calls her Becky.' His mind fogged as he thought about

Becky. It took him a while to realize Carol was talking.

'– about next Saturday?'

Ryan lifted one eyebrow questioningly.

'The Black and White Ball,' she explained. 'Will you still be my escort? It would be difficult to find another this late.' Her eyes glittered and her red lips curved in a tight smile.

As always, he admired her cool beauty. Carol was both stunning and successful. Why couldn't they have fallen in love with each other? It would have been so much simpler. And then he thought about Becky and grinned. Simpler, maybe, but he would have missed the excitement and plain frustration of loving Rebecca Hansen.

'Of course.' Escorting her to the ball was the least he could do. 'I would never leave a friend in the lurch.'

'I appreciate it.' Her gaze was diamond bright. 'We were good together, weren't we, darling?' Her hand trailed across his shoulder and she touched his cheek with one finger, more than a hint of seduction in her voice.

'Well . . . I . . .' He leaned away, then jumped to his feet when Hallie bustled in.

'Tsk, tsk, tsk. Just look at this mess.' She picked up the half empty cups of cold coffee abandoned on his desk amid the drifts of crumpled paper. She dumped them in the garbage can, then moved it back out of sight under his desk. Hallie's lips were pursed in disapproval. She'd obviously noticed how close they'd been sitting and she'd never liked Carol much. 'Becky and the kids are here, Ryan.'

'Thanks, Hallie. Could you please get the disks on the new program from the safe for me after you show her in? They're in the red-tagged envelope.'

'Of course, Ryan.' She opened the door again and called out in the direction of the reception area. 'Come on in, honey.'

'We were downtown and I thought – ' Becky appeared behind Hallie but her smile vanished when she saw Carol. 'I'm sorry. You're busy.'

'No. Come in. Where are the kids?'

'They are – '

'I'm here, Ryan.' Nicky's head poked around the door jamb and his body slithered into the room after it. 'We're all here. Now I want to see the computers. Please.' The last word was accompanied by a 'see-I-remembered' glance at his mother.

'I should get back to work.' Carol slipped her cigarette case into her bag and rose gracefully. She slipped the clutch under one arm and extended her hand. 'You must be Becky. Ryan told me all about you.'

Becky looked at her blankly before she shook the other woman's hand. 'He did?' She glanced at Ryan. 'What did he say?'

In a moment of panic he felt as if his stomach hit somewhere around his ankles then bounced up to his throat before it relocated immediately below a seriously wobbling diaphragm. He broke in before Carol gave away his plans when he hadn't yet talked to Becky himself. 'Becky Hansen, this is Carol Hill.'

'I know. Hello.' Becky smiled politely at the other woman then turned to face Ryan. 'There was no school today so we all went to Science World. Since we were already downtown, they wanted to see your office.'

'I want to see the computers.'

Ryan glanced down at the little boy whose hand gripped his trouser leg, then back at Becky and the other three kids clustered in the doorway at her back.

'See you Saturday, Ryan.' Carol waited until Becky and the other children backed out of her way, then left before he realized he'd forgotten to say good-bye.

'I like this.' Nicky had picked up the heavy crystal box that graced the corner of Ryan's desk, and was playing with its lid. 'It sparkles.'

'Be careful, honey.' Becky carefully replaced the expensive ornament and smiled apologetically at Ryan. 'We should leave. You're busy.'

'No. They can have the penny tour but you look tired. Why don't you sit down while the kids look around?'

Becky looked longingly at the soft leather couch and wiggled her burning toes. After a three hour stint looking at science exhibits with four children, all with different interests and too much energy, she was exhausted. The prospect of walking another inch, even if it was only around Ryan's office, was more than she could face.

'I should probably come with them but remember, you offered. Thank you.'

He waved the children to go ahead. 'Coffee? Iced tea?'

'Iced tea would be heavenly.'

'Coming up. Make yourself comfortable.'

She put her purse on the coffee table and dropped into a corner of the big couch, snuggling her shoulders into the over-stuffed cushions. She wrinkled her nose at the lingering aroma of Carol Hill's heavy but expensive perfume.

She kicked off her sneakers and sighed as she propped her feet on the coffee table, careful to put a magazine between her heels and its black lacquered surface. The desk and every other piece of furniture had the same high gloss finish. Even the casing of his computer was black. The only ornamentation was a surrealistic painting hung on one of the pale walls and the crystal box squatting on one corner of his desk.

Ryan's office was very elegant if cold and certainly expensive. He must be doing well, she thought as she closed her eyes and listened to the silence. Oh, bliss. The office door clicked open and shut and she looked up, expecting to see Hallie with the drink.

CHAPTER 6

Ryan loomed over her, a tall glass coated with condensation in each hand. She jerked upright and swung her feet to the floor.

'I thought you were going with the kids.'

'Two of my employees are giving them a guided tour.' The ice cubes tinkled against the glasses as he sat beside her, holding out one for her to take.

'Thanks.'

'I thought Nicky would drive them crazy, which is why I delegated two guides. But once Mike was assured I wouldn't be along, he really opened up and Nicky isn't getting many questions in. Your older son is very knowledgeable for someone with little access to computers.'

'Mike is fascinated by technology. The instructor at his school's computer lab has allowed him extra time on the terminals. As for his attitude to you, well, it's nothing personal.'

Ryan nodded and they sipped in silence while Becky tried to keep from staring at him. With mussed hair and dark shadows under his eyes, he looked tired. Probably working too hard, judging by the state of his office.

His hand rested on one muscular thigh next to her own and she watched his fist clench and flex slowly, repeatedly, the only outward sign of tension in the man lounging at her side. He raised the glass to his lips and downed the rest of the liquid before setting it on the table with a sharp click.

'What did you mean, "I know"?'

'Pardon me?'

'When I introduced you to Carol, you said "I know".'

'Oh. Jan described your girlfriend and when I saw her . . .'

'How does Jan know about my personal life?'

'Hallie worries about you and when she worries, she talks. She cares as much about you as your real mother.'

'Not likely,' he said in a frosty tone.

'You shouldn't get angry. She only talks to Jan because she cares about you.' She twisted around to glare directly at his face.

'That's not – ' He broke off, then nodded toward the piece of crystal she'd rescued from Nicky's scrutiny. 'That's the only thing my mother ever gave to me.'

'It's very beautiful.'

'It's an empty box.'

The hostility in his voice startled Becky.

'Never mind. That's not what I wanted to talk to you about. Carol is a friend. We once had a . . . closer connection but that's over.'

Becky refused to admit the relief she felt at his denial, even to herself. 'I can't imagine why you're telling me this.'

'Can't you?'

When she looked up he was smiling, with one eyebrow tilted in disbelief. She bent forward, allowing her curls to fall across her eyes to hide the blush she couldn't control. She shoved her feet back into her shoes and tied the laces.

The door opened and Hallie rushed in. 'They're not there.'

Becky held back a sigh of relief as his attention switched to his secretary.

'What's not – '

'The file's empty. The disks aren't in the safe.'

'Yes, they are. I put them there myself before I went to Miami. I saw them yesterday.'

'If you did, they're gone.'

Becky and Hallie both stared in shock when Ryan uttered a crude phrase and stood up so quickly he knocked his glass over. He set Hallie aside and ran down the hall. A minute later he was back.

'What's the matter, Ryan?'

'Dammit, can't I trust anyone around here?' He sat on the edge of his desk and massaged the deep furrows between his brows with one hand.

Becky's gaze went from the frozen hurt on Hallie's face to the angry frustration on Ryan's. 'I'd better leave.'

Neither seemed to hear her. Neither moved to let her past to the door.

'How could you say that to me?' Hallie clasped her hands tightly together at her waist and watched him for a long, silent minute before she spun on her heel and marched to the door.

'Hallie, don't go.' He leapt to his feet. 'I didn't mean you.' He touched her shoulder to stop her, then reached around her to shut the office door.

'I'm sorry.' He rubbed the back of his neck. 'I seem to be saying that to someone every day lately, if not twice. Remember when I told you about PasComm undercutting our bid on the Horizon deal by a few thousand dollars? When it happened again with the Johnson deal and Smith Corporation? When Paul, Dick and Susan all received offers from PasComm, with salaries I couldn't possibly match, and they couldn't refuse because of their particular family situation?'

'Yes, but . . .'

'When my apartment was robbed, the only other copy of the new program went missing, too. I can only assume they've both been stolen by the same person.'

'The program you said would make us a fortune?'

'Yes. I'd bet it's about to make a fortune for PasComm.'

'Oh, my goodness.' Hallie reached toward the telephone. 'I'll call the police.'

'And tell them what? That PasComm's new program is mine? They already know the other disks were stolen and that I suspect Pastin. As the detective pointed out, it's not unusual for two people, working separately, to come up with similar ideas. What I need to know is how, for the last few months, Pastin has always known where to hit me, right where I'm most vulnerable.'

'What's going on, Ryan?' Becky asked. The way his head jerked around in her direction made it clear he had forgotten she was in the room.

'PasComm is paying Judas money to someone I trust.'

'Who?'

'I have no idea.' He slumped into the chair behind his desk, long legs stretched out. His lips twisted in a self-mocking grin when he spoke. 'Do you, Hallie?'

Hallie shook her head.

'I hear the kids coming back. I'd better take them home.' Becky waited a moment, wondering if she should offer sympathy and support. Wondering if she was crazy to think he would want either from her.

'I'll see you later.'

'Well . . . Good-bye then.' Becky said. She hesitated again but left when Ryan only nodded.

'That wasn't very polite.' Hallie shook her head.

'Sorry.' He groaned. 'I'm getting tired of that word. I'll apologize to her when I pick Dani up tonight.'

'What are you going to do now?'

'If I don't work something out soon, you and I will both be unemployed,' he said. 'I have an idea that might help but it's going to take time. The board meeting with the money men is only two weeks away.'

'What can I do to help?' she asked.

He smiled warmly at the woman who until recently had meant more to him than anyone else, Carol included. Today Hallie's hair was an improbable red, carefully styled. She still dressed like a respectable matron of thirty years ago, as she had done since the day he hired her, right down to the single-strand pearl necklace and knitted cardigan.

'Field as many calls as you can. I'll need all of that two weeks to get ready. I think we should aim our strategy at having an even better product ready for the trade show in a few weeks. A good showing there might make all the difference and get us over this fiscal hump.'

'I've been meaning to ask you, Ryan. Is Dani happy? Is Becky suitable?'

Distracted from his problems, Ryan heard himself chuckle. 'Yes, she's very suitable. In every way. Rebecca Hansen is quite a woman.'

Something in his tone caught Hallie's attention and she studied his face. He grinned innocently.

'Ryan McLeod, does that smile mean what I think it means?'

'I don't know. What are you thinking?'

'You'd better be careful, young man. Rebecca Hansen has had a wretched time. She isn't like Ms Hill or any of your other women.'

'I could tell. Three children are impossible to miss.'

'Ryan, if you hurt her I'll regret I ever set up that interview. Then I'll make you very, very sorry.'

'I have no intention of hurting her. As a matter of fact I want exactly the opposite.'

She tried to say something more but he interrupted her. 'Now don't scold any more. I have a company to save.'

She pursed her lips in disapproval but left. For the rest of the afternoon he tried to concentrate on his work but Becky's image drifted in the back of his thoughts.

From the first she had judged him on the basis of his looks and decided he was precisely like her ex-husband. Nicky was only five and since Hallie had said Becky was divorced over six years ago it seemed likely that she'd been hurt by both her ex-husband and Nicky's father.

Ryan shook his head ruefully. It was chastening to realize how he'd subconsciously counted on his physical assets to give him an edge. Worse to know those assets were acting against him. He leaned forward and pulled the keyboard closer. Starting tomorrow he would have to show her there was much more to him than a pretty face. He needed a way to get close to her without scaring her off.

Then it hit him.

Years of experience, both in business and in life, had taught him to target an opponent's weakness. Ryan chuckled in anticipation, then picked up the phone.

'Are you sure you don't want a fire?'

'No, I don't want a fire,' Becky snapped.

'There's something really cosy about sitting in front of a fire in the evening, listening to the wood spit and crackle. Especially when it's cool or raining outside.' Ryan leaned back and stretched out his long legs toward the cold grate.

'Cosy? You? Ha!' She avoided the empty cushion beside him and sat down in the old bucket chair beside the hearth. 'I can't imagine you seeking out anything because it's cosy.'

'You'd be surprised. Any man learns to appreciate the warm things in life, especially if he's a bachelor like myself.'

She knew a leading comment when she heard one and refused to react. No way was she going down that conversational road again. Besides, she had two far more important bones to pick with him.

'About the computer – '

'If the kids have any trouble with it, let me know. I can always have a look at it in the evening when I pick up Dani.'

'It's too expensive.'

'Nope. It's an old unit we weren't using in the office any more since my staff upgraded. Dani can use it, too, when she's here.'

'I know the programs must have cost a lot of money.'

'Samples. I have to stay aware of what the competition is doing.'

'Even the games?'

'What can I say? They're fun.'

'The kids really appreciate your generosity, especially Mike. Thank you,' she said stiffly.

'About dinner – '

'It sure was good.' He patted his lean stomach. 'I like Chinese food. It has something for every taste. Even the kids liked it.'

'My children like anything even faintly resembling junk food.' She kicked off her slippers and curled her legs under her. 'Especially take-out.'

'Sour grapes?'

'You knew I didn't want to have dinner with you. I've told you so often enough.' Hating herself for responding to his jibe, she pursed her lips and turned her shoulder, trying unsuccessfully to block him from her peripheral vision.

He linked his fingers over his stomach and wiggled deeper into the cushions without answering her.

'You shouldn't have turned up with all that food. I might have already started cooking dinner. It would have been wasted.'

He still didn't say anything.

'Inviting the children without first asking me was despicable and you've done it three nights this week. You're manipulating the situation and persuading them to conspire with you. You knew they would agree.'

'Sure did.'

'Don't do it again.'

His smile was affectionate and tender when he replied. 'Yes, Ma'am, I will.'

'What?'

She spun around and was caught by the instant attraction she felt whenever she looked at him. He was really the most outrageously beautiful man she had ever seen, even rumpled and tired with jacket discarded, sleeves rolled up to reveal strong arms lightly dusted with blond hair, and loafers kicked off.

He was the picture of relaxed masculinity. She, however, felt as if a boulder had settled in the pit of her stomach.

'What did you say?'

'I said, yes, I will do it again.' He rolled his head sideways on the cushions until he gazed right at her. 'I will do anything that keeps me in the same room with you. I'm attracted to you. I want to get to know you. And I think you would feel the same if you would only let go of the past.'

'Don't be . . .'

He held up one hand to halt her denial. 'I know you won't agree but it's true. I feel your response to me. Every time you look at me, it's as if you touched me.'

'No.'

'Please, honey, reconsider. I know you've been hurt, probably more than once.'

'Yes, I have,' she said, her voice strained. 'I have to make sure it never happens again.'

'Do you still think I'm like your ex-husband?'

'Yes. No. I don't know.' Becky twisted her fingers together in her lap. 'You're very easy on the eyes, you have to know that. So was he.'

'Is that fair? Would you like to be judged and rejected on the basis of your face? An accident of birth?' He stopped speaking and his very silence demanded her answer.

'No,' she answered reluctantly.

'I decided to show you the real me. Heaven knows I've tried every way I can think of. Talk with me, Becky. Get to know me for myself, the man inside the body. I won't push. Or rather, I'll try not to. I might slip now and then because I want you so very much and,' he gave a small self-mocking laugh, 'self-denial is new to me.'

She felt herself weakening, giving in, and that would be terrible. Wouldn't it? She was having difficulty remembering why she had to keep him at a safe distance. Fighting a losing battle with herself, she grasped at anything to use as a shield against his appeal.

'What about Carol?'

He cocked his head at her and grinned. 'I told her about you and we're just friends now. You know that.'

She couldn't believe it. Just friends? Ha! And there was a pile of gold to be found at the end of the rainbow, too. What woman could be 'just friends' with Ryan McLeod, especially after being more?

'Please, Becky?'

She searched his face and saw something that called to her, something that made her want to try. 'Okay.'

'Can I take you out to dinner next Saturday?'

She hesitated before she answered. He was probably an expert in man-woman relationships and her life with Eric didn't put her in Ryan's league.

There would be dim lighting, probably a candle or flowers on the table, soft music, with expensive wine to muddle her good sense. Not to mention sitting across the table from that face. No, no, no. She couldn't do it. At least in her own home there was always a multitude of children in and out of the house. She wouldn't be alone with him.

'I can't get a baby-sitter at such short notice so I'll make dinner here.'

'I'm glad you didn't reject the idea out of hand. Let me bring the food and you've got a deal.'

'But I invited you . . .'

'No, you didn't. I invited you. I'll bring enough steaks, salad stuff and dessert for everybody. We'll cook it together. Four o'clock?'

'Seven.'

'That's too late for the kids. Five?'

She wanted to argue but he smiled that mesmerizing smile and said 'please' so persuasively she cautiously agreed. Besides, she couldn't bring herself to turn down steak to eat macaroni and cheese.

Becky stopped pacing the living room floor when she saw Ryan's car pull into the driveway. He wasn't early, in fact he was almost fifteen minutes late. She'd been watching for him, off and on, ever since three that afternoon. Every time she'd come to stare out this window, she'd been annoyed at her own lack of control and pride. But she hadn't been able to stop thinking up one more feeble excuse why she had to peer out at the street.

She watched him get out of the car and walk around to the trunk where he leaned into its depths, probably to get the groceries he'd promised to bring.

Dani hovered behind him, trying to help but only getting in the way. When he turned his head to laugh at her antics Becky could see his grin, the white teeth, the way an errant lock of golden hair fell across his forehead. His jeans were sinfully tight and the royal blue polo shirt fit snugly across the muscles in his arms and chest.

When he turned toward the house she whirled and almost ran into the front hall, hovering to one side of the door where he wouldn't be able to see her through the glass. She hated the crazy ideas about him that were gaining strength in her brain. Why had she allowed him to talk her into this in the first place?

Her heart felt as if it was ricocheting off her rib cage as the doorbell rang. Her hand reached out to the knob but her sweaty palm slid slickly on the metal and she let her arms drop to her side. She scrubbed her fingers up and down her denim covered hips.

What if she didn't answer the door? Would they go away? Then she could go back to seeing Ryan only when he picked up or dropped off Dani. That would be so much safer.

Safer. Becky's palms stilled on her thighs and she stared hard at the veneer of the wooden door, her gaze centered on but not really seeing the tiny nail that supported a wreath every Christmas. Is this what she had come to? Judging everything on the basis of whether or not she would be safe?

Well, not any more. She sucked in a deep breath and put out her hand. This time the knob turned easily and she opened the door.

'Hi.' His eyes twinkled at her over three huge brown paper bags stuffed to overflowing and balanced precariously in his arms.

'Hello.' Once again all she could see were his eyes and below his waist. Only this time he wasn't coated in soot from her fireplace. Until he spoke Becky couldn't drag her gaze away from his legs and the well-worn stress points on his jeans.

'Can we come in? These are awkward.'

'Oh, sure.' She jumped back and pulled the door open.

Ryan's grin widened, safely hidden behind the shield of groceries, and he stepped by her into the hallway. He hadn't missed the way her gaze traveled down his body and he felt a small thrill of hope at this renewed evidence she wasn't unaffected.

Dani edged by and headed straight for the kitchen, another grocery bag banging against her knees as she walked.

'Put it on the counter, Dani, and then you can go find Sarah,' he said. He maneuvered around the bottom stair and a pile of Nicky's action figures heaped in the middle of the hall. After a minute he realized Becky wasn't following him and he glanced back.

'Coming?'

She realized she was still standing in the open doorway, her fingers clenched around the door knob that was once again slippery in her palm, and staring as world-class buttocks clad in worn denim walked away from her.

'Sure.' She jerked alert and slammed the door behind her as she followed him down the hall. 'What on earth did you buy? There's a lot more than salad, a couple of steaks, and some dessert in those bags.'

His reply was muffled and she followed him into the kitchen. Dani carefully placed the packages she carried onto the counter and skipped out of the room. Becky listened to the sound of her feet on the stairs until Sarah said hello, then switched her full attention back to the man who was busily unloading groceries onto the kitchen counter.

'What are you doing, Ryan?'

'What does it look like?'

Her heart melted a little around the edges when he grinned at her over his shoulder.

'Come on, get to work, lady. I'd put these away but I don't know where you want everything.'

Becky frowned as she scanned the array of vegetables and junk food he'd spread across the counter space in her kitchen. 'You bought way too much, Ryan.'

'Yeah, well.' He took a better look at what he'd bought and smiled. 'I didn't know how much fun grocery shopping could be. Maybe I got a little carried away. Everyone was so helpful. One lady helped me pick out fruit and another gave me a fascinating lecture on the different cuts of meat.'

She picked up a package of steak. 'These are filets.' She lifted another package. 'These are rib eyes. My kids have never even tasted these cuts.'

'Yeah, she showed me how to pick out some good ones. When did they start having those free samples? Dani and I both had lunch right in the store. One demonstrator was serving oriental chicken and when I said it was delicious she offered . . . well, never mind. Here,' he handed her a heavy plastic bag, 'better put this in the freezer before it melts.'

She just bet there were helpful women in that store, she thought as she peeked inside and saw four three-pint buckets of ice cream. 'Chocolate, vanilla, strawberry and wild cherry cheesecake?'

'I decided to go with the basics because I didn't know which flavors your family preferred.'

'Wild cherry cheesecake is a basic?'

'It is for me.'

'There's someone at the door for you, Ryan,' Mike called from the front hall.

He glanced at his watch and shoved the second bag of groceries in her direction.

'Could you finish these up? There's some more frozen stuff and it'll thaw. I'll be right back.'

She looked at the bag then back at him. 'I guess so, but . . .'

'Sorry, I'd better get that.' He smiled and hurried out of the room.

She starting laying food out on the counter, mentally listing the items. A dozen packages of steak, sliced ham, sausages, boneless chicken breasts, brown and white rice, red potatoes, linguini noodles, six tomatoes, three of the skinny expensive cucumbers, jelly powder in eight different flavors . . .

'Mom? He asked me to bring these in. Where do you want them?' Mike stood in the door, holding two more full bags. Wordlessly she pointed to a spot on the floor by the stove.

Twenty minutes later she stared around at the counters and the table heaped with food. The man had only said he'd bring enough for one meal, she thought. What is all this?

Did he think she was a charity case? She had never accepted charity from anyone in her life. She sure as heck wasn't going to start now with a man she barely knew, especially when she wasn't even convinced she wanted him in her life at all.

Or was he trying to buy her companionship?

Anger slowly built up inside her head until she was afraid if she didn't release it, her brain would fry. So she went looking for the person who deserved to have it fall out all over him.

There was no one in the living room or the front hall so she snatched open the front door, determined to search until she could order him to pack up all his food. He could go find some other woman, one who wanted to be bought. 'Ryan? Ryan!'

'In the driveway.' His reply came from the other side of the lilac bushes that proliferated at the corner of her house without any encouragement.

She was out the door, around the side of the house, and pushing through the bushes before the door swung shut.

'Who do you think you are? I want you to march right in the house and get those . . . Oh, my God! What's going on here?'

She had been so angry and so determined to have it out with him that at first she hadn't noticed the big blue step van in her driveway or the man who was so efficiently removing the tires from her station wagon.

'What do you think you're doing?' She forgot all about the groceries and walked past Ryan, outraged to find someone messing with Matilda. 'That's my car, you get away from . . .'

He grabbed her arm and swung her around. 'It's okay, he's only mounting the new tires.'

'New tires? New tires! I didn't order any tires.'

The mechanic had looked up when she yelled but Ryan waved him on and he started removing the old tires from their rims. As each one came off, the man tossed it into the back of his van.

'I've got to stop him before he wrecks something. I can't afford to pay for this.'

'You're not. I am.' Ryan wrapped an arm around her shoulders and steered her into the back yard.

'What? You're not buying me tires!'

The shivers that spiraled from her throat to her stomach at his touch scared her, and she pulled away.

'Yes, I am. The old ones are so bald that if you hit a sharp rut you'll blow one, if not all. They're not safe.'

'You are not buying me tires! You're not buying me a month's worth of groceries, either. You can pack up the food, and your tame little tire man, and get off my property. I will not be bought!'

'Bought? I'm not trying . . .'

'Right now, Mr McLeod.' Becky crossed her arms over her chest and glared at him. 'I am not that kind of woman.'

'What are you talking about? You needed tires, so I arranged to have them put on today. You didn't even have to take your car to the garage. And what's a few groceries?'

'A few? You bought enough food to feed two basketball teams.'

'It was fun. I hadn't been inside a grocery store in years and I got carried away. Is that a crime? Dani eats here more than she would at any other sitter's.'

Then he smiled that smile.

'Oh. I never thought of that.'

Ryan made the mistake of allowing triumph to show in his eyes. She straightened her shoulders and lifted her chin. 'But absolutely no tires. Those aren't all that bad yet, and I can't afford . . .'

'Mr McLeod?'

Becky stopped mid-sentence and they both turned to look at the mechanic who hovered at the gate.

'All done. Sure was a good thing you got those changed now. They wouldn't have lasted more than a few miles, even on the city streets.'

Ryan read the rebellion simmering in Becky's eyes, then looked back at the man wiping his greasy hands on a rag. 'Blow-outs are dangerous, aren't they?'

'Yes, very.' He handed Ryan the work order to sign and smiled at her. 'You should have had them replaced a long time ago, Mrs McLeod. Why, one time I saw an eight car pile-up caused by a blow-out. What a mess. They needed six ambulances.'

'I'm not . . .'

'Thanks,' Ryan read the name tag sewn to the front of the man's uniform, 'Stan. We really appreciate the good job you've done.' He walked around her to guide Stan back to his van. 'I'll make sure your boss knows.'

After he waved good-bye to the mechanic and turned back toward the house, she was ready for him.

'Why did you do that?'

'Those tires weren't safe.'

He was going to go past her when she put her hand on his chest to stop him. Immediately the tingle started in her fingertips and raced up her arm but she ignored it.

'I didn't ask you to change them and you didn't ask me if you could.'

He put his hand over hers to trap it, then pressed it against the hard muscle that covered his heart. 'It didn't occur to me you'd mind.'

'I do mind.'

'Why?' He reached out for her other hand and tugged until they were standing so close together she felt woozy.

The rain had held off all day but now it began to drizzle, flattening her curls and darkening his hair.

Becky noticed but couldn't seem to care that they were both outside in the rain without coats. When he touched her she didn't feel the cold. She couldn't feel anything but him.

'Why?' It took her a moment to remember what they were talking about. 'I can't accept them. They're too expensive.'

Ryan remembered the emerald earrings, the diamond necklace, and the exotic vacations the women in his past had expected, women whose names he couldn't remember when he stood so close to Becky.

How could he get this contrary female to accept something as inexpensive and necessary as new tires? He darn well wasn't going to back down and have the old ones replaced. It would be a waste of money and dangerous, especially with a car full of kids to drive around.

That was the answer!

'I can't let you drive Dani on bald tires. It is too much of a risk. I'll write it off.'

Her eyes rounded and she stared up at him. He was right, she thought. If they were as unsafe as the tire man had said, and a blow-out as bad as the one he described happened, one or all of the children could be hurt or perhaps killed in the accident.

'I . . . I didn't think. Can you do that? Write off the expense?'

'Of course,' Ryan lied easily as he wrapped his arms around her shoulders and pulled her against his chest. She had to tip back her head to look at him and his heart began to beat faster as his glance roamed her concerned face, then settled on her lips. Damn, how he wanted to kiss her.

'Then I guess it would be okay. If you're sure. If your accountant tells you it won't be allowed, make sure you let me know and I'll pay you back.'

'Sure.' His whole attention was so focused on her lips he barely heard what she was saying. Dare he? Was it too soon?

'I don't know how, but I'm . . . sure . . .' Her voice trailed off. His heart was racing hard under her palm, his eyes blazed, his fingers slowly kneaded her spine. She was sure he was going to kiss her. She forgot what she was saying and stared back in helpless fascination. Should she pull away? For weeks she had dreamed about being kissed by him, about being in his arms.

'I'm going to kiss you.' It was not a question.

'Are . . . are you?'

He lowered his head by slow degrees and, though she trembled, she didn't turn away. His lips touched hers, firm yet tender, moving lightly yet generating a heat that spread until her toes curled and her scalp tingled. His hand stroked fire up her spine and her thought processes tangled, shutting down when he buried his fingers in her hair.

CHAPTER 7

Ryan had expected the whirl of passion but he hadn't known she would taste like this, make him burn like this. He slanted his mouth over hers and dragged her that last inch closer until their bodies clung together. He groaned and she shuddered as shared needs built, and built, and built –

'Mom?' The door banged open and she jerked away, turned her back, and wrapped her arms around her stomach. 'Mommy? Telephone.'

'Yes . . .' She gulped for air when he gripped her shoulders and pulled her back against his chest. 'I'll be right in.'

'Okay, I'll tell them.' The door slammed shut.

'Becky.'

'No.' She forced herself to step away but she didn't look at him. 'Not now.'

'But we have to talk.'

'Not now!'

He touched her arm and she finally turned halfway toward him. 'Later?'

Her shoulders were stiff and she didn't meet his eyes. 'I don't know. Maybe.'

She still wouldn't look at him so he moved until he stood in front of her again. It wasn't hard to see the shock and the fear in her eyes. He knew he couldn't push too hard when she was so vulnerable, no matter how much he wanted to.

'Later?' he asked again.

'Later.'

Becky saw the headlights of Ryan's car and went to the door. When she heard the dull thud of two car doors, she knew he was coming in with Dani.

How did she get herself into these situations, she wondered. Somehow she had agreed to baby-sit so Ryan could go out with another woman.

If ever she was tempted to swear, she knew this was exactly the situation that might drive her to it. She found herself praying he hadn't picked up Carol before he drove out to Richmond. It was one thing to know about something. It was quite another to have to watch it happening. One of the more colorful phrases Nicky had invented for cursing came to mind and she said it out loud, hoping it would relieve some tension.

'Pifflelumpawonk.' No relief there.

Ryan rapped briskly on the door and she swung it open.

'Thanks for letting me come,' Dani said.

'You're always welcome, honey.' Becky stared at the man standing behind the little girl, his hair glinting gold under the porch light. She tightened the sash on her robe and opened the door wider so Ryan and Dani could come in. 'Sarah's upstairs waiting for you. Remind her that you guys have to keep the noise down. Nicky's already asleep.'

'Of course, Becky.'

'Are you sure you don't mind?' Ryan asked as Dani took her small suitcase from him, said good-bye, and walked quickly up the stairs.

'No, no, of course I don't mind.' Becky gritted her teeth and pasted a smile on her face. 'I told you so when you called earlier. Sarah loves to have Dani sleep over. I hope your housekeeper is going to be okay.'

'Mrs Estevez' son called again just before we left the apartment. She's in hospital for an emergency appendectomy but the doctor believes everything will go smoothly.' Ryan shoved back the sleeve of his tuxedo and glanced at his watch.

'I'm keeping you. Go. You'll be late.' Becky's jaw began to hurt.

'Can I borrow your phone? I'd better tell Carol I'm running late.'

'Sure. Go ahead.'

He walked down the hall to use the phone in the kitchen. Becky sank into the side chair she kept by the hall table and, elbows on knees, rocked forward to press both hands over her mouth.

Nothing, absolutely nothing on this earth could have prepared her for the way he looked in a tuxedo.

She thoroughly disliked the idea of him escorting Carol Hill to a fancy charity ball tonight. The Black and White Ball had been a fixture in Vancouver ever since Becky could remember, one of the most exciting and glamorous social events of the year and always reported in detail by the media. To get an invitation a person had to be powerful, wealthy, famous, or infamous, if not all four.

Granted he'd made the promise before he'd met Becky and she was glad he was the kind of man who kept his word. Granted she believed he'd ended his . . . personal arrangement with the other woman.

Those facts didn't make his 'date' with Ms Hill any easier to bear. Even scarier was the fact that her feelings tonight wouldn't be so strong if she wasn't beginning to care for him.

She didn't want to care.

'She's going to take a taxi to the hotel and I'll meet her there.'

Still dazed by her thoughts, she looked up. He stood under the chandelier and the crystal prisms sparkled almost as much as his eyes. Her breath hitched as his lips tilted into a smile.

'Huh? Oh. Ms Hill.' She gathered all her strength and stood up. 'That seems practical.'

'This thing always goes late. Maybe as late as one o'clock but Carol and I could come by here to get Dani afterward.'

'No.' She sucked in a breath and let it out slowly, through her teeth. Anything would be better than seeing him in that tuxedo again tonight. 'They'll have fun together. Tomorrow morning's soon enough.'

He glanced at his watch again. 'I'd better get going.'

She walked him across the hall and waited, hand on the doorknob, for him to leave.

'There's just one thing. Tomorrow, when I pick up Dani . . .' He paused rocking back on the heels of his shiny leather loafers. His hand lifted, hovered in the air beside her face.

'Yes?'

'I was wondering . . . Is it "later" yet?'

'Later?'

'Tomorrow, when I come to get Dani. Can we talk?'

'No.' She stiffened. After her lecture to Mike on 'later' here she was using it herself. She hated knowing she was a hypocrite. Her hand twisted on the metal knob. 'No. I don't think . . .'

'It's okay.' He cupped her cheek and rubbed his thumb across her full bottom lip before stooping to kiss her forehead. 'Good night, honey. Let me know when later comes, will you?'

He tapped her nose and ran down the stairs.

She watched as he climbed in his car and backed down the driveway. She lifted one hand as he tooted the horn. Several seconds passed until she closed the door.

Becky went upstairs, checked on the children and headed for bed. She tried not think about Ryan laughing and dancing with Carol Hill, holding the other woman in his arms. Spending his evening surrounded by the most interesting and powerful people in the city. Probably dining on fancy canapes and sipping champagne.

He was probably having such a fabulous night that he didn't even give her a second thought. Eating in her kitchen with four noisy children, followed by an evening watching television, could not even begin to compare.

She crawled into bed, punched her pillow into shape, and wriggled until the blankets were bunched around her in the manner most conducive to falling asleep. No way was she going to spend another night thinking about him.

Sleep was a long time coming.

Ryan sipped champagne, restraining a grimace as bubbles tickled his nose. He wasn't in the mood for bubbles. Why couldn't they serve a decent scotch at these events?

And the food! He eyed the silver trays and tried to ignore his growling stomach. The only thing he recognized on the whole table was the caviar and a salmon mousse. He loathed caviar and the mousse had been dressed up with so many spices he couldn't taste the salmon.

He'd been distracted all evening. Earlier Carol had seemed slightly annoyed, commenting on his lack of attention. Eventually she'd given up on him and concentrated on making business contacts, which was her reason for attending this shindig in the first place.

He'd decided not to explain. Telling her about the anonymous note he'd found in the car when he left home would have added nothing to the evening. At least he could be grateful Dani hadn't noticed the piece of white paper lying on the driver's seat when he unlocked the car. It had been no more vitriolic than the e-mail messages he'd been receiving for several months but knowing that the person had actually been inside his car would have frightened Dani. She'd only just stopped mentioning the robbery every night at bedtime.

He'd notify the officer in charge of his case in the morning. In the meantime, the note and its envelope were sealed in a plastic bag he'd borrowed from Becky's house while he phoned Carol. He patted his jacket pocket and heard the reassuring rustle of plastic.

He swirled the liquid in the glass, contemplating the bubbles as they rose to the surface. Becky had been very supportive when he'd explained his commitment to escort Carol to the Ball, even going so far as to have Dani for the night. All evening one thought had been niggling in the back of his mind.

Why?

In his experience, women did not like the man in their life to spend the evening with another woman, especially at an affair like this one. The only logical answer to his question was no more palatable than the caviar.

She still didn't care how or with whom he spent his time.

Ryan drained the glass and slammed it down on the table with enough force to draw the attention of his dining companions.

'Ryan? Is something wrong?' Carol asked.

'No. Sorry. It slipped.' He smiled easily at the men and women seated around the table and they resumed chatting.

God, he wished he was cuddled up with Becky on her old sofa right now. He'd be comfortable, his stomach pleasantly full after one of her delicious meals. Maybe he could have even convinced her that the time had come for the conversation she'd postponed until 'later'.

Instead he had to listen politely to the macho boasting of the mayor's husband on his left while Carol flattered the potential client on her right. He glanced at his watch. Three more hours. He lifted the bottle from the ice bucket standing at his elbow and refilled everyone's glass, including his own. It was going to be a very, very long night.

Two weeks had passed and it still wasn't 'later'. She was a coward and she knew it but she still didn't want to talk about what she'd felt when he kissed her.

They were seated side by side on the old couch, Ryan sprawled in one corner, his drink balanced on his stomach. Becky leaned back in the other corner facing Ryan, her head pressed to the couch's back. Her bare toes curled into the upholstery fabric only inches from his thigh.

Since 'The Kiss' he had stayed to dinner almost every night he didn't work late. Sometimes she gave in to Ryan's persuasions and allowed him to take everybody out to eat. He hadn't kissed her again and she couldn't decide if she was glad or sorry. Maybe the feelings evoked by the kiss had scared him as much as they had her.

Today the chill of late fall outside was a comfortable contrast to the warmth of camaraderie inside the old house. Only an occasional interruption from one child or another had broken their concentration on each other. Conversation flowed easily, any silences were tranquil. She'd chatted about her children and he'd talked about work.

Both were enjoying the glimpse into what seemed, to them, an alien lifestyle. She grumbled a little about how a teenage boy's actions sometimes seemed to border on insanity. He told her how it felt to have employees leave him in the lurch.

He was an enjoyable companion and she was learning to like him even though she still had no intention of ever trusting him or any man with her heart. Perhaps he could be her friend.

'You still don't know who's behind it all?'

'No.' He ran his fingertips through his already tousled hair. 'Only that he or she is working for PasComm and probably taking a salary from me. It might be any one of six or seven people, as far as Hallie and I can figure.'

'What is PasComm?'

'One of my biggest competitors. If my expansion had progressed as expected the stolen program would have cost them a big chunk of their market share. The owner also seems to feel he has a vested interest in breaking me.'

'Why?'

'When I was much younger I worked for a large company. I was a very insignificant cog in their computer department. Pastin was my boss. He had a bad habit of taking credit for his employees' ideas.'

'That's dishonest.'

'It happens. Just not to me. I made sure the president of the company knew the true identity of the brains behind Harold Pastin's newest innovation. I was promoted. Pastin received a slap on the wrist and a lateral transfer. He left the company soon after. Every time our paths have crossed over the intervening years he's made it clear he intended to get even some day.'

'Is that the only reason he's so angry with you?'

He didn't answer and moved restlessly in his seat, surprising her with the flush darkening his cheek-bones.

'Ryan?'

Still no answer.

'I get it. Is there a woman at the heart of this tale?'

'Damn.' He downed his drink. 'I don't want to talk about it.'

'I'm right, aren't I?' she chortled, pleased to have him at a disadvantage for the first time since she'd known him.

'You're going to push this, aren't you?'

'You bet.'

'His wife offered . . . She said she wanted to have sex. I turned her down but that's not the way she told it to her husband. There's been bad blood between Pastin and myself ever since.'

As she listened she was by turns surprised, then curious, then thoughtful. 'Has it always been like that? Women chasing you?'

No longer able to resist touching her, he put down his empty glass and slid closer to take her hands in his own, thumbs rubbing gently on her knuckles, his palms cupping her fingers.

'Would it sound egotistical if I said yes? I can't lie to you, Becky. There were times in my life when they didn't have to chase very hard. And when I was younger they didn't have to chase at all. Actually that's how my relationship with Carol began.'

Her fingers trembled in his and he hesitated.

'Do you want to hear this?'

'Part of me does, part of me doesn't,' she answered honestly. 'But perhaps if I did it would help me understand you better.'

'I was tired of it all and Carol offered to keep the vultures away by pretending we were involved. Most of the time it worked.'

'Is that all she meant to you? A means to that end?'

'No, of course not.' He stopped, then backtracked, determined to be honest with her. 'Maybe, but only at first. Long before we were lovers we became friends. And make no mistake, Becky, it worked both ways.

'Carol is a very beautiful, successful woman and there were men creating some of the same problems for her. It solved difficulties for both of us, so we could concentrate on business. Plus there is the health risk of casual relationships.'

'It sounds so . . . so cold.'

'It was practical.' He shook his head. 'Nothing in my past experience, both with other women and my own family, had shown me a relationship could be any different. Until I met you.'

She blushed. He squeezed her fingers then forced himself to let her go and they sat back, sipping their drinks in companionable silence. In the distance they heard the faint sounds of children playing elsewhere in the big house.

As always lately, he restrained himself with difficulty, afraid to let her see how his need grew stronger every time he was with her.

He wondered about Becky's marriage and about Nicky's father. How had her husband hurt her? Was Nicky the result of a love affair gone bad? As bad as her marriage?

Was Nicky's father still around? Could she still be involved with the other man?

That thought had bothered him more and more lately. A straight question would get a straight answer, he knew. Becky was too honest to play games with him. He wanted to know, needed to know, but did he want to hear the answer?

He put down his glass and poured out an inch of scotch from the bottle still standing on the coffee table. He turned the triangular bottle in his hand, scrutinizing its label as if his life depended on his ability to repeat every letter of the small print.

She had called him at work this afternoon to suggest he bring his favorite brand and leave it at her house. Ryan had enjoyed the domestic sensation of receiving something he knew married men often complained about, a request to run an errand on the way home.

For a little while he let himself pretend Lilac House was his home. Ha. What an idiot he was. He picked up his glass and threw back the neat scotch, grateful for the way it burned down his throat.

'Is there someone else, Becky?'

'Someone else?' she asked, puzzlement clear in her eyes.

'Another man?'

'No.'

His fervent 'thank you, Lord' made her laugh.

'Will you tell me about them?'

'Them?'

'Your ex-husband and Nicky's father. The men who hurt you so badly you can't bring yourself to trust me.'

'Nicky's father?' Her eyes opened wide in surprise then her cheeks went white. 'Oh.'

'I'm sorry if I've embarrassed you. I know you were divorced before Nicky was conceived.' He poured another ounce or two into the heavy tumbler. 'I thought if you told me about them and how they hurt you I could understand why you pull away from me.'

She ducked her head and lifted her knees, wrapping her arms around her ankles. Her whole body coiled into a tight bundle, shutting him out.

He waited, listening to the old mantel clock tick away the minutes. Waited, hoping she would open up to him.

Hurting for her when he realized his questions had caused her pain.

He scooped her up in his arms and leaned back, holding her against his chest. One large hand rubbed a warm circle on her back, the other wrapped around her legs and rested on her hip.

She sighed and rested her head on his shoulder. Her fingers curled around his neck. He wondered who was comforting whom.

'Never mind. Forget I asked.'

Becky lay in his arms, absorbing the freely given care and concern. And finally succumbed to the urge to tell him about her past.

Gradually the tension dissipated and her body relaxed. From somewhere deep inside she dragged up the courage to talk, to tell this man about another, very different, man. When she spoke her voice was low and he rested his cheek on her hair while he listened, elated because she was starting to trust him.

'My husband's name was, is, Eric. We married very young, right out of high school. Every girl wanted him but he chose me. At first we were like two children playing house. No worries, no responsibilities. When I got pregnant life was still a game and when Mike was born he was our doll. He ate and slept. I changed his clothes three, often four times a day for the fun of it and Eric had a son to show off to his friends as proof of his masculinity.

'But as Mike began to grow, the bills multiplied. Jobs were scarce for people with no skills and good day-care even scarcer. I couldn't find work that paid enough to cover the expenses incurred by a working mother so I had to stay home with the baby. Eric was out most of the day and part of the night, working two jobs.' She lifted her head so she could see Ryan's face.

'Make no mistake, I loved Mike and Eric but there were lots of problems. Then I got pregnant again. It was unintentional but Eric accused me of doing it on purpose. He said I wanted to ruin his life.'

The bitterness was acid sharp in her voice and Ryan kissed her brow lightly, soothingly, to remind her she lay in his arms now. He left his fingers tangled in her curls after he pressed her head down onto his shoulder.

'Then what happened?'

'The day I brought Sarah home from the hospital Eric went missing for thirty-six hours. Over the next few months he began disappearing for several days at a time. He complained I paid more attention to the children than to him. Sarah was colicky and her first three months were a nightmare. I tried so hard . . .'

Ryan had to make himself keep silent; listening to Becky recite her painful history was very difficult.

'I tried to keep the kids quiet when he was home but he hated listening to the baby wail. Always telling them to leave him alone. It wasn't fair to Sarah or Mike and I hated it. One time when Sarah was sick he threw on his clothes in the middle of the night and left in a rage. He didn't come back for eight days. That was only the first in a string of unexplained absences over the following year.'

'How did it end?'

'On the evening of Sarah's first birthday the doorbell rang. The woman, girl really, was perfectly cool as she announced she was Eric's lover and he had moved in with her. He'd sent her to help me pack up his belongings.' She twisted to look up into his face. 'You know what I remember best about that night?'

'What?' With one hand he brushed damp curls away from her eyes.

'Her strong musk scent. I was grateful that my kids were occupied in the kitchen. I felt mortified to have his pretty young mistress see me at the end of a long, hectic day.' She managed a grin of sharp-edged pleasure. 'I refused to let her in the house and told her Eric could come the next morning and pack up the stuff himself.'

'Did he come?'

Her grin widened until her teeth were bared in an expression of irreverent joy. 'After the kids went to bed I dumped everything of his onto the front lawn. In the rain.'

'What did he say?'

'Nothing to me. I wasn't home when he came. I had the locks changed, then packed up the kids and went to Jan's place in San Diego for the weekend. When I got back I filed for divorce.'

He waited, knowing there had to be more.

'Not that it was much of a marriage anyway, at that point. I was glad to be finally rid of his constant complaining and humiliating absences. Eventually the judge decreed Eric was responsible for the house payments and minimum monthly child support.'

On the last word her voice quavered and she burrowed her face in Ryan's neck, seeking the strength she sensed was there for her. A sob shook her and warm tears trickled down his neck to pool in the hollow where her lips pressed against his skin. His arms convulsed around her.

'Stop, Becky. I don't need to know any more. Let me help you forget.' His voice was husky as he shared her anguish. She shook her head and quickly told him the rest.

'About a year later she kicked him out. He showed up here past midnight and drunk, battering on the door, shouting and screaming at the top of his lungs for me to let him in.

'I was afraid the noise would wake the children and scare them so I opened the door. Once inside the house, he told me since he was paying good money to support me he should get something in return. We fought but he forced me . . . he . . . oh, God . . .'

Sobs racked her body.

'Your ex-husband is Nicky's father.' Shock settled heavily over Ryan. Though his hand still moved in a slow, automatic caress on her spine, his thoughts exploded furiously. The bastard had made her life hell. Then he humiliated her. Then he raped her.

A red haze tinged his vision and his arms tightened around Becky until she was pressed tightly to his heart. Except her pain was ripping it out of his chest.

'Where is he now?' His words dropped into the quiet room like rocks down the icy crevasse of a glacier. He promised himself then that if he ever found the man, he'd make Eric pay for what he'd done to Becky.

'I don't know. After Nicky was born he quit making the support payments and . . . and I couldn't endure explaining things to the court so they would force him to do so. In September he stopped the mortgage payments and left town. I haven't heard from him since.'

'Did you have him arrested and charged?'

'For neglecting his children? For neglecting his financial responsibility to them? There are women all over the world in the same position and there is little they can do through the courts.'

'No. Because he . . .' Ryan swallowed. Hard. 'Because rape is a criminal offence, dammit.'

'How could I? The scandal would have hurt the children unbearably. Richmond might be a suburb of a big city but it's like living in a small town. Everyone would have known. He is still their father.'

Had she done the right thing, he wondered. In a small town environment the children might have heard gossip but he was sure they'd heard some anyhow. Could the truth have been so much worse than what people said now? That she'd been reckless and ended up with an illegitimate baby?

'Perhaps if you had reported it you would have received professional help to deal with . . . everything.'

'I did go to a therapist at the rape crisis centre in the city. They helped me a lot. They suggested I report him to the police but this way only my reputation was hurt. If he had been arrested and then a trial . . .'

'But – '

'I'm not saying my decision was the right one, but back then things weren't the same as they are now. I'm not the same.'

'Your friend, Hallie's niece, she would have – '

'I didn't tell Jan. She was having a really rough time right then. The man she loved had been killed a few weeks before, then her mother died. She couldn't handle any more pain. I think she suspects the truth but we haven't talked about it.'

'What did you tell people when they found out you were pregnant?'

'Nothing. To no one. Luckily Nicky resembles me, not his father, so I assume they all think I had a fling after the divorce and got careless.'

He winced. She was right. After all, it was what he himself had thought. Her words were cool and uncaring but he knew what the rumor mill had probably done to her pride. His respect for the woman in his arms grew. Becky had weathered the storms in her life and had come out on the other side a warm and loving mother. She never treated Nicky any differently than her other children and seemed to love him equally.

'Is that why you decided to do day-care? Because you needed the money?'

'Yes.'

'How have you survived? What I pay you can't be enough to support your family.'

'I have a small trust fund from my father and I have a job, sort've.' The comfort she'd found in his arms gave Becky the lift she needed to throw off the distressing memories. 'Come on, I'll show you.'

She dragged the backs of her hands across her face, scrubbing away the tears. She took his hand, tugged him to his feet, then towed him down the hall and into a small room he'd not seen before, tucked behind the dining room and under the stairs. In the doorway she stood back and, in a grand manner, waved an arm for him to enter.

'Ta da!'

He stepped inside, Becky close on his heels. He stared around but saw nothing to explain what she used this room for.

An old desk filled most of the tiny room, its top overflowing with loose sheets of paper. When he turned his hip bumped a pile of papers and they began a slow slide to the floor.

'Ooops,' she said and grabbed for them quickly. 'That's always happening. Hand me that, would you?' She pointed with her chin.

He saw a small model of a train steam engine on top of a bookshelf. He picked it up, then as quickly almost dropped it. He hefted it with two hands. It had to weigh four or five pounds.

'This is heavy.'

'It's brass. Put it right here.' She moved sideways so he could reach over her shoulder to place it on the stack of paper. 'My great-grandfather played with that model when he was a little boy. I use it as a paperweight. Nicky is fascinated by its detail and working parts.'

'An antique?'

'Well, it is really old but not valuable, thank God.'

'Why?'

She ran her fingers across the brass detailing. 'I would have had to sell it.' She was silent for a moment, then shook herself and turned to him with a smile. 'Well, have you figured out what I do here?'

He didn't know what to say about the sadness in her comment about the train, so he said nothing and looked around the tiny room again. Behind the door he saw a bookcase, its shelves so heavily loaded they sagged in the middle. A quick perusal of the titles on the spines of the heavy tomes did not clear up his confusion.

There were five or six different dictionaries, two complete sets of encyclopaedias, and several paperbacks for translating English into foreign languages. Balanced precariously at one end of the desk was a manual typewriter of a brand he hadn't seen for years. Open boxes held reams of graph paper and two enormous, wobbly piles of reference books were stacked on the floor.

'I give up. What is it? Besides a fire hazard.'

'Can't you guess?'

'No way.'

'I create crosswords.'

'Crosswords?'

'And word puzzles.'

'Puzzles?'

'What are you? An echo? My favorites are the acrostics.'

He was amazed. This woman made those mind twisters for a living. 'I love puzzles. Of all kinds. I wonder if I've ever done one of yours?'

'Do you do the ones in *The Times*? I've had several published there and in a few of the local newspapers, magazines, that sort of thing. Occasionally a company wants one for their newsletter or a contest. I specialize in theme puzzles.'

'I'm impressed. How long have you been doing it?'

'Seems like forever but I didn't start earning money for them until after Sarah was born. I needed an income and Jan suggested this. The money is erratic but there was enough until I had to find the mortgage money from somewhere. And it let me stay home with my children.'

She sparkled merrily up at him. His hands lifted to caress her flushed cheeks, his thumbs rubbing across lashes still spiked from her tears.

Becky's hands quivered and her knees were weakened from the effort required to keep from touching him. The fragrance of his cologne made her aware of the cramped space in which they stood. She backed out and spun on her heel, leading the way to the front hall.

'Anyway, now you know all my deep dark secrets. It's late. I'll call Dani.' She tossed the words over her shoulder as she hurried away from what he made her want.

He strode after her, stopping her with one large hand on her shoulder. He was so close his breath stirred the curls on her nape when he spoke.

'Don't run away. Please.'

Fear. Embarrassment. Panic. All these and more coursed through Becky. She couldn't let him close to her, close enough to touch her heart. He was too sophisticated for her. He would hurt her and she knew she couldn't bring herself back from the edge of the abyss again.

'No, Ryan. Go home. I'm grateful you listened, I guess. And maybe you do care. But right now I want you to please go home.'

'Becky.'

She heard the longing in the one word and turned around. 'Maybe we can be friends,' she promised. 'Some day.'

'We are friends, damn it! In fact, we are more and you know it. Stop fighting this!'

She studied a smudge of ketchup on the front of his white shirt, put there by Nicky when he leaped on Ryan's back for a piggy-back ride after dinner. Ryan had laughed it off but she'd been mortified and ordered Nicky upstairs to get cleaned up.

He was right but he was pushing her and both habit and necessity made her pull back. 'You're exaggerating. There's nothing to fight.'

Ryan could hear the fear behind the words. And

the uncertainty. He knew he had to ease off, give her time to accept him as a friend before she could want him as more. He would leave. For now. He would make her believe in his love. Soon.

Every minute he spent with her he became more aware of how necessary Rebecca Hansen was to his own happiness. He would convince her.

He had to.

CHAPTER 8

'Do adults get tired of having kids around?' Dani kept her face averted as she studied the rack of dresses. The store's public announcement of a special sale in the hardware department almost drowned out her voice.

Ryan resisted the urge to pretend he hadn't heard her. This must be one of those moments of deeply emotional communication Becky had warned him were so important between kids and their parents. And since he was *in loco parentis* for Dani, he'd been duly designated as responsible for supplying suitable, uplifting, and encouraging answers.

He abhorred deeply emotional communication. He'd already talked more about emotional subjects to Becky than to everyone else in his entire life put together. How the hell was he going to cope now it had started with Dani?

'I guess. Sometimes people do get angry and wish they didn't have to be with another person. I imagine that kids get tired of the adults in their lives sometimes, too.'

'My aunt and uncle didn't like me. That's why I came to live with you, isn't it?'

Yup. Deeply emotional. A minefield.

'You came to live with me because your parents chose me to be your guardian.'

'I like living with you, Ryan. I don't want to go away.'

Nothing in his life had prepared him for saying the right thing to a distraught little girl. The situation was fraught with peril. He'd rather be almost anywhere else on earth than standing in the aisle of this department store, having this conversation. Dangling from a rope on the side of a mountain would be preferable and he hated heights.

What to say? He had to say something.

'You won't go away until you're grown up. Until you want to.'

'Okay.' She stroked the shoulder of the dress she held. 'Can I have this one?'

That was it? No big long discussion that left his stomach in knots? No teary scene to draw the disapproval of every woman around him? The anticlimax was almost overwhelming. It took him a moment to understand.

His simple reassurance had been everything required.

He was good at this fatherly stuff. He felt like puffing up his chest and strutting with pride.

'Do you need to try it on?' Ryan glanced around the girls' clothing department of the big store. 'I'm sure they have a fitting room here somewhere.'

'Becky showed me where it was when we shopped for my new school clothes.' She pointed into the next department. 'It's over there.'

In the lingerie department. Ryan shuddered. He might have known.

'Are you sure you wouldn't rather do this with Becky and Sarah?'

Dani hung the dress back on the rack. 'Okay.'

He sighed with relief and turned to walk away. Then he saw her pat the dress. She looked so damned sad. He couldn't do this.

'No, sweetheart. You can try it on today.'

He followed her through the racks of nightgowns, past the shelves of bras and panties, and around the display of slips and those skimpy tops that looked like a man's undershirt. Just his luck the fitting rooms were in the back corner.

She paused by the locked door. A clerk came by, punched in the combination, and opened it.

'Aren't you coming in?' Dani asked.

'No!' Ryan blanched. 'I mean, no, sweetheart. A man can't go in there.'

'Oh.' She stared inside the door the clerk was holding open but made no move to enter.

'What's the matter? Have you changed your mind?'

'Becky told us not to go off alone at the mall.'

He crouched at her side. 'Are you scared? You don't have to be, I'll be right here.'

'I can help her, if you like.'

He looked up at the young woman who was still waiting. 'Would you? Thanks.' He put one hand on

Dani's shoulder. 'Okay with you?'

She solemnly studied the clerk for a moment before she nodded. The door shut behind them.

Five minutes passed while he listened to Dani's highpitched voice discussing her new party dress with the clerk. Five long minutes. Amazing how a man can feel so intimidated by plastic female bodies wearing scraps of fabric, he thought. They didn't even have heads.

Ryan shifted from one foot to the other. His movement accidentally knocked a stack of packaged stockings off the shelf. He quickly stooped and swept them into his arms, then looked helplessly at the spot they'd been.

The other stacks on the shelf had tilted, then fallen sideways to fill the space. Where was he supposed to put these? Eventually he just dumped them on top and stepped back, afraid that another incautious movement would knock over the wobbling pile. Unfortunately he hadn't noticed the mannequins immediately behind him.

His shoulder connected. When that mannequin fell over it knocked into the next one. It fell sideways into a third one. Just like dominoes. Ryan grabbed for the fourth one, catching it just before it hit the floor. Only the body slid right out of the scrap of satin and bounced twice before it came to a rest across the aisle, naked and wobbling on its pointy plastic breasts.

Except for its left arm, which had stayed with the nightgown in his hand.

'Can I help you?' The clerk stood behind Dani, who had obviously come out to model the dress for him. Dani's mouth was a perfect 'O' of surprise. The clerk was trying not to laugh.

Ryan glanced at the plastic bodies tumbled at his feet, then at the sexy satin nightgown and graceful arm he still clutched. He shook his head. 'I think this is beyond help, don't you? I'm really sorry.'

'It's not permanently damaged, sir. The arms are detachable to make it easy to change the display garments.'

'Can I have this one?' Dani asked.

She had evidently grown tired of the discussion and wanted the adults to focus on the far more important subject of her new dress.

'You look beautiful, sweetheart. You go change, and we'll buy it.'

This time she went back inside the fitting room alone quite happily while Ryan helped the clerk gather together the mingled body parts he'd spread around the area. That was when he noticed. The nightgown he still held was the same warm pink of the shorts Becky had worn that first day in front of her fireplace.

He rubbed the fabric between his fingers and thumb. So soft. So silky.

He closed his eyes. Becky would look so beautiful in this.

No.

No way would she accept this from him.

He resolutely gave it back to the clerk, who replaced it on the mannequin she'd reassembled.

While he watched she adjusted the lacy neckline and the skinny straps. Then she smoothed the fabric down over the hips and twisted the bottom half so one plastic leg showed through the lace-edged slit.

Lord, would Becky look a knock-out in that thing. He snorted. Yeah, sure, in your dreams, buddy. As if she'd ever wear it for him. As if she'd even let him buy it for her. He tapped his mouth with one finger as he contemplated the rack of identical nightgowns just behind the display. Of course he did owe her something for the night-shirt he kept forgetting to return.

When he and Dani left the store she was proudly carrying a large bag. He'd slipped his much smaller bag, paid for when she wasn't looking, inside his jacket pocket. He whistled as they drove home.

Becky dropped onto the living room sofa, lifted her feet with great difficulty until she could rest them on the coffee table, and allowed her spine to sag until it fitted the curve of the old cushions. Today she felt shabbier than those cushions and older than dirt. It was a mystery to her where she was going to find the energy to climb the stairs to bed. At least it was quiet in here. The kids were either in their rooms or watching television in the play room.

The door bell rang but she couldn't find the energy to move. Someone else could get it, she decided, after trying unsuccessfully to lower her legs. She lay there waiting but no one came and after a minute it rang again. She knew she really should shout up the stairs to one of the kids, asking them to answer it, but even that effort felt onerous.

It rang again. She sighed and began the laborious task of getting to her feet but dropped back when the door opened.

'If you're a criminal, turn around and leave. I don't have the energy to deal with you right now.'

'And if I'm not?'

Ryan! A spark of energy generated her smile but it fizzled out quickly.

He came into the room and set his elbows on the back of the couch beside her head, then leaned forward until he could see her face. 'Bad day?'

'The worst. At five this morning Sarah started throwing up, joined by Nicky at six. The flu has made its dreaded presence known and felt. Dani seems to be fine, though.'

'How are they now?' With one hand he smoothed the damp curls back from her forehead.

'Much better. They no longer feel insecure about leaving the immediate vicinity of the bathroom.'

She managed to find the energy to smile at him again but the effort sapped her strength and her eyelids slowly drifted shut. She tried valiantly to arrest their downward motion so she could keep looking at his face but it proved impossible.

'I had a ten o'clock appointment with Mr Ellford so I spent the hour between eight and nine begging my friends to baby-sit sick kids. On the way back from the bank Matilda stalled in front of the entrance to the mall parkade and I had to sit there while I waited for the tow truck. I was not very popular.'

'You need a new car.'

His tone made her eyes blink open. 'Forget it, Ryan, you are not buying me a new car. It was a faulty generator that has since been replaced and none of your concern.'

'Sorry.' He grinned and shrugged. 'Habit.'

'Then break it,' she ordered.

'Yes, Ma'am.'

'That was only my morning. There's more but I'm not going to talk about it because merely thinking about today makes me as cranky as those monsters upstairs.'

He brushed one finger down her cheek as her eyelids drooped again, then pressed a kiss to her temple. 'I'll get Dani and go home. You're too exhausted for company tonight.'

'Okay.' A strange awareness that she didn't want him to leave settled at the back of her mind but she couldn't spare the strength to think.

'Go to bed early.'

She was dozing before he left the room, unaware when he left the house. Four hours later she kissed her kids good-night and dragged herself into her bedroom. She stripped off her clothes without turning on the light, hauled a nightshirt over her head, and fell across her bed.

'Ouch!' Something hard and pointed dug into her scalp. She jerked upright and snapped on the bedside lamp.

'What on earth . . .?' A small gift-wrapped box lay on her pillow. Slowly she placed it in her lap and lifted out the small silver card stuck into its blue and silver bow so she could study the strong irregular handwriting.

Dream of me as I dream of you. Yours, Ryan

'Yours, Ryan,' she repeated the last two words out loud. Ryan was hers. Now there was food for fantasy. Her hands tightened and the shiny wrapping paper crumpled under her fingers. Suddenly not as tired as she'd been a few minutes before, she tore away the packaging.

She stared for a few minutes at the shimmer of pink before she lifted it out of the box. Lace trimmed silk that felt like rose petals slid through her fingers and flowed across her lap to the floor.

Immediately she stooped and picked it up again, allowing her fingers to glide back and forth across the silk for a few minutes before she folded it back into the box and closed the lid on temptation. It was lovely but she would have to return it when he dropped off Dani in the morning. She wouldn't accept such an expensive, intimate gift from any man. Especially not from him when both her resolve and her body melted when he kissed her.

Becky put the box on the dresser so she wouldn't forget to take it downstairs in the morning. Before she got into bed she saw the small silver card on the floor where she'd dropped it. She picked it up and held it, staring at his writing. She knew she should put it in the garbage tomorrow with the ribbon and the wrapping, but she slipped the card into the bedside table's drawer before she went to bed.

'Why?' His breath misted in the cold morning air as Ryan looked at the paper bag she had thrust through the open car window. Dani had already run into the house.

Becky stepped away and put her hands behind her back. 'I can't accept a gift like this.'

'Why?'

She could feel unwanted emotions building inside her. Why wouldn't he take the darn thing and leave? 'It's too expensive, too personal, too . . .'

'Do you like it?'

'Of course. The nightgown is very beautiful but you shouldn't have bought it for me.'

'I can't return it.'

'I'm sorry. My mind is made up.'

'What should I do with it, give it to someone else?'

She could see his exasperation.

'Yes,' she said and her lips felt unnaturally stiff when she spoke. Pain shot through her at the thought of some other woman wearing her nightgown. It was worse when she thought of that faceless, formless woman modelling it for him but she pushed both the image and the regret away.

She waited while he sat there, the engine of the expensive car rumbling quietly as if it wanted to be on the road. She sucked in a mouthful of the exhaust flavored air, air so wet that even though it wasn't raining, she felt as though she'd swallowed water.

'I won't do that. See you tonight.'

'No!' She could see he was as startled as she was by the way the word burst out of her mouth. 'I've decided we shouldn't see each other so much. If you have Hallie call when you're leaving, I'll have Dani waiting at the door.'

'Why are you doing this, Becky? Are you so afraid to spend even those few minutes a day with me?'

'I think it would be best for you to honk and she'll come out.'

'Don't bother. You don't have to hide from me.' His hands tightened on the steering wheel. 'I'll have someone else pick her up. Six o'clock?'

She agreed and his eyes glittered but he didn't say another word. He put the bag on the seat beside him, slipped the car into gear, and backed down the driveway.

Becky sighed as she headed for the house. She must finally be getting through to him, she thought. He was finally realizing that a relationship between the two of them wouldn't work. But she couldn't quite stamp out the flutter of joy she'd experienced when he'd said he wouldn't give the pink silk gown to another woman. Then she remembered the look in his eyes and shivered a little.

She wished she could have kept and worn the nightgown.

She wished he'd smiled before he drove away.

'You haven't seen him in over a week? And yet you still insist that this temper tantrum has nothing to do with Ryan?' Jan asked.

Becky's spoon punished the sides of the aluminum bowl filled with cookie dough.

'Are you sure it's safe for me to be here?'

'Don't be an imbecile.' Becky's voice snapped with irritation. One vicious swirl of the spoon and the bowl slipped out of her hands, crashing to the floor. Two bounces later half the dough splattered across the tiles.

'Darn.' She picked up the bowl and pressed her fingers into the large dent caved into its metal side. 'Exactly what I needed on this really quite wonderful day.'

'Sarcasm, Becky?'

'Now I have to buy a new bowl. I promised Mike I would make him cookies if he would do errands for me. Here it is, almost six o'clock and the dough is ruined.'

'Be glad. If it had been made of glass instead of aluminum you would have splinters all over the floor as well as cookie dough. Get out your other mixing bowl and make some more.'

'I can't,' she muttered. 'I broke the glass one yesterday.' She glared when Jan clapped both hands over her mouth, her shoulders heaving in silent giggles until Becky's mouth curved reluctantly.

'Okay, woman.' Jan swung a kitchen chair around and straddled the seat, crossing her arms on the high back. 'Suppose you tell me what your problem is. I have never seen you so clumsy in your kitchen, or so irritable. Ellford on your case again?'

'Yeah but, boy, was that fun, waltzing in there and dropping a check for October and November on his desk. I even got a start on the repair bill for the furnace.' Becky started scraping dough off the floor.

'Having trouble with one of the kids?'

'Mike is hanging around with some people I don't like but I'm dealing with it.'

'Do I have to drag it out of you? What is the matter?' Jan's voice rose in pitch with each successive word.

'Fine! You win. It is Ryan.' She dropped the bowl and cookie batter into the garbage. 'I couldn't even concentrate on Wilbur's puzzle today and I have a deadline.'

'Wilbur?'

'Wilbur's Fantastic Chocolate Factory in North Vancouver wants a puzzle contest to introduce some new flavors. Do you have any idea how impossible it is to come up with a puzzle about candy without craving the stuff? I've gained four pounds and it's all his fault.'

'Wilbur's?' Jan asked. 'If it was going to be a problem, why did you agree to do it?'

'No, not Wilbur's. Ryan's!' She wet a rag and knelt on the floor to scrub up the sticky mess left by the smeared cookie dough.

'What does he have to do with your chocolate puzzle?'

'Because if he wasn't making me crazy I would have finished it in a couple of days but it's already taken more than a week. I've gained four darn pounds!'

'And that's Ryan's fault?'

'Yes.' She rinsed out the rag and hung it over the edge of the sink to dry.

'Oh. What's he done now?' Jan asked.

'It was bad enough when he dropped Dani off early, picked her up late and sent messages asking me to take her shopping for everything she needs,' she complained as she sat down again. 'A couple of times he asked if she could sleep here because he had to go out of town.'

'I know. You told me he pays you very well for those extras.' Jan ticked off Ryan's reported sins on her fingers. 'He sends you flowers every Monday – '

'Not this week,' Becky muttered.

'Be quiet. You'll make me lose track,' Jan ordered. 'He gave the kids a computer, put new tires on the old rattletrap, and has a bag of groceries delivered once a week. For Dani, he claims.'

'That's not what I meant.' Becky got up and started searching through the kitchen cupboards for a new bag of store-bought cookies. When she found one she dumped them in the cookie jar, then crumpled the bag into a ball and tossed it in the garbage with an impressive rim shot.

'Tell me, does she enjoy the fresh imported coffee beans processed in her own grinder?' Jan frowned. 'Do you think the kids notice the steak is filet rather than chuck?'

'I didn't ask for any of that stuff.'

'You're right. The man's certifiable. He's abusing you shamelessly. You'd better tell him the whole thing's off.'

Becky blushed but said nothing.

'What brought on this particular fit of anger?'

Becky sat down, then leaned forward across the table.

'Every day this week he sent Ms Hill to pick up Dani.' Becky grimaced when she remembered how the woman had sharply corrected her for referring to her as 'Miss' Hill.

'Oh.' Jan's pause was long and silent. 'The woman he used to be involved with. She's pretty.'

'Gorgeous. So what?'

'You seem to be taking this personally. You weren't this angry about the other things he's done.'

'It is obvious she doesn't like Dani any more than Dani likes her. It's equally obvious Ms Hill doesn't know how to deal with a child. He should pick up Dani himself.'

'Why?'

'Why? Because he should, that's why.'

'That's no answer. Why should he? Are you and Dani told if and when you should expect Ms Hill? Does she arrive on time?'

'Yes, but . . .'

'Does Ms Hill seem like a responsible adult?'

'Yes, but . . .'

'You wanted to see him more often?'

'No!' She noticed Jan's lifted eyebrow. 'I told him that we were seeing too much of each other.'

'Then what's your beef?'

'Dani misses him.'

'She does?' Jan looked surprised. 'I didn't think she was overly emotional about anything, much less him.'

'She doesn't show it much but I think in her own way she loves him and wants to be with him.'

'Seems to me you're mad because of who picks her up, not because it happened. Maybe you're afraid of what Ms Hill means to Ryan, personally.'

'No!' The indignant denial burst explosively out of Becky. 'I don't think of him that way at all.'

'Does he still ask you out all the time?'

Becky bent to pick up a toy car that lay on the floor. When she was sure she had her facial expression under control she straightened and spun its wheels along the table top. 'No.'

'Aha.'

'What do you mean "aha"?' Becky plunked the car down on the table with such force it bounced back to the floor and promptly rolled under the stove.

'Never mind. I'm thirsty.' Jan reached for the glass jug on the table and poured herself a glass of Koolaid fruit drink. She held it up to the light and admired the ruby colour. 'I still can't believe you talked me into drinking stuff made from a box of sweet powder, much less liking it. I even bought some last week. It's a great mixer with rum or gin. I've decided to serve it at my next party.'

'Jan!'

'I think you need to go out Friday night.'

'I told you. I am not going to date anyone.'

Jan raised her eyebrows at Becky's heated words. 'I meant with me.'

'Oh.' Her anger deflated fast. 'I have nothing to wear.'

'You should have time to sew a new dress.'

'I'll need a sitter.'

'Get one.' Jan waved her glass expansively. 'My treat.'

'Since when do you have a Friday night free? What happened to Simon, or Vince, or Peter, or whoever it is you're dating this week?'

'Richard.'

'Fine. What happened to Richard?'

'It wasn't working. We decided not to see each other again.'

'Jan!'

'Don't start, Becky,' she warned.

'Ralph – '

'I know Ralph is dead, okay? He was wonderful, but he's dead. Now tell me why you want me to settle for less in another man when, because of Ralph, I know how terrific a relationship can be?' She slammed the glass down on the table and the liquid geysered over its side.

'Look what you made me do.' Jan shook her hand and red drops glistened as they flew through the air. 'Hand me the damned rag.'

Becky tossed her the damp dish cloth.

'At least I'm willing to give men the benefit of the doubt. That's more than you can say.'

Becky didn't answer. She couldn't. On one level Jan was right. She wasn't willing to give another man the chance to break her heart.

'I'm sorry. I shouldn't have said that. Look, you're my best friend. I don't want to fight.' Jan dropped the cloth into the sink, then hugged Becky. 'But you started it.'

Becky tried to think of something she could say to refute her friend's accusation. It wasn't worth it. She returned the hug with interest, and a smile. 'Where should we go for this girls' night out?'

'People are always friendly at the Unicorn Pub.'

'You know, it might be fun!' Becky's smile grew and her eyes began to sparkle.

'You bet. Lots of Ds there.'

'Ds?'

'Dine and Dance with Dark and Debonair. I also think you should do something about mending fences with Ryan. What's that old saying? She bit off her nose to spite her face? You've let old fears take the nose from your face. Not very attractive. In the meantime, get to work on Wilbur's puzzle.'

'Wilbur?'

'How soon she forgets.' Jan shook her head sadly. 'Chocolate, my dear, chocolate.'

'Oh. Right. Go home, Jan.' She jumped up to hug her friend. 'And thanks.'

Becky hesitated outside the big glass doors, studying the gilt writing that spelled out McLeod Systems on its surface while she tried to decide whether she should go in or scurry on home. Jan's pointed comments last night had inspired this visit today.

Becky had planned to apologise to Ryan for over-reacting about the nightgown. She probably could have refused the gift without shooting the giver. But now she wasn't sure. Why hadn't she gone tamely home after her dentist appointment?

'Rebecca honey? Could you grab the door for me?'

'Sure.' She stepped aside to hold the door. Hallie's arms were stacked high with two briefcases and a potted plant, its delicate purple blossoms withered and brown around the edges.

'Thanks. Friday mornings are always so crazy – Oh my, oh my.' One briefcase started to slip and Becky released the door to grab it before the plant toppled to the floor. It wasn't until Hallie was thanking her profusely that she realized she was inside the office. The decision had been made for her.

'Thank goodness you were here. That poor plant is almost on its last legs and would've been a goner for sure if its dirt spilled out, not to mention the mess on the floor.'

Hallie tucked her scarf in the sleeve of her coat and hung it in the closet. She patted her hair, absently tidying stray curls back into place, and tugged at the material of the prim black and white dress.

'Somebody put this poor violet out with garbage, can you believe it? I saw it beside the canister when I parked my car, so I rescued it. The cruelty of some people.' She shook her head and picked up the plant, leaving the briefcases beside the reception desk. 'Thank you, my dear.'

'You're welcome.' Deciding she'd made a terrible mistake giving in to the urge to see Ryan even though she was downtown without the kids, Becky smiled and sidled back the way she'd come.

'Did you want to talk to Ryan?'

'Never mind, I've changed my mind. I've got to get home.' Her lips flexed in a poor semblance of a smile. 'I thought, since I was downtown I'd . . . No, never mind. He's probably busy and I'd be interrupting.'

'Nonsense. He'll be glad to see you. He's probably down the end of the hall in the lab, as always at this time in the morning. If not, try the boardroom around the corner to the left. You can find your way alone, can't you? I need to get this poor thing some water and TLC.'

'Uh, okay.' Becky stood there another minute, watching Hallie bustle off in the opposite direction, then started down the hall. Ever since she'd missed the kids' tour she'd been curious about Ryan's offices. Cautiously, she peeked in the other open doors as she passed.

The first room held metal shelves stacked to the ceiling with high tech gadgets and gizmos, most of them with purposes and uses totally unknown to her. Electric cords and power bars hung from the racks like garlands on the mantelpiece at Christmas. Men and women in white lab coats were stooped over crowded work surfaces.

The second room held a maze of desks, low dividers, and huge white boards covered in notations, flow charts, and mysterious symbols. Every desk held one or two computer monitors. She gawked for a full minute at the muted bustle of people and machinery before she recognized Carol Hill perched on the corner of one man's desk.

The other woman crossed her perfect legs at the poor guy's eye level and she leaned forward, her hands resting on the desk either side of her knees. The gaze of every man in the room was drawn to her when she laughed throatily and shook back her blonde hair. The women studiously ignored her.

While Becky watched, Carol leaned even further forward and her jacket gaped open, exposing more than the sheer camisole she wore. The poor man in the chair below her flushed an alarming shade of red and his eyes bulged.

Hope he doesn't have high blood pressure, Becky thought cynically. He might drop dead after that show.

Just then Carol slid off the desk, knocking his working papers to the floor. Amid gracious apologies, she immediately stooped between his knees to pick them up. The guy looked like he was going to choke on his own saliva as he stared down at her head bobbing between his thighs.

Becky couldn't bear to watch any more and hurried on down the hall, determined to get this ill-advised visit over with before Ms Hill decided she wanted to see Ryan. The door to the next room was closed but the glass wall's venetian blinds were open. Ryan had his back to her while he and two other men worked at a big table, consulting several massive tomes from the shelves that lined two of the walls.

Today he wore jeans. While she watched he unbuttoned the cuffs of his black shirt and rolled up the sleeves. She blinked when he leaned over the table to point out something in a book to one of the men.

Her heart began to beat faster. Sweat broke out on her palms. Just nervous, she told herself.

Nonsense, herself retorted. It's been a while but you know darn well what causes that sensation in your belly. It is not nervousness. This is something a lot more basic.

Some of her mother's favorite sayings ran through her head as she stared at him. To be wise you must be cautious. Discretion was the better part of valor. She who runs away lives to fight another day. Or if not fight, at least lives, she thought. Time to leave.

But she didn't move.

No. Hallie would tell him she'd been there and then he'd know she'd chickened out. And she'd know he knew. And he'd know she knew he knew.

Becky shook her head. Get a grip, woman. Let's be practical here.

She'd say hello, make some excuse or other, slip in an apology. Maybe then if things were going well, she'd invite him and Dani to drop by Sunday for lunch and an afternoon of videos. Then, whether he accepted the invitation or not, she could leave quickly, clucking silently all the way home.

One of the men noticed her standing outside the glass wall and he said something to Ryan who twisted to look back over his shoulder.

She lifted her hand in a weak wave.

Even knowing what was coming, she knew she wasn't well enough prepared. After all she hadn't seen him for a week. Yes, there it came.

His cheeks creased, his mouth tilted, the corners of his eyes wrinkled. Unattractive words for something so wonderful. But those were only physical aspects of his smile. The real impact was how it conveyed the sheer charm of his personality. He smiled at her like there was nothing else he wanted to do right at that moment.

As if seeing her filled him with joy and made his day.

Horse feathers and she knew it. But if it were true? She lowered her hand and pressed it to her chest. Would she ever get used to how she felt when she was the focus of his smiling attention?

He said something to the men and they chuckled as he strode quickly to the door.

'Becky!' He halted at her side.

'I was wondering if you had a few minutes. If you're too busy,' she nodded toward the men who were now watching them avidly through the window, 'I can talk to you later.'

'No. No. Now is great. Let's go to my office.' He took her arm to urge her back down the hall. After only a few steps he halted abruptly. 'No, that won't do. Someone else is using my office. How about . . . No, that won't work either.'

'You're busy. I understand.' She made a move to pull her arm free of his hand but he resisted. 'Perhaps you could spare a few minutes when you pick Dani up tonight?'

'I can pick up Dani?'

She could feel the blush forming on her cheeks. 'Yes. I wanted to say – '

'No. Wait.' He spun them both around and headed back toward the glass wall. He shoved open the door and said one word to the two men inside. 'Out.'

They looked at her curiously as they left and Becky knew her cheeks were fiery red.

'Ryan, you didn't have to do that. I only wanted to – '

'Just a sec.' He'd noticed a few staff members looking in as they wandered by. He swore just beneath his breath, went to the end of the window wall, and yanked a few times on a chain. The blinds jerked shut.

'Here, sit down.' He pulled two of the upholstered chairs out from the table and swung them around to face each other. He managed to get her into one and himself in the other before she could say another word.

Becky felt dizzy, as if she'd been swept up in a whirlwind and then set down gently but firmly.

'Becky? You wanted to talk?'

'Yes, I did. I wanted to discuss what happened – ' She stuttered into silence when he settled back in his chair, legs spread, elbows resting on the chair's arms, fingers linked on his lean stomach.

She glanced down. They were sitting so close to each other that her own knees were almost between his. Resisting the urge to move back, she closed her eyes briefly, then started over.

'The other morning I over-reacted about the . . . about your gift. I shouldn't have said what I did.'

'You'll let me give you the nightgown?' He leaned forward.

'No.' He was too close. At her refusal he leaned back and she breathed easier again. 'What I meant was that I could have returned your gift and explained it was too personal without ordering you to stay away from the house. I spoke without thinking and I am sorry.'

'So am I. I've missed you.' He leaned forward again.

'I was . . . that is, the kids and I were wondering if you and Dani would like to come for lunch and videos on Sunday.'

'I'd like that very much,' he said, taking her hands. 'I've never been good at what you call emotional communication but, thanks to Dani and to you, I'm learning.' He tugged, pulling her closer until their faces were only inches apart.

'Being with you is very important to me, Becky. If nothing else, this last week has taught me that. Would you be willing to give this thing between us, these feelings, a chance? See where it leads?'

She was glad he hadn't asked her if she missed him. She couldn't answer that question honestly in her own head, much less say it aloud to him.

'We can be friends.' She hoped the eagerness in her voice wasn't as clear to him as it was to her.

'Just friends? Not good enough,' he said and released her fingers to slide his hands up to her shoulders. 'How 'bout kissing friends?'

The last coherent thought she had as his lips touched hers was to be glad he'd shut the blinds.

Fire licked at her skin, scorching away inhibitions. Cool air caressed her back as he tugged her shirttails free of her jeans and slipped his hand up her spine. This hunger was madness, a wonderful insanity. Her fingertips clutched greedily at his bare shoulders where she'd shoved his shirt aside.

The intercom buzzed and they both went still as Hallie dryly informed them that Ryan's expected guests had arrived. Becky struggled free of his arms, not sure of her feelings except for horror and maybe terror at what they'd almost done in his boardroom.

'What time?'

She paused. Ryan leaned nonchalantly against the table, one side of his mouth tilted in a faint smile, making no effort to tidy his clothing as he watched her frantically trying to tuck her shirt back in her jeans.

'Do up your shirt, for heaven's sake,' she snapped at him.

'I wish I could.' He grabbed the tails of his shirt and held it away from his body. That's when she saw the two gaping holes where there used to be buttons.

She felt her mouth drop open. 'I did that? I couldn't have done that.' She stopped fumbling with her own shirt and stared at him. 'What are you going to do? Those people are waiting.'

He chuckled. 'Don't worry about it. I keep extra shirts in my office. What time?'

'Time?' She tugged at the button on her jeans, trying to loosen them enough to slide the shirt hem back where it belonged.

'Sunday. Lunch and movies?' He straightened and took two lazy steps forward. He moved her hands away from the twisted cotton.

'Oh.' She trembled as he opened her jeans and smoothed the cotton fabric of her shirt down her sides, over her hips. She stopped breathing as he slowly, notch by notch, raised the zipper. Her heart cartwheeled as he closed the brass button.

'Becky?' His hands lingered on her hips. 'What time?'

'Noon.' Her voice squeaked as she stepped back. 'Noon will be fine.'

Without looking him in the eye, she grabbed up her purse and walked quickly away.

'Becky?'

Halfway down the hall to freedom, she glanced back. He was standing in boardroom doorway, a hand propped on either jamb, his chest bared by the torn shirt.

Carol and several of his staff were peering from office doors along the hall.

'We'll be there,' he called after her. 'I'll bring the pop.'

She ducked her head and fled. She could hear the whispers of his staff as she picked up speed, passing Hallie with an embarrassed nod.

'Becky?' Hallie asked. 'Is something wrong?'

She shook her head. Embarrassed to the bone and unwilling to linger a moment longer, Becky jabbed frantically at the elevator call button and squeezed into the crowded elevator when it finally arrived. Once downstairs she didn't stop running until she was safely inside her Matilda.

Her hand shook so much she dropped the keys when she tried to locate the ignition. She sagged back, closed her eyes, and tried to convince herself that what had just happened, didn't really happen.

It didn't work. She could still smell his cologne on her hands and face.

She'd never been any good at lying to herself. She'd ripped off the man's shirt in his office, and might have done worse if Hallie hadn't interrupted them, with his staff in the next room. They'd tell Hallie about the torn shirt and within seconds she'd be on the phone to Jan.

Jan would never let it die. She'd still be tormenting Becky about this when they were eighty-two. Becky groaned. It was twenty minutes before the trembling of her hands eased enough so she could drive home.

CHAPTER 9

A bird crashing into the mirrored window broke Ryan's concentration. He glanced at his watch. Ten past four on Friday. He took one look at the untouched papers still piled on the 'in' tray and groaned. Hours more work. He'd better call Becky and warn her he'd be late again.

Thoughts of Becky and how she'd actually dropped in to see him that morning immediately lightened his fatigue. He wished she could have stayed longer although, remembering the heat they'd generated in the boardroom, perhaps it was for the best. He was smart enough to know that he had to slow things down a little. Her invitation to lunch on Sunday hadn't exactly been the same as an offer to model the pink nightgown for him, but hey, a guy had to get encouragement where he could.

He felt wonderful after the banishment he'd barely survived this last week. He'd been thinking about his father a lot lately, wondering why the old man had stayed married to his mother all these years, how he'd survived a life of virtual exile. He could still remember his father muttering a string of 'bloody hells' when he was ordered to the spare room to sleep.

No matter how angry she was, Becky could never be insulting like his mother.

Becky. Rebecca. He said her name aloud, rolling the sound on his tongue much like a connoisseur would sample the flavor and bouquet of a superior wine.

He should have offered to pick up a late dinner for two on his way to her house tonight and they could share a meal without four extra sets of ears listening to every word. Much as he was learning to like and enjoy the company of Dani and Becky's three children, it would be bliss to spend a few hours alone, talking with Becky.

It would be nearly impossible for anyone to resist the happiness, warmth and acceptance that filled that old house and during Becky's recent cold spell he'd missed their time together, with or without the four children. Asking Carol to drive Dani to and from Becky's house had been tough on him. Thank the Lord his plan to back off and wait for the thaw had proven successful.

His eyebrows lowered in a frown. Carol hadn't been drawn to the residents or the environs of Lilac House. She'd complained about the mess and the mayhem and was glad to get off delivery duty. He wouldn't ask for her help again. Plus both Dani and Carol had expressed, subtly, that they would prefer their meetings to be as seldom as possible.

He grinned slyly as he wondered what Becky had thought when Carol picked up Dani. If she was jealous. He frowned again. Or if she cared.

She was so good at keeping him at a distance he couldn't be sure if she had even noticed his efforts to get her attention. Lately he had felt like an awkward adolescent again, performing crazy stunts to get the girl in his eighth grade history class to notice he was alive. Although she'd sure noticed him in the boardroom.

He laughed at himself as he dialed Becky's number. Slow and easy, McLeod. Then you can get her attention, full-grown man to full-grown woman. And once you have her undivided attention . . . Tonight they'd have a little wine, some tasty tidbits from the deli. Maybe they'd light a fire. In his imagination he could see flames reflecting off sleek skin where her breasts were bared to his lips . . . Heat curled low in his abdomen while he listened to her phone ring.

'Hello.'

'Hi. It's me,' Ryan said, his voice hoarse because he'd slipped into the passionate daydream and the brutal jerk back to reality had been too swift. 'I'm sorry but I've a got a ton of work. I'm going to be late again. Why don't you put the little monsters to bed and light the fire. I'll stop by the deli and pick up some . . .'

'No. You have to pick up Dani on time tonight.'

Stopped cold by the finality of what she'd said, Ryan's mind was a blank, shocked from his heated imaginings back to an even crueller reality than he'd been expecting.

'Why?' he asked baldly.

'I have a date,' she said.

And then she giggled.

She giggled, dammit.

'A date,' he repeated.

'. . . to dinner at the Unicorn.' The first part of her sentence was drowned out when Mike began shouting at Nicky.

Dinner? Wasn't there dancing at that restaurant? His Becky was going to spend hours in the arms of another man?

'Don't be late, okay?' And then she giggled again.

'I'll be there,' he snarled, enraged as much by her chuckle of anticipation as the incendiary words that preceded it, and slammed down the receiver.

The plastic telephone fell off the desk, broke on impact and small metal parts pinged as they ricocheted off the furniture. The trailing cord whipped against the crystal box and knocked it off his desk to the floor where it shattered, cascading sparkling shards of glass across the room.

He stared at the pieces of crystal scattered around him like useless, frozen tears, expecting a deluge of emotion now his mother's gift was gone forever. He was surprised to feel nothing except maybe peace. His symbol, his cross, was gone. The turmoil stirred up by this threat to his relationship with Becky put the old pain where it belonged. In the past.

He swore and snatched up a pen. He scribbled a note to Hallie asking her to order him a new phone but leave the broken glass for the janitorial service. He picked up his jacket and stormed out of the office.

His fury was at flash point, out of control, but he didn't even try to rein it in. He had invested a lot of time and emotion in Becky and he would be damned before he let another man get close to her.

The wheels of the Mercedes squealed as he took the corner out of the parkade too fast for safety. He fought the steering wheel for control as he raced along rain-slick roads to her home.

Becky belonged to him. And tonight he would make sure both she and this guy knew it.

He spent the forty minute trip tormenting himself with visions of Becky being touched by another man, trying to deal with the blinding betrayal he felt.

At her house he slammed on the brakes and forced the car to a sharp stop only inches from the bumper of the brand new yellow Corvette that blocked the driveway. His upper lip curled back in a sneer. He might've known. Most men on the prowl drove expensive sports cars. This guy sure had the wrong woman if he thought a fancy car would impress Becky.

He took the porch steps in one leap and yanked open the door without ringing the bell. The sight that met his eyes made him feel like the day he'd been alone in an elevator that suddenly dropped a few floors; his heart hit his throat and his stomach twisted in knots.

She stood in the front hall, talking on the telephone. Her curls were swept up and held back on the left side of her face with a sparkly star. Earrings glinted as she moved. Her dress had the dull sheen of antique gold. Long tight-fitting sleeves. Ivory lace ruffled around her small hands and edged the low neckline of the draped bodice that outlined the curve of her breasts. Her full skirt flirted around her knees when she turned to face him.

Becky wasn't merely pretty, she was ravishing. He held one hand to his chest, silently urging his heart to start beating again.

He hadn't planned what he wanted to say when he arrived. What came out of his mouth would not have been his first choice.

'Bloody hell.'

Obviously his father had been on his mind a lot lately. Why else would his subconscious have blurted out the old man's favorite cuss words?

'Don't worry about it, Ann.' Becky glanced at the man standing inside her front door before her attention was drawn back to the phone. 'Take care. I hope you feel better soon.' She dropped the receiver into its cradle before she turned around to face Ryan.

'Where is he?' His voice was gritty and strained. 'Who is he?'

She didn't hear his actual words at first, so stunned was she by what she saw. Gone was the smiling, suave, almost obnoxiously self-confident man of the world. In his place stood an unshaven, dishevelled, and very angry male. If he'd been a lion his tail would be twitching and his ruff would be standing on end, was her first thought.

He could be dangerous, was her second.

'What?'

'Where is he?' Ryan stalked forward and grabbed her arm above the elbow.

'Who?' She tried to resist as he hustled her into the dining room. The glass panes in the French doors rattled when he kicked them shut.

'Let me go. What do you think you're doing?'

Ryan barely heard her question. Now he held her in his hands the sweet scent of her perfume and the texture of her flesh combined to blur his mind. His grip shifted to her shoulders and tightened. Slowly Ryan drew her nearer until their bodies were pressed together, from shoulder to thigh.

Becky put her hands on his chest and pushed but he was relentless. As his greater strength brought her closer, her hands slid to his shoulders, where they tightened in the damp wool of his jacket. A fleeting image of what another angry man had done years ago briefly reared its ugly head but she took one look into the past and put the memory away for ever.

Ryan was not Eric and he never would be. Slowly her arms weakened until they rested on his chest as she fought her own need for this man.

Ryan wrapped both arms around her body and rested his chin in her soft hair. She felt marvelous in his arms but soon simply holding her was not enough. He lowered one hand to cup her bottom, braced his legs, and lifted her to fit snugly into the cradle of his thighs.

Becky quivered and Ryan's body shuddered as his erection nestled against her softness. Her head fell against his wide shoulder and Ryan buried his mouth in the scented hollow below the delicate line of her jaw.

She shivered as he breathed her name against her skin. He said something unintelligible and barely audible as he slowly ground his hips against her pelvis. Sensations long forgotten swamped her as his kisses climbed her neck and found her mouth.

And she forgot, simply forgot, everything. The past, the kids, Jan. Everything was as mist before the heat and passion this man aroused in her.

Ryan's lips alternately caressed and nipped. His tongue traced the closed line of her teeth, urging, compelling, until she opened up slightly on an urgent moan. Needing no further invitation, his tongue plunged forward, withdrawing to delve deeper again.

He kissed her as he'd burned to do since . . . since forever. He slid his hand to her breast and lightly rubbed his palm in small circles, arousing the nipple buried beneath layers of fabric. Then he felt her come alive in his arms, responding to his touch as no one ever had before.

A small part of him, the part that in the past had never really believed in any woman, stood back and watched the madness take over, the need to touch her bare skin, the desperation to have this woman. The passion grew and grew until the cynic wavered and was lost, overwhelmed as never before.

But before Ryan lost total control a child's voice rose loud and clear, laughing in the distance, forcing him to remember where they were. He tore his mouth from hers with a ragged groan, pressed her cheek to his chest, and rested his jaw on her forehead. Gently he tugged the fabric back up to cover the breast he'd bared. Slowly his mind regained some good sense. Oh, God, what had he almost done?

Still holding her in his arms, he stepped forward until he reached the table, where he lowered her to sit on its edge.

Becky listened to the heart thundering under her ear and knew it beat no faster than her own. Slowly his arms loosened and he brought his hands up to cup her face. He tilted her head until he could see her face, his gaze wandering hungrily from her swollen lips to her flushed cheeks.

He pressed a kiss between her passion-glazed eyes. Gentle, but hot as a brand. So sizzling that afterward she felt her forehead for the mark.

'So sweet, so sweet.' Passion and determination darkened his silvery eyes to slate and he growled at her. 'You are mine. Mine. You hear me?'

Becky paled then flushed with anger as his words sank through the erotic haze left by his caresses. She shoved violently at his chest. He staggered back a couple of steps until he regained his balance. She slid off the table, rested her hands on her hips, and scowled fiercely.

'I do not belong to you or anyone else. Who do you think you are?'

Ryan moved forward and reached for her again but her slitted glare dared him to touch her. His arms dropped to dangle loosely at his sides until his own anger rose again and he shoved his hands into his pockets. He felt as helpless as his father ever had when dealing with Ryan's mother.

'More to the point, who is he?' he snarled.

The picture of an angry lion rose in her mind again and she bit off an unexpected chuckle. 'Careful, your tail is twitching.'

'What's that supposed to mean?'

'Never mind. Who is who? I mean, who are you yelling at me about?' Never one to hold on to anger, Becky's calm was returning. She felt amused by his crazy questions and irrational behaviour, even as she set aside her physical response to examine later when she was alone.

Ryan gritted his teeth, trying to control the rage that filled his head with a red haze. Was she trying to pretend he hadn't courted her? Were all his plans and hopes so much data lost on a crashed hard drive? Even worse, what kind of macho idiot had she got herself involved with?

He ignored the fact he knew very well who was acting like a macho idiot right now. He swallowed hard and tried again, asking the question with a stilted voice and careful but unnatural enunciation.

'Who is the guy you are going out with? Where the hell is he?'

Her eyes lit with amusement and her lips turned up at the corners. The red haze in his brain thickened. Would she dare laugh at him? Before he could stop himself the thought popped out of his mouth.

'Are . . . you . . . laughing . . . at . . . me?' He spaced the words out like bullets from a machine gun. A fast, rising crescendo.

'No. Well, yes, but not at you.' Becky saw something through the glass doors behind him and changed another laugh to a cough. 'Do you want to meet my date?'

'Just long enough to kick him out of your house and tell him not to come back. Where is he?'

'Right behind you.'

Ryan spun on his heel, his stance aggressive, and yanked open the French doors. Coming down the stairs was a gorgeous redheaded . . . woman.

He stood speechless, his hand still clenched on the door. Becky's giggles broke over the back of his head. He flushed a deep brick-red and hunched his shoulders inside his jacket. He said only two words.

'Bloody hell!'

'He's a hunk, isn't he?'

'Who?' Becky avoided Jan's eyes. It was past one in the morning and they were heading back to Lilac House in the yellow Corvette.

'The guy you've been thinking about all evening. Ryan McLeod.'

'I haven't – '

'Don't try to lie, it won't work. Ryan's a real winner in the personality stakes, too. How many men would stick around after they'd embarrassed themselves so thoroughly? He apologized very nicely, once you stopped giggling. And when he found out we were going to miss our night out because your baby-sitter was sick he even offered to stay so we could go.'

'Yes, it was very nice of him to offer.'

'Nice! Nice? Don't you mean terrific? A wealthy bachelor offering, of his own free will, to baby-sit four kids must come close to amazing. And if the mother of three of the kids in question has consistently refused any and all offers of . . . of companionship from that self-same bachelor, it's positively amazing.'

'Jan – '

'Maybe it even warrants sainthood.'

'I will not listen to any more nagging from you. Yes, Ryan was wonderful to baby-sit tonight. And yes, he is very good looking. Now drop it.'

The two women finished the ride to Becky's house in silence, the passenger indignant, the driver amused. In her driveway Becky paused with one foot in and one foot out of the car.

'Do you want to come in for some coffee?'

'No. I'm not cut out for the role of chaperone.'

'That's painfully obvious.' Becky slammed the door and stomped up the driveway, past Ryan's car. Jan's voice floated after Becky before she gunned the engine and drove away.

'Ask yourself why you didn't dance with any of the men who offered tonight. Ask yourself who was on your mind all evening. Then answer with the truth.'

Jan's comments rang in Becky's ears as she waved good-bye. The truth. What was the truth?

She loitered along the sidewalk and up the steps where she paused with one hand on the cold door knob. Her mom had always said only a fool tried to fool herself. And the truth was she had spent most of the evening thinking about Ryan. He was handsome, he spent most of his time chasing a dollar, he reminded her of Eric. So why did she like Ryan?

Shivers traveled up her spine as she recalled her body's response to his touch, to his kisses. If she was being honest she had to acknowledge that when she first met Ryan he had reminded her of Eric. But lately the only man she thought of was Ryan himself.

Telling Ryan about Eric, and Ryan's comforting and protective response, had acted as a catharsis. Now she saw the two men as entirely different people.

Eric had always either rejected or yelled at his children. Becky had never been sure when, or if, Eric would show up. He had treated their home like a hotel, the kids like barely tolerated pests, and herself as a convenience or worse. Since the divorce his attitude had not improved.

Ryan always had a kind word or helping hand for Dani and the others. He let Becky know when he was going to pick Dani up late and he was appreciative, always thanking Becky for the extras she provided.

He let her know that to him she was special. The way his eyes were filled with wanting when she turned unexpectedly and caught him staring. A caress on her cheek as they passed. His erratic breathing if their bodies brushed. The occasional kiss that drifted lightly across her lips.

And then there were the presents. Ranging from the prosaic to the outrageous. From new tires, which Jan knew about, to the slinky pink nightgown, which she didn't. Becky felt a pang of regret for refusing the filmy swathe of silk and lace but she squashed it firmly.

All his gifts had been the result of his concern for Becky's comfort or safety, regardless of the little fictions he invented so she wouldn't be able to refuse them. Except the nightgown. That little item had nothing to do with comfort or safety.

She felt her cheeks heat and a smile curved her lips until a chill breeze eddied around her knees and lifted her skirt. Goosebumps sprang to life on her arms and she realized she was standing outside her own house daydreaming about Ryan. She quietly opened her front door.

The house was dark except for a light at the top of the stairs, one lamp on the entry table and another that shone palely in the living room. All was quiet, which she hoped was a sign the children were asleep and the evening had gone well for her rookie babysitter.

As she stepped forward her high heels clicked loudly on the hardwood floor so she slipped them off and dangled them from her fingers.

Moving quietly, she walked into the living room. As soon as she saw Ryan her fingers fisted around the shoes with the force of restraint necessary to keep from touching him. Stretched out full length on the couch, her baby-sitter slept soundly. At some point he had removed his jacket and kicked off his shoes.

The lamp on the table behind him turned his tousled hair into a cap of gleaming gold. His tie trailed from one hand, the top buttons of his silk shirt were undone, the cuffs loosened. His features, fully relaxed in sleep, were boyish, even vulnerable.

Becky chuckled quietly. He must have drifted off even as he was trying to get comfortable. An uncontrollable urge drew her closer until she was standing in the space between his body and his out-stretched arm.

Those glinting eyes were closed and she felt a deliciously naughty sense of power. She could look her fill and he would never know. Becky let her gaze drift slowly down his unconscious form. His head lay in profile, the clear-cut lines of cheek, jaw and nose sharp in the weak light. The late night stubble of his beard glinted red. One arm was draped across his flat stomach, his thumb hooked beneath the belt buckle, the long fingers draped across his . . .

She jerked back and her glance darted nervously to his face. His eyes were still closed. She squeezed her own eyelids shut in gratitude he would never know how lustfully she had ogled his body. When she opened them again she saw past his beauty to the dark circles and the grey hue in his skin. He was exhausted.

The hand she'd put out to shake him awake dropped to her side. He needed sleep, not a long drive home after midnight and another back here in the morning to pick up Dani.

Becky dropped her high heels beside his shoes and tiptoed out to get the quilt she kept in the front closet because the old house was always so chilly at night. She'd needed the warmth of her grandmother's quilt on the many long, lonely nights when she stayed up to watch old movies on the late show.

Back at the couch Becky slipped his tie from between his fingers. Then she placed his dangling hand on his chest, covered him up, and tucked the quilt around his shoulders. Unable to resist, she pressed a kiss to his lips and brushed an errant lock of hair off his forehead. Frightened by her impulse to crawl onto the couch with him, she leaped to her feet and hurried upstairs. With luck and co-operation from the children he would be able to sleep late in the morning.

Safe in her own room she took off her clothes and reached down into the bottom of her drawer for a warm nightgown. Reached for flannel but touched silk. She hesitated then pulled it out. Pink silk spilled from her fingers.

How did this get into her drawer, she wondered, until she remembered the angry glint in his eyes when she'd made Ryan take it away. Stubborn man. He must have hidden it in her drawer tonight. Becky rubbed it along her cheek, relishing the sensation of luxury after wearing flannel and cotton for so many years. She was tired of always staring in the windows of lingerie boutiques, envying those wealthy enough to wear silk and lace and satin next to their skin.

Why not wear it? Ryan would never know whether or not she'd found it, whether or not she wore it. She slipped it on over her naked body and whirled to admire her reflection in the long mirror behind the bedroom door. The straps were so narrow they were almost invisible against her skin. Wide lace trimmed both bodice and hem and the slit that climbed to her thigh.

The gown was so special. More exquisite and expensive than anything she had ever owned in her life, it made her feel attractive. Sexy. She spun on her toes. The gored skirt twisted around her knees then drifted down to her ankles again when she stopped. She swayed then whirled in circles again, then danced a few steps of sheer happiness.

She stopped and gaped in the mirror at eyes wide with surprise, her fist pressed to her heart. Happy? Sexy? The eyes didn't blink and the wide grin melted away. Was she happy? Could she really feel sexy again?

Yes, she decided, a new grin slowly tipping up the corners of her mouth. Yes, she could and it was because of the man asleep downstairs. In a hundred ways he let her know he found her desirable. And right now she was happy.

Becky stifled the laugh she felt bubbling up inside and sashayed around the room, out-vamping the vampiest starlet in any of the late night movies. Tonight she felt truly glamorous, for once in her life.

She clicked off the overhead light, threw back the covers, and flopped down on the mattress in an extravagant pose. Feeling ridiculous, but enjoying it, she giggled and rolled over on her stomach. Tentatively her fingers reached out and slid across the cool cotton surface of the empty pillow beside her.

If only . . .

Becky fell asleep to dream of sharing love and loving with the man downstairs.

Ryan shivered and, half asleep, tugged at the blankets, trying to cover his shoulder but succeeding only in baring his feet. What's the matter with this thing, he wondered irritably, groggy with sleep. And why is it so cold in here?

He turned over, trying to get comfortable, but his knee bashed into something sharp. What the heck? He fumbled his hand free of the blanket and reached out. A table?

Then he remembered. Baby-sitting. Becky's house. He must've fallen asleep. He opened his eyes and stared around. The room was dark. Hadn't he left on a light? Groping over his head he found the lamp and turned it on. His hand dropped back onto his chest and touched something cushiony. He plucked it up and craned his neck. A quilt?

He propped himself on his elbows. Somebody had covered him with a quilt. When? Who? And then he spotted the high heels sprawled on top of his own shoes. A grin spread across his face and he lay down with arms crossed behind his head. Becky had tucked him in. A laugh rose in his throat but he smothered it.

He wondered what she was going to say in the morning. Especially when Mike began asking questions about why Ryan had slept in their house. Thinking of the morning made him practical. Unless he took them off now, tomorrow he was going to have to wear the clothes he'd slept in.

Tossing back the quilt he stood up to unbutton his shirt then hung it on the back of a chair and put his watch down on the coffee table. After he pulled the belt through the loops he shoved his hand in his trouser pockets to pull out his loose change.

Ouch! He'd stabbed his finger on something sharp. What on earth? Oh, yeah, Sarah's tooth. He reached in again, more carefully this time, and pulled it out. He tossed it in the air and caught it again. The production that child had made over a loose tooth!

She had wiggled it all evening. Then the others had discussed their pet methods for tooth removal and compared toothfairy rates. Only his promise to make sure her mother would be told had convinced Sarah to get into her bed and go to sleep. His solemn, cross his heart, hope to die promise.

But he had been asleep when Becky came home. He sat down and eyed the small jagged tooth in the middle of his large palm. He picked up his watch and confirmed it was late, almost three in the morning. He stared at the tooth again.

Silently he addressed the tooth.

Do you justify sneaking up to Becky's room? Waking her up in the middle of the night? No? What about my promise to Sarah? I crossed my heart, you know. What terrible things might happen to someone who broke a cross-your-heart promise?

He grinned at his behavior. What was he coming to? Talking to a tooth! Then he thought about Becky upstairs in her bed. Sound asleep. He could wake her up, give her the tooth and come back down. Maybe, if he was real lucky and she was real sleepy, he could sneak a quick kiss.

But then he'd come right back downstairs.

Deliberately he put the tooth back in his pocket and stood up. Very, very quietly he climbed the stairs and pushed open her door.

Moonlight lay like a silver bar across the foot of her bed but Becky herself lay in deep shadow.

'Becky?' he whispered. 'Becky?'

She didn't stir. He crossed the floor to the side of the big bed. He scarcely touched her arm and she stirred restlessly.

'Becky? Wake up, honey.'

His palm cupped her bare shoulder. Was she naked? All the times he'd thought about what she slept in, he'd never considered she might sleep nude. The night-shirt she'd loaned him that first day still resided in his bedside table. The Becky he thought he knew would always sleep in pyjamas or a night-gown of some kind in case her children woke in the night.

As he moved his hand in a gentle caress his heart started to thump loudly in his ears. His fingers trembled when he felt the thin strap of her night-gown where it had drooped off her shoulder. One finger followed the slender ridge of fabric across her shoulder blade but stopped short when it disappeared under the sheet.

Was she wearing it? He bit back a groan and sat down beside Becky. His weight on the edge of the mattress rolled her unconscious body toward him; the sheet slid down her back until it lay at her waist.

'Honey, please wake up now. For my sanity's sake,' he pleaded. 'Sarah's tooth came out while you were gone.'

She uttered little meaningless, sleepy sounds and turned over. As his eyes became accustomed to the darkness, he saw her eyelids flicker and slowly begin to lift.

'Hi.' An enchanting smile curved her lips and her voice was like velvet, both soft and rough.

He opened his mouth to speak but Becky's eyes drifted shut again and she snuggled her body into a curve around his hip. He wiped at the sweat beading his upper lip. He felt like he was a nuclear reactor going into melt down. When she said something so quietly he couldn't make out the words he bent his head lower.

'What did you say?'

'Come back to bed, Ryan.' Heavy with sleep, her voice spiraled around his senses and enticed him closer. With every bit of control he possessed, he held onto his good intentions. But . . .

Come back to bed? Had she been dreaming of him?

His leg shook when her hand touched his knee. Eyes still closed, her fingers caressed his leg, then curled into his groin. Touched so intimately his body surged to life. With everything he possessed Ryan fought the urge to take her in his arms.

Tortured by her nearness he lifted her hand away and leaned over to switch on the bedside lamp. The moonlight tore at his self-control. He thought brighter lighting would dissipate the atmosphere of intimacy and romance.

He was mistaken.

Brown curls tumbled on her pillow; pink lace played peek-a-boo with creamy skin. The cotton sheet lay across her waist below the fullness of her breasts straining the fabric of the gown. White sheets. Pink silk and white cotton.

His fantasy had come to life.

He hung his head and pinched his eyelids shut. Harsh breaths shuddered through lungs abruptly starved of oxygen.

'Sweetheart,' Ryan said, his voice rough with longing. 'Wake up. Please?'

Becky was so sleepy and her eyelids so heavy she had trouble opening her eyes but she managed. What a strange look on Ryan's face. Was he in pain? Her mind still foggy with sleep, her gaze dropped to his chest. The weak light glinted on the tight blond curls.

She had been dreaming that he belonged in her bed and they'd made magnificent love. Was this reality or still dreams that he should be here now? Asleep, she had been free to touch and be touched as never before. If she touched him now would he prove to be an illusion?

Her fingertips glided across his skin, fanning out in the thicket of hair that matted his chest.

Ryan's muscles clenched, his nipples beading at her exploring touch. The pain, the agony of wanting her was intense.

'Becky love, you have to stop.'

His voice grated loudly in the quiet room, waking Becky to reality. So this was no mirage from her sleep, with husky whispers and promises, but the real man.

Her first instinct to pull away was halted by the suffering he exuded. And the passion. Staring directly into those silver-blue eyes reminded her of how special Ryan was. He tried to be there when she needed him. He'd been kind to her children and tender the night she cried in his arms. He wanted her.

Tonight she could accept that woven through the fabric of emotions she felt for this man ran a sparkling, rainbow-hued, fragile thread of . . . something. Not love, never love, but she cared for him and about him and he had shown in so many ways he cared for her.

She wanted him.

CHAPTER 10

Fire hurtled through her veins and she reveled in the sensation. She was free! No longer would she allow passion to be a prisoner to the past. She lifted her hand from his chest to his cheek, then curved it around his neck, threading her fingers through his golden hair.

'Honey, please. I can't take much more.'

'You don't have to,' she whispered and pulled his lips down to meet hers.

'Becky?' He whispered her name against her lips, first with shock then twice more. With doubt, then desire.

'Becky, Becky!' His arms circled her, lifting her close. And then his mouth was on hers, intense and hungry. She tasted sweet, so sweet.

Her mouth opened, welcoming and encouraging. Eager, taking from him, the years of abstinence and manacles of fear washed away as if they had never been.

Pressed firmly to his hair-roughened skin, separated from his naked chest only by silk, her nipples were almost unbearably sensitized. She gasped when Ryan reached to cup the weight of her breast in his hand, his thumb brushing across its crest.

Impatient with the gown's slight barrier, Ryan leaned away and slipped first one then the other strap off her shoulders. The lace bodice dipped and caught on swollen nipples. He slowly lowered her to the pillow, his mouth nuzzling her flesh until the fabric fell and her breasts, full and firm, were bared to the cool night air.

His hair brushed her collarbone as his tongue drew one straining nipple into his mouth. Pure sensation rushed through his body when her back arched off the bed in response. Urgent hands ran up and down his spine, finally tightening in the thick strands of hair at his nape, holding him to her.

Ryan reclaimed her mouth with his, continuing to roll her nipples between finger and thumb, thoroughly enjoying her uninhibited response. Pushing the sheet to the bottom of the bed he lay down beside her.

'Becky,' he said, his voice whisky smooth. 'Becky, open your eyes.' She focused with difficulty on his face.

'Keep them open, honey. I need to see your response to my touch. I need the passion in your eyes. Do you want me?'

'Yes, oh, yes!'

One hand left her breast and traveled down across the velvet smoothness of her belly. His fingers trembled as he hesitated briefly at the silken barrier formed by the nightgown bunched at her waist, then with one smooth motion his hand vanished, seeking the nest of curls beneath.

He shuddered again as he reached heat and wetness. Oh, God, she was ready for him.

A whimpering cry was torn from deep within her as his finger slipped inside her. Stroking, withdrawing, plunging ever deeper. Heat raged and her hips arched into his hand.

His name burst from her lips, a cry for fulfilment. Her hands fumbled frantically with the clasp of his trousers, clumsy in her haste to touch him.

'Easy, sweetheart.' He soothed her with small kisses trailed across her lips, down her neck to the tip of her breast.

Quickly he stood and stripped off his pants and briefs. A sharp tug had the gown down over her hips and tossed on the floor beside his clothing.

Stretched out beside her again, Ryan pulled her into his arms. Intensely aware of him, rigid and pulsating against her flesh, Becky slid her hand down to his waist, hesitated, then retreated to the neutral ground of his shoulders.

'Touch me, Becky,' he urged hoarsely.

Once more her fingers dipped until she cradled him in both hands. Then on a full-throated groan his tongue invaded the moist heat of her mouth and he moved himself in her palms. A shudder rippled down his body as he thrust once, twice.

Ryan knew he was losing it and forced himself to be still. But Becky wanted him as out of control as she was herself. She moved her hands, fingers caressing, arousing, pushing him to the brink.

'Too fast,' he whispered as he jerked away from her, trying to slow his breathing, to regain some control over his own body. 'Oh, God, what your touch does to me.'

He slid one muscular leg between hers and moved deliberately against her, his hair-roughened thigh rubbing erotically against her moist curls. As she matched his motion he froze.

'Becky, you're not on the pill, are you?'

Immediately her encircling arms fell away and tears of frustration and fear wet her cheeks. 'No, no. We've got to stop.' Frantic hands shoved at his shoulders. 'I might get pregnant.'

'Wait, honey.' He groped for his trousers and pulled a small packet from his pocket.

Through her tears a grin appeared. 'Sure of yourself, were you?'

'Nope,' he responded sheepishly, 'hopeful.'

With a small kiss on her lips he moved over her, supporting himself on elbows and knees, rubbing himself against her without entering. Waiting until he felt the warm, moist heart of her opening to him. Rebuilding the heat, the need for oneness that churned in both of them.

Then he was inside her, driving deep, restraint lost. Her legs came up around his waist, thighs gripping, urging him harder, deeper. The burning needs they had held back boiled through them, searing their flesh, erasing all thought. Ryan slid one arm beneath her, arching her back as he leaned down to suckle first one nipple, then the other. Pulling strongly, matching the rhythm of their bodies.

She arched, her mouth open, and cried out. The moonlight exploded into a million blazing stars, her body pulsing in release. Ryan moaned on her breast as he reached his own intense completion and they spun into infinity together.

Eventually the earth slowly steadied on its axis. He collapsed on her, his lips buried in the hollow of her neck and breathed in the scent of woman, loving, and passion. He stirred.

'I'm too heavy.'

Her arms tightened around him before reluctantly releasing him. He slid out of bed, went into the bathroom for a minute, then came back to cradle her in his arms, her cheek pressed to his heart. They lay silent, listening as two heartbeats slowed and steadied. Two bodies, slick with sweat, clung at every point they touched.

'That was . . . glorious.' His voice was filled with wonder.

'Mmmmmm.' Her response was a small sound of contentment. She wriggled until her curves fit comfortably against his rugged lines and rubbed her nose in the hair on his chest.

Becky felt so good. Sleepily she thought about Ryan, and the loving, and the night. Again she felt the overwhelming brilliance of pure joy. Such moments were gifts from fate and so very rare. An instant in time when everything was so exactly perfect you knew, right then, right there, you were supremely happy.

She hugged the emotion to her, holding on as long as she could until it began to dissipate. As it always did.

It had to. No one could live forever in that state. Although, she thought, she would have liked the opportunity to give it a try. But two brief moments of bliss in one day, in one night, was almost more than any woman could ask. Had the right to ask.

She tilted her head and kissed the angle of his jaw. The fact that he was here, now, with her, was special all by itself. But hold on, she thought, other than the obvious, why was he here? She had a vague memory of him saying something about Sarah.

'Ryan?'

'Ummmm.' His sigh of pleasure was a deep throated purr.

'Why are you here?'

'Mmmm?' Ryan was still lost in a sensual daze, not really heeding her question. He rolled his head and buried his nose in her hair and kissed her forehead.

'Why are you here?' This time her question was louder and she jerked her hair away from his face.

'I baby-sat and you tucked me in when I fell asleep on the couch.' His tone was sweetly reasonable and one long arm reached around in an attempt to scoop her onto his shoulder for sleep.

Becky's kiss was soft but her elbow was sharp. 'I know why you're in the house. What are you doing in my room?'

'We made love.' This was said with immense pride and satisfaction.

She sat up and glared down at his fatuous smile. 'Pay attention. Why did you come to my room? Something about Sarah?' Her words were evenly spaced and sharply enunciated.

'Oh. I almost forgot.' He laughed. 'Sarah lost a tooth and she made me promise, cross my heart, I would make sure you knew tonight. Or else. For some reason she fears your ignorance of this important event would lead to the absence of the toothfairy. Since you didn't wake me up when you came home I was afraid she would be awake before me. And right now I don't want to imperil my heart.'

'But . . .'

'There's something I've always wondered and you seem to be an authority on children's rituals. What happens to a heart when you cross it but break the promise?'

'Ryan . . .'

'Never mind,' he said, and kissed her. 'You looked so adorable in the moonlight. Then you told me to come back to bed, right before you touched me. I tried to wake you up but next thing I knew . . . Did you know you wake up most delightfully?'

She blushed and dipped her head but one strong finger under her chin soon brought her face back into his view. He feathered kisses along her cheek, finishing with a potent kiss that promised wonderful things.

'I adore you.' His voice was low and cracked midsentence. 'Cross my heart.'

She said nothing but her lips parted in surprise. He chuckled and dropped a kiss on her nose.

'Don't look so shocked, my sweet.' His tone turned brisk as he swung his legs over the edge of the bed and sat up. He reached down to pull his pants onto the bed and searched in the pockets until he found the tooth.

'Here it is. Shall I be toothfairy? You can coach me in the role. I'll be gallant and chivalrous for my lady and hurry, shivering, through chilly halls while you wait here for me, snug in bed.'

'Trying to earn a place at the Round Table?'

'No. I want to hold you in my arms while we sleep.'

She had propped herself on her elbows to follow his search but now she smiled dreamily and lay down, heavy lids masking her anticipation and a sultry smile curving lips swollen by his kisses.

He leaned over to brace his hands on either side of her head. His eyes gleamed like molten silver.

'Forget about sleep. I am going to make love to you all night. You won't get any sleep,' he warned, baring his teeth in a wolfish leer, 'until we both collapse from too much loving.'

Her forefinger followed the line of his profile, across his brow, down his strong nose. When she traced his lips, her touch as light and elusive as a butterfly's, his sharp teeth nipped then kissed her fingertip.

'Then in the morning, I'm going to wake you slowly, with my lips, and my fingers, and then . . .'

Ryan continued, his husky whispers dark and erotic, making promises until her body throbbed in anticipation. She wanted him again. Now.

'You will, will you?' Becky grabbed his shoulders and hauled him down until his lips touched hers. 'You know what they say about big talk.'

He grinned and pulled her hand into his lap to prove he was ready for more than talking.

'You wait until morning . . .' He stopped when she blanched and jerked her hand away. 'What's the matter?'

'I can't. You can't. I mean, you can't sleep with me, there can't be a morning. The children sometimes come in here early. How would we explain . . .? You can't.' Her tone revealed equal parts longing and regret.

But he was already pulling on his briefs, then his pants. She watched regretfully as he very carefully zipped them up. He bent to press a kiss to her palm before he placed the tooth in it.

'Don't be upset, darling. I understand. I'll go down and try to stay warm with only a quilt. You take care of the toothfairy.' The heavy pathos in his voice, the not-quite-fake tortured sigh he heaved, and the dejected slump of his shoulders made her giggle.

Pleased he'd managed to bring back her smile, Ryan left quickly before stronger urges took over and he convinced her to let him stay. At the door he turned back. Their passion had tumbled the sheets into wild disarray and, skin naked and rosy from lovemaking, Becky lay curled in the tumbled nest of white cotton.

He felt strange. During that long night when he decided to marry Becky, he'd been so sure he loved her. He knew now that he hadn't had a clue what that word meant. He did now. Ryan wrenched his gaze away.

Leaving her was the toughest thing he'd had to do in a long, long time.

'Do you think he's awake?'

'I don't know. Do you think he's awake?'

'Maybe. Should we check?'

'Mommy said we should be quiet. She said he was tired.'

'Why don't you check?'

'How?'

Fatigued by a night of intense gratification followed by intense discomfort, Ryan was at first only vaguely aware of the whispering at the door. He decided to keep his eyes closed, hoping they'd get discouraged and leave. He needed at least another hour of sleep before he could feel human, he thought, thanks to the lumpy couch he'd endured plus an arousal that just wouldn't die until long past dawn.

No, he'd probably need two hours sleep and a cold shower.

'What are you guys doing?' The new voice didn't try to be quiet.

'Shhh, Nicky. Ryan's sleeping. We think.'

He was. He will be again, Ryan thought. Go away.

'Mommy told us to be quiet until he woke up.'

'Where's Mommy?'

'In the shower. I don't think she slept very good, 'cause she's sure cranky.'

She didn't, hmmm? Ryan wondered why. Perhaps the rest of her night had been as restless as his own?

'I want to watch cartoons.'

'Shh, Nicky!'

'But it's not easy to be quiet.'

'Mommy made us promise not to make any noise if he was still asleep.'

'Is he?'

'We don't know.'

'Why don't you find out?'

'How?'

'Look and see, silly.'

Expecting them to come closer, Ryan made sure he was breathing normally and his eyelids didn't flicker. Time dragged and his skin prickled as he felt the weight of their inspection.

Shock held him immobile as a small grubby finger pushed up one of his eyelids. Two brown eyes stared into one blue eye. An impish grin curved jam-smeared lips.

'Hello.'

He said nothing, staring grimly at Nicky's face.

'Are you asleep or awake?'

'Asleep.'

'Oh.' His eyelid snapped shut when Nicky's finger released it. There was more whispering and Ryan held back a grin with great effort. Then his eyelid was carefully lifted again.

'Are you sure?'

He attempted a loud snore and Nicky giggled. Ryan swept out long arms and pulled Nicky closer so he could tickle him. Dani and Sarah couldn't resist the urge to jump into the fray.

When Becky came downstairs she was drawn to the doorway by roars and laughter. When she looked into the room she saw the heap of wiggling, giggling bodies on the couch.

'What is going on here?' Becky's stern question caused an immediate cessation of hostilities. From where she stood behind the couch all she could see was a mass of disjointed arms and legs.

'I thought I told you not to wrestle on the furniture.' Her voice was severe as she waited. One by one, four apologetic faces appeared over the back of the sofa. Becky's jaw dropped when she saw the appealing grin of the largest offender. Six steps took her close enough to see the children were sitting on his quilt draped form.

'I thought I told you to let Ryan sleep? Get up and go into the play room right now or I will be really angry.'

Relieved to get off so easily, all three scrambled to their feet and out of the room at top speed. She turned her head to follow their escape and when she turned back to Ryan her nose bumped into a very masculine, very naked chest. Two strong arms pinned her to him.

'Whaaat?' Her mouth opened in protest and her lips grazed Ryan's skin.

'You said to get up. I'm up.' His hips, clad only in black briefs, pressed his erection against her stomach, proving his statement. 'You have quite an effect on me lady. You walk in the room and . . .'

'Ryan! What if the children come back?'

'I hate to admit it but . . . you're right.' He enveloped her in a quick hug, then his arms loosened as he searched her features. He needed some sign of her feelings about their lovemaking the night before. He needed to know she felt no regrets this morning.

Becky leaned forward to drop a kiss on the centre of his chest. He growled and made to gather her up again but she skipped backward to evade his arms.

'No, Ryan.'

'Then I had better make use of your cold shower.'

She was unable to pull her attention away as he bent to pick up his pants. He noticed her ogling him and smirked.

'Wanna help?'

Becky blushed and fled.

'Mike, call Nicky.' Becky felt breathless as she scurried around her kitchen preparing breakfast, refusing to acknowledge the man methodically burning the toast. Ryan's hair was still damp from his shower, the thick strands showing marks from the teeth of his comb. She was exhausted from trying not to see his suggestive grin, being deaf to the double entendres, and eluding his sneaky hands.

'He won't come.' Mike ran back into the kitchen and skidded to a halt. 'He told me to go away.'

'Go back up there and tell him if he wants breakfast he'd better get down here, pronto.'

'I already told him. He said it didn't matter.'

'I can't go up there, the food will be ruined.' Becky waved a hand at the bacon she was frying and the eggs she was scrambling and the hashed potatoes that would burn and stick to the pan if she left the room for even one second. 'Go back and tell him to come now, or else.'

'I'll go, Becky.'

She jumped when Ryan spoke from immediately behind her, his breath stirring the tiny curls on her nape.

'Thanks.' Anything to get him out of her kitchen before breakfast was totally ruined because she was paying more attention to him than to the food. 'I'd appreciate it.'

On the landing upstairs Ryan called Nicky and received no answer. It took a second search around the boy's bedroom before he saw the legs sticking out from under a pillow at the foot of his bed.

'What are you doing?'

Nicky's answer was unintelligible and Ryan tried to lift off the muffling pillow. Two small hands held tightly to the pillow case but lost the fight to Ryan's superior strength.

'Is something the matter? Your Mom has breakfast ready.' Nicky lunged for the pillow but Ryan held it high out of reach. 'Why are you hiding?'

'I'm not hiding.' Nicky's stiff body and stiffer voice expressed his outraged indignation. 'I'm waiting for the toof'airy.'

'The toof'airy?' Ryan wondered what on earth Nicky was talking about.

'She's going to bring me a lot of money. Like Sarah got for her toof, only more.'

Ah, enlightenment, Ryan decided. 'But you don't have a tooth to put under your pillow.'

'One toof is no good.' Nicky's scornful glance raked the big man who had loosened his grip on the pillow while he listened. 'I need lotsa money.'

With one swoop Nicky grabbed back the pillow and pulled it over his head. When he continued his explanation for the dumb grown-up his voice was once again muffled by feathers. 'So I'm putting them all under together.'

Ryan couldn't hold back his laughter. Nicky lifted the pillow, glared his displeasure, then turned to face the wall, his head once again hidden away.

'I'm sorry,' Ryan lifted the pillow off once more and laid his hand on the boy's stiff shoulder, 'but it won't work.'

'Why not?' Nicky was resentful and suspicious but willing to listen.

'Do you know what happens to the teeth the toothfairy pays for?'

'No.'

'She takes them away. You'd have no teeth left in your mouth.'

Much struck by Ryan's statement, Nicky thought it over, obviously pondering the consequences of such a thing. 'Okay.'

'But, Nicky, that means no popcorn, no corn on the cob, no apples. No toffee.'

'No apples?' Nicky was visibly upset. 'No candy?'

'It's not too late. You can change your mind, the toothfairy only comes at night.'

'Really?'

'Really.'

'Thanks lots.' The small hand slipped trustingly into the big one and Nicky's smile was blinding as he beamed up at Ryan. 'I'm sure glad we talked 'bout this. I could've had a big problem.'

'Glad to be of service.'

'You know?' An expression of concentration and deep thought settled on Nicky's face. 'This must be what Mommy meant when she told Mike us kids should always talk about important stuff with a grown-up who cares about us.'

'Yes, I believe you're right.' The long-time bachelor had to swallow a lump in his throat as he squeezed Nicky's hand. 'Let's go get some breakfast, tiger.'

'Okay!' Nicky leaped off the bed and raced to the door where he stopped, turned and held out his hand. 'Coming?'

Monday morning Ryan drove to work, windows wide open, CD player going full blast, fingers tapping out the rhythm on the steering wheel. On Saturday, for the first time in weeks, the sun had decided to make an appearance and it still shone today. Traffic was light, the other commuters were behaving themselves and he felt good.

Euphoria bubbled up inside him, his grin widening until his jaw ached.

He felt great.

Whizzing over the Burrard Street bridge he wound down the window and dragged in a lungful of the ocean air. The wind gusting in off the water had blown away the smog and today the air was salty. Tangy. Exciting. At the stop light he let loose an irrepressible rebel yell.

Dammit, life was good.

A car horn tooted on his left and he glanced out his side window. In the next lane a sexy redhead in a white Ferrari offered her best come-hither smile. Ryan grinned.

He wasn't the least interested. Who cared about a redhead when he could have Becky? He laughed out loud as he accelerated away on the green light.

Forgetting the redhead the instant she was out of sight, he laughed again for sheer joy. How many years had it been since he'd felt this enjoyment in simply being alive? Since university? Or later when he formed his own company? Or had he ever? Traffic crawled along bumper-to-bumper. His mind drifted back over the weekend.

Dani and he had spent both days together with Becky and her kids. Saturday Becky had made a picnic and they drove both cars to Lighthouse Park where they occupied several exciting hours climbing rocks and pulling Nicky out of tidal pools. At dusk they camped out on a large bolder, exhausted but cheerful, to ooh and ahh as the sun set over Georgia Strait.

The Gulf Islands, and beyond them Vancouver Island, were misty purple lumps crowned by rosy, glowing clouds. Becky leaned back into the arm he had placed around her shoulders. Even the kids were silent as they watched nature's familiar, extravagant performance.

On Sunday, instead of the lunch and movies at home she'd planned, he'd rented one of those big family-style vans so there would be enough seat belts in one vehicle for everyone. They drove the Sea-to-Sky highway, up the coast and into the mountains. They hiked the nature trails around Whistler until a persistent drizzle and hunger pangs drove them back to the van.

On the edge of a small lake, surrounded by forest, they found an empty rest stop built for stray tourists. No more than a rough roof set on four poles, it kept off the wet even if its lack of walls meant they weren't protected from the chill breeze.

Becky and the kids huddled on cement benches while he produced his version of a picnic: a barrel of Kentucky Fried Chicken, a bag of rolls, and a dozen cans of soda he'd picked up at the drive-through restaurant on their way out of town.

Becky had only laughed when he couldn't produce napkins or ketchup, both necessities when feeding children. She'd pulled packets of finger wipes out of her purse and told the kids they ate too much ketchup anyway. Then she sneaked him a kiss and told him the picnic was perfect. All six of them had consumed the food with one hand while they kept the other buried in a warm pocket.

All weekend he had suffered. Wanting her, knowing he couldn't have her with four children underfoot. Tormenting them both with stolen kisses, secret touches. Two days and one interminable night had passed since they had made love. Until last night.

Last night . . . He groaned as he remembered Sunday night. A dinner of hot dogs, carrot sticks, potato chips and a bad joke contest. Later Jan had taken all the kids out to see the new Disney movie, though Mike complained about being seen at a little kids' show.

Ryan had waved them off while Becky started washing dishes.

She'd had both hands in soapy water when he walked up behind her. One large hand gripped the rim of the sink on either side of her and his body leaned into her. He trailed open-mouth kisses down her neck, nudging aside her collar with his chin.

'What do you think you're you doing?' she asked.

'Helping you do the dishes. I promised I would.'

'That's not helping.' The last word ended in a squeak that coincided with a powerful push of his pelvis against her bottom.

'Sure it is.' One hand lifted the hem of her sweat shirt and crept underneath to cup her bare breast, allowing a callused thumb to stroke across her nipple. He touched the tip of his tongue to her ear lobe and she gasped.

'You once told me doing dishes is boring, so I thought I'd provide some entertainment.' His lips trailed down her shoulder and back up to her ear, where his breath tickled her skin as he spoke. 'I've had this fantasy . . .'

'A fan . . . fantasy?' Her voice broke mid-word.

'Ever since that first Sunday when I sat here and watched you wash the dishes.'

Her breath faltered when he brought his other hand to her belly and slid those long fingers inside the elastic waistband of her fleece jogging pants. When his fingertips toyed with the lace trim on her panties her hands froze on the dish she still held submerged.

'What . . .' her voice trailed off then she gulped and tried again. 'What . . .'

'Shhh . . .' His fingers slipped beneath her panties and quested through the nest of hidden curls.

'But . . . Ohhh.' He had found her. A quiver started where his tongue explored her ear and ran straight down to where her toes curled into the worn linoleum. She arched into his hand, her head turned, her mouth blindly seeking his lips.

'So wet, so ready.' His words were uttered into her mouth, his hand on her breast trailing fire. His other hand moved lightly on her moist warmth, rubbing, massaging. Long fingers parted her and hesitated, waiting.

'Becky?'

Her answer was an inarticulate moan and the frenzied movement of her hips. He growled in his throat as he fastened his lips on hers and slipped his fingers inside her. He stroked harder, deeper, bringing her to the brink and then he held her as she fell into the whirling depths.

She whimpered into his mouth as her body pulsed around his hand, her bottom instinctively rubbing against his erection, trying to share what he had given her.

He withdrew his hand and pressed her against the counter, halting the arousing motions. Her body stilled and he wrapped both arms around her waist, supporting her weight when her increasingly weak knees gave up the job. Her head fell forward until her chin rested on her heaving chest.

When she'd somewhat recovered, Becky lifted her hands out of the water and gaped in disbelief. Each fist clenched her new glass mixing bowl, now snapped in half. She muttered something about the cost of another bowl but she set the pieces on the counter and forgot all about them when his hand cupped her breast once again and he rested his cheek on the crown of her head.

'Oh, Ryan.' Her whisper was low but the yearning in her voice was strong. 'I want you.'

He spun her around in his arms so fast soapy water splashed on the floor, soaking their legs.

'What did you say?'

'Make love to me.'

Blue eyes stared down into brown. Their mouths met, open searching. Tongues meeting, entwining. Hearts pounding.

Feet apart, she went on tiptoe, the better to cradle his rigid length against her warmth. He groaned, the pain of his arousal intense. Succumbing to the needs clamoring so savagely, he sent his glance sweeping around the big room. Then he lifted her in his arms and walked over to the sturdy table where he swept the kids' coloring books to the floor.

He put her on her feet and crouched to yank off her pants and panties. His hands shook as he tugged open the button fly of his jeans and fished a foil packet from his pocket before he pushed them to his knees. He lifted her to the table top, bracing her hips with his hands, then thrust hard into her welcoming warmth. She gasped and he stilled, deep inside, waiting until she adjusted to the size of him.

'I'm sorry, but you make me so crazy I couldn't wait,' he said, his voice thick and unsteady. 'Did I hurt you?'

She shook her head. After a moment she lifted her legs and anchored them around his waist. At her unspoken urging his hips started to move slowly, then his own need demanded release and he plunged fiercely. His hands dug into her thighs, holding her close.

Her fingers slipped beneath his shirt and curled into his wide shoulders, clinging to her only support in the wild maelstrom of passion he aroused. Head back, eyes closed, both were drawn into the seething whirlpool of color centered where their bodies joined.

His shout jerked their eyes open and they stared fascinated at each other, their faces transformed as he spent himself in her. This time she held him as he went over passion's cliff. His release triggered another of her own and they waited, still joined, propping each other up until the aftershocks of their completion had abated enough to allow coherent thought.

A horn blared outside and Ryan jumped, yanked back to the present. Vision blurry, it took him two minutes to realize he wasn't in Becky's arms but in his car, blocking an intersection in Monday morning rush-hour traffic. A few seconds later he drove off with an apologetic wave out the window at the impatient drivers behind him.

'Becky.' He said her name aloud, savoring it, tasting it, as last night he had savored her. He recalled with satisfaction the kiss they had shared when he'd dropped off Dani this morning. The vividness of his memories had him stirring restlessly in the car seat, uncomfortable with an almost painful arousal.

In the parking space under his office building he adjusted himself, trying to ease the constriction of his clothing. Eventually he gave up and decided to hold his briefcase in front of his hips if he met anyone between the car and his office.

Keys in hand, he paused with one leg out the car door as he pondered what Becky had come to mean to him.

She could arouse him as no other woman had ever been able to. Her passionate and honest response to his touch was heady stuff. Yet her love for her family and the affection she shared so generously with Dani and himself pierced his heart in a way completely foreign to his experience.

He wanted to protect her, to be there for her, to fulfil all her wants and needs. He needed her and he wanted her to need him. For himself. Not for his money, impossible as he knew that to be, and not for his face. He wanted her to need his love; he wanted her love. When they had resurfaced last night and realized passion had swept them away, on a kitchen table no less, they had both been a little shocked and disconcerted.

Then he had kissed the red marks his hands had put on her thighs and Becky had lovingly cleaned the bleeding crescents her fingernails had carved in his shoulders. Clothing restored, faces washed, hair combed, he had helped her finish the dishes.

Ryan slammed the car door and whistled as he walked to the elevator. He held his briefcase strategically and flipped his key ring in his hand. A song on a distant radio echoed through the underground cement cavern and, his feet light with happiness, he danced a few steps and jabbed the call button with his elbow.

He felt a little ridiculous to be dancing in the basement of his office building. That thought made him pause. Dancing?

Of course! He'd take her dancing!

He'd make a reservation at Rick's, the private dinner and dance club. She'd enjoy the atmosphere of elegant decadence reminiscent of the late thirties and early forties. He could introduce her to some of his friends. Every man in the place was going to be envious because the most extraordinary woman in the room was there with him.

Later, much later, he'd take her home to his penthouse where they could be alone.

There, if he was feeling really brave, he would finally tell her he loved her.

Two elderly women already occupied the elevator when it came up from the lower parking level and he stepped inside. They both moved back, worried and concerned, when he first growled, then laughed out loud. He noticed how they sidled out of his way and laughed again.

'Sorry, ladies. I'm not crazy, just in love. And I'm taking my special lady dancing on Saturday night.'

The nervous looks faded into little smiles. Then they used the trip upwards to give him tips on the proper way to court a lady.

CHAPTER 11

The lights of Vancouver twinkled a long way below as the revolving room inched around, presenting a panoramic view of the city's skyline to the patrons of the exclusive Rick's. The staff and the room both wore finery from the thirties and forties, a very different era from the present. Fans circled lazily overhead. The music ebbed and flowed, muffling the voices and laughter around them. White rosebuds on every table scented the air. The cuisine pleased the eye and the tongue.

Ryan was thoroughly enjoying the amazed delight of the woman seated across the small round table. He slid a little closer on the curved, upholstered bench.

When the four piece orchestra took their breaks, a single pianist played, sliding from one old wartime song into another.

'I know that song. *Lili Marlene*.' Her eyes sparkled. 'Remember I told you about Emily, the friend of my grandmother's who owned Lilac House? They used to listen to the old records all the time when we visited. I think it made them feel young again. This one was Emily's favorite.' She hummed along with the piano.

'Thank you for bringing me here, Ryan. This place is wonderful. I feel as if at any moment Humphrey Bogart will walk into the room and sweep Ingrid Bergman into his arms.'

'I'm glad you like it.' He toasted her with his glass of scotch. 'I want to thank you.'

'For what?' Becky asked.

'For being so great with Dani but especially for helping me to understand her a little better. I can't say it's a completed process but lately I feel we are growing closer.'

'You don't have to thank me. I didn't do anything.'

'Yes, you did. When she first came I was very uncomfortable around her. Didn't know what to say or do. Now we have fun whether we're with your family or on our own. Thursday night we went for a walk after dinner and we both had a good time.'

'I don't think . . .'

'Dani and I might never have made it past the polite stage. I owe you and I thank you.'

'You're welcome, kind sir.' She dipped her head with mock formality.

He sipped his drink and listened to her reminisce about her childhood visits to Lilac House.

Her dress gleamed like old gold. In the candlelight her curls weren't an ordinary brown but strands of copper woven through sable. He felt if he stayed close enough he could warm himself with her presence. 'I'm glad you wore that dress. I wanted you to wear it for me.'

Becky laughed self-consciously and smoothed one hand down her skirt. She knew the other women in the room were probably wearing designer fashions and real diamonds. Whenever he introduced her to a friend passing their table she could feel the women, and some of the men, judging her appearance.

She looked back at Ryan and, just for a second, stopped breathing.

He was an outrageously beautiful man.

One lock of bright hair had fallen over his forehead, his blue eyes appeared dark in the candlelight, and his lips lifted at one corner in a perpetual tempting grin. His black suit looked tailor-made. Every woman in the place probably wished she could be at his table tonight, if not in his bed. A tide of doubt and despair washed over her, deep enough to wash the sparkle out of her eyes.

What did he see in her? She was a thirty-five year old mother. No glamor, no mystery, far too many stretch marks. She wouldn't be able to hold him. When he left her she would be devastated. Should she break if off now, before she got in any deeper? Could she?

He stretched his free hand across the table and played with her fingers, his smile adding warmth to those perfect blue eyes. And she knew the answer to her question. It was already too late. She would stay with him until he left because she could never be the one to end it.

'It's a home-made dress. Not like the others here.' She gestured around the room. He obediently scanned the small intimate tables but he brought his eyes back to her almost immediately. He longed to erase the shadows that had appeared on her face.

'You remind me of the angel on top of our Christmas tree when I was very young. Beautiful, remote, fragile. I always insisted on being the one to place her on her perch so high above the rest of us. She belonged to me.' Possessiveness resonated in his voice.

'Forget it, Ryan. Everyone knows the angel is always blonde. Pretty, perfect and blonde.'

'Nonsense. You shouldn't listen to retailers' propaganda. You are perfect. Beautiful and, like that angel so many years ago, you are mine.'

The delicate blush that stained her cheeks and the shy smile that curved her lips bewitched him. The waiter had removed their empty plates and Ryan couldn't wait any longer. He had to hold her in his arms.

'Let's dance,' he ordered abruptly and stood.

Exasperated by the curt demand, Becky was all set to decline when she made the mistake of looking at him. His glinting smile dared her to refuse but the expression in his eyes begged her understanding.

'Please, Becky. I want to hold you.'

She nodded and he pulled her to her feet. On the dance floor he wrapped both arms around her waist and held her so tightly the only movement possible was a swaying shuffle. The orchestra was playing a fast waltz and she felt flustered when the other couples spinning past gawked at their teenage-style clinch.

'Ryan, not so tight.' With difficulty she wedged both hands against his chest and tried to lever a few inches of air between their bodies. 'Everyone's staring.'

At first she thought he was going to disregard her protests but eventually he loosened his grip with a sigh.

'Fine . . . but I don't have to like it.' He backed off until he was holding her in a more conventional way and expertly swung her into the intricate steps of the dance.

She caught one glimpse of his face and burst out laughing. 'You're sulking!'

'I am not sulking.'

'You are.'

'Am not.'

'Are too.' Becky's laughter rose over the music and he had to smile.

'Maybe a little. I want you so much that holding you in public is going to drive me mad.' His leg slid between hers and he spun her around.

She leaned back in his arms until she could see his expression. Heat blazed in his eyes and she felt desire burgeon in her own body. Why not? Jan was baby-sitting and before Ryan's arrival her friend had teasingly offered to stay all night.

'Ryan, let's leave now. I'd like to be alone with you.'

He stopped dancing and stared down at her, ignoring the crowd swirling around them. The shadows he had seen in her eyes earlier were gone.

Now they held only promises. Promises of love and passion and joy.

He'd made Becky happy.

He felt a familiar pride of accomplishment swell up inside himself. But this time it was different. This was not the pride of a teenager forcing obedience from a gang of cut-throat toughs. Nor the pride of a man besting the competition and earning the biggest percentage. This was more. More vital to his existence and happiness.

After years of uncertainty and pain Becky deserved happiness. She deserved to be courted. And he was the man to do it!

'No, sweetheart.' The arm around her waist tightened as he spun her into the music again. 'The most beautiful woman in the room is going to dance all night. And if I go a little mad while she does it, so what? I read somewhere a little madness is good for the soul. Not to mention, learning patience should be good for what some consider my oversized ego.'

He held her in his arms and twirled her around so fast and so often that when at last he stopped they were both breathless and dizzy. Her eyes sparkled more brilliantly than the rhinestone star nestled in her curls. She deserved real diamonds. A big diamond for the third finger of her left hand.

His conscience twinged when he remembered the trouble at McLeod Systems. If his efforts failed, his backers would put their money elsewhere. Then the banks would call in the demand loans he'd taken for the expansion and he would lose everything because all he owned was tied up in his attempt to save his company.

If he was broke how would he buy groceries, much less a diamond for Becky? She didn't need another failure for a husband. He shook his head, shedding the doubts. You'll pull it off, McLeod, he told himself silently.

He wouldn't fail. He never had.

'Let's sit down.' He dropped a kiss on Becky's lips. 'It's time for the champagne.'

'Champagne?'

She sat down on the banquette and slid around the table, Ryan close behind. He called over a waiter to take their order then looked at her. Once again he was captivated by the picture she made.

'We have to celebrate.' He tasted the champagne, nodded his approval for the waiter to pour the golden liquid into their glasses.

'What are we celebrating?'

'I managed to get the new software ready to present at the business trade show next week,' Ryan chuckled. 'I'm going to blow PasComm out of the water.'

'That's wonderful.' She had lifted the glass of expensive imported liquor but went still when Carol walked into the room with an older man. 'Ms Hill is here.'

'Where?' He twisted in his seat.

'The maitre'd is seating them at the corner table.'

'Why, yes it is her.' He half rose from his chair. 'I should say hello. I haven't seen her since . . .'

His voice tapered off and he sank back. Abruptly he turned to face her and uttered a succinct but comprehensive string of curses, his face as tense as his body.

'What's wrong?'

'Do you recognize the man she's with?'

'No. Should I?'

'Harold Pastin. President of PasComm, the company so successful at sabotaging and undercutting me. Damn her.'

'I don't understand.' She stared, baffled by Ryan's quiet fury. At the corner table Carol Hill leaned against her tall, silver-haired companion, their comfortable intimacy very obvious.

'Now I know how he always knew exactly where I was vulnerable.'

'But, Ryan, she's your friend. You used to be . . . You don't think . . .?'

'You bet I do. Very few people had access to both my office and my apartment. She had plenty of opportunities to copy my keys and she knew when I was going out of town. They had a clear field.'

'You don't seem very surprised.'

'No. I did wonder if she . . . I dismissed her as a suspect because she was supposedly out of town when the theft occurred. May they both rot in hell.'

Becky chewed on her bottom lip as her heart twisted with jealousy. Maybe he was angry for more than one reason. Maybe he disliked seeing Carol Hill and Pastin so intimate.

Oblivious to her withdrawal he was still growling, disillusionment and betrayal tightening his jaw and lowering his brows. 'I wonder how long she's been conspiring with Pastin? I remember when we first got together she said he was one of the men she wanted to avoid. Do you suppose he set us up together from the beginning?'

'Ryan?'

He still stared at the far corner of the club. 'Hindsight sure is twenty-twenty. She played me carefully and I was arrogant enough not to question why she wanted to make the relationship physical. She wanted access to my apartment. What a fool,' he condemned himself fiercely.

'No, you are not a fool. If you love someone, and they say they love you, you have every right to trust them. If she deceived you then she is the fool. Not you.'

He focused on the woman seated across from him. What was Becky saying? Did she think he had loved Carol? He'd felt affection and pleasure, yes. Love, no. Not even close to what he felt for Becky.

'I'm sorry, it's none of my business. I've presumed too much.'

Startled by her apology, Ryan noticed her cheeks had lost the delicate bloom they'd worn most of the evening. She kept her face averted and her fingers alternately pleated and smoothed her linen napkin.

'What do you mean?' He knew the question was abrupt, but he wanted to know what she was thinking. Her skin whitened even further and a small dot of red welled where her teeth pierced her bottom lip.

'When I'm with you I'm never sure what I mean.'

Instinctively his hand lifted and his thumb soothed the rich flesh, wiping away the blood. Her lips parted in surprise and his thumb slipped inside, exploring the sharp edge of her white teeth and the damp warmth, brushing against the tip of her tongue. Desire shot through him and he decided to forget both Carol and Pastin for tonight.

His betrayer had been identified and thus neutralized. Tomorrow morning was soon enough to call the police detective and deal with the situation. Now he knew the truth Pastin and Carol were both supremely unimportant, especially compared to Becky.

Besides, his body was making demands he didn't want to ignore any longer. His breathing was ragged, his vision glazed, and his powerful response pressed insistently against the zipper of his slacks. Leaving his thumb against her lip, he curved his fingers around her jaw and ear. His hand and his voice shook when he tried to say her name.

'Becky?'

She couldn't say a word. One smile, one touch, and she was drowning in the depths of passion he aroused, uncertainty forgotten. Oh, how she wanted this man. Her body leaned toward his in helpless yearning.

'Oh, Becky, what you do to me. No matter where we are, at your touch I go up in flames.'

He slipped his free arm around her waist and pulled her around the curve of the bench. Behind the long tablecloth he took her hand and pressed her palm to his arousal.

His eyes closed to slits and he swallowed a moan when her fingers curved around his hardness.

Need for this woman surged through him. His body jerked and a low growl escaped through his tense throat. He pulled his thumb away and brushed his lips over hers.

'Let's go to my place, honey.' His breath held the flavor of champagne and his arousal pulsed in her palm, almost as strongly as her heart thundered in her breast.

Becky forced her eyes closed, trying to resist temptation. She had to think. There was a reason to say no, but what was it? She couldn't think when he was touching her, when she was touching him.

'Excuse me, Mr McLeod. May I serve you and your guest some dessert?'

She opened her eyes with a gasp, jerked her hand out of Ryan's lap, and slumped into the support of the bench's high back, embarrassed at what the waiter might have seen. Ryan curled his fingers into a loose fist under her chin and nudged upward, trying to read her expression.

'Rebecca? Would you like dessert?' The question was innocuous, but his eyes gleamed as they asked a different question. Confusion swirled through her mind. Finally she shook her head. Disappointment darkened his eyes before he turned to the waiter.

'No, thank you. Coffee and the bill, please.'

They sat in silence until after the waiter brought the coffee.

'What's the matter?'

'Nothing. I think we should leave.'

'No. I want to know what happened. You wanted me. What changed?'

Consumed by mute despair, she didn't answer his question. Her eyes, earlier bright and filled with promises, were now muddy and dark. They had lost the gleam of joy when . . . when? He ran through their evening in his mind and then he knew. Becky had changed when Carol came in with Pastin. Why would their presence affect Becky?

Then he remembered her saying that he had trusted Carol because he loved her.

He put down the coffee cup and reached over to pull a resisting Becky back into his arms. He dropped a quick kiss on her forehead and laid his cheek on her silky curls. The fragrance of her perfume drifted past his nostrils and he took a deep breath, trying to absorb her scent into his body.

'Darling Rebecca. I never loved Carol.' She stiffened in his arms, trying to pull away. 'I liked her, we had many interests in common and we were friends and occasional lovers. She used me and I am ashamed to admit I used her. I never loved her.'

He felt a huge sense of relief as Becky slowly relaxed and snuggled into his arms.

'If she is my thief and helped Pastin cause the recent trouble, I regret the loss of a friend and am angry I was stupid enough to trust her. No more than that.'

'Are you sure?'

'Yes. I feel something for you I have never experienced before. I promise . . .'

She cupped his jaw with her hand. One finger drifted across his lips. 'Hush, my darling. No promises.' She pressed her fingers to where his pulse beat in his throat. 'I've changed my mind. Let's have dessert . . . at your place.'

And then, not caring where they were or who watched, she kissed him. Thoroughly.

In the lobby of the dinner club, Ryan waited impatiently for the clerk to retrieve their coats. Becky would be back from the ladies' room soon and he wanted to be ready to leave. His need for her was a fever in his blood. An evening alone with her in his penthouse, in his bed . . .

'Hello, Ryan.' Carol's voice doused his thoughts like ice water on a fire. He tipped the clerk, put on his own overcoat before he picked up Becky's jacket, and slowly turned to face the other woman.

'Hello, Carol.' Suspicion and anger raged beneath his carefully blank expression. 'How are you?'

'Great. Business is better than ever. Remember the de Creva brothers you steered my way last month? They finally signed a two year contract.' While she talked Carol stepped closer and idly smoothed his lapel before letting her fingers trail down his chest to rest on his arm.

'I owe you a big one,' she purred. 'Say the word, any time.'

Disgust was bitter on his tongue as he acknowledged to himself she was making all the usual moves. Once upon a time her nearness, the scent of her perfume, and the blatant invitation would have brought his arms around her.

He wasn't interested. Now he had finally convinced Becky to be part of his life he could see Carol's actions for what they were, a carefully calculated attempt to bring him into line. He stepped away, not bothering to hide the distaste he felt.

A few yards away in the ornate ladies' room, Becky put down the phone. Jan had said the kids were fine and she had no problem with how late Becky arrived home, she'd use Becky's bed herself. She congratulated Becky on finally finding her courage and began giving advice on what to do and how to do it. She'd still been making absurd suggestions when Becky broke the connection.

She washed her hands and tugged the brush through her hair, impatient to get back to Ryan. She leaned toward the mirror, lipstick in hand. And paused, caught by the image reflected there.

The woman in the mirror had been absent a long time: her eyes shone, her cheeks glowed, a smile curved lips swollen by her lover's kisses. All these things were visible on the outside. Anticipation hummed in her veins and Ryan's touch had put heat in her belly and lower. She dropped the lipstick back into her purse unused. Why bother with lipstick? It would be gone as soon as Ryan kissed her.

She froze when she stepped into the lobby and saw him standing with Carol Hill.

Most of the illumination in the large room came from pot lights hidden behind the lush foliage that lined the walls but Ryan and his former lover stood directly beneath a spot light that turned his hair to gold and the other woman's to silver. Carol's hand lay on his arm and his head was bent slightly. The intimacy of the picture brought tears and pain stabbed at her heart.

Then his head lifted and he gazed straight at Becky as if primal instinct had told him where she stood. It wasn't until his eyes blazed with welcome and sudden passion that she understood precisely how grim and stiff he had been while he talked to the other woman.

He walked toward Becky and Carol's hand dropped away unnoticed. He held out his hand and, her flash of doubt erased, she went into his arms.

Ryan gathered her close and wrapped her in her coat with tenderness and an instinct to protect no one had ever inspired in him before.

'How sweet. It must be true love.' Carol's spiteful voice cut through their absorption in each other.

He lifted his head to scowl at the blonde woman and his voice held a warning when he spoke. 'Good-bye, Carol.'

Carol's manner was bright but brittle as she patted his cheek. 'Oh, darling, don't be silly.' She slipped her hand through his arm with a calculated intimacy while she turned to Becky.

'Hello again. I'm sorry, I've forgotten . . . no, it's Becky, right? Such a quaint name. Ryan told me you are a wonderful mother, so perfect for Dani. So convenient.'

'Convenient?' Becky faltered on the word. Had he discussed her with his former lover?

Ryan was furious when he saw the pain in Becky's face. He shook off Carol's hand and stopped Becky when she would have pulled away.

'You're a little confused, Carol,' his smile mocked the other woman. 'I love Becky. *You* were convenient.'

He dropped a kiss on Becky's lips, enjoying her shocked expression. 'I *do* love you. I didn't want to tell you this way. I thought . . . I had planned . . . Later, when we were alone . . .'

'Oh, Ryan.' Overwhelmed by the roller coaster ride her emotions had taken during the evening, she buried her face in his shoulder and breathed deeply of the mingled scents of wool and spicy cologne, trying not to cry.

He smiled lovingly and tightened his grip on Becky's waist but the smile grew threatening when he faced Carol.

'If you ever try to hurt Becky again, I will make you sorry. She can't deal with someone like you . . .'

'But I can.' Becky had lifted her head and Ryan and Carol stopped glaring at each other as they turned to look at her in surprise.

'Or rather, I could but I refuse to deal with her.' She astonished herself with the truth of what she was saying. No longer was she the meek wife afraid to confront Eric and his mistresses. Ryan was not Eric. 'Ms Hill is unimportant. If you love me then she has no power.'

Ryan was overwhelmed. Becky trusted him! He felt like shouting his delight to the world. A wide grin spread across his face but Carol's cynical laughter reminded him they had company. Annoying company that had to be dealt with. The fact that this woman had tried to wound Becky made his anger all the stronger.

'I saw you with Pastin, Carol. Leave us alone,' he snarled, 'or you will regret it.'

'Oh, I don't think so.' His threat seemed to amuse Carol. 'You never suspected a thing, did you?'

'No, I didn't.' He hesitated but decided to ask the question. He'd probably never get another opportunity. 'Why did you do it, Carol?'

The façade of a sophisticated, controlled woman slipped as her lip curled in an unattractive sneer. 'You never considered marrying me, did you? I could tell there were days you didn't even like me much. Even though I was already involved with Harold, how do you think I felt when you dumped me for *that*.' She lifted her chin in Becky's direction.

He jerked forward but Becky restrained him with a hand on his arm. 'We had an agreement, an agreement you proposed, if you recall. If you'd changed your mind all you had to do was tell me.'

'Why should I? Harold asked me to marry him but we had to wait until he completed his plans for McLeod's. As long as his wife thought you and I were a couple, she wouldn't suspect he was leaving her for me. He wants me and if I can use my relationship with you to help him, why shouldn't I?'

'Do you know what that makes you?' His expression was grim as he contemplated her.

She lashed out but Ryan ducked the slap.

'You've gone too far, Carol. It would take only a few words from me in the right places and your firm would start losing clients.'

'You couldn't!'

'No?'

She studied his face and laughed scornfully. 'If you want to try, go ahead. I'm good at my job and my clients know it. I might have needed your help getting my agency off the ground but that time is past. I'm glad your company is collapsing,' for the first time she raised her voice. 'Glad!'

'My company is far from collapse. You can tell Pastin his efforts have failed. As a matter of fact, quite the reverse. And I suggest you both watch your own backs.'

Something primitive and more than a little savage in his voice got through to Carol and she blinked warily. He smiled with genuine humor as he observed the dawn of understanding and fear in her face. Also the sick recognition of how much she had almost admitted.

'What do you mean?' she asked. 'What have you done?'

'I'm not going to tell you. I advise you to stay away from Becky.' He grinned maliciously. 'Good luck.'

Carol's fingers curled into talons as she lunged at him but a long arm snaked around her waist and hauled her back against an immaculate shirt front.

All three had been so absorbed in the confrontation no one had noticed Harold Pastin's approach. When Carol tried to speak the older man covered her mouth with his free hand, his fingertips white where they bit painfully into her cheek.

'You must get control of yourself, darling.' His voice held no inflection, a featureless monotone. 'You're causing a scene. Think of the poor maitre'd.' When her struggles ceased he released her with a pat on the shoulder. 'That's better, dear.'

The tall, elegant man glanced over to where Ryan still stood with his arm around Becky and examined her face, feature by feature, before impassively scanning her body.

'So this is the new little playmate,' he said with a smile when he finally spoke.

Becky shuddered, disturbed by the ugliness he oozed with such a charming, careless manner. She felt violated, as if he had stripped her naked in public.

Ryan clenched his fist, his arm lifting as if to strike a blow.

Becky felt his movement and wrapped both of her hands around his forearm, holding him back. 'Please, Ryan? Let's leave.'

He dropped his fist but it didn't relax. 'Whatever is between us has nothing to do with her, Pastin. Let's leave it that way.'

'Between us? My good fellow, whatever are you referring to? Is it my relationship with Carol? You can't resent my enjoyment of your discards. After all, I'm accustomed to the experience.'

'You sicken me,' Ryan spat out, his face a mask of loathing.

'You have no idea how the thought of your dislike pains me. Perhaps it bothers you to know Carol has been my lover for months. How does it feel, McLeod?'

'I told you then, and I'll tell you now. I did not have an affair with your wife.'

'Though you are an accomplished liar, you must not forget I saw you together.' His smile was unpleasant as he glanced at Becky. 'I hope you've not given in too easily, Mrs Hansen. McLeod is ruthless when he wants something. Until he gets it. Then, when the novelty wears off . . .' He spread his hands out in a physical expression of doubt and dismissal.

'Ryan is trustworthy and responsible, sometimes too much so. I know he would not have become involved with a married woman.' Becky shook her head. 'You really shouldn't say things like that, Mr Pastin. You're only hurting yourself.'

Pastin shook his head pityingly. 'You're very naive, aren't you?'

'Keep your poison to yourself, Pastin,' Ryan said.

'On the other matter, I trust you aren't going to give Carol's words any serious consideration?'

'I have nothing more to say to you. Come, Becky, let's get out of here.'

As they stepped onto the elevator Becky saw Harold Pastin speak and Carol began to weep. He shook her by the shoulder, hard, then turned and strode rapidly away, leaving Carol standing alone.

Pity stirred and Becky put out her hand to stop the closing doors.

'No, you don't!' Ryan said and pushed her hand down.

'Don't what?' she asked but she knew he'd already seen and understood the expression of sympathy on her own face.

'She isn't worth your compassion. Remember she did her best to destroy my company and a few minutes ago she tried to hurt you. She deserves what she gets.'

'From you? Will you try to ruin them both?'

'Yes.'

'Can you prove anything against them?'

'I don't know. It's doubtful. But there is more than one way to skin this particular cat. A few words here, a hint in someone's ear there . . .'

'What did you mean about watching their backs? What have you done?' The doors opened and she stepped out, gathering the collar of her coat around her neck as they went out into the night air.

'Nothing . . . yet.'

'Hasn't there been enough trouble already? My mother always said "as you sow, so will you reap". People usually proved her right.'

He looked at her with amazement. 'Do unto others and all that?'

'Yes. They are betrayers, they will be betrayed. If you wallow in revenge and hatred it will change the man you are. I couldn't bear that. Besides, you say your new program is better than the one he's using and as for Ms Hill . . .' she squeezed his hand, 'she doesn't have you. That's bad enough for any woman.'

His mouth twitched with amusement, then he began to laugh.

'All right. Have it your way.' He swung her around by the hand and quick-marched her down the street to where he'd parked the Mercedes. 'Let's go have dessert.'

CHAPTER 12

Becky slipped out of Ryan's bed, leaving him to sleep peacefully. She was curious about his home and too restless to fall asleep herself. The evening had ended as sweetly as any 'dessert' she'd ever enjoyed. Tonight had been even more incredible and satiating than anything that had gone before. Awesome, in more ways than one. Alone together. No kids who might wake up and wander in.

She bent and feathered a kiss across his lips, pulling back when he stirred and smiled in his sleep. She tucked the sheet around his waist and turned away to pull her dress from the clothes scattered on the floor. She held it in her hands, then laid it on a chair. She didn't want to get dressed, not yet.

In the armoire, the second drawer she searched held his T-shirts. She selected a white one with a university logo, pulled it over her head, and tugged at the hem where it skimmed her thighs, uselessly trying to stretch it longer, then gave up. There was no one to see her and Ryan's apartment wasn't cold.

She blushed when she remembered how he'd hurried her into his bedroom and into his bed, offering only fleeting glimpses of the apartment as he stripped first himself, then her, leaving a trail of their clothes from door to bed.

She hadn't protested. Indeed she wondered whether she would have allowed him to slow down. By the time they'd arrived here from the dinner club, they'd both been aroused beyond bearing. She looked once more at her lover, then left his bedroom. As she walked down the hall she peeked inside each door she passed.

The room next to his bedroom was obviously an office. She smiled. Beside his large desk stood a much smaller one with its own computer. The keyboard was pushed aside and an arsenal of crayons stood in a carousel next to a stack of white paper.

Across the hall she was drawn into a little girl's dream land. In the centre of the room she wrapped her hand around the post supporting the filmy white canopy over the bed.

She'd always wanted a canopy bed. Even as an adult she would give almost anything to be able to afford a bed as beautiful as this one.

Dani had two. One full size for herself, one in miniature for her dolls. And the dolls! Porcelain dolls with silken curls, cloth dolls with wool braids. Barbie dolls in a fully furnished castle three feet high. Teddy bears dressed in satin and velvet that appeared to have stepped out of the pages of a medieval fantasy.

Becky hoped Sarah never saw this room.

At the next doorway she flicked the wall switch, then blinked and shaded her eyes from the strong fluorescent lights. Gradually the room came into focus. The kitchen. White laminate and granite counter tops. So cold. Except for the artwork.

Crayon drawings and blurred water colors were taped to most of the cupboards and the fridge. She chuckled as she snapped off the light. Obviously the man recognized talent when he saw it.

Becky wandered into the living room, pausing at the end of the hall where she flicked the light switch by the door. Art deco wall sconces illuminated a room both stark and sleek, a frame for his other art collection.

Pale grey walls, steel grey carpet. The splashes of colour in some of the paintings and the oriental area rug in the centre of the room provided the only visual relief in the austere surroundings. Even the leather furniture was dark, a deep rich burgundy. Judging by the empty spaces on the walls and empty display cabinets he hadn't yet replaced the artwork and statues stolen or damaged during the robbery.

She sniffed. The aroma of freshly painted walls still flavored the air. She flicked the lights off again and curled up in a comfortable chair near the huge expanse of glass to watch dawn break over the darkened city. Almost morning. Almost the end of their night. She lay her head back against the leather upholstery and thought about what Ryan had said.

In the lobby of the dinner club he'd said he loved her. Calmly. Stating a fact. Then later, as he thrust into her body, he'd said it again, his voice rough with passion. And it had been the last coherent thing he said before he fell asleep on her breast.

Ryan Loved Rebecca.

It was carved on her heart in capital letters but she hadn't been able to say it back to him, despite the questions visible in his eyes as he waited for her to offer the same words.

Why?

During the confrontation with Carol she had accepted the truth behind his words and had learned how much she had come to trust him. He was a lover and a man like no other. Why had she hurt him by holding back the words he wanted to hear? Becky thought back over the months since she'd met Ryan and knew the answer.

She was a coward.

Whichever way she twisted and turned in an effort to avoid the truth, she knew she loved him. By not saying the words, she had subconsciously tried to keep a barrier between her heart and the possibility Ryan would hurt her. It wouldn't work. She was only hurting them both.

She felt a weight lift off her soul as she made her decision to take the last step toward him and what they might have together.

'Becky? Why are you out here?'

She glanced over her shoulder. He stood behind her, yawning, gloriously naked.

'I was restless and didn't want to wake you.'

Ryan stretched his hands over his head and yawned again until his jaw cracked. 'You should've woken me.' He dropped his hands and leered happily. 'We could've made good use of the time.'

'I love you, Ryan.' She stood and faced him.

Shock wiped the silly expression from his face. He took two steps forward then stopped. 'I'm not sure whether to grab you and kiss you madly or collapse in shock on the nearest flat surface.'

'I'm sorry I didn't tell you sooner but . . .'

He grabbed her and wrapped his arms around her as if he would never let her go, burying his face in her neck. 'Don't be sorry. I don't care why you hesitated to tell me, I'm just glad you finally did. Oh, baby, you make me so . . .'

'Please, let me finish.'

He relaxed his grip on her enough to allow him to see her face.

'It's important to me.'

He nodded, then scooped her into his arms and sat down, arranging her carefully on his lap. When her naked bottom came into intimate contact with his rising manhood he gasped but swallowed bravely.

'Fire away.'

'I was afraid. I thought . . .' She felt him squirming. 'Am I hurting you?'

'No,' he wheezed. 'Hurry.'

She twisted a little until she could look in his face and he moaned.

'Are you okay?' she asked.

'The woman I love told me she loves me and now she's squirming practically naked in my lap but she wants to talk.' He shrugged philosophically. 'But, hey, I can take it.' His erection nudged upward as he spoke.

She choked back a laugh. A serious talk could wait until later. Anticipation shivered up her spine. Yes, much, much later, she promised herself.

'I'm glad,' she said, oh so innocently, 'because I have so much I want to tell you.' And she wiggled a little, more purposefully this time. 'It might take hours and hours and hours and . . .'

He groaned. 'Becky, please hurry. Or I'm going to embarrass myself right here.'

'We can't have that.' She turned until she was kneeling astride his lap and gradually lowered herself until her wet softness was teasing at his hardness.

'Becky . . .' Her name was a long drawn out moan of agony. His head fell back, and his fingers clenched on her hips.

'I . . .' She whispered as she sank a little lower and this time they both gasped as he entered her.

'Love . . .' She stopped when he was deep inside, so deep she knew she'd never feel empty again.

'You . . .' And she began to move.

'If you wangled a day off on a Monday, why are you at the mall with me and the kids?' Becky waved at Nicky where he balanced on the top rung of the climbing poles. 'Be careful!'

'What's up with Eric?' Jan winced as a group of toddlers squealed at a nearby table. 'Any sign of the money he owes you and the bank?'

'He's called a couple of times. To ask for money.'

'Doesn't that guy have any grasp on reality?'

'I guess not. When I tried to talk to him about the mortgage payments he pretended we had a bad connection and hung up. Now tell me why you're here.'

'You're here, aren't you?'

'I don't have much choice. School's closed for the day. Spending a few rainy hours at the indoor playground wears the kids out a little so I can have some peace for the rest of the day.'

'You know why I'm here, Becky. You are going to tell me what happened Saturday night. I've waited two days for all the gory details and I refuse to wait any longer. Now you're playing games with me.' She swirled a French fry in the puddle of ketchup beside her burger and pointed it at Becky. 'It's not nice to toy with Auntie Jan's curiosity. I canceled a date so I could stay overnight with all those kids and this is the thanks I get.'

'I thanked you. Ryan sent you flowers this morning. I'd say that was a handsome acknowledgment.'

'Now, Becky, you know what I mean. I set you two up and I insist that you keep me informed about the relationship's progress.'

'Isn't your own life complicated enough?'

'Not at the moment.'

'Oh, Jan! Did you break up with . . . with . . .'

'His name is Stanley. And, no, I didn't. As a matter of fact, things are going pretty good. Stan's a really nice guy. Caring, giving, loving . . .' She dipped another fry in the ketchup and her eyes glinted while she slowly, suggestively, put it between her lips.

Becky glanced around to see if anybody had observed Jan's actions, then she chuckled. 'You're crazy. Am I to assume this guy might last a while?'

'He might.' She leaned forward and lowered her voice. 'Sometimes . . . late at night when I'm alone . . . I'm scared, Becky. It's good with Stan. Almost like it was with Ralph.'

'Jan – '

'What if I lose him, too?'

'Maybe instead of worrying about the end, you should stop comparing him to a dead man.'

'I don't – '

'You do. You compare all the men you date to Ralph. Or rather, to your memories of Ralph.'

'What's that supposed to mean?'

'Ralph wasn't perfect, Jan. He had faults like any other man. But you seem to have forgotten them over the years.'

'How can you say – '

'I liked him, too, because he made you happy. But what about the yardwork that had to be meticulous? What about the hours he spent watching sports on television?' She pointed a pickle at Jan. 'He wouldn't dance.'

'Petty annoyances.'

'What about the motorcycles?' The pickle crunched emphatically as she bit into it. 'How many times did you ask him to stop racing?'

'Rebecca Marie Hansen! How could you . . .'

Becky sat back and bowed her head meekly to the storm. Hopefully by the time Jan finished scolding she would forget to ask any more questions about Saturday night. Even better, perhaps she would take Becky's observations to heart and really think about allowing Ralph's ghost to come down off that undeserved pedestal.

The poor guy had been nice enough. And he'd certainly loved Jan right up to the day he died on a dirt race track one hot Sunday afternoon in Oregon. Too bad the accident happened right after he'd lied to her about spending the weekend with his old granny when he'd really been there to compete. Too bad they'd had a blistering argument only the week before about his racing and he'd promised to quit.

'. . . and don't think I'm going to let you change the subject. We were discussing you and Ryan, not my love life. Who are you to talk about comparing men? You've done it for years. You wouldn't even give Ryan a chance because he reminded you of Eric.'

'He's nothing like Eric.'

'Sure, you admit that now.'

'What do you want from me?'

Jan ceremoniously slid aside the tray that held the remnants of her lunch and leaned across the table. She moved Becky's milkshake and gripped her hands. 'I want the whole truth and nothing but the truth,' she intoned solemnly.

'Carol Hill was at the restaurant . . . with Harold Pastin.'

'I think Hallie's mentioned him. Isn't he the guy who hates Ryan?'

'Yeah. As soon as Ryan saw them together, all lovey dovey, he knew who'd betrayed him. When we decided to leave, things got nasty.' She shivered. 'Pastin is creepy.'

'I think a heck of a lot more happened that night than a run-in with those two.'

Becky pulled her hands free and picked up the milkshake. She gulped too fast and pain bloomed in her temples. 'Urrghh!'

'What's the matter?'

'Give me some of your coffee, quick.' She grabbed Jan's mug and swallowed a mouthful, then pressed her palms to her face and waited a few seconds until the ache subsided. 'Darn, I hate ice cream headaches.'

'Evasion won't work, my dear.'

'You're a nag,' she scowled. 'He told me he loves me.'

'And then you said . . . what?'

Becky opened her mouth to speak but no words came out. Shock gave way to anger as she stared across the restaurant at the group of teenagers loitering outside the record store.

'And then . . .?' Jan prompted

'I told him to stay away from that guy.'

'You told Ryan to do what?'

'Not Ryan. Mike.' Her fingers tightened on the milkshake in her hands, squeezing until the thick liquid bubbled over the edges of the paper cup. 'That guy's real bad news. He makes my skin crawl.'

'Who?' Jan twisted in her seat, scanning the crowded mall until she saw Mike.

'The white-haired kid. Joe Brasky. He dropped by the house once to talk to Mike.'

'Pretty boy. He's got to be at least eighteen.'

'He's nineteen but still in school. He's failed a grade at least three times according to school legend, as reported by my admiring son. Why do teenage boys consider anyone so obviously a failure to be "cool"?'

'What does he want with a gaggle of twelve and thirteen year olds?'

'Ego.' Becky glared. 'There's a whole group of young boys who look up to him, think he's so damned wonderful. Around them he's Mr Big Shot. Most of his gang are sixteen and older.'

'Is he a bad kid?'

'That day he came to my home it seemed to me he was checking out whether we were worth robbing. And when he looked at me . . .'

'Insolent?'

'Worse. Like I was naked and available. Made me ill.'

'What are you going to do now?'

'It obviously did no good to forbid Mike to hang out with them. It's time to go home.' Becky began gathering the litter from lunch. 'I'll drop this stuff in the garbage. While I go get Mike will you collect the other three kids?'

'I don't think having his mommy drag him away is going to separate your son from his new friends. I'm getting an idea.' Jan propped her chin on her hand while she thought. 'Wouldn't you agree Mike is fond of me, like an aunt?'

'You've always been his favorite.' Becky put her hands on her hips. 'And not merely because you treat him to Canucks hockey games.'

'Wait here.' Jan picked up her bag and went into the washroom.

Becky finished clearing the table. She'd decided not to wait any longer when Jan reappeared. Her coppery hair had become artfully disordered, her lips scarlet and her eyes emphasized by thick black liner. She'd removed her bulky sweater and wore only a white exercise leotard with her jeans. She sauntered back to the table, hips swaying seductively, sex personified.

'Well?

'What the heck are you doing?'

'The trick is to show Mike exactly how puny and stupid Brasky really is. A guy like him will always put his foot in his mouth . . . if you give him the opportunity.' Jan dropped the sweater and her purse on the table. 'Take care of these for a moment.'

Becky watched as Jan strolled over to Mike. She put her hand on his shoulder, said a few words, and pointed back toward the restaurant.

Brasky eyed Jan's body, nudged his buddies, grinned cockily, then spoke. Mike looked shocked by his friend's comments, then confused.

She couldn't hear what Jan replied but her contempt was clear even from a distance. Then Jan and Mike walked away.

Anger swept across Brasky's face as the group around him roared with laughter.

'Was that smart?' Becky asked Jan as soon as she reached the table. Mike had gone to collect the younger kids from the indoor playground.

'It was effective.'

'Mike looked so unhappy.' Becky clenched her hands. She hated it when her children were hurting. She felt so helpless.

'Yes, he is. Disillusion is always painful. That doesn't make it a bad thing.' She pulled the sweater over her head and picked up her purse. 'He apologized and made excuses for his friend's remarks. But the next time that guy pulls something similar, Mike will start to see him for what he really is. It won't be long before your son will find new friends.'

While they packed up and went home Becky couldn't get Jan's words out of her head.

Disillusion *was* painful. But she was right. It wasn't always a bad thing.

Becky looked up from the menu when she heard his voice in the noise emanating from the area around the hostess desk. At last.

Two weeks had passed since their wonderful night alone at his apartment and she was not looking forward to another evening of frustration for them both. They had agreed to be discreet which meant spending time as a family. She simply had to convince her body to be sensible.

'Ryan, over here.' She waved one hand in the air until he turned in their direction and smiled. He bent his head slightly to say something to the hostess, then walked to where she and the kids occupied two booths near the back wall.

'Hi.' He winked as he slid onto the bench opposite her.

'Hi.' She smiled and laid down the menu as she slid one hand across the table to clasp his. 'This was a good idea. The kids have been in seventh heaven ever since you called and said you were treating us all to dinner at Oscar's tonight. They love it here.'

He looked over at the kids' table where all four munched on crackers. The younger three were drawing with crayons on paper supplied by the restaurant. Even Mike seemed to have put aside his poor attitude for once and was enjoying himself as he helped Nicky trace his way through the printed maze.

'Why the crackers?'

'It keeps their tummies and mouths occupied until the food arrives.'

'Good idea, but let's order fast before they start complaining that their food supply has been cut off.'

Becky waited patiently while six meals were ordered. She waited not quite so patiently while he talked about work until his beer and her glass of wine were set in front of them.

'Okay, that's enough.'

He put down his beer. 'What's enough?'

'You have been chattering aimlessly for the last twenty minutes but that grin tells me something is up. What are we celebrating?'

'I can't fool you, can I?' he asked with a smile.

'No. Come on, 'fess up.'

'Something kind of funny happened.'

'Funny, ha ha, or funny, strange?'

'Funny weird. At least it felt weird to me.'

'Well, what is it?' Becky glanced over at the other table. 'Put the salt down, Nicky.'

'You're hungry. It can wait until after the food comes.'

'Talk, buster.'

'The police called me. They arrested Harold Pastin yesterday.'

'Arrested? What happened?'

'Stupidity. He told his staff he'd come up with a new inventory program, then asked one of my former employees to work on it. Pastin knew that once Paul worked on the program any changes he made would alter it enough from my original so I couldn't prove anything.' He fell silent while the waiter served the salads and put a basket of rolls in the middle of each table.

'What he didn't know was that Paul still felt some loyalty to me and, despite the huge paycheck, was regretting the move because of Pastin's shady methods.' Ryan grinned. 'When Paul recognized my technique he called the cops and turned over the disks.'

'Is Mr Pastin still in jail?'

'The company lawyer bailed him out last night.' He paused. 'Today PasComm was absorbed by a New York conglomerate.'

She shushed the kids without taking her eyes off him. 'Why?'

'The board of directors didn't like PasComm's president and chairman to be associated with even a whisper of wrong-doing. They couldn't overlook an actual arrest.'

'How could they get rid of him? I thought he owned the company.'

'It seems that Pastin was in the middle of a fast, slightly illegal deal. He'd given Carol nominal control of some PasComm shares. This morning she took advantage of a loophole and sold them out from under him. Left with only twenty-four percent of the remaining shares he was voted out of his position as chairman of the board and fired.' He sipped some beer and buttered one of the buns.

'Stop eating and tell me what happened.'

'For some strange reason I'm ravenous.' His sharp teeth crunched on a celery stalk. 'A member of the board called the police anonymously to report the illegal deal and Pastin was arrested again. This time PasComm's lawyer didn't return his call so I gather he's still in jail.'

'That's . . . that's . . . weird, all right.'

'There's more.'

'More?'

'This afternoon he called his wife. When she and her lawyer arrived to bail him out, she discovered he'd lost his job and the company. Then she found out about his affair with Carol. The detective told me that, after a screaming fit that rattled the police station's windows, she threatened to take him for everything he owned. She left with the lawyer, supposedly to file for divorce. Then Carol was arrested.'

Becky choked on a mouthful of salad. She gulped some water while Ryan patted her on the back. 'Oh, my Lord . . . why?' she asked as soon as she could speak.

'With nothing more to lose and a lot of rage to spew, Pastin gave the police documented proof of Carol's criminal actions while she was his mistress.'

'Oh, my God. Was there anything about robbing you?'

'I don't know yet. The detective wants me to go down to the station first thing in the morning. I do know that with Pastin and Carol out of the way, things should smooth out some at the office.'

'This is so . . .' Becky looked at him, an odd little smile twisting her lips. 'See I told you. The Golden Rule. It always works. We all get back what we give.'

'I expected to feel jubilant or avenged or something. But I didn't feel much of anything at all except relief.'

'That's understandable. You got on with your life and forgot about them.'

'I guess I did to a certain extent. You've been keeping me busy.' At that moment the waiter arrived with their orders so he sat back until they had all been served. 'Punishing Pastin didn't seem so vital any more.'

She looked up from where she was carefully drizzling vinegar over her French fries. 'That's because it isn't.'

He took the bottle out of her hands then nudged the straw baskets containing their fried chicken to one side so he could hold both her hands.

'I love you, Becky.' His voice was clear and not at all hushed in deference to their public location. Luckily the kids were involved in a fight over the vinegar and ketchup.

She blushed a little and glanced around self-consciously at the other diners before she smiled at him. 'And I love you,' she whispered.

'You've helped me to learn what is really important and I owe you for that.'

'Ryan,' she said, her eyes glinting warningly. 'You're not going to give . . .'

'No, no presents. Only my love.'

She curled her fingers into his and squeezed tightly. 'And mine, honey. And mine. Besides, it's my turn.'

'Your turn?'

'To give you a present.'

'What – '

'Tomorrow night, love. Tomorrow.'

Becky hovered nervously in her room, half-afraid to go downstairs. All the kids, even Dani, had been invited for a birthday party sleep-over next door.

Ryan waited for her downstairs, probably setting up the video machine as planned. For some reason his expensive shirts and designer jeans didn't seem so out of place in her home as they used to.

Beer for him and wine coolers for her were chilling in the fridge. Only half-an-hour ago she had made a big bowl of popcorn and set it on the coffee table.

She sniffed. A trace of smoke drifted in the air. He must have built a fire. What had he thought when he saw the cushions she'd piled on the floor, a nest for them to lie in? She listened carefully until she heard the faint spit and crackle of burning wood.

Why was she so jittery tonight? Other than the absence of the kids, everything was the same as other times they'd talked late into the night. Everything was the same except one thing. What she wore. Tonight she had determined on a new role for herself in their relationship.

She wiped damp palms down her sides and turned to face her reflection. In one corner of her bedroom stood the massive mirror she had inherited from her great-grandmother, its oval surface wavy and splotched.

She studied her image. Did she dare wear this? The role of seducer was new to her but Ryan had taught her so much. Had given her so much. Dear Lord, she felt absurdly young again. Desirable and feminine. Scared.

No. Make that terrified. When Ryan told her he'd dreamed of her in pink silk and white cotton she'd laughed, flattered to think she starred in his fantasies.

Her whim to make the fantasy into a reality had grown from a scene in a book she'd read.

She wore the pink silk nightgown he gave her. But over it she wore the new robe she had sewn last week. Of white polished cotton, it fell to the ground in graceful folds. The sash, the lapels and the quilted insets on the shoulders were made of a deep rose silk. The gown's lace bodice showed at the deep opening between the lapels.

Embarrassment at her own daring made her cheeks as rosy as the gown. She chewed her lip in misgiving. Should she wear it or not? Behind her reflected image she caught sight of the jeans and blouse she had worn all day. Normally she would have kept them on for her evening with Ryan.

She recognized and hated her uncertainty. Believe in yourself, she thought. Resolution filled her and she left the bedroom before she could change her mind. She had made this robe with Ryan in mind and she would wear it for him.

Ryan shoved another log on the fire, closed the screen doors and stretched out on the pillows he'd found piled so cosily on the floor. She must have gathered them from all over the house. He picked up the icy beer and took a long swallow, then crunched on a handful of popcorn while he remembered the first time he'd seen Becky, almost in this very spot. He had wanted to touch her then and he yearned to touch her now.

No matter how often they made love, each time he wanted her more. It was a miracle she wanted him, loved him. She was warm and caring, loyal and passionate. Special, so special.

As soon as they were married, he would buy her everything her heart desired.

Idly he put his hand on his pocket and, through the fabric, rubbed the small metal object he had put there earlier. He was a different man lately. Not so driven, thanks to Becky. No woman had ever loved him so openly, so completely. He would try to make sure it would always stay this way.

He heard a footstep and knew she was there. He turned his head and looked to where she stood in the shadows at the end of the room. The flickering light of the fire picked out the gleam of her curls and the shimmer of white fabric.

Keeping her gaze steady on him, she reached behind her and pushed shut the double doors. The lock snicked as she turned the small brass knob.

When she smiled he straightened to sit upright among the pillows. He could see her chest move as she inhaled deeply and released it in a breathy sigh. She inched forward, stopping when she stood in the circle of light cast by the flames.

His breath caught and held. Becky's bare toes peeked out from beneath the hem of a white robe that glimmered as she moved. Pink framed the upper curves of her breasts and her slender neck. Her nervous grin hovered and white teeth bit at her bottom lip.

At first he was so stunned he couldn't speak, then he breathed her name. 'Becky?'

'Do you like it?'

'Like it? Yes, Ma'am. Come here.' He put down his beer and stretched out one hand. She laid her fingers in his and he pulled her down beside him until she lay against the cushions in a pool of white.

'Where did you find it?'

'I made it. To wear for you.'

'It's beautiful. You're beautiful. I've got something else I want you to wear for me.'

'Not another present, I hope. You're far too extravagant.' She struggled to sit up, protesting all the while, but he kissed her until she weakened and fell back in his arms.

'No, it's not a present.' He stuck his hand in the front pocket of his jeans with some difficulty because they were considerably tighter than they'd been before Becky walked into the room.

'This,' he said and held up an exquisite pear-shaped diamond solitaire.

'Oh, Ryan,' she breathed.

'Will you marry me?'

'Oh, Ryan.'

'I love you.'

'Oh, Ryan.' She blinked so she could see his face without the obscuring fog of looming tears.

'Is that all you can say? I'd much rather hear "Oh, yes" than "Oh, Ryan".'

'What will the kids say?'

'I like your kids. They seem to like Dani and me. We can live here, if you want. I'll pay off the mortgage and you'll be rid of that idiot bank manager.'

She flung her arms around his neck, laughing and crying at the same time. 'Should we? Are you sure?'

'Yes, I'm sure.' He kissed her then pulled her left hand from behind his neck. 'Can I put this ring on your finger?'

'Oh, Ryan.' Becky grinned when he pretended to frown. 'I mean, yes. Oh, yes.'

'I love you, cross my heart.' He put the ring on her finger, then kissed the knuckle. 'Now, where were we?'

'Right here.' She slid one finger down his neck, pausing to test the fast pulse, venturing on to play with the mat of hair curled in the open neck of his shirt. She toyed with the top button before slipping it loose.

'There's one thing,' her breath whispered across his skin, 'I am paying off my mortgage. Not you. You have enough to worry about with the hassles at your office. I can take care of my own problems, understand?'

'I don't like the idea of you struggling to pay off all that money when it would be so easy for me to . . .'

'No. No. No.' Her pointed finger prodded his chest on each denial. 'And I don't want to hear about this again.'

He hesitated, studying the determination in her eyes. Then he relaxed and smiled. 'Whatever you say.'

He'd leave it for a while until he could change her mind. But if he couldn't convince her to let him pay it off, he'd do it anyway and persuade her he was right after the fact. 'What about Eric?'

'What about him?'

'Yesterday Nicky told me his dad called you. Where is he? Was he bothering you for money again? I'll talk to him, tell him to stop – '

'Eric is a small problem and definitely not yours.'

'I need to make sure he never comes near you again.'

'He won't. He wasn't even in Canada when he called. Now, stop bringing up all these depressing subjects. I want to make love.'

Ryan smiled, mentally added Eric to the list of things he'd take care of later, and drew one hand down her back, caressing her spine through the layers of cloth.

She pressed a kiss to the hollow of his throat, her tongue darting out to taste him. She undid all the buttons on his shirt, tempting, teasing him with small kisses after every one. He stirred and reached for her but she pushed his hands away.

'No. Tonight I want to make love to you.'

He leaned back. 'I'm all yours, lady.'

CHAPTER 13

She nudged the shirt from his shoulders then started on one broad shoulder and kissed her way down his body. She reached his lean stomach and he groaned when her fingers tugged at the brass button on his waistband. She paused.

'Ryan?'

'Don't stop, honey. Never stop.'

The button was stiff so she slipped her fingers inside the waistband to work on it. Her fingers combed through the wiry curls below his navel and he sucked in a gasp of air as her fingernails grazed him.

His face felt tight and his fingers dug into the pillows at his sides as he resisted the urge to take over. Come on, Becky, it's only a button, he urged her silently. You probably undo them for the kids a hundred times a day.

Finally it popped loose and she slid down the zipper so slowly he moaned as the ache in his groin came close to real pain. At her urging he lifted his hips and she tugged his jeans and briefs down long muscular legs. She dropped a kiss high on his thigh and he trembled as the muscle flexed in response.

Crouched at Ryan's feet, she stared up the lean length of the man she loved. Her gaze traveled up from his toes, her finger tracing the outline of bone and sinew, pausing at his hipbone. He was magnificently and totally aroused. She paused then slid her fingers to his side and on up his body. When Becky's hand reached his chest she met his fixed look. Desire raged in the icy blue depths.

'Touch me, Becky. I burn for you.'

She straddled his thighs. Slowly she brought her hands back down his chest and belly in small massaging circles, moving lower until she held him in her palms. Her fingers stroked satin flesh over steely strength, then she bent until her curls tickled his stomach and tasted him.

His hips arched at the touch of her lips. He couldn't keep his hands off her any longer. He wrapped his hands around her upper arms and slid her into his lap.

Cool silk and cotton dragged across his body, snapping what little control he had left. Ryan growled low in his throat and twisted until she lay underneath him. His hands shook as he yanked open the sash of the robe and pushed the nightgown up to her waist. One savage thrust and he was deep inside.

'I'm . . . sorry . . . I can't . . . wait . . .' The words were dragged from him, each one punctuated by the drive of his body into hers. His mouth swooped down and took possession, his tongue plunging, teasing, taunting her own. His fingers curved under her hips, lifting her to meet his thrusts, even as her body began to shake with passion.

Becky wound her legs around his hips, tasting beer and man, her senses drugged by the building tension. His breath rasped in his throat and she clung to him, fingers digging into his shoulders, something inside her reaching, reaching . . .

His harsh cry echoed in the room, followed immediately by her own, as he drove into her for the last time, his spine arched, his body shaking with the force of his release.

'Wake up, Mom.'

Becky turned over and snuggled her arms around the pillow she held. Her nose burrowed into its fluffy contours, absorbing the lingering scent of Ryan's cologne. So it *was* real. He had been in her bed last night. After their mind-shattering lovemaking in front of the fire, he had come to her bed, where they had made love again and again until dawn.

Too bad Jan was out of town until tomorrow night. She was going to be impossible to live with once she found out her manoeuvring had paid off in an engagement. Becky smiled. She could hardly wait to tell her.

'Mom. Wake up.'

A hand shook her shoulder and Becky jerked upright. She blinked once, twice, then slowly focused on Mike's face.

'I need to talk to you,' he said.

'Whaaat? Mike? Why are you home so soon?'

'Mom, you knew the Jordans were sending us home before they went to church.'

Muddled by the dregs of sleep, she squinted at her clock. 'Is it nine o'clock already?'

'Mooomm.' He dragged out her name in disgust.

'Okay, okay. Give me a minute.' She rubbed her eyes and dragged herself up to sit against the headboard. 'Okay, shoot. What do you want to talk about at nine o'clock on a Sunday morning?'

'My friends make fun of me because I have to walk Nicky and the girls home from school every day.'

'Why?'

'It's baby-sitting.'

'Not cool?'

'No way.'

'But I explained about those bullies tormenting the little kids and you understood. Last week you thought it was a good idea for you to make sure they got home okay.'

'Yeah, I guess.'

'That's not it, is it?' She lay her hand over his on the quilt. 'What's really bothering you, honey?'

'He slept here again. Why is he here, Mom?' His face was white with red blotches burning high on his cheeks. His eyes were glazed with tears, manfully held back. 'I went downstairs to make breakfast so you could stay in bed. He was sleeping on our couch.'

High-pitched giggles and the banging of pots echoed up the stairs.

'It was late when our movie finished so I told him to stay. He had to come back this morning anyway to pick up Dani.'

'But, Mom, he said he'd make breakfast. He told them he'd make French toast and they cheered. They said it was better than ordinary toast.' A single tear trickled down his cheek and he angrily wiped it away.

'Mike, you know Sarah and Nicky love French toast. I don't understand why you're upset. You love it, too.'

He didn't answer and her heart ached at his wounded look. 'Come here.' She patted the bed beside her. 'Tell me what's the matter.'

He sat down on the edge of the bed, carefully beyond arm's length, teeth clenched against the quiver of his lips. He blinked and sniffed.

'Tell me.'

'It's my job to make breakfast on Sunday so you can sleep. Now he's here all the time.'

Very conscious of ring on her finger, she slid her left hand behind Mike and hugged him. 'I thought you were starting to like Ryan.'

'He's okay, I guess. But we don't need him. I can take care of you, Sarah and Nicky.'

'You know you are very special to me. All of you are. But you are old enough to understand how I can love my children and still fall in love with Ryan.'

'You love him?' His voice was tight as he glared at her.

'Yes, I do. Very much. He's asked me to marry him.'

'We were doing great without him. He's only another man. We don't need Dad or Ryan.'

She hesitated, not sure of what to say to show Mike that if she loved Ryan, she wouldn't love Mike or her other kids any less. Her son's pain and anger caught her by surprise and the words didn't come easily.

'Why do you feel this way?'

'He'll hurt you and make you cry. Just like Dad.'

She was horrified. How had she become so caught up in her own feelings she hadn't noticed how much Mike hated Eric and resented Ryan?

How could she show Mike that Ryan was nothing like Eric?

Movement caught her eye and she glanced at the open door. Ryan stood there holding a tray. Breakfast in bed? She melted a little inside. No one had ever made her breakfast in bed in her life.

A quick check assured her Mike couldn't see Ryan. She smiled but warned him away with a slight shake of her head. He balanced the tray on one hand and, with an expressive movement of head and free hand, asked if he should come in.

She hesitated. Should she ask him to join them? Would Mike be hurt if Ryan became part of this conversation or would it help? Finally she shook her head 'no'.

He nodded and blew her a kiss before he left with the tray. Tears misted her vision. As always he accepted her decision without disparaging or questioning her reasoning, as Eric would have done.

'Mike, Ryan is nothing like your father. He likes you and Sarah and Nicky very much. He wants to be a father to them and a friend to you. Please try to understand, honey. I love him.'

'What about Dani?' he asked sullenly.

'She will be like an extra sister. I thought you liked her almost as much as the others do.'

'She's just another girl,' he mumbled.

'Do you dislike Ryan?'

He hunched his shoulders and scowled at the floor. 'He's okay, I guess.'

She cupped her hands around her son's face and pulled him down for her kiss. 'I love you, Mike. Please remember that.'

When the metal of the ring on her finger touched his cheek, Mike grabbed her hand to examine the glittering stone. Hurt and confusion swirled in his eyes.

'You already said yes, didn't you? When were you going to tell me?'

'Ryan only asked me last night while you were next door asleep. We planned to talk to you all together right after breakfast.'

'You don't care about us. I'm never going to use his stupid computer again.' He shoved her away from him and ran to the door. Before he went out he turned and glared with helpless fury. 'If he hurts you I'll kill him. I'm old enough, now.'

'Mike? What are you talking about?' Her question bounced back from the door he had already slammed shut. She listened as his footsteps pounded down the stairs and the front door slammed.

He'd probably gone to complain to his friends. Maybe it was for the best. Give them both time to cool off. Thank God he seemed to have stopped hanging around with that kid who made her skin crawl.

In a few hours Ryan and Dani would go home. Tonight, after the two little ones went to bed, she and Mike could have a long talk without interruptions. They would find a way to work through her son's resentment.

They had to.

Becky buried her face in the pillows. Thank God he didn't actually hate Ryan. She couldn't, she wouldn't, be put in the position of having to choose between hurting her son and sending away the man she loved.

Ryan heard Mike dash down the stairs and out the front door.

'You guys finish your breakfast. When you're done get washed up and turn on the television.'

'Where are you going?' The question came from Sarah, of course.

'To talk to your mother.'

Nicky and Sarah swung around to face each other. Two seconds of silent communication, eye-to-eye, were followed by two sharp nods. Agreement had been reached.

'Ryan?' He winced at the syrupy hand that clutched his pant leg as he passed, then glanced up at Sarah's face. He reflected that, once upon a time, syrup on his clothes would have made him feel violently ill.

'What, Sarah?'

'Can we talk to you, please?'

'I'll be right back. I want to talk to your Mom.'

'No.' The grip on his jeans tightened as he tried to pull away. 'We need to talk to you now.'

He forced down a surge of frustration. If he wanted Becky to fit him into this family, he would have to learn to deal with her children. Mike, Sarah, and Nicky had been Becky's number one priority for years and even if she did marry him, which he knew Mike's attitude made a question rather than a certainty, he would have to learn to accept that fact.

Listening when Sarah wanted to talk was a good start. Ryan glanced once, longingly, down the hall, then sighed and shoved back the swathe of hair that hung over his forehead. 'What is it?'

'Please sit down.'

He swung a chair away from the table, turned it around and straddled it, resting his elbows on its back. 'Shoot.'

He was amazed at the ensuing subtle shift of positions as Dani and Sarah moved to stand one on either side of Nicky. He had no trouble reading their body language. His training in the criminal world followed by a lifetime in the corporate jungle had made him an expert. The two older girls intended to protect the younger kid and they considered Ryan their adversary.

'Do you love our Mommy?' Sarah asked.

He felt his jaw drop. For the first time in his life he'd been caught totally by surprise. Scratch that, he told himself. He'd been continuously stunned ever since he met Rebecca Hansen. Why wouldn't the feeling carry over into his relationship with her kids, too? After all, they were a lot like their mother. Especially Sarah.

What should he do? Put off this conversation or be honest? A picture of Becky, upstairs alone, worried and upset after talking to her son flashed into his mind. His chin firmed. She'd had enough for now. He could get through this conversation without her.

Maybe the worst would be over before she came down.

'Yes, I do.'

'Do you like us? As much as you like Dani, I mean.' He heard some roughness in Sarah's smooth self-possession. 'I know she's your girl but could you like us, too?'

Taken aback, he studied Dani. Her mouth was tight, her total attention riveted on his face.

Was she his? He thought back over the time that had passed since he'd 'inherited' her and realized, yes, he did consider Dani to be his. He had been careful of her physical comfort but was it enough?

'Dani?'

'Yes, Ryan.'

'Would you come here?' Dani obediently circled the scarred wooden table to stand at his side.

'Remember the conversation we had a few weeks after the first time we came to this house to meet the Hansens? About what you should call me?'

'Yes.'

'I was wrong. I would be honored if you would call me Dad.'

Dani stood silent and unmoving for so long he grew afraid he'd left this too late or misjudged what she wanted. Then she slowly nodded and her body shook with a soul-deep sob. He swept her into a hug, pressing her head to his shoulder.

'Are you my girl, Dani?' he whispered.

Unable to speak, she nodded. He gave himself up to the stranglehold she had on his neck. Then, still holding her loosely in his arms, he considered Sarah, who was grinning with smug satisfaction.

'Sarah?' His harsh tone and stern expression wiped away her smile until she saw the amusement in his eyes. When she grinned he saw that a new tooth had poked through her gum, half filling the empty gap.

'Yes?'

'I like Mike and Nicky and you. Very much.'

The three of them smiled at each other and him, then grew very serious before Sarah spoke again. He braced himself for whatever might come.

'We all like you very much, too. Except for Mike. He's acting a little weird right now.' He could see her pondering that mystery, then she seemed to decide it wasn't worth worrying about.

'We were wondering . . . if you would please marry us?' The last words whooshed out in one breath. A fiery blush rose in her cheeks but she stood straight and tall, calmly waiting for his answer.

Ryan was lost. Should he tell them Becky had already agreed to marry him or did she want to tell them herself? Or would she change her mind because of Mike? He couldn't say yes to these kids, if she had decided to give him back his ring.

Questions ran in circles through his brain, making him dizzy. If he handled this wrong, he might screw things up with Becky. Royally. Oh, God. Why had he decided to handle this conversation by himself?

While he remained silent, Sarah's cheeks went white, Nicky lost his grin, and Dani's shoulders sagged. Frantic, he tried to think of what to say. Dani pulled out of his arms and went to stand with the others.

Ryan cursed his own indecision.

Becky crawled out of bed, yanking on jeans and the first shirt that came to hand. She had to go downstairs and have a talk with Ryan. They had to decide how to deal with Mike.

In the hall outside the kitchen door she stopped and sagged against the wall when she heard Sarah speaking to Ryan.

'Do you love our Mommy?'

She felt like she was living through several lifetimes worth of agony while she waited for his answer.

'Yes, I do.'

She started to breathe again when she heard the strength of purpose in his voice.

After a minute she edged closer so she could see into the room. Ryan sat with his back to her at the table and the kids were out of sight around the corner. Should she go in and rescue him from Sarah's inquisition?

No. If he became part of this family, he would have to learn to deal with this little quirk in Sarah's personality.

Besides, she was curious how he would hold up, three against one.

But she almost broke into the conversation when she heard Sarah's next question about Dani and she loved him the more for the honest way he dealt with the little girl. Then she slid bonelessly to a crouch against the wall when Sarah asked Ryan to marry them.

Why didn't he answer them? Had he changed his mind?

It was a few seconds before she realized he couldn't answer the question without talking to her first. He couldn't say yes, he couldn't say no. He didn't know how to explain.

She stood up and inched her way into the room. The children noticed her but didn't acknowledge her presence. With their whole being, they were waiting for his answer.

Ryan, unaware Becky stood directly behind him, felt inept. Damn it! Where were his vaunted negotiating skills now? But he knew the answer to that one. They had deserted him because he cared so much about this family. This was not merely another business deal.

A kiss feathered over his ear and Becky's hand slid around his shoulder to rest soothingly over the frenzied beating of his heart when she came to stand at his side.

'Will you, Ryan? Will you marry "us"? Because I love you with all my heart.'

He turned his head to look up into the velvety brown eyes of the woman he adored, then relaxed and leaned sideways to rest his cheek on her breast.

'Yes. I will.'

Becky kissed him. The kids dashed around the table, laughing and cheering, and leaped on him. The kitchen chair crashed over sideways.

Ryan spent the first hours of his engagement in the emergency room of the local hospital getting eight stitches in the back of his head where his scalp had connected with the business end of Nicky's toy bulldozer.

'Hi. I didn't expect to see you.' Jan's smile was thin, her tone one of false cheer as she took a moment to hug Becky. Then she grabbed a cart for her suitcases and began jostling for position beside the airport's luggage carousel.

'I really wanted to tell you something and when Stan couldn't come – '

'The flight was good though I'm glad I didn't waste my money on first class. Judging by the noise coming from the front of the plane, somebody up there was drunk and disorderly.'

Becky stepped out of the way of one man balancing two sets of skis on his shoulder and carrying a huge duffel bag slung from the other. With four flights all arriving at the same time, the airport was rather more crowded than she expected it to be in the middle of the night. She glanced around and sighed with envy. All these people traveling to and fro.

When she'd parked the car earlier and walked toward the terminal the people streaming by her on their way out to the parking lots were tanned, smiling, and wearing flower leis, obviously on their way home from Hawaii. The down'n mean jealousy had felt like a punch in the stomach.

She'd never been any further south than Portland or further east than Saskatoon. Saskatoon and Portland had been interesting but she didn't believe they could compare to Hawaii.

'You didn't have to come and get me.' Jan stood on tiptoe and scanned the ramp down which the luggage would come. 'I could've taken a taxi home.'

'When Stan called – '

'My suitcase is so full I thought I'd never get it closed. I bought some great things for the little monsters. I might even get a hug from Mike when he sees the hockey jerseys. They were such a deal, I bought two. Nicky's present is . . .' she paused and glanced sideways at Becky, 'well, plenty of time to show you that later.'

'You don't have to give them – '

Jan waved her hand in a shushing gesture. 'I wanted to. I bought Sarah this cunning little jewelry box with secret compartments. It's going to drive Nicky crazy when he snoops in her room.' Her laugh was brittle. 'I bought one for Dani, too. Have to keep things equal, especially if you and Ryan smarten up and make them sisters.'

'Nicky doesn't – '

'Yes, he does. He's nosy as heck but so darned clever about it you don't catch him. Oh, there it is, the big red one.' She moved closer to where the suitcases trundled slowly down the ramp. Hers wobbled for a moment, then tipped over to slide down to the rim of the moving carousel.

'Let me help – '

'No, no. I've got it.'

She could tell Jan was hurt by Stan's absence. Now she refused to listen as Becky related his reasons. Time to change tactics.

'No.' She blocked Jan as she leaned forward to grab the suitcase's handle. Immediately another woman elbowed in to take her spot.

'Why did you do that? Now we'll have to wait for it to go around again.'

'It's not going to disappear forever.' Becky waited until her friend stopped glaring after the red case. 'You haven't let me finish a sentence since you got off the plane.'

Jan looked startled, then rueful. 'I haven't, have I?'

'No, you haven't. And furthermore,' she crossed her arms and looked stern, 'we're not taking that suitcase out of this airport until you tell me what disgusting gadget you bought for Nicky this time.'

'Look, Becky, it's a simple toy.'

'A simple toy that does what? Last time you bought him trick candies that tasted like hot peppers. The time before it was a pen that squirted fake ink back onto the chest of the unwary user unless they pushed the secret button. That one earned us a session with his school principal.'

'I said I was sorry about that.'

Becky lowered her brows and waited. If Jan sensed even a glimmer of weakening on her part, there would be no end to this debate.

'Fine. I'll tell him if he takes this one to school I won't bring him another treat until he's twenty-two. Good enough?'

'That depends. How nasty is this one?'

'I guarantee there will be no lasting damage or stains.'

'Okay. You can give it to him.' Becky shoved her hands in her coat pockets. 'Aren't you going to ask me where Stan is?'

'Nope.'

'You're not the least curious why I'm here instead of him?'

'Nope.' Jan's feet shifted restlessly. 'Here comes my suitcase.'

'I don't believe you.'

'Fine.'

Becky grabbed her sleeve and pulled. Jan's fingers closed on air as the handle slid smoothly past. She swore as she again lost her place in front of the machinery spewing out suitcases.

'Look, Becky, can't you wait until we're in the car to tell me I've been dumped?'

'You haven't been dumped.'

'Look. Stan and I had a . . . a slight disagreement before I left but he promised he'd be here. He's not. I'd say that sends a very clear message.'

'That's why he called me. Although he described your "slight disagreement" as a doozy of a fight. He knew you'd imagine the worst if he wasn't here. But his sister and her kids were in a car accident near Williams Lake and he had to drive up there to take charge of things.'

Jan stopped watching for the suitcase. 'I've been a selfish idiot, haven't I? Are they badly hurt?'

'No. He called an hour ago and everyone's going to be okay. His sister and two of her kids were shaken up with a few cuts and bruises. Her little boy has a slight concussion but the hospital is only keeping him overnight to be safe.'

'I feel terrible. I was thinking all these bad things about him while he . . .' Her body sagged as the thinly concealed anger and fear seeped away.

'You were tired and cranky. Besides, no one except me will ever know what you thought.'

Becky noticed the approaching red case out of the corner of her eye and reached between a fat man and a skinny teenager to snag the handle as it passed. As she set it on the cart the latches snapped open and the contents erupted into the air.

It was as if the next few seconds passed in slow motion. They watched, stunned and helpless, as Jan's clothes rose over their heads before settling to the dusty floor around the feet of the other people waiting for luggage. Assorted items of her clothing festooned the surrounding carts. The skinny teenager blushed furiously when a bra landed on his shoulder. Her cosmetic bag slammed into the fat man's back as if it had been shot from a cannon.

The strange silence that had accompanied the explosion of the suitcase was followed abruptly by laughter as everyone in the immediate area helped gather Jan's belongings. Even the skinny teenager helped until he found himself with a handful of silky panties. Then he turned an even brighter shade of red, dumped them into Jan's suitcase, and fled. A woman offered a plastic bag to hold the excess that wouldn't fit now the items were no longer folded.

By the time they scooped up everything and thanked those who had helped, Jan had shaken off her dejection. When they left the arrivals area she was as volatile as ever, claiming if she didn't get a chocolate bar she was going to faint.

They were passing the immense glass wall that separated the lounge area from the aeroplanes when Jan noticed the diamond on Becky's left hand as she carried the suitcase.

Her squeal was pitched slightly higher and louder than the engine of the Lear jet preparing to take off on the other side of the glass. She dropped her bags and flung her arms around Becky's neck in a wild hug. Becky laughed but shushed her as they drew the attention of every person in the area, including the security guards.

'You finally did it, didn't you? That sly dog. He must've kept it a secret from Hallie. Why didn't you tell me? What did the kids say? When's the wedding? What are you going to wear?'

'How about you ask one question at a time?' Becky picked up the bags, handed her the suitcase, and nudged her into walking again. 'It happened while you were gone. The kids all think it's great except Mike. He seems really angry.'

'You're not considering canceling the whole thing because of Mike, are you?'

'It crossed my mind but how can I? I really love Ryan and so do Nicky and Sarah. Dani asked me if she could please call me Mom after the wedding, like the other kids. If I did what Mike wants, five people would be made unhappy.'

'Have you asked Mike why he doesn't want you to marry Ryan?'

'He's not being too receptive when I ask him to talk to me about his feelings but I intend to keep trying. I've just got to find the right moment.'

'If you want me to talk to him, let me know. I'll get him alone at a hockey game where he might tell his Auntie Jan what the problem is.' Jan hugged Becky with her free arm. 'Don't worry. We'll figure something out.'

'I'm going to wear Grandmother's debutante dress.'

'What dress?'

'The one in the picture on the mantel in my bedroom. Years ago, when I was a little girl, she had it specially packed so it would stay nice until I was an adult. She said it was her wedding gift to me since she knew she probably wouldn't be here when I was old enough to get married.'

'But you didn't wear it when you married Eric.'

'No, I didn't, did I? I wonder why?'

'Probably because in your heart you knew you were making a bad move.'

'Perhaps,' Becky said. She fished her keys out of her purse as they entered the parking lot. 'I think the car's down this way.'

'Have you chosen a date or where you're going to have the ceremony?'

'We've decided to have a small civil ceremony at Lilac House with only a few good friends.'

'Absolutely not. You're going to have a Cinderella wedding this time even if I have to organize the whole thing myself. Between the groom's bad attitude and your parents' dislike of the groom, you didn't get to have a real wedding when you married that jerk, Eric.'

'It was all we could afford. I was perfectly satisfied.'

'Satisfied isn't good enough. This time we're doing it up with all the pomp I can afford. No, no, no,' she overrode Becky's protest, 'I'm not going to listen to you preach economy this time, my dear. If I have to, I'll let Sarah loose on to you.'

'Oh no, not her, anybody but her.' Becky pretended to cringe in terror, then unlocked the car.

'Uh, huh. So you'd better behave.'

'Seriously, though, it's important to me to be married in the front parlor at Lilac House.'

'I know. You've only talked about it since we were kids.'

'Will you be my maid-of-honor?'

'Of course I will. Just try to stop me.'

Jan dropped her suitcase in the back seat. As they climbed into the front and fastened their seatbelts, she spoke. 'Eric.'

'What about Eric?' Becky asked.

'I wonder what he's going to say when he finds out you're getting married again.'

'There's really no doubt. He'll swear – '

'– never to pay you another penny for those kids,' Jan finished the sentence for her. 'And if he finds out Ryan has money, he'll probably try to sue you for support.'

'Even he wouldn't have that much gall.' Becky started the car and pulled out of the parking lot.

'Don't count on it.'

'Let's not talk about him any longer, it gives me a stomach ache. Time to go home. I've got a long day tomorrow and I need my sleep. I promised to sew matching dresses for two little girls we know and love.'

CHAPTER 14

'Hello, Becka.'

Becky's hands froze on the fabric she was feeding through the sewing machine. Only Eric used that version of her name.

'It's been a while,' he said.

The machine began to whine against the pull she was exerting but it wasn't until the needle snapped that her foot lifted from the peddle and she released the fabric. Slowly she lifted her head.

He stood in the doorway, between her and the front hall. He was still a very good-looking man, she supposed.

If only he possessed substance beneath the good looks and charm. Who was he trying to be today? Despite the backpack hanging from his shoulder, he'd achieved a 'look' somewhere between James Dean and Elvis. Very picturesque. Although the number of gold studs on the leather jacket seemed a little excessive, even for him.

She watched silently with a cold knot in her stomach as he removed his sunglasses.

'How did you get inside my house?'

'Hey, the door was open. I'm not one to refuse an invitation.' He twirled the glasses by one earpiece.

'I locked the doors myself after the kids left for school. Either you broke in or you got a key from somewhere.'

'So I remembered you kept a key in the shed for the kids. So what? It's partly my house. I sure paid through the nose for it.'

'Not lately.'

'Hey, crap happens. I had to leave town.' He hung the glasses from the neck of his T-shirt, then sauntered to the table and picked up the strip of lace she planned to attach to Sarah's new dress. 'A man can't let anything get in the way of a real good opportunity.'

'An opportunity? I almost lost the house, Eric. The kids and I wouldn't have had anywhere to live.'

'Naw. They have to give you four or five months before they can kick you out. I came back in time, didn't I?' He slid the lace through his fingertips.

'Have you got a check for me to give to the bank?'

'Huh? Yeah, sure. Right here.' He patted his pocket.

'Why didn't you tell me you were leaving town?'

'Be still my beating heart.' He clasped his hands together against his chest and tilted his face upwards, as if in prayer. 'She cares.'

'I don't. The bank, however, does.'

'Oh, well.' He abandoned the pose and moved nearer.

'That's close enough,' she snapped.

'Aw, hell, Becka. I'm not going to touch you.'

'Where have you been?' She turned off the sewing machine and pushed away from the table. When she stood up she stepped sideways, keeping the wooden expanse between them, hesitating when her hand was only inches from the shears. After a moment she closed her fingers into an empty fist, left the potential weapon on the table, and kept moving.

'Vegas. With Margaret.' He tossed the lace onto the table and shoved his hands into his pockets. 'She saw me in the bar of the hotel where I worked and must'a liked what she saw. We had a hot'n dirty weekend, if you know what I mean. Next thing I know her business trip's over and she's begging me to come home with her.'

'So you quit your job, dumped your girlfriend, and left town. I take it Margaret's wealthy?'

'Filthy rich. She's my ticket outta here, babe.'

She gave him as wide a berth as possible as she went past, hoping he'd follow her out into the front hall. When he did, she sighed, relieved not to be trapped with him in the dining room or any other room. She opened the front door wide and gripped the sturdy wood. 'Why are you here, Eric?'

'Thought I'd drop in to see the kids.'

'Try another one. You know they don't get home from school for another half-hour. Furthermore, you seldom came here to see them even when you lived in town.'

'Oh. Well, you and I can visit a while. You know . . . talk over old times?'

'You and I don't have any old times I care to remember.'

'Dammit, Becka, that all happened years ago. Are you going to bitch about it forever?'

'It wasn't like you broke a window, Eric. You *raped* me. I should have called the police and had you arrested.'

'Do you really want to get into that again?' He shook his head, sighed, and looked disappointed. Another pose.

She looked at him. Really looked at him. Sure his hair was a beautiful shade of chestnut. But it was so thick with hairspray that the breeze from the open door didn't move a single strand. Apparently he still worked out every day. He hadn't gone to fat the way his former team-mates had. If anything his muscles were bulkier than ever. Too bulky.

His teeth were even and white. But she knew exactly how much the caps had cost because she'd help pay for them. Sure his dimples were cute and he could charm most women out of their clothes. So what? He had a whole list of assets he knew how to use to his advantage.

But none of them made him half the man Ryan was.

And thanks to the self-defense course she'd taken after the last time he'd caught her alone, she wasn't scared of him any more. The topsy-turvey state of her stomach came only from old, very bad memories and the abruptness of his appearance.

'No, I don't. I want to you to tell me why you're here and then I want you to leave.'

Before Eric could answer, her youngest son barreled through the door, followed more sedately by the other three kids. When Nicky saw his mother wasn't alone he stopped running but it was too late. The area rug skidded out from beneath his feet, sending him directly into Eric's knees.

It was as pretty a tackle as any Becky had seen on televised sports. Nicky ended up at her feet, smiling sheepishly. Eric went over with a mighty thump to lie cursing, spread-eagled on the wooden floor.

The toy train engine that had belonged to her great-grandfather tumbled out of the satchel on his shoulder. When Eric grabbed for the train, Mike scooped it up.

'So. You came to steal the train. Why, Eric?' she asked.

'Money, my dear. Money.' He got to his feet, tucked his shirt back in, and casually adjusted the fit of his jacket. He picked up the satchel. 'Margaret's little hobby, other than myself, is antiques. I saw a toy exactly like that one in a Christie's catalogue. It's worth a fortune.'

'No, it's not.' Dismay filled her heart. 'You're lying.'

'We don't want you here, you jerk.' Mike stood between his parents, his jaw jutting belligerently as he faced his father, while Nicky, Dani, and Sarah ranged themselves beside Becky. 'You . . . you get the hell out of this house right now and never come back.'

'You can't talk to me like that you little – '

'No!' Becky grabbed Mike's arm and tugged him behind her as Eric raised his fist threateningly. 'Is there anything else in your pockets that belongs to me?'

'No, there's not,' he snapped. 'Why shouldn't I have the damn toy? I sure as hell didn't get anything else out of this marriage except a lot of grief and debts.'

'Give me the check for the bank and get out, Eric.' He didn't answer, nor did he reach into his pocket. 'You lied about that, too, didn't you? You have no intention of making the mortgage payments.'

'If that's going to be your attitude, I'll leave.' They watched as he pulled on a dignified attitude as if it were a cloak and swaggered out the door.

'And if you ever raise your hand to one of my children again, I will call the police and have you charged with assault,' she shouted after him.

After his rental car had pulled out of the driveway, she knelt and gathered the kids into her arms, even Dani. Sarah shed a few tears and Mike patted her back awkwardly.

'Are you guys okay?' Becky asked.

One by one they assured her they had survived the ugly scene, though only Nicky looked relatively calm. She kissed them all and sent the youngest three into the kitchen for their after-school snack. She held Mike's hand, keeping him beside her until the others were out of earshot.

'You shouldn't have talked to him that way, honey.'

He slipped out of her hold and put the toy train in her hands. 'He's a jerk.'

'He's your father.'

'Well, I don't want him to be. And nothing you say will make me say I'm sorry. I don't care if he ever comes back,' he yelled. Then he ran upstairs before she could say anything more.

She let him go. They both needed time. Time to calm down and think before they talked about what had happened.

She plopped down to sit on the floor with the toy in her lap, thinking about the past and how, if Eric was right about the value of the train, he had managed to hurt her again. Because of course she'd have to sell it. She couldn't justify keeping it when her family needed so many things.

She was still sitting there when Ryan walked in the door fifteen minutes later.

'Becky?' He crouched and put his arm around her shoulders. 'Honey? Is something wrong?'

'Eric was here.' Her voice was listless.

'Damn.' His arm tightened around her instinctively but he eased his grip as soon as he realized he was holding her too tightly.

'Did he hurt you?' He could feel his teeth grate as he ground out the question.

'Do you know where I go to get an antique toy appraised?' Her fingers traced the raised numbers on the train engine she held. A tear splashed on its surface.

'Becky, you're scaring me. Talk to me.' He reached around, gripped her other shoulder and turned her to face him.

'He didn't touch me.' Her eyes were dark with misery when she finally met his gaze.

'The kids.' He couldn't see anyone else, but he heard dishes banging around in the kitchen. 'Are the kids okay?'

'They were scared but they're okay now. He almost hit Mike.' She shook her head slowly from side to side, bewildered. 'Mike . . . erupted. I've never heard him talk like that.'

'Where is Eric?'

'He's gone. To Las Vegas, probably. For good, I imagine, since he didn't get what he came for.'

'Where is he right now?' Ryan could hear the barely suppressed rage in his voice. He sucked in a breath and counted slowly down from ten, struggling for calm. He had to find out the facts, make sure everyone here was safe before he tracked down the bastard and helped him to a new understanding of pain.

'Why? So you can go after him and beat him up? He's not worth it and you might get hurt. The man's still built like a tank with muscles.'

'Big muscles won't help him against brains.' He knew his smile was unpleasant.

'How could I explain to the kids that it's okay for you to settle things with your fists, but not them?' She gripped his forearm.

He felt himself weakening. Then she said something that almost reduced him to mush.

'You have to start thinking and acting like a father and role model now. After I change the locks – '

'I'll change the locks. Today.'

She grimaced and looked as if she was about to argue, but then her shoulders slumped. That scared him. Never before had she given in so easily when he'd tried to do something for her.

'I'm worried about Mike. His reaction was . . . too strong. Almost as though he hated his father more than ever. As if when he saw Eric in the house it triggered an emotional explosion.'

'Should I try to talk to him?' he offered. Although what good it would do, he didn't know. Apparently the boy tolerated him only slightly better than he tolerated Eric.

'No. Thanks. I'll talk to him tonight, after the other kids are in bed. We'll both be calmer then.'

'What did Eric come for?'

'This.' She patted the engine.

'The toy? Why?'

'He says it's worth a lot of money.'

'But you said – '

'I know.' Her sigh shuddered as if she was holding back a sob. 'I was wrong. He saw one like it in a catalogue from Christie's auction house. Isn't that great?'

He'd never heard her sound so sad. 'But, Becky – '

'If it's worth so much he'd come here to steal it, I imagine after I sell it there'll be enough money to do some long overdue house repairs.' She wiped her eyes with the hem of her sweatshirt, then offered him a wavering but determined smile. 'So. Do you know where I should take it for an appraisal?'

Damn. He couldn't let her sell something that meant so much to her. But she'd made it very clear that giving her money was not an option.

'Let's go sit down.' He urged her to her feet and led her into the living room. He lowered her into the wing chair in front of the window. The puddle of sunshine would help her feel better, he thought. Then he pulled the footstool over beside her feet and sat down, resting his hands on her knees.

'Are you sure you want to do this?'

'Yes.' She closed her eyes and lay her head back against the worn upholstery. 'The sun feels heavenly.'

'You haven't asked why I'm here before six o'clock today.'

Her eyes blinked open in surprise and she glanced at the mantel clock. 'You are early. Why?'

'I have to go away tomorrow morning on business. I'll be gone almost two weeks. Can Dani stay with you again?'

'You know she can. I'll miss you.' She wedged the toy between her leg and the chair's arm and squeezed his hands. 'Where are you going?'

'I have six or seven stops on the East coast.' He leaned forward. 'Including New York.'

'Ryan! Could you – '

'Yes. I'll take the train with me and have them look at it.' He rubbed his thumbs across her fingertips. 'If you're sure.'

She leaned forward and wrapped her arms around his neck, burying her face against his neck. 'I'm sure.'

Ryan heard the conviction in her tone, but he also felt her tears against his skin. He decided then that no matter what it took, he'd find some way for her to keep her great-grandfather's toy train.

Another spate of shivers racked Becky's body. It wasn't because she was cold. The evening had been dry and mild, almost balmy for a fall day. She'd been shivering off and on for the last hour, ever since the firemen forcibly escorted her out of Lilac House.

It was much quieter now. No more shattering glass. No more shouted orders or thumps or ripping wood.

She knelt on the sidewalk in front of her house, her arms around the girls and Nicky. Mike huddled alone on the curb several feet away, his face buried in the arms crossed on his knees after refusing to sit near her and the other kids. She'd have to talk to him, but later. Much later, when she could be calm and reasonable while she demanded what the heck he'd been thinking of . . .

No. Too much anger. She needed to let the fear and adrenaline abate so she could be calm. Raging at him for teenage stupidity would gain her nothing and he would become even more sullen.

She focused on her home again. The front door stood wide open. Puffs of smoke still meandered their way skyward from the broken attic window but everything else looked normal. Two firemen came out of the house carrying coils of heavy hose which they dumped on the front lawn. Thank God they hadn't needed to use it.

Over the years she'd seen footage of fire and water damage on the evening news many times. Lilac House and all their belongings would have been ruined. Smoke smells and stains she could deal with. Starting over from scratch would have broken her heart. She watched as two more firemen carrying axes came out her front door and all four began storing equipment on the fire truck.

Axes! She thought about the ripping and rending she'd heard earlier and tried not to cry as another bout of shivers traveled through her body.

'Can I go talk to them now, Mommy? Can I?'

She tightened her arm around Nicky's wiggling body. 'No, honey. We can't get in their way.'

Jan's yellow Corvette screeched to a halt behind the fire truck and she hopped out. 'Becky? I came as soon as your neighbor called me. Are you and the kids all right? What happened?'

'A fire in the attic.'

'It was Mike's fault,' Nicky piped up. 'The biggest fireman carried Mommy out over his shoulder.'

'Carried? Were you hurt?' Jan exclaimed.

'No, I wasn't hurt. I made sure all the kids were safely outside, then I used the fire extinguisher to put out the flames.'

'An idiotic thing to do,' a gruff voice interrupted them.

She glanced away from Jan to the man who'd ordered the others to get her out of the way. Behind the helmet, heavy boots, and bulky clothing she recognized the face of Roger Chalmers, now Lieutenant Chalmers. He'd changed a lot from the boy who used to torment the girls in grade eight cooking class and played high school football with Eric. Last winter he'd asked her out several times but she'd turned him down.

'You should have left the house with the kids right after you called 911.'

'And then Lilac House would be a ruin now instead of just dirty.'

'You could have been hurt or worse. With all the stuff you had stacked in that attic the fire could have traveled behind you and cut you off from the door. It's usually best to leave immediately, Becky.'

'Is the fire out?'

'Yes.'

'Is there much damage?'

'Luckily someone had fairly recently put fire resistant insulation in the roof and walls. There is damage to the attic walls because we had to check inside to make sure the fire was completely out. Because of your quick, if risky, action the flames were confined to one end of the attic. You'd better get the roof checked right away, just to make sure it's still weather proof.'

'The big wardrobe against the North wall,' afraid of his answer she had to gulp enough air to finish her question, 'is it okay?'

'I'm sorry. Everything at that end of the attic was destroyed.'

She didn't say anything as tears filled her eyes and trickled down her cheeks.

'Becky?' Jan asked.

'Grandmother's dress.' She wiped her cheeks with the hem of Nicky's shirt. 'I kept the dress box in the wardrobe. They said the cedar lining would protect it from the m-m-moths.'

'Your wedding dress!' Jan handed her a tissue from her purse and Becky blew her nose.

'Never mind. It's just a dress. The kids are safe and Lilac House is still standing. The stores have lots of beautiful wedding dresses I can choose from when the time comes.'

She noticed Mike had lifted his head and was staring at her. The misery and regret in his expression hurt *her*. She dug deep inside and found a smile for him. Whatever he'd done, he was her son and she loved him.

She turned to Roger. 'Can we go back in the house?'

'Yes, but there's still smoke in the air. It would probably be better for the kids to sleep somewhere else.'

'I'll take them to my condo,' Jan volunteered. The younger three agreed immediately and happily.

'I won't go.' It was the first time Mike had spoken since the fire. 'It's my fault and I'm staying to help.'

Becky thought about what he'd said. And about what he hadn't said.

Mike had asked if he and his new friends could play in the attic and, much as she disliked them, she'd wanted to avoid another fight with her son right now and reluctantly agreed. She knew how the rooms under the roof fascinated all the kids, especially at dusk. The shadows cast by the sinking sun made the clutter and shrouded furniture into a place of mystery and adventure.

She'd been sewing in the dining room when Joe Brasky and the others thundered down the stairs and out the front door, with Mike swearing and yelling after them. Then the smoke alarm shrilled out its warning. She ordered Mike to get the girls from Sarah's bedroom while she got the fire extinguisher and Nicky from the kitchen.

He tried to make her listen to a scrambled explanation of dares and cigarettes and accidents but she refused to listen. Time enough for that when she knew the kids were safe and just how bad the situation was.

While Mike herded the younger children out to the road she ran up the stairs, dropping to her knees in the dark attic and crawling through the smoke toward the orange and yellow flames. When she was near enough she aimed the extinguisher and prayed.

The last bright flicker died a few seconds before the firemen burst in through the door. Next thing she knew she'd been tossed over a broad shoulder and carried quickly down two flights of stairs, dumped on the sidewalk beside her children, and ordered to stay put.

Maybe Mike did need to remain with her. He needed to see the results of his carelessness and she sensed he needed to try to make it better. He was still boy enough to be afraid but she was proud that he was mature enough to face the consequences of his actions.

'Okay. You can stay.' She hugged the girls and Nicky. 'You be good for Jan, you hear?' Luckily the girls had been playing hopscotch on the driveway so Matilda had been parked on the road. Jan moved the Corvette down the road, locked it, and loaded the kids in the station wagon. A short while later the firemen finished packing up their gear and left.

Becky and Mike watched from the end of driveway until all the activity had ceased. Then she slung her arm around his shoulders and squeezed. 'Let's go, honey. We've got lots to do.'

He resisted when she tried to moved them toward the house. 'I'm sorry, Mom.'

She put both hands on his shoulders and looked him in the eyes. 'I know, sweetheart. I know.'

'I shouldn't be doing this.' Becky tightened her grip on her purse as Jan swerved, narrowly avoiding scraping Matilda's fender against a telephone pole. 'I'd planned to have another talk with Mike today.'

'About the fire?'

'We worked that out. He's promised to stay away from those boys and will help me work on cleaning up the mess for as long as it takes.' She clenched one hand on the edge of the seat to brace herself. 'No, I meant the marriage. I still can't get him to tell me why he's so angry about me marrying Ryan.'

'When are you going to realize Mike's almost a man? Raging hormones, bossy attitude, and a deep-rooted resistance to any conversation about his feelings. Typical immature male. Give it up.'

'Maybe you're right.'

'I know I'm right. Let it go. He'll get over it as soon as he decides the whole thing was his idea. Sooner or later you'll have to listen to him congratulate himself on your great second marriage.'

'If you say so.' Becky closed her eyes as they almost hit a mail box. 'Ryan called last night and he was furious.'

'Oh, oh. He must have found out about the fire. Hallie and I both told you it was a mistake not to tell him. Who told him?'

'Nicky answered the phone.'

'And of course he spilled his guts. Nicky hasn't stopped talking about the fire truck since it happened. I'm surprised you managed to keep the news from Ryan this long. What did he say?'

Becky glanced in the back seat. The girls were concentrating on their own conversation but she lowered her voice anyway. 'He was perfectly polite. Too polite. Sort've frozen. I would almost have preferred him to yell a little. He was going to fly home immediately but I convinced him there was no need.'

'Oh, no. Big mistake.'

'What are you talking about?'

'You shouldn't tell a man like Ryan that he's not needed.'

'I didn't say that! I meant he shouldn't cut his business trip short when there's nothing he could do here. Everything was over and done with.'

'Even worse.'

'Humpf. This whole conversation is foolish.'

'Promise me you'll call him back tonight and get this settled. If you let it wait until he comes home he'll have almost a week to build up to being really mad.'

'Fine. I promise.' Becky crossed her arms and glared at Jan. Silence reigned in the front seat until she noticed they were driving through Stanley Park toward Lion's Gate Bridge.

'Don't you think it's time you told me where we're going?' Becky asked sharply.

In the back seat Sarah and Dani exploded into giggles.

'That's for us to know and you to find out.' The light turned green and Jan stepped on the gas. Hard. Matilda backfired in protest. Jan thumped her fist on the dash and the station wagon surged forward.

'Could you please remember whose car you're driving? This is not your Corvette.'

'Believe me, I'd noticed.'

'I don't understand why I couldn't drive.'

'That's simple, Mommy,' Sarah piped up. 'You don't know where we're going.' The two girls were giggling so hard she could hardly finish the sentence.

'Very funny.' Becky put her nose in the air and sniffed. 'Humpf.'

'How long is Ryan going to be out of town?'

'A few days.'

'We're here.' Jan spun the steering wheel and scooted into a parking space only inches ahead of another car. With the attendant noise of the other driver's car horn and angry shouts, they all jerked forward against the seat-belts when Jan slammed on the brakes.

'That's it. I'm driving home,' Becky said, as soon as she could breathe easily again.

'Be my guest.' Jan dropped the keys into her hand, then unsnapped her seat-belt. 'Everybody out.'

Becky scolded Jan about her driving in whispers as they followed the girls into a nearby store. She'd only been vaguely aware that it was a dress shop until the girls gasped in wonder.

They were surrounded by mannequins clad in little girls' dreams. Not to mention big girls' dreams.

Floating veils, satin shoes, glittering tiaras, Juliet caps embroidered with luminous pearls. Lacy umbrellas, wrist and elbow-length gloves, ring pillows. And those were only some of the accessories.

The gowns. Becky turned in a slow circle. Sophisticated, ornate, simple, elegant, and cute. White, ivory, palest pink, daffodil yellow. Emerald green, ruby red, and sapphire blue. From what she could see the store held something in every color and any style.

Then she noticed the little elderly lady, dressed all in black, smiling at her from beside the glass counter.

'This is her, yes?' the woman asked.

Becky blinked.

‘Yes,’ Jan said. ‘And these are the bridesmaids.’ She shepherded Sarah and Dani forward.

‘Yes, yes, I see, I see.’ She scurried closer and peered into the girls’ faces. The tiny woman was only a few inches taller than Sarah.

‘This is the blue,’ she tapped Dani’s chin, ‘and this is the rose.’ She patted Sarah’s cheek. Then she bowed, pointed to a cluster of chairs facing a half-circle of mirrored panels, and backed away as quickly as she’d come. ‘Please to sit. All is in readiness.’ She vanished back into the nether regions of the store.

When they were alone again Becky turned to face Jan, hands on hips. ‘What have you done?’

Jan was running her hand over the brocade upholstery on the chairs. ‘Aren’t these beautiful? I’ve decided to ask her where she bought them. They’d be perfect in my sitting room.’

‘Forget the chairs, Jan. I want to know – ’ Just then she noticed her two girls approaching the heavily embroidered gown displayed on a raised dais in the centre of the store. Sarah’s hand reached out to touch the crystal beads woven into the lace.

‘Sarah? Dani? Please come and sit down. That dress probably costs more than I make in a year.’ She waited until they’d chosen a chair.

‘Isn’t that Madame de Moor?’ she whispered to Jan, who nodded. ‘I’ve read about her in the newspapers. She’s famous! I can’t afford anything in her store.’

'For heaven's sake, Becky, Madame de Moor wouldn't own a store. This is a salon.' Jan gestured regally.

'Fine. I can't afford anything in her salon.'

'You don't have to.'

'You can't afford it either. I don't care how immense a salary you make at that big shot job of yours.'

'Remember I told you about Stan's buddy Petrov? Madame de Moor is his grandmother and she's giving us the family discount. Plus she wants to use the little chapel on Stan's father's estate to shoot the photos for her spring line. So we worked out a deal.'

'You and your deals.'

'Yeah, I'm good.' Jan blew on her nails, then polished them against her shirt. 'Anyway, it's all settled. The day after you told me you were engaged to Ryan, I sneaked Sarah's and Dani's measurements out of that notebook in your sewing room. Madame and I sat down, she asked me a few questions, then I left everything in her hands. Everyone gets a new dress. My treat.'

Madame scurried back, two plastic wrapped garments over each arm. With a flamboyantly regal gesture, obviously the original Jan had been imitating earlier, she whipped off the plastic and hung each child's dress on a separate hook set into the mirrors. Jan, Becky, and Dani all gasped. Sarah's eyes filled with tears.

Madame smiled. 'It is always thus.'

The two dresses were the same empire-waist style and yet subtly different. Becky, with her years of sewing experience, could tell at a glance that each would enhance the girls' own best qualities. Sarah's dress was as rosy as her cheeks and fashioned of velvet. Dani's rustling taffeta dress matched her blue eyes exactly.

'Please to wait one little minute longer.' Madame scurried away again. When she came back she carried only one garment bag.

'This for the crazy lady who talks me into giving away my work.' Madame shook her head sadly, but then she smiled as she removed the plastic.

'Oh, Jan.' Becky covered her mouth with both hands.

The ivory linen suit was cut on slim lines, with ivory satin accents on the lapels. Matching satin buttons followed the diagonal closing of the jacket and finished off each sleeve.

'Well, you like?' Madame asked.

'I like.' Jan gently touched a finger to one of the buttons.

'It's absolutely beautiful. You're going to look wonderful.' Becky reached out and clasped her friend's hand.

'More like a bride than a maid-of-honor, wouldn't you say?' Jan turned her hand in Becky's and held on tightly.

'You mean –? You and Stan –?'

Jan grinned. 'He asked me to marry him and, thanks in part to your nagging, I decided not to be stupid any longer. Ralph's dead and Stan is a truly terrific man. So it looks like I'm finally going to get married.'

Becky whooped with glee. 'When?'

'Well, we were kind'a wondering how you and Ryan felt about a double ceremony.'

'In the parlor at Lilac House?'

Jan nodded.

'I think that's the most wonderful idea you've ever had.' Becky jumped up, paced in a tight circle, then sat down again. 'This wedding is really going to happen, isn't it? I'm really starting to believe in this,' she thumped her chest, 'in here where it counts.'

'You bet, kiddo. Nothing's going to stop us now,' Jan said.

'One more little minute.' Madame hung the suit on another hook and scampered away. This time when she reappeared she had a mousy assistant with her, who pushed a wheeled mannequin to the centre of the viewing area. The mirrors reflected it on all sides as together they solemnly unwrapped the plastic covering. At last they'd finished and stepped aside.

'It's exactly like Grandmother's dress.' Becky couldn't believe her eyes. Her hand tightened on Jan's. 'You copied it from the picture of her and Emily at their coming out ball. When?'

'I sneaked it out and had it photocopied the day after the fire. You were so busy I knew you wouldn't notice if it was gone for a few hours. Madame de

Moor did the rest.' Jan grinned and repeated Madame's earlier question. 'You like?'

'I like.' She hugged Jan. 'I like it so much my heart hurts. Thank you, dear friend,' she whispered.

'Good.' Jan sat back and briskly patted her eyes with a tissue. She handed a second tissue to Becky. 'Now the real work begins. It's time to accessorize.'

CHAPTER 15

Ryan paid the cab driver, picked up his keys and suitcase then raced up the sidewalk. It had been raining for most of the four days of his absence and his feet skidded as he leaped up the stairs. The water-slick wooden porch steps were worse than banana peels or ice for the unwary.

Hanging on to the screen door handle, he fought for balance. Safely inside at last he put down his case and listened for the sounds that would tell him where everyone was. He'd worked like a maniac but it was worth it. He was back home a day early.

Now if only he could convince Becky to let him pay off the mortgage, maybe he could believe it was his home, too.

'Becky? I'm back,' he called out. Someone had to be here. The door stood wide open to let in the unusually mild breeze.

'Sarah? Dani?' he yelled from the bottom of the stairs. No answer meant no one was upstairs. How about the backyard?

'Nicky?' He held open the back door and called again. 'I brought you a present,' he added temptingly, in case the little imp was hiding.

'Mike? Anyone?' Inside again, he sat down on the bottom stair. All around him the big house echoed into silence. He propped his elbows on his knees and rested his chin on his hands. How do you like that? A man labors at his job, travels thousands of miles, rushes home, and no one's there. Becky must have been crazy to leave the house unlocked. Anybody could have walked right in and helped themselves.

He was on his way to a major panic when he heard a faint, uneven tapping. He stood up and followed the sound. Outside the closed door to her office he paused then twisted the door knob, pushed open the door, and there she was.

With the earphones of Mike's precariously balanced stereo covering her ears, she hummed along off-key to music he couldn't hear. Her fingers picked out the rhythm on the old manual typewriter, followed, half a beat out of step, by her wiggling bottom and feet.

Pages of graph paper were scattered haphazardly around her. Reference books lay open on every available surface. He jumped when she belted out the final line of the song's chorus.

'She loves you, yeah, yeah, yeah!' On the last note she tossed her hands up in the air, yelled at the top of her lungs, shoved herself back from her desk, and spun the old secretary's chair around on its squeaky pivot.

Then she caught sight of him.

'Ryan!' A smile split her face and she leaped up, her arms flung wide to give him a hug, forgetting the earphones that anchored her to the desk. The earphone jack snapped loose, a Beatles' song blared out. The radio crashed to the floor and the music cut off.

'Oh, no! If it's broken Mike is never going to let me forget it.'

'Never mind.' He drew her into his arms. 'I'll buy him a new one.'

'No, you won't, I'll get it fixed. You've got to stop throwing your money around,' she scolded.

'I like to buy things for you. That's what husbands do. Especially for wives like you and I've only got a few weeks 'til the wedding to get the husband role down pat. I can't have you changing your mind.'

'Where did you get these crazy ideas? I don't want you to keep doing this.'

He thought back to his youth, when for years the level of serenity in his home rose and fell with the fluctuations in his father's salary. Learned in childhood, the concept had been constantly reinforced by every woman he'd known since. Even though he knew, intellectually, that Becky wasn't like his mother, emotionally he was still determined she and the kids would have everything his money could buy.

'Come here, you,' he growled. He kissed her with all the passion he'd stored up while he'd been away on business. Only when they had both run out of air did he pull back. 'I needed that. Now I know I'm home.'

'You have to stop kissing me whenever you want to change the subject.'

'If you say so. Finished working on your puzzle?'

'Ryan!' She sighed but gave in. She'd let it go for now. 'I am now. It's based on Beatles' music for a fanzine.'

'I love the way you get right into the research for your puzzles.' His lips hovered in the air above her ear lobe, his breath stirred the curls and she shivered in reaction. 'Is there any likelihood *Playboy* or *Cosmopolitan* will hire you for a puzzle about all the ways of making love? I'd be glad to help with your research.'

She pulled back a few inches and laughed. 'You're in a good mood.'

'You have no idea. Where're the kids?'

'Next door. They were all invited to a party.'

'Oh?' His lips nuzzled her throat. 'How much longer are they going to be gone?'

She turned his wrist around so she could see his watch. 'About two hours. What are you . . .?' Her voice rose to a shriek when he swung her high in his arms and strode out of her cubby-hole workroom. At the bottom of the stairs he stopped long enough to kiss her again.

'I missed you. Talking on the phone every night is not enough.'

'Are you suggesting,' she glanced up the stairs, then fluttered her eyelashes, 'what I think you're suggesting?'

He grinned and kissed her again. 'I knew you were a smart woman.'

'I missed you too. Now put me down. You're wasting precious minutes of our two hours.'

He put her on her own feet and she flew up the stairs. At the landing she paused, winked sassily over her shoulder, and scooted around the corner.

He exhaled on a long, low whistle. By God, how was he supposed to wait six more weeks to marry her?

With clumsy fingers he stripped off his tie and jacket while he dashed after her, flinging them back over the railing in the general direction of his suit-case.

'I'm glad the police recovered the items stolen from your apartment.' Becky lay on her side and scooted up against his body, resting her head on his shoulder.

'Yeah. It seems Pastin's wife decided to liquidate some of his things while he was still in jail. She didn't know the mask and abacus were mine, although I doubt that would have stopped her trying to sell them. I'm not exactly one of her favorite people. The gallery recognized them from a police bulletin listing recently stolen art and antiques.'

'You must be glad to get them back.'

'I've decided to sell the mask.'

'I thought that mask was important to you?'

'Yeah, it was. When I looked at her, the face seemed to hold some universal truth about women. Very comforting, as if she illustrated or perhaps affirmed, the way I had chosen to live my life.' He tightened his arm around her, drawing her closer to his body. 'Recent events have changed my thinking.'

'What happened at Christie's?' She swirled one finger in the chest hair close to her nose.

She hadn't really wanted to think about the train so she'd put off asking but the time had come. A mature, responsible woman should be able to handle selling a family heirloom if it meant financial security for her children. Too bad she didn't feel very mature about her train.

'Jeez, Becky, why would you want to sell something that means so much to you?'

'You did have it appraised, didn't you?'

'I want you to remember I had a lot of options with this.' He fidgeted with the sheet they'd pulled over themselves as their bodies cooled.

'What options?'

'I could've said they appraised it under a hundred bucks, not worth their time or your regrets. I could've put it in a safety deposit box, said it was sold, and handed you the appraised value from my own money. On our tenth anniversary you would have been real happy to get it back.'

'What did they say, Ryan?' She selected one hair and tugged.

'Ouch!' He rubbed his chest. 'They figure it would sell for between five and eight thousand dollars. The other one went for seven.'

She propped herself up on one arm so she could see his face. 'Oh, my Lord. Why so much?'

'Good quality and it's really old. Made in 1898 by a German company, I think. The details are in my briefcase.'

'I'm going to get eight thousand dollars.' She didn't believe it, so she repeated it. 'Eight thousand dollars.'

'Maybe less. If it's consigned to one of their sales.'

'If it's consigned? Didn't you – '

'I brought it home.'

She collapsed onto her back and flung one arm over her eyes. 'Why? This was hard enough to deal with when you left for New York. Now I'll have to work myself up to selling it all over again.'

'Listen, Becky, okay? You don't need that money now we're together. I don't want you to sell it.'

'You don't want me to sell it. What about what I want?'

He winced at the flatness in her tone. 'Give me a little credit here, Becky. I'm trying.'

'Sure. A very little credit for how little you're trying.'

'You've got to let me in, Becky. Give me a stake in your home. Maybe then I wouldn't feel so much like I'm trespassing.'

'Trespassing?' She rolled away and his heart froze.

She sat up on the side of the bed. It was all he could do not to slide his hand up her naked spine. Her shoulder blades moved as she leaned forward and covered her eyes with her hands, muffling her words.

'I can't hear you, Becky.'

'I said I didn't know.' Her head lifted and she turned to face him. 'I'm so sorry. I don't know which is worse. That you felt that way or that I had no idea.'

'I didn't say that to make you feel bad. I love you.' He reached out and dragged her into his arms and back under the sheet next to him where she belonged. 'I understand it's going to take time for us both to get used to being half of a team. Just cut me a little slack now and then.'

'A little slack?' She winked and nudged him with her hip. 'I don't think so.'

He laughed. 'Does this mean if things change you'll keep the train?'

'If things change how?'

'I don't know. Maybe the bank will get rid of that jerk manager. You didn't answer the question. If things were different, would you keep the train?'

'I guess so. Because you ask, I won't sell it right now. But I reserve the right to sell it later if I decide it's necessary.'

'If we decide.'

'Yes. If we decide, you big bully.'

'Isn't this the point where you're supposed to thank me for going to Christie's?' He slid over her, grinning suggestively.

'No, Ryan. The kids are going to be home in fifteen minutes.' Becky spread her fingers on his chest and pushed. He settled his weight between her thighs, his upper torso propped up on straight arms.

'Phone your neighbor,' he whispered fervently. 'Ask her if the kids can stay a little longer.'

‘I can’t. They’ve been there all afternoon already. It wouldn’t be fair.’ Of their own volition her fingers burrowed through the hair on his chest, massaging the sleek muscles. ‘Anyway, we’ve already made love twice.’

Electricity rocketed through him at her touch. Ryan gasped and rotated his hips, seeking her, needing her all over again.

‘This trip was hell. I didn’t sleep. I could barely concentrate. I lived on coffee and visions of you. Erotic visions. You were like a ghost in my bed, in the office, in the taxi, in every restaurant and all you wore was that damned pink nightgown. Twice isn’t enough. Three times won’t be enough.’

She felt his sex, fully aroused, rigid against her flesh.

‘I felt like a horny teenager again. Always hard, wanting you. Thank God for pleated pants, or I would have humiliated myself.’

She stared up into his face. Hooded blue eyes glittered feverishly. Taut lips whispered what he wanted to do to her, with her. What they could do to each other. It was so amazing, so marvelous, to be loved equally as much as she gave love. Without looking away, she groped for the phone beside the bed and dialed.

‘Sally? Can the kids stay a little longer? Why? Oh. Ummm, the sink backed up and flooded the kitchen floor. I’ll call you when I get it cleaned up. Thanks. Bye.’

Becky fumbled the receiver back into its cradle. Still holding his gaze with her own she placed her open palms on his chest and slid them slowly down his belly, along lean hips and around to cup firmly muscled buttocks.

'Now.' Her whispered command was accompanied by a forceful squeeze of her hands as she brought him into her.

Ryan stopped just inside the heavy glass doors of the bank and looked around, aware that he was attracting the staff's attention. Four women worked at desks behind the counter and a male teller was helping the only other customer, an elderly man.

He'd deliberately chosen to arrive immediately after opening, determined to get this contemptible situation resolved before another day passed.

'Can I help you, sir?' asked a woman standing beside a desk to his left.

'Yes. I'd like to see Tom Ellford.'

'Do you have an appointment?'

'No.'

He could see her consider, and reject, telling him that her boss only saw people with appointments. He wasn't surprised. Few people had the temerity to put him off.

'May I have your name, please?'

'Ryan McLeod.'

She disappeared into an office beyond her desk. She shut the door behind her but the latch didn't catch and it bounced open an inch or two.

'Why are you bothering me, Marie? I told you to leave me alone this morning. If you can't do as you're told, I'll fire you and find someone who can. Now get out of here and stop wasting my time.'

Ryan was startled by the man's tone, which was as offensive as his words. Even in a time of chronic unemployment, how did anyone get away with being so rude to his staff? Sounded like this man bullied his staff as well as harassing vulnerable clients.

When the clerk came out of the office Ryan saw she was blinking back tears.

'I'm sorry, sir. Mr Ellford is busy at the moment. Can I make you an appointment for later today?'

'No, I think this has waited long enough.' He gently set her aside and strode past. He thrust open the door, slamming it against the wall with enough force to knock askew a velvet painting of Elvis. He was aware that the other staff and the customers were moving closer but it appeared none of them intended to interrupt.

'Whhaaat!' The pudgy man behind the desk sputtered outrage through a mouthful of powdered donut.

'Tom Ellford?'

'Who the hell are you? Marie, get in here!'

'My name is Ryan McLeod.'

'Leave my office now, or I'll call the police. Marie?'

Ryan moved a chair that stood between him and the other man.

'Marie!'

'I don't think she's coming. Do you? Why should she protect you? You treat her like dirt.' He advanced slowly, steadily, until he was standing over the man who by now was cowering in his padded leather chair. 'I want to talk to you.'

'What could you possibly want with me? I don't even know you.'

'Rebecca Hansen is my fiancee.'

Fear leapt into the other man's eyes.

'I see you recognize her name.' Ryan shoved aside the donut box and stack of paper napkins so he could rest one hip on the corner of the desk. He placed his elbow on his thigh and leaned forward until his face was only inches from the bank manager's. 'I thought you might.'

'Of course I do. She and her family have been customers here for many years. I feel the utmost respect for her and how well she's managed through trying times.'

'I doubt respect enters into any of your dealings with defenseless customers or staff, if you even know the meaning of the word.'

'But . . . but . . .

'Your behavior toward my fiancee has been both lewd and improper.'

'I refuse to sit here and listen to another word.' He tried to stand up but when Ryan put one finger in the center of his chest and shoved, he plopped back down.

'Let me tell you how it's going to be from now on.' Ryan picked up one of the paper napkins and wiped off the hand that had touched the manager's chest. 'You will always refer to her as Mrs Hansen or, after our wedding, as Mrs McLeod. If she ever again has the bad luck to meet with you in your office, the door will be open.'

'This is outrageous.'

'You will never again attempt to humiliate or insult her in any way. Your dealings with her will be strictly professional and stick to accepted business practices. If not, I will contact your head office and have you fired.'

'You couldn't – '

'Actually, I could. Perhaps you should run my name through your computer before you say anything more.' Ryan stood up, deliberately looming over the other man. Aware of the avid audience outside the office, he lowered his voice so only Ellford would hear his next comment.

'And if you ever again suggest, by word or tone, that Becky should have sex with you,' he balled up the napkin and tossed it in Ellford's lap, 'you'll suffer such pain that you'll no longer be interested in sex.'

'You can't threaten me.'

'Of course I can. I just did.' He took out his wallet and tossed a check onto the desk. 'That should cover Mrs Hansen's mortgage. When you have completed the paperwork, send it to my address on the front of the check.'

Ellford eyed the check but didn't touch it as Ryan turned to leave.

'Oh, one last thing. I suggest you treat your staff with more respect or they might decide to inform bank authorities about your behavior.'

'They wouldn't dare. They'd lose their jobs.'

'You should keep in mind that newspaper reporters are always interested in human interest stories and right now banks have been getting a lot of bad press.' He smiled. Ellford winced. 'I don't think your superiors would appreciate that type of media coverage, do you?'

Ryan walked out of the office, through the silent cluster of staff, and straight toward the exit. His heels cracking smartly against the tile floor were the only sound in the oppressive hush. As he put out his hand to the door he heard a sound that made him stop and turn.

Marie was applauding, slowly at first, then gaining speed as a broad smile spread across her face. Then, one by one, everyone else joined her.

He grinned and saluted them before he left. Outside he climbed in his car but didn't start it right away. He felt good. He'd done the right thing for Becky and if he'd helped the bank staff and other customers, so much the better.

Now, if only Becky would agree. He hoped he'd be able to come up with a convincing argument soon. Having the paperwork sent to his own address would only delay the inevitable confrontation for a while. He'd made the decision to act, and believed he'd been right to do so, but he could see trouble coming.

Ryan frowned but didn't look up as the door to his office swung open.

'Hallie, the trade show is next week and it's so damned important I get this perfect. I told you I couldn't be disturbed.'

'Oh?'

The one word reply was quiet but the voice jerked his head up anyway. 'Becky!'

It only took one glance at her face for him to understand the stormy expression. Oh, oh. Trouble. She must have heard from the bank.

'Why did you do it, Ryan?'

Yup, she'd heard from the bank.

'Today I received a letter, thanking me for payment in full on my mortgage. But . . .' She stomped closer until she was standing directly beside his chair, put a hand on the arm rest on either side of his hips and leaned forward until her nose was only two inches from his.

'I didn't pay off my mortgage. Immediately I wondered, did Ryan pay it off? Then I thought, no, he wouldn't have done something I specifically asked him not to. So then I thought, perhaps a mistake at the bank?'

'Becky . . .'

'I went to see Ellford. Do you know what he said?'

He thought back to his meeting with Ellford, a man who had obviously striven with more than moderate success to make up in girth what he lacked in height. Ryan shifted uneasily when he guessed what was coming next.

'He refused to see me. I was worried enough to march past his secretary and into his office anyway. The poor man practically became hysterical when I shut the door. He leaped up and ran, Ryan. That fat little man ran to the door and opened it.'

'Becky . . .'

'It seems he was afraid to be alone with me behind a closed door. Someone promised bodily harm because of improper, lewd behavior, and then threatened to complain to the bank's head office if it happened again. Sound familiar?'

'The man wouldn't leave you alone.' He jumped in with his explanation, hoping he could talk fast enough and persuasively enough before she took his head off, which was imminent if he judged the expression in her eyes correctly.

'When you told me he came on to you again last week it made me angry. No one insults my fiancee. I decided to take care of the situation.'

'You decided?' She straightened abruptly and stalked away to stare out his office window. 'Who gave you the right to make unilateral decisions about my life?'

'Who knows how many other women are in the same vulnerable position you were? The bastard needed to be taught a lesson.'

'Maybe so, but you shouldn't have gone behind my back.'

When he stood and moved to stand behind her the afternoon sun blinded them both, though neither cared. 'I love you. You have to understand. A man needs to protect the woman he loves. I couldn't stand to sit back and do nothing. Is that so bad?'

She didn't answer and he smacked his fist against his thigh as he began to pace the width of the office.

'I want to make you happy. I saw what I thought would be a way to achieve that, so I did it.' He stopped behind her and grasped her elbows, pulling her back against his chest. 'I'd do anything, buy you anything, give you anything . . .'

'I told you I would take care of both my mortgage and Eric. You have enough troubles right here in the office.' Becky jerked her arms out of his hands and turned to face him. The sun was so dazzling her face was a dark shadow against the brightness. 'I don't want anything your money can get for me. I only want you to love me!' Her voice cracked on the last word.

'Can't you understand? I needed to do this for you.' Ryan reached out to wrap his arms around her but she spun away and went to stand on the other side of the desk.

Becky stared at the tall man who was now only a silhouette against the sun-glazed windows, his golden hair a halo.

'Why, Ryan? I've asked you and asked you to stop buying things. At first it was exciting, then it was merely nice. Now my children are starting to expect expensive presents and I don't like it.'

'I have to.' He dragged a hand through his hair and turned away. 'I have to make sure you always have everything you want. You must believe me, I know what will happen . . .'

'No. You have to stop doing this. I don't need you to rescue me. I want to marry you because I love you. I am a capable, independent woman who wants you to be part of my life. My lover, not my parent. We have to be equal partners for our marriage to work. If you can't live with that, then . . . then I won't see you again.'

His first instinct was to force her to listen, to make her understand, using his own past to prove he was right. Then he saw the bleak determination in her eyes and knew that she would neither listen to nor accept his explanation. He had to concede or lose her. But how could he agree?

How could he not? Whatever he believed to be true and inevitable, she would not marry him if he didn't give his word here and now. He came around his desk and stopped when he was so close they could touch, if either reached out.

'I'll try,' he promised.

The bleakness faded from her eyes and a tentative smile curved one corner of her mouth. At this sign she was softening he wrapped his arms around her and hugged her tightly.

'You have to do more than try. The next time you buy a gift it will be returned. It will be painful both for you and the person you gave it to.'

'What if I ask you first? You will allow me to buy the kids and you a present now and then?'

She anchored her hands on his hips and kissed him lightly. 'Okay. But only if you ask me first,' she warned.

He returned the gossamer kiss but it took only seconds for heat to blossom and passion to rise. They forgot where they were so thoroughly, they were both startled when his phone buzzed. Unable to let her go, he waltzed her backward until he could pick up the receiver.

'Hello? Which line? Thanks, Hallie. Stall for a minute, okay?' Ryan put down the phone and kissed Becky again. 'A client, honey.'

'Never mind. I have to get home before the kids get out from school. I'll see you tonight at dinner.' She returned his kiss with interest and waved before she closed the door behind her.

He was about to push the button on the phone when the door opened and Hallie came in.

'Before you get bogged down in business, I thought I'd better tell you the private detective reported in by fax. Eric Hansen is still in Las Vegas where the detective contacted him and delivered your message. In their opinion, he will no longer have time to cause trouble for Becky. He's about to marry a very rich, very possessive woman fifteen years older than himself.'

Ryan dropped into his chair so hard it rocked back into the wall. 'Oh, my God. I forgot.'

If Becky found out . . .

He would swear Hallie to secrecy, and wait until after the trade show next week, perhaps even until after the wedding, to tell Becky he'd had Eric investigated and dealt with. Maybe by that time he would be able to think of a way to tell her that wouldn't make her angry all over again.

Ryan sat slumped in his office chair, concentration fixed on the pencil he was flipping end over end on his blotter. Thump, the eraser came down. Thwack, the lead point bit into the leather. Thump, thwack, thump, thwack.

It was late Thursday night. The last day of the trade show was over. Five hours ago he'd returned to the office, sent his staff home and told them not to come back until Monday. Then he'd fallen into this chair. He'd been there ever since. Thump, thwack, thump, thwack.

A failure.

Hard to swallow, McLeod? he asked himself. No one had been interested in his ingenious new program. No one.

The brainchild of a young kid from a university back East had taken the computer industry a quantum leap into the future. Everybody was being cautious about purchasing technology and he couldn't blame them.

Damn! Once he had been the kid genius, scaring the pants off the establishment. Where had that kid gone? Chasing the big bucks had cost him more than he'd ever realized.

And now it was going to cost him the best woman he'd ever met, the only woman he would ever love.

How was it going to feel when he told Becky he was a failure? He needed money for the easier life he'd promised her. Where would it come from? Monday morning he had to report to his backers on the results of the trade show. They were going to be very . . . he searched his mind for the right word . . . unhappy. Thump, thwack, thump, thwack.

'Why are you still here?'

The pencil stopped. Hallie stood in the doorway, coat on, black hair carefully protected by a silk scarf that depicted cavorting puppies and kittens.

'Where else should I be? Why are you here? I sent everyone home hours ago, including you.'

'Go home. You're so tired you look five, maybe ten years older than you did a week ago. Things will look better in the morning.'

'No, they won't. I'm thirty-six years old and washed up. A used up old hack.'

'Go home. Better yet, go to Becky's. Kiss her a few times and you won't feel old. I guarantee it.'

'No. I can't. I want to pretend she's mine one more day. If I see her tonight, I'll have to tell her it's over. Tomorrow is soon enough.'

'What are you talking about?' she asked, baffled.

'I'm broke.' He restarted the pencil on its endless journey. Thump, thwack, thump. 'Finished.'

'You are not!' she exclaimed.

'Close enough. Becky needs someone with a solid base to support her and her kids. To give her the security she deserves. Thanks to a pimply kid I will have a difficult time taking care of only Dani and myself.'

'You're blowing this out of proportion. This is a setback, sure. But we've pulled out of those before and ended up ahead every time. Even if you have to cut back, you're far from a poor man. Sell the penthouse and that pretentious car. They're worth enough to keep you all, plus the business, for a year or more.'

'Go home, Hallie. I'm not going to debate my decision with you. I'm tired. You're tired. Go home.'

'You're making a terrible mistake. Becky loves you, not your money!'

'I said, go home!' He slammed the pencil down and stood up, his voice shaking with rage. 'I don't need you to second guess my decisions!'

'Oh, yes, you do. You're acting like a spoiled brat.'

'Hallie,' he stalked over to the couch, 'leave me alone.' He lifted one of the cushions that formed its back and angled it across the low arm.

'What are you doing?'

'What does it look like?' he asked sarcastically as he kicked off his shoes and lay down with his head on the improvised pillow. 'I'm going to get some sleep.'

'Aren't you supposed to pick up Dani?'

'I knew I'd be working very late for the entire four days so Becky suggested that Dani should sleep over. We included today because I knew, one way or the other, I would be very late tonight. Now, if you don't mind, I want to be alone.'

'You do this and you'll hurt Becky,' she warned him. 'You promised you wouldn't hurt her. And what about those lovely children?'

'If I marry her now, things will be worse for her, and them, than if I don't go through with the marriage. Believe me, I know.'

'This is dreadful. What can I say . . .'

'Hallie, there's nothing you can say I want to hear right now.' He closed his eyes and a faint smile curved his lips then faded away. 'Except maybe good-night and good-bye.'

She stared down at him.

'I said, good-night.'

She sighed in defeat then picked up his discarded suit jacket, used it to cover his shoulders, and turned out the light before she left.

Ryan cruised down the street Friday afternoon. Half-an-hour ago he'd changed out of the wrinkled suit he'd spent the night in, shaved off two days growth of beard, and rinsed his red eyes with cold water, trying to reduce the visible effects of exhaustion.

He hadn't slept after Hallie's departure the night before. He couldn't. To sleep he would have had to relax his uncompromising control over his emotions and he was afraid if he let go he'd start shouting or crying, or something equally awful.

Once started, he might not have been able to stop.

He needed to be calm when he talked to Becky. To explain to her he couldn't give her what she needed. To tell her he was sorry.

To say good-bye.

It was only two o'clock and she wasn't expecting him until five or six but he couldn't procrastinate any longer. He'd never been one for putting off unpleasant tasks and he needed time to talk to her alone before school let out for the day. This was going to be bad enough without having all those kids listening.

Damned if he knew how he was going to stay away after today. At least Mike was going to be pleased the wedding was off. Ryan chuckled sourly as he fought back the misery washing over him in waves. Now he wouldn't have to figure out a way of telling Becky he'd chased down Eric.

Or maybe he should tell her. Perhaps she'd be so angry she'd kick him out and save him telling her the truth about the trade show debacle. Then he could find a way to hire her a good lawyer so she could pin the louse to the wall for back child support and the missing mortgage payments.

At least if Becky could manage financially he wouldn't have to worry about her and the kids. Much.

CHAPTER 16

Becky glanced up at the Garfield clock on the wall of her office when she heard the distinctive rumble of the Mercedes. He's early, she thought.

She looked down at the puzzle she'd been trying to work on and a happy grin danced across her lips. Who cared about missed deadlines when she could spend some time alone with Ryan before the hordes descended. The doorbell rang while she was tidying away her papers. She paused for a moment. Must not be Ryan, he'd have used his key.

When she swung the door open, she was shocked at Ryan's appearance. His face was grey with exhaustion and he looked . . . The only word she could come up with was disheveled, though his clothes were tidy.

'What's the matter? You look terrible.' She reached for his hand but he shoved them both deep in his trouser pockets.

'May I come in?'

'Of course. Why did you ring the bell? It wasn't locked.' She stepped back. 'Was it jammed again? I'll have to get a repair man out here. Mike couldn't get it open yesterday so Nicky decided he would kick it in like they do on television. You can probably imagine how indignant he was when I made him scrub off the scuff marks . . .'

He didn't respond and her voice died away as she realized she was chattering nervously.

'I need to talk to you.' He didn't kiss her as he always did, he didn't even look at her. When she moved closer he backed up a step, his face almost as stiff as his body.

'What's the matter, Ryan?'

'Can we sit down?'

She stared at him, her heart contracting painfully when he spoke so coldly.

'Come in the kitchen. We can talk while I do the dishes.'

A spasm of pain crossed his face, so quickly she thought she'd imagined it.

'No!' A tic appeared at the corner of his left eye. 'I would rather sit in the living room, if that's acceptable.'

'Of course.'

After she sat down he positioned himself in front of the windows on the far side of the room.

'Becky, I . . .' He coughed, swallowed, and began again. 'I have something to tell you.' Then he stopped.

'What is it, Ryan? What's the matter?' Fear choked her throat as all the possibilities scrambled for first place in her mind.

'Are you sick? Or . . . is it the kids? Did something terrible happen to one of the kids?' She leaped to her feet and rushed to him, her hands out, reaching for comfort and reassurance.

'No! Calm yourself.' He gripped her hands in his own and held her away from his body, not allowing the hug she so desperately needed. 'Please sit down.'

Her knees trembled as he led her back to the sofa. As soon as she was seated his hands dropped away and he walked back to the window. She waited while he stared at her, his eyes bleak and hungry.

'You're scaring me. Please, tell me what's wrong. Don't leave me at the mercy of my imagination. If the kids are fine it can't be too terribly . . .'

'I can't marry you.'

His words hung in the air between them and she could see the wall they formed as if something tangible blocked him from her.

'Why?' As soon as the word was out of her mouth she realized she had been waiting for this. From the beginning a part of her had known the happiness would disappear. She couldn't let it crush her. She would survive but this time she needed to be told why her world was falling apart around her. 'Explain.'

'I'm broke.'

She waited for him to continue but he didn't. 'I don't understand.'

He lifted his shoulders and rotated them, as if trying to relax some of the tension in his body.

'The trade show was a flop. The computer industry is in shock and things are going to change drastically, very soon. Some young . . .' he broke off. 'Never mind, that doesn't matter. What does matter is my new program isn't going to sell.'

'I'm sorry. I know how much you wanted it to succeed.' The words were as strained as her expression. 'But what does that have to do with our wedding?'

'It's going to be difficult, perhaps impossible, to make up what Pastin has cost me over the last year. I'm not going to be able to give you all the things I promised.'

'So?' She didn't bother trying to hide her bewilderment.

'Look, Becky, don't make this any harder for me.' For the first time he showed some emotion as he deliberately allowed anger to bolster his resolve. 'We both know how money problems wreck marriages. You lived through it with Eric. I grew up with it. My mother made life hell whenever my father's salary was inadequate for her needs.'

'And you think the same thing will happen to us?'

'No. I know it will.'

'I am not your mother and you are not Eric. It's not fair to expect – '

'Don't you know this is tearing me apart?' He shoved his fingers through his hair and Becky felt herself shrink back as he began to pace. 'I love you. I feel like I'm dying inside but I will not go into a marriage that will bring pain to everyone. You and your children and Dani have suffered enough.'

'You're running out, aren't you?' She knew him well enough to know that nothing she could say would change his mind. She let her frustration show. 'You're too damned scared to work at this.'

'I'm being realistic.'

'No! You're being cruel and absurd.' She stood up and grabbed his arm, forcing him to face her. With every second word her finger poked his chest. 'This is something you decided. Well, buster, I'm sick of you making decisions and expecting me to sit there and say yes, sir, amen.'

'You don't understand.'

'No, I do understand. You are leaving me. What you don't understand is I have never cared how much money you make. I don't care if we spend our holidays in Tahiti or picnic at the park down the road. I don't care if I drive a twelve year old Toyota with rust spots or a brand new BMW.'

'Becky . . .'

Now he reached out to her. Now when he'd already told her he was leaving her. Now when the pain in her heart was so excruciating that she couldn't let him touch her because if he did she'd probably fly apart.

She jerked away.

'Get out of my house.'

'Becky . . .'

'I don't want to see you again. Jan or Hallie can chauffeur Dani back and forth until you find her another sitter.'

'Let me . . .'

'Get out!' she shouted.

He went.

Becky waited until she heard his car screech out of the driveway before she relaxed enough to let the tears fall.

Ten minutes later she was still waiting for the tears to fall. Why wasn't she collapsed into a sodden heap? she wondered. It took her a little while to figure out the rather simple explanation but when she did, first her lips twitched, then she grinned.

There were no tears because she didn't believe their chance at happiness together was gone.

Stupid man, she thought tolerantly. Dealing with his single-minded determination to direct their lives was becoming very frustrating.

If that wonderful idiot thought she was going to sit back and let him ruin their lives, he had a richly deserved lesson coming. A lesson he'd made so painfully obvious he desperately needed. She was no longer the woman who had let Eric stomp all over her and she owed a lot of her strength to the man who had allowed a bunch of emotional garbage from his past to confuse him into walking away from her.

Her grin softened as she recalled how he had stood there and told her what he couldn't do. As if she would let him be so foolish.

Even as she began making plans for how she was going to fix the situation, she realized how difficult it was going to be to convince him he was wrong. It didn't take her long to decide she would succeed. He had given her something to base her hope on.

If he really wanted to break off their relationship, he shouldn't have told her he loved her.

Ryan realized he was driving far too fast and eased back on his speed as he steered the Mercedes around a busy corner. Today he felt strangely at home among the grotesquely shaped oak and elm trees lining both sides of the road as they reached out to grasp futilely for heaven. The winter sun slanted through the writhing and naked branches, casting distorted shadows.

It was done, it was over. He tightened his hands on the steering wheel, twisting his fingers around the soft leather cover. Oh, God, why did it hurt so much?

A few blocks from Becky's house he caught a glimpse of red out of the corner of his eye. A singular and spectacularly vile orange-red. The same color as the new ski-jacket Nicky had sworn he couldn't live without and cajoled Ryan into buying for him last week.

He put his foot on the brake, slowing the car to get a better look at the running child.

Why was Nicky running down the street by himself? Mike was supposed to ride his bike as far as the playschool, then walk his little brother home. Lately, with the increased threat of violence from youth gangs moving into the area, the two girls had also started walking home with Mike.

Where were Mike and the girls?

He stepped on the brake, swerved into a parking space in front of the flying figure, jumped out of the car and waited for Nicky to see him. When he realized Nicky was going to barrel on past, blinded by tears, he bent and swung the little boy into his arms.

'Whoa, there. Where's Mike?'

Nicky wrapped his arms around Ryan's neck, sobs shuddering through his body.

'They're going to hurt him. I need Mommy, get Mommy . . .' He ended on a wail and buried his wet face in Ryan's shoulder, weeping loudly.

Fear squeezed at Ryan's heart and he lifted Nicky away until he could see his face.

'Who's going to get hurt?'

At first Nicky didn't answer, merely cried louder.

Ryan fought down panic and gave Nicky a small shake. 'Tell me. I have to know so I can help. Is it Mike? Is Mike in trouble?'

Nicky nodded, unable to speak.

'Where is he? Can you show me?'

He nodded again, dragging in a shuddering breath. Ryan jerked open the passenger door, strapped Nicky into the seat and raced around the hood of the car to his own door. He started the engine.

'Which way?'

With the hiccups finally subsiding Nicky pointed back in the direction he had been running from. 'In the back lane down there.'

Ryan pulled the car around in a tight circle, gunned the engine, and raced back the way Nicky had indicated, pausing at the entrance to every lane they passed.

'Where are the girls?'

Nicky swiped the back of his hand beneath his runny nose. 'They went to Sally's.'

Ryan whispered a thank you to whichever powers were listening. At least, whatever was going on, it didn't involve Sarah and Dani. They were safe.

Seven blocks later he saw a large group of people milling among the garbage cans in the middle of a tree-shaded lane between a row of houses.

'There? Is Mike there?'

Nicky peered over Ryan's arm. 'Yes.'

He sized up the situation quickly. Fifteen or so people, aged anywhere from twelve to twenty, and they all looked like trouble. He rested a hand on Nicky's leg while he surveyed the crowd of youths, most of them clad in identical jackets.

It had been a lot of years but Ryan's sense for this kind of danger still functioned. He felt a prickling at his nape and his adrenaline kicked into overdrive automatically. He couldn't take a little boy in there and he couldn't leave him alone in the car. And with so large a group to face, he'd definitely need help if there were trouble.

He pulled the car into the driveway of the nearest house and grabbed Nicky out of his seat, then ran to the front door. He held his thumb on the doorbell, ringing it repeatedly.

About to try the next house, he saw a drape in the side window twitch. 'Ma'am? Please, I need help!'

A young woman, children clinging to her knees, cautiously opened the door only the inches allowed by the chain. 'Mommy, it's Nicky. Hi, Nicky, did you come to play?'

The childish voice from inside the house was an unexpected blessing. Maybe the fact that her child knew Nicky would persuade the woman to overcome her natural fears. 'Please help me! My older boy is in trouble in your back lane. A gang.'

She inspected him carefully, then pushed the door closed to release the chain before she opened it wider. He put Nicky down at her feet.

'Call the police,' he ordered.

'Of course,' she said. 'Go. I'll call.'

He didn't bother with thanks but ran. He raced back to the mouth of the lane, then forced himself to slow to a walk as he neared the group of both boys and girls. They noticed him immediately but he disregarded their jeers, surveying the crowd for a sign of Mike.

His heart stopped, then began to beat madly when he recognized a crumpled heap of metal as Mike's bike.

Where in God's name was Mike? What had they done to him?

Bile rose in his throat as he thought of what could have already happened to the boy. Lately there had been frequent and horrifying news reports of the random and senseless violent crimes perpetrated when such gangs moved into a community.

A chill breeze eddied close to the ground, stirring dead leaves. Torn pieces of paper lifted on the wind, twisting and turning in a lazy ballet. A capricious gust pinned one against his leg and he reached down to brush it off. But the picture on one side seemed familiar so he picked it up.

It was part of a painstakingly traced and colored map of the Canary Islands Mike had been working on last weekend. Now it was torn and muddy. Ruined. Ryan crumpled the paper in his fist, then moved forward again. The crowd parted as he pushed through.

Finally he saw Mike.

The boy lay in a foetal ball in the dirt, his arms crossed protectively over his face and head, his knees drawn up tight against his belly. His jacket was torn and his school books scattered.

A young man, probably nineteen or twenty years old, at least three years older than anyone else in the group, stood over Mike. The black leather collar of his blue jacket was turned up around the face of an angel. Hair so pale it appeared white curled around his forehead; a dimpled, impish grin curved his lips.

Before Ryan could get closer, he kicked Mike in the kidney.

'I'm really sorry 'bout this, man,' his tone was sweetly reasonable, 'but I can't have people refusing to do as they're told. I'm gonna have to use you as an example.' He lifted his foot and drew it back to kick Mike again.

With a roar of rage, compounded by the fear and despair he'd been living with, Ryan leaped forward. Perhaps he intended to kill the young tough? He didn't know or care. For a second or two his logical brain malfunctioned. All he wanted was to stop the person who dared to hurt one of Ryan's own.

Any way he had to. At that precise instant eighteen years of civilized living fell away and he was once more back in his own youth. Roaming the seamy streets of half a dozen American cities. Searching for excitement with his friends. Acting out his own frustrations with the system. Angry at anyone daring to trespass on his turf. Surviving.

Mike's tormentor jerked back in surprise but soon recovered his poise. He reached inside his jacket. The younger kids retreated when their leader pulled a knife.

Sunlight glinted along the jagged edge of the blade, reminding Ryan he was thirty-six, not sixteen. Sensing a good show, everyone else pulled back in a ragged circle. He stepped closer to where Mike lay, his gaze fixed on the eyes of the guy wielding the knife.

'What'cha doing here, suit?'

'I came for my son.' And that easily Ryan accepted that he could never walk away from Becky or her children. 'I'm leaving now and taking him with me.'

'Oh, ya are, are ya?' the kid with the knife sneered. 'I don't think so.'

A loud raspberry resounded in the crowd and although most of the kids looked uneasy, one voice in the crowd began urging him to 'hurt the suit good'. Their leader crouched slightly, tossing the knife back and forth between his hands, the expression on his angelic face twisted into something cold and ugly.

'Come on, big guy. Come get me. I'll cut your pretty face for ya.'

Ryan glanced down to where Mike lay unnaturally still. Was he badly hurt? Was he alive? He hadn't responded to either the kick or the threat. He crouched near the boy's head.

'Mike, can you hear me?'

Mike's body jerked when he heard Ryan's voice, then inch-by-inch he lowered his arms.

'Ryan?' His swollen eyelids lifted, then drifted shut again as if the effort to keep them open was beyond his strength.

It was only one word but Ryan felt intense relief course through his body. Mike was alive. Then he looked closer at the tears and the terror and the bloody scrapes on the boy's face.

Deep, cold rage awoke, twisting inside him, then went deathly still.

He turned his head to stare at the knife, then studied the face of the man who stood on the other side of Mike as if through a strangely distorted window. They silently assessed each other for the space of several heartbeats. In the gang leader Ryan recognized some of the evil he'd seen in his life on the streets so many years before. He knew this wouldn't be done the easy way.

He casually slipped off the jacket of his tailored linen suit and draped it over Mike before he rose to his feet. Hopefully the thin cloth would provide a little warmth for the boy. Slowly Ryan lifted his hands and slipped off his tie.

'What's your name?' He asked while he unfastened the heavy silver cuff links, dropping them on the ground beside the tie. He rolled his sleeves up, exposing sinewy forearms.

'What's it to ya?' The gang leader stretched forward and took a swipe at his ribs. Ryan swayed slightly, allowing the knife to miss by less than an inch.

'Because I need to know, buddy boy.' Ryan's fingers made quick work of the top five buttons down his shirt front, loosening the snug fit of the imported shirt, giving himself room to manoeuver. The chill wind still blew but rage kept him warm.

'I always like to know the name of my adversaries. It makes it easier for the coroner and the police to do their jobs.'

Ryan's calm preparation and lack of fear startled his opponent, who halted the constant moving and involuntarily retreated a step. After a quick glance at his audience, he scowled and swaggered forward.

Ryan smiled grimly. Good. The hoodlum had realized that the coming fight would not be an easy one. That small amount of doubt in the other's mind would work to Ryan's advantage.

'Let's get out of here, Brasky. We don't need the kid,' said one of the spectators.

'Shut the hell up.' Brasky danced in and tried to bury his blade in Ryan's side, feinting to the left then jabbing upward from the right.

'Ah, yes, the young man who thought it would be smart to smoke in a crowded attic.'

Ryan slid away, keeping himself between Mike and his abuser. He avoiding the knife easily but couldn't duck the fisted blow to his left eye when his leather soles skidded in the gravel. He kicked off the hand-sewn loafers and bounced lightly in his stocking feet, knees bent and toes curled into the uneven surface, testing for balance.

Keeping his attention on the knife, he tried to stay aware of the movements of the rest of the gang as all but the oldest melted quietly away in ones or twos. Only the most hardened gang members remained. A mixed blessing.

'Think you're tough, do you?' Ryan smiled mockingly, trying to make the other angry and careless.

Reacting to the taunt, his opponent leaped in close and stabbed at Ryan's side. Ryan stepped back, his motion agile enough, but a rock rolled under his heel and while he was off-balance the knife slashed at his face.

He felt the sting of the blade, the wetness on his cheek. Disbelieving, he touched his face then stared at the dark red blood on his fingers. Must be getting old, he told himself. Was he too slow to hold him off until the police arrived?

'See, old man? You should give up right now. If you say you're sorry, real nice, I might not do it again.' The number of his friends had shrunk to a handful but those howled encouragingly when their leader grinned evilly. 'But then, maybe I will.'

On the last word he brought up his arm and swept his blade toward Ryan's stomach. He leaped back and Brasky followed, thrusting and lunging, getting in the occasional punch with his free hand.

Ryan evaded the worst cuts and blows but soon his lip was split and little flecks of red appeared here and there, soaking through cuts in the silk fabric of his shirt. Once or twice he landed a punch to Brasky's body. A blow to Brasky's face stunned him enough to allow Ryan to throw three rabbit punches to his stomach.

Brasky backed off, one hand to his abdomen, using the back of the other to wipe at the blood trickling from his nose.

Through the satisfaction at landing the blows, Ryan could feel himself tiring. He knew it by the breath rasping in and out through clenched teeth, searing his lungs. He was beginning to feel waves of pain from the cut on his face. Sweat soaked his back and he was moving slower.

How much longer could he last? Ryan wondered. When would the police come?

Ryan staggered back a step as Brasky landed a kick to his kneecap but stayed on his feet, wiping the sweat and blood from his eyes, once again circling warily. Then very faintly Ryan heard sirens.

He gritted his teeth and smiled grimly. Brasky thrust forward with the knife and Ryan grabbed his arm at wrist and elbow. He yanked Brasky's arm in close and spun him around, wedging the hand holding the knife high up against Brasky's spine.

'Old man, eh?'

Brasky's answer was a chain of curses.

He squeezed Brasky's hand until he could pluck the knife from the man's loosened fingers.

'You'd better let me go,' Brasky spoke over his shoulder as the sirens drew closer. 'My people will make you sorry you interfered. I'll get Mike another time, you know, and his mother . . . whoooeee, I can hardly wait to try her out.'

Ryan gritted his teeth and shoved Brasky's arm up his back. Viciously. Brasky's shrill scream was drowned out by the wailing sirens as police vehicles blocked both ends of the lane.

'You broke my arm, you asshole. I'll sue you.'

'Self-defense. No court in the land is going to fault me for disarming you. No pun intended.'

Brasky responded with a mixture of whimpers and threats.

'I've forgotten more tricks than you will ever learn, scum bag.' He lowered his head until his mouth was beside Brasky's ear. 'If you go near my family, I will find you and take great joy in breaking every bone in your body, one at a time, even if I can't prove you were involved. I don't think you'll fancy life as a cripple.'

Brasky screamed again when Ryan released the useless arm.

'As for your people, I don't think I have to worry. Look around. You're all alone, boyyo.'

Ryan dropped him in a heap on the ground. He turned his back and limped over to where Mike lay, ignoring the police as they rounded up fleeing gang members and herded them into the police van. He knelt beside the boy he'd claimed as his son, allowing the knife to fall from numb fingers. His hand trembled as he touched the boy's ashen face.

'Mike? Can you hear me?'

Mike's eyes flickered open. 'Nicky?' he asked hoarsely.

'He's safe. He told me the girls were at their friend's house.'

'Yes.' The single word was whispered so low Ryan had to put his ear next to Mike's lips. The boy struggled to say something more but Ryan shushed him.

'Nicky told me they went to Sally's.'

Mike nodded weakly.

'Then don't try to talk.'

'We've sent for an ambulance, sir. It should be here in a few minutes. Could you answer some questions?'

He glanced up. The young uniformed police officer blanched when he saw the blood still seeping slowly but steadily from the cut that laid Ryan's cheek open from the corner of his mouth to below his eye.

'Does it have to be right now?'

'No, ah, no. Someone will talk to you at the hospital. I'll stay with the perp.' He started toward where Brasky lay but paused. 'Is there anything I can do for you?'

'No. Thanks. We'll wait here until the paramedics arrive. I don't know how serious my son's internal injuries are.' He shifted and heard metal clink against rock. He picked up the knife and handed it to the officer. 'Here, you'd better take this.'

The officer took it gingerly with a handkerchief, then put it in a plastic bag one of the other cops brought him from the patrol car. Then they both went to stand beside Brasky, who still lay huddled on the ground, whining about lawsuits and lawyers. One of the cops told him to shut up.

Ryan sat down heavily in the dirt and gravel next to Mike. He leaned forward to pick up his shoes and other belongings, but stopped mid-motion, too tired to bother. Neither said anything more while they waited.

'Ryan, Ryan, Ryan!'

Wearily he lifted his head in time to brace himself for the weeping whirlwind that flung itself into his arms. He wrapped one arm around the small shaking body, pulling Nicky close to his uninjured side.

'I was watching from the fence. Is there anything I can do for you?'

Ryan looked up. The mother who'd opened her door to a stranger had followed Nicky into the lane. 'No, but thanks for taking care of my son.'

'Glad I could help.' She handed him a clean tea towel. 'Here. I thought you might need this. Throw it away when you get to the hospital.' He thanked her again and placed it against his cheek as she walked away.

Nicky was still crying.

'Shhh. Mike's safe.' Awkwardly he rubbed his hand up and down Nicky's spine, trying to soothe him. Gradually his sobs abated and he nestled against Ryan's chest.

Ryan felt a small movement on his thigh and looked down. Mike had inched closer. Ryan wrapped his larger fingers around the smaller ones that crept into his hand. Tears trickled from beneath Mike's closed eyes, through the dried blood and grit that caked his skin.

Then the three of them sat there on the ground, waiting for the paramedics.

Ryan rested his good cheek on Nicky's head, staring at the torn scraps of paper still pirouetting in a mad ballet with the wind, until finally he gave into the pain and sheer exhaustion and closed his eyes.

CHAPTER 17

Becky's heart was pounding as she walked into the hospital's emergency ward. She identified herself and the trauma nurse directed her to a case room. Her hand shook as she reached out to pull aside the curtain.

Mike lay on his back in one of the two high white beds. Ryan slouched uncomfortably in a chair beside Mike's bed with Nicky curled in his lap. One of Ryan's arms curled protectively around Nicky's body, while he held Mike's hand with the other.

All three were blood-spattered, filthy and asleep. Even in their sleep both her sons had a tight grip on the man she loved, would always love.

Mike's face was swollen, his chest bare except for the bindings on his ribs. Nicky was unhurt, merely dirty and exhausted.

'Ryan?' she whispered.

His eyelids lifted slowly. 'Forgive me? Marry me?'

She'd been existing in a twilight of hope and uncertainty and sheer terror ever since the police had showed up at her door. Now that she was finally in the same room with her family and could see and touch them herself, it lifted. She smiled back when he tried to grin. 'No more decision making on your own?'

'No more. I obviously need intelligent help anyway. I was so wrong, but . . .'

'Shhh. Yes, I'll marry you but we can talk later.'

'The girls?'

'Jan's picking them up from Sally's and will tell them where we are.'

He saw her glance at the gauze bandage taped across his cheek, from eye to jaw. 'Not so handsome now, honey. Will you love me anyway?'

'You look beautiful to me.' She bent to kiss his lips, gently, tenderly, trying not to hurt his battered mouth. 'I'll always love you. You rest a little longer. I have some forms to fill out, then the police want to talk to us both. Have the doctors examined you yet?'

'No. I didn't have the boys' medical numbers. Plus they became hysterical when the hospital staff tried to separate us, so I told them to forget it until you got here. My injuries could wait.'

'Did they tell you what's wrong with Mike?'

'No, because I'm not his legal guardian. Not yet.' Ryan sighed heavily and his eyelids started to droop. 'Needed you,' he muttered.

She felt the sting of tears and she blinked, willing them not to fall. 'Give me Nicky. I'll lay him in the other bed. You're exhausted.'

'Better not.' His arm tightened protectively. 'He started to cry when the nurse tried to move him. Leave him with me until you can hold him.'

'What happened? Nobody seems to know exactly.' She felt terrible when he forced open blurry eyes. 'Never mind. I'll find out later when we talk to the police. I'll be as quick as I can.'

After she left Ryan stopped trying to stay awake. He was too old for this kind of exertion. He still had to explain things to the cops but they could wait. Sleep wouldn't. At least Becky had forgiven him, though he knew he owed her an explanation and a better apology. He was so darn tired . . .

The bustle and confusion of the emergency ward faded away as he drifted into sleep.

'Ryan?'

He moved incautiously and bit back a groan. Someone had whispered his name to wake him up. Was Becky back already? Then he realized his arms were empty. Where was Nicky? Panic spurted through him and he lurched up to look around groggily.

'Ryan?' Mike whispered again.

'Yeah, sport?' He dropped back into the chair, too dizzy and nauseous to search for Nicky. 'Where's your brother?'

'Mom came for him when a nurse woke me up to take my temperature.'

'Oh. That's okay then.' Gratefully he settled back into the support of the chair.

'Thank you for rescuing me.'

'Try not to let it happen again. I'm too old for this.'

'I'm real sorry.'

'What happened?'

'They were going to . . . They wanted me to do something and I wouldn't. Joe said he had to make an example of me. I guess he wanted everybody to be afraid of him and do what he said.'

'Do you want me to arrange a transfer to another school? Or we could buy a house somewhere else after your Mom and I get married. It would get you right away from them.'

'No, thanks. Mom loves Lilac House too much to move.'

'For you, she would.'

'I can handle it.'

'Let me know if you have any more problems.'

'Sure.'

Silence settled over the small curtained area once more. But not for long.

'Ryan?'

'Yes, Mike?'

'Do you love Mom?'

'Very much.'

'Oh.' Mike was quiet while he thought it over. 'Will you hit Mom? Cause if you do, I'm old enough to protect her now. Even if you did take care of me today.'

He jerked upright. 'I'd never hit Becky, Mike. I'd never hurt any of you. Why do you think I would?'

Mike went deathly pale. 'Dad did.'

Ryan was shocked mute.

'A long time ago I woke up real late, must've been after midnight. I wanted a glass of water and when I went to the bathroom I heard Dad's voice downstairs.'

Ryan could hear tears in the boy's voice even though his eyes were dry.

'I was so excited. I hated them to be divorced. I thought maybe he was home to stay so I went down to see him.'

Mike stopped talking. Ryan clenched his maltreated hand into a fist, dread and horror masking the pain that shot up his wrist from the damaged fingers. Mike's next words answered the question Ryan was afraid to ask.

'I saw Dad . . . I saw him hurting Mom.' He reached out blindly for Ryan's hand. 'I didn't know what to do! I didn't understand. I ran away. I ran away.' His face crumpled and he dropped his head to hide his face on their joined hands. 'I ran away.'

For a second Ryan was paralyzed when he realized Mike blamed himself for something he couldn't have changed. He'd been carrying a massive load of guilt all these years for not protecting his mother the night Eric raped her. Too heavy a burden for a young boy to bear all alone.

'It wasn't your fault, Mike. You were too young to help her. Even if you had gone downstairs, he probably wouldn't have stopped. And he might have hurt you too. That would have been worse for your Mom than what he did to her.'

Mike didn't acknowledge Ryan's statement.

'You have to believe me, Mike.'

The boy lifted his head and Ryan smiled crookedly.

'Are you sure?'

'Yes, very sure. If you talk to your mother, she'll say the same thing.'

'I couldn't!' He looked horrified.

'Yes, you can. Haven't you talked to her before about . . . private things?'

'Sure.'

'Then you can talk to her about this.'

'She'll hate me. I should've done something.'

'No, she won't. She loves you. Your Mom knows you will always, and have always, done your best. She expects no more.' He heard the truth in what he'd said and, finally, saw how wrong he'd been.

Becky would never judge him on the basis of how much money he earned. She judged people on how they lived their lives. Thank God he'd learned, and accepted, that fact before he'd walked away from her. Before either of them had said something to make his stupidity irrevocable.

'But what if he comes back? I've always been afraid he'd . . . you know . . . again. I tried to make sure I was there whenever he came to the house. That last time, you know, when he tried to steal her train? I wanted to kill him.'

'You're forgetting that from now on I'll be there too. Don't you think between the two of us we can protect her?'

'You mean after you get married.' Mike hesitated, then his cheeks reddened. 'I'm sorry I've been so dumb. Are you mad at me?'

'Of course not. You were only trying to protect your Mom. Do you feel differently now?'

'Yes.' Relief glimmered in Mike's eyes.

Ryan thought he could feel the weight of the boy's assumed burdens shift to his own shoulders. It felt good. But good or not, he'd do anything for Becky's family. For Becky.

'I'm glad you're going to marry her. I think you could take care of all of us and Mom, too. Real easy.'

'I'm going to need someone to show me the ropes around there, though. How about it? Would you be willing?'

'You bet!'

Their embrace was impulsive and awkward and, though it was physically painful, they both felt better for it. Then, embarrassed by the strong emotions, they pulled apart and laughed sheepishly.

Ryan lay back on the couch and lifted his legs to rest his ankles on the low coffee table, listening to Becky move around upstairs as she settled the children for the night. A difficult task after all they'd been through. His entire body was one big ache, but that was nothing compared to the throbbing agony in his cheek.

A doctor had bound Mike's bruised ribs, treated his various cuts, and prescribed a mild sedative. The emergency room doctor had treated most of Ryan's own injuries but the cut on his face was so severe Becky had insisted on a plastic surgeon. Even so, he would probably have a scar for the rest of his life.

Or rather two scars, counting the one Nicky's toy truck had cut in the back of his head. Rather strange that these were his first, considering his misspent youth.

He closed his eyes and waited for the painkillers to have some effect. While he waited, he relived the day. Becky had been terrific from the minute she'd arrived at the hospital. Brisk, efficient, strong.

Even after they were released from the hospital, she had scoffed at his concern he was causing her too much trouble and insisted, over his objections, that he and Dani spend the night so she could keep an eye on him. So here he was, back in the house he been ordered out of, with the woman he thought he'd lost forever.

'All asleep at last.' Becky sighed as she said the words and walked over to stand beside him. 'How are you feeling?'

'My face is starting to feel a little numb.'

'What can I get for you?'

'Not a thing, except maybe you right here,' he patted the cushion he was sitting on, 'right now. I need some comfort and the best way I know to get it is to hold you in my arms.'

'I shouldn't, you must hurt all over.' But she sat down even as she objected.

'I'd rather feel good all over,' he hinted, leering outrageously.

'Forget it, you'd be no good right now anyway. The doctor told me the side effects of that prescription.' She tentatively laid her hand on his thigh but relaxed when he didn't flinch.

He forced up one of his arms and placed it around her shoulders, urging her into his embrace, moaning as her shoulder came in contact with his side. She stiffened and tried to pull away but he shook his head, refusing to release her.

'Don't make any fast moves and we'll manage. I need to hold you.'

They sat in silence for a long time, staring into the empty fireplace. There were still ashes heaped beneath the grate from the last fire they'd enjoyed together. He thought how symbolic it was. If he had gone through with his intention to leave Becky his life would have been empty of everything but the cold ashes of his plans and hopes.

Even now, after all they'd been through and what she'd said, there was a persistent fear deep in his gut that wouldn't let him believe. How could she love a broke failure? 'We have to talk about this afternoon.'

'Yes.'

'I was wrong.'

'Yes.'

His ribs hurt when her blunt answer made him laugh but he wished he could see the expression on her face because her short answers were making him feel uneasy. Was she changing her mind? 'You are going to marry me, aren't you?'

'Weeellll . . .'

'I'll do anything. Give me another chance, please.'

'Oh. . . .' she drew out her pause as he tried to hide his anxiety. He knew he wasn't succeeding very well.

'Okay, I'll put you out of your misery but there's one condition.'

'Anything, as long as you marry me.'

'I'm going to have the marriage ceremony changed.'

'To what?'

'You will promise to honor, cherish, and share decisions.'

He shared a smile with her. 'Sounds fair.' He pressed a kiss to her forehead. 'I'm going to sell the penthouse and the car. The two of them should clear enough to get us through the tough times if we're careful.'

'Not your Mercedes! You love that car.'

'Not as much as I love you. Besides, it's a ridiculous car for a father of four,' he said as he squeezed her shoulder. 'You were magnificent today, Becky.'

She turned her face away and her voice was strained when she answered him. 'No, I wasn't.'

'Yes, you were and don't try to deny it. By the time we got to the hospital I was a basket case. If you hadn't arrived to take care of everything, we would have been in a real mess.'

'No, I wasn't!' She leaped to her feet and stood over him. Her arms were stiff at her sides, her hands clenched into fists. She shook with anger as she glowered down at the man staring up at her, his mouth hanging open in astonishment. 'And if I was, it was because I had to be. But I don't want to be.'

Her sudden anger perplexed him. He was even more astounded when the anger dissolved into tears and her stiff posture collapsed. Ryan bit off an agonized groan when she hurled herself back onto the couch beside him and cast her arms around his neck.

'I'm so damned tired,' she said with her lips pressed to his throat.

'Tired of what?'

'Of being everything to everybody. What if you weren't there? What would have happened to Mike? My baby, my baby . . .' Her grief-filled words faltered and faded into sobs.

Awkwardly he tried to shift himself until he held her in his arms, his bandaged hand rubbing up and down her spine in a gentle massage, his lips buried in her hair whispering brokenly in an attempt to comfort her.

'But I was there, honey. Don't cry, I was there.' He said the words over and over, as if they were a magical incantation, until she sat up, laughing self-consciously as she wiped her face.

'I'm sorry. I hope I didn't hurt you. I guess a person never knows how they'll react . . .' The facile platitude tapered off into silence when he said her name, a little harshly, a lot reprovingly.

'Becky.' He waited, his face stern, until she looked at him. 'You're allowed to lose control when your children are in danger, it's part of being a parent. What about me? I lost control, too, when I saw Mike hurt and bloody and I'm not even his real father. I came real close to killing that monster.'

Her hands dropped to her lap and she met his direct gaze openly. 'Thank you for being there. I don't know what I would have done if . . . if . . .' She stopped, unable to continue.

He lifted her tear-wet hand to his lips and pressed a kiss to her palm. 'But I was there.'

'I know.' She turned his bandaged hands over and cradled them in both of hers. 'But at the hospital it was weird. I kept expecting to lose it but somehow, because of you, I didn't.'

'I don't see what I . . .'

'You don't know what my life's been like,' she said, her face serious and intent, the urgent need to make him understand pushing her along. 'I have always been solely responsible and answerable for the lives of my children. They depend on me totally. And now, finally, there is someone else who cares what happens to them. And to me.'

'But . . .'

'Even though you were hurt, and Mike was hurt, I felt light, buoyant.' He still looked baffled. She withdrew her hands from his and leaned closer to carefully cup his face, her fingertips memorizing the slight roughness of stubble on his chin, the gauze bandage that covered his wound.

'Don't you see? I'm not alone. You were there. *You*, not your money.' She tried to smile.

He searched her expression, finding the truth in her words. She needed his presence in her life. His love, his help, to know he cared. Her definition of love didn't place a dollar value on kind words, on hugs, or even on making love.

He took her hands from his face and held them loosely, his swollen fingers brailing their length and shape and texture.

'Becky, I have a confession to make.' He hesitated, wondering how to tell her what he'd done. Wondering how angry she was going to be. 'I hired a private detective to find Eric. When they found him, I had them convey a warning. He won't show up here uninvited again.'

She didn't say anything for a long time.

'You threatened him?'

'Yes.'

'I asked you not to interfere.'

'Yes, you did.

'You know what? I think I'm too tired to be angry. Let's talk about this next week. Or maybe next year.'

He smiled in relief. That hadn't been so bad.

'Don't think this lets you off the hook, though. I want your promise this kind of thing won't happen again.'

'Becky,' he paused to kiss the blue vein on the inside of her wrist, 'I wish I could give you everything I promised.'

'Yes, you can, silly.' She smiled lovingly and feathered a kiss along his eyebrow. 'You promised to love me forever, cross your heart.'

EPILOGUE

Ryan slid the card into the lock on the hotel room door and slipped silently inside, locking it behind him. He stepped out of his shoes, then put down his briefcase and the vase of pink roses that had cost him a fortune because he'd bribed the night manager into opening up the flower shop after midnight. He padded across the vast expanse of white carpet to the side of the bed, stripping off clothing as he moved.

The entire room was decorated in white. White furniture, white draperies. So much whiteness had been blinding when they'd checked in that morning, with the sun shining in through the floor-to-ceiling, wall-to-wall windows. It would have been painfully bland except for two things.

First were the lush textures. Nubby linen fabric hung at the windows and the over-stuffed chairs were upholstered in leather. All the painted surfaces were slick with glossy lacquer. The carpet was a thick plush that begged you to bury your naked toes in its pile. The walls were covered with rough sacking and painted the ever-present white.

Second was the bed. It was scarlet. The lacquered headboard was scarlet, the quilt was scarlet velvet, the sheets were scarlet satin. It was dramatic, it was erotic, it was utterly provocative.

But, to Ryan, the most important, delightful thing about that bed was the woman asleep in it. After two years of marriage, the love and the passion grew stronger every day he spent with Becky.

She lay curled on her side, a book still propped in slack fingers. Her white skin, visible above the drooping satin sheet, gleamed in the light cast by the bedside lamp.

He tossed his briefs on his discarded clothes, set her book on the bedside table, and slid into bed beside her, pulling her into the curve of his body, nestling her spine to his chest. Then he stretched out his arm and touched the base of the white ceramic lamp, plunging the room into darkness.

Unable to resist her allure, even though he knew she was tired from a hard day of shopping and sight-seeing, he touched his lips to her bare shoulder, trailing the kiss to the nape of her neck.

'Mmmmm, feels good,' she murmured, turning in his arms until she lay on her back, entwining her legs with his, and snuggling into his arms. 'Do it some more.'

'I'm sorry I woke you, honey,' he said, not sorry at all. 'Go back to sleep.'

'How did the meeting go?'

'Go to sleep, we can talk in the morning.'

'No,' Becky said, and rolled over to turn on the light. He smiled as she sat there blinking sleepily, naked above where the scarlet satin sheet pooled around her hips. 'It's important and,' she yawned mightily, 'I want to know now.'

'You'd better cover up or we won't be doing much talking,' he teased, staring pointedly at her rosy-tipped breasts.

'That's what you think, buster,' she said threateningly, but she pulled up the sheet and tucked it under her arms.

He bunched the pillow behind his shoulders and reclined against it, half-turned to face her. God, she looked seductive wrapped in a scarlet satin sheet. As soon as he got home he was going to find her a nightgown in that same shade of satin. Pink silk was okay but scarlet satin . . . Remembering she wanted to talk, he dragged his thoughts away from where they were heading.

'Did you phone home? Kids okay? Jan surviving?'

'They're fine. Jan says we owe her and Stan a million dollars for baby-sitting this week.' She poked him in the chest with her fingernail. 'Now stop teasing. What happened?'

'McLeod Systems is now officially working for IMS Inc.'

'Ryan,' she squealed and, sheet dropped and forgotten, flung herself onto his chest, 'they signed the contract!'

'Finally.' He smiled up at her.

'See? Aren't you glad you listened when I told you to leave Pastin and Carol alone? I told you they'd get what they deserved and I was right. You worked hard and got what you deserved.' She propped herself up with her arms so she could see his face. 'That's the way life works. What goes around, comes around. Do unto others as you would have them do unto you.'

His heart began to pound as he admired the way the light gleamed on the white breasts suspended so temptingly in front of him, their pink tips brushing through the hair on his chest. 'Becky?'

'Yes?'

'Does it always work that way?' He lowered his eyelids to mask the glitter of anticipation he knew was probably visible in his eyes. 'I mean the do unto others bit?'

'I believe in it,' Becky answered, her flesh starting to tingle where his gaze caressed her.

'Good.' He scooped her onto her back and lay over her, trapping her with his weight.

'Good?' Her voice was a mere breath of air as she held onto his shoulders.

'Because,' he lowered his mouth until his lips were only a heartbeat away from hers, 'I'm about to do unto you.'

And he did.

THE EXCITING NEW NAME IN WOMEN'S FICTION!

PLEASE HELP ME TO HELP YOU!

Dear ***Scarlet*** Reader,

As Editor of ***Scarlet*** Books I want to make sure that the books I offer you every month are up to the high standards ***Scarlet*** readers expect. And to do that I need to know a little more about you and your reading likes and dislikes. So please spare a few minutes to fill in the short questionnaire on the following pages and send it to me.

Looking forward to hearing from you,

Sally Cooper

Editor-in-Chief, ***Scarlet***

P.S. Make sure you look at these end pages in your ***Scarlet*** books each month! We hope to have some exciting news for you very soon.

Note: further offers which might be of interest may be sent to you by other, carefully selected, companies. If you do not want to receive them, please write to Robinson Publishing Ltd, 7 Kensington Church Court, London W8 4SP, UK.

QUESTIONNAIRE

Please tick the appropriate boxes to indicate your answers

1 Where did you get this Scarlet title?

Bought in supermarket ☐

Bought at my local bookstore ☐ Bought at chain bookstore ☐

Bought at book exchange or used bookstore ☐

Borrowed from a friend ☐

Other (please indicate) ______________________

2 Did you enjoy reading it?

A lot ☐ A little ☐ Not at all ☐

3 What did you particularly like about this book?

Believable characters ☐ Easy to read ☐

Good value for money ☐ Enjoyable locations ☐

Interesting story ☐ Modern setting ☐

Other ______________________

4 What did you particularly dislike about this book?

____

5 Would you buy another Scarlet book?

Yes ☐ No ☐

6 What other kinds of book do you enjoy reading?

Horror ☐ Puzzle books ☐ Historical fiction ☐

General fiction ☐ Crime/Detective ☐ Cookery ☐

Other (please indicate) ______________________

7 Which magazines do you enjoy reading?

1. ______________________

2. ______________________

3. ______________________

And now a little about you –

8 How old are you?

Under 25 ☐ 25–34 ☐ 35–44 ☐

45–54 ☐ 55–64 ☐ over 65 ☐

cont.

9 What is your marital status?
Single ☐ Married/living with partner ☐
Widowed ☐ Separated/divorced ☐

10 What is your current occupation?
Employed full-time ☐ Employed part-time ☐
Student ☐ Housewife full-time ☐
Unemployed ☐ Retired ☐

11 Do you have children? If so, how many and how old are they?

____

____

12 What is your annual household income?

under $15,000	☐	or	£10,000	☐
$15–25,000	☐	or	£10–20,000	☐
$25–35,000	☐	or	£20–30,000	☐
$35–50,000	☐	or	£30–40,000	☐
over $50,000	☐	or	£40,000	☐

Miss/Mrs/Ms ______________________________
Address __________________________________

____

____

Thank you for completing this questionnaire. Now tear it out – put it in an envelope and send it before 31 August, 1997, to:

Sally Cooper, Editor-in-Chief

USA/Can. address
SCARLET c/o London Bridge
85 River Rock Drive
Suite 202
Buffalo
NY 14207
USA

UK address/No stamp required
SCARLET
FREEPOST LON 3335
LONDON W8 4BR
Please use block capitals for address

MAPLA/2/97

Scarlet titles coming next month:

TIME TO TRUST Jill Sheldon
Cord isn't impressed by the female of the species! And he certainly doesn't have 'time to trust' one of them! It's just as well, then, that Emily is equally reluctant to let a man into *her* life – even one as irresistible as Cord. But maybe the decision isn't theirs to make – for someone else has a deadly interest in their relationship!

THE PATH TO LOVE Chrissie Loveday
Kerrien has decided that a new life in Australia is just what she needs. So she takes a job with Dr Ashton Philips and is soon hoping there can be more between them than a working relationship. Then Ashton's sister, Kate, and his glamorous colleague, Martine, decide to announce his forthcoming marriage!

LOVERS AND LIARS Sally Steward
Eliot Kane is Leanne Warner's dream man, and she finds herself falling deeper and deeper in love with him. When Eliot confesses to having memory lapses and, even worse, dreams which feature . . . murder, Leanne begins to wonder if she's involved with a man who could be a very, very dangerous lover indeed!

LOVE BEYOND DESIRE Jessica Marchant
Amy is a thoroughly modern woman. She doesn't want marriage and isn't interested in commitment. Robert seems as happy as she is to keep their relationship casual. And what about Paul – does he want more from Amy than just friendship? Then Amy's safe and secure world is suddenly shrouded in darkness and she has to decide which of these two men she can trust with her heart . . . and her future happiness.